The Road From Elephant Pass

D0050438

Vijitha Yapa Publications
Unity Plaza, 2 Galle Road, Colombo 4, Sri Lanka
Tel. (94 11) 2596960 Fax: (94 11) 2584801
e-mail: vijiyapa@gmail.com
www.srilankanbooks.com
www.vijithayapa.com

Copyright © Nihal de Silva

ISBN 955-8095-38-9

All rights reserved. No part of this book may be reproduced, stored in a retrieval system or transmitted by any means, electronic, mechanical, photocopying, recording or otherwise, without written permission from the publisher.

First Edition September 2003
First Reprint June 2004
Second Reprint October 2004
Third Reprint September 2005
Fourth Reprint March 2006

Printed by Tharanjee Prints, Maharagama

The Road From Elephant Pass

by

Nihal de Silva

Vijitha Yapa Publications
Sri Lanka

Also by Nihal de Silva

The Far Spent Day
The Ginirälla Conspiracy

For Elmo Jayawardena,
aviator and philanthropist,
author and friend

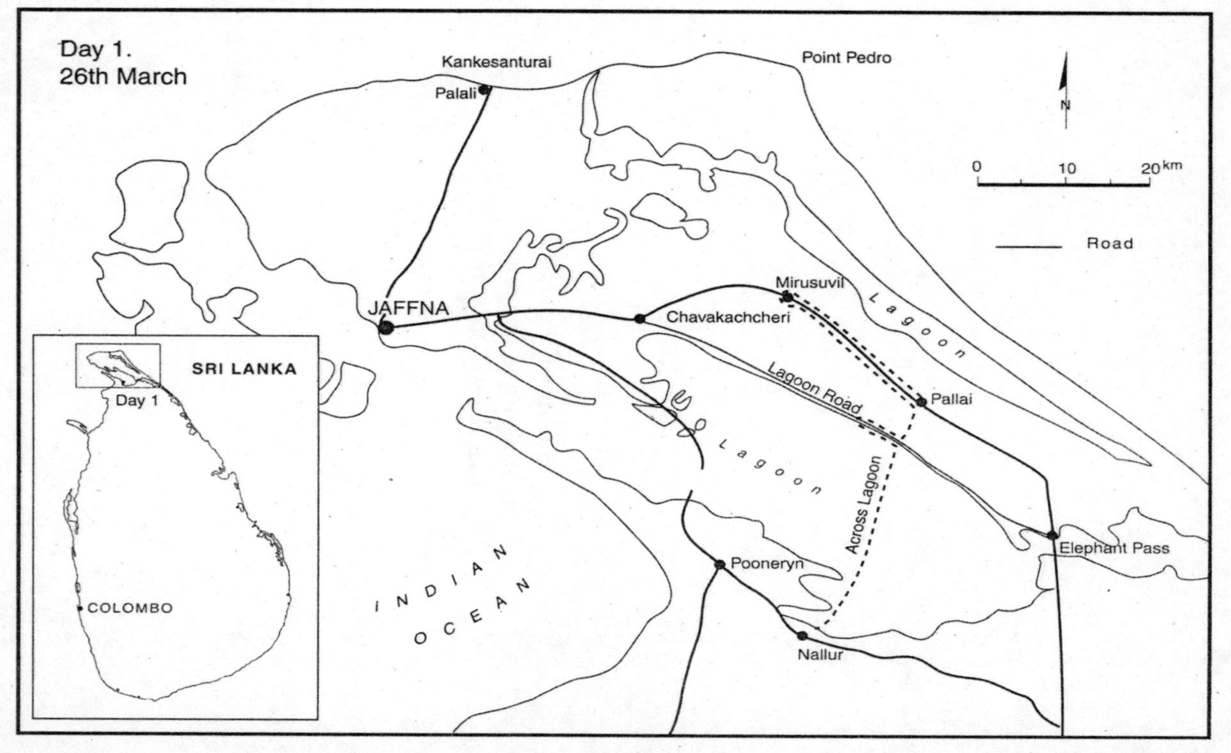
Day 1.
26th March
Kankesanturai
Palali
Point Pedro
N
0
10
20km
Road
JAFFNA
Mirusuvil
Chavakachcheri
Lagoon
Lagoon Road
Pallai
Lagoon
Across Lagoon
Elephant Pass
Pooneryn
Nallur
INDIAN
OCEAN
SRI LANKA
Day 1
COLOMBO

1

26th March 2000

The woman was late.

I'd been waiting at the checkpoint near Pallai, on the main road from Elephant Pass to Jaffna. A wooden barrier had been thrown across the road with barbed wire fencing on either side. A crude hut stood on the side for the troops to shelter from the sun. Sandbags, piled up around the hut, gave the illusion of security.

The checkpoint was in a grove of coconut palms, many of them with their crowns blown off by cannon fire in bygone battles. I had been standing by the barrier for nearly an hour. The late afternoon heat was oppressive, harsh and dry. The baked countryside, and the road running through it, seemed to shimmer and dance in the heat. I tried, without success, to stifle my irritation.

An elderly man dressed in a white verti walked up to the barrier, had his papers scrutinized, and was allowed to pass. Two men on bicycles rode up and then three elderly women with two children came from the other direction. All movement, by the villagers at any rate, would cease after dark.

Still no sign of the woman!

*

My boss, Major Kiriella, had summoned me to his office last evening. Most of the troops from our regiment were stationed in the east. Two companies headed by Kiriella had been, for some unknown reason, posted to Elephant Pass. The camp there was a massive, sprawling fortification manned by troops from a number of regiments, some ten thousand men in all.

Kiriella was a man of average height, several inches shorter than I, but immensely broad at the shoulder and hip. A bear-like man with a temperament to match.

'Wasantha, I have some information that may lead to something,' he said.

He called me Captain when it was strictly business and Wasantha when he had something unpleasant in mind.

'My contact tells me he can produce a senior woman activist who has turned against the movement. She claims to have vital information and wants to negotiate a deal with us. It might amount to nothing, but I think it's worth looking into.'

For seventeen years the Liberation Tigers of Tamil Eelam, the LTTE, had been fighting the Government to establish a separate state for the Tamil minority of the country. The peninsula of Jaffna is the stem end of our pear shaped island. It was the home base of the Tamils but now was occupied by our forces. The rebels held the heavily forested region called the Wanni, the landmass south of Jaffna extending up to the centre of the island. The camp at Elephant Pass controlled the isthmus between the Wanni and the Jaffna peninsula.

'Is your informant reliable, sir?' I had asked, scratching around for some pretext to drop the project.

'He has given me some useful stuff, yes! But you can

never tell,' he had looked at me earnestly. 'It seems that this woman had a brother who was with a combat group in the east. He has been executed for some reason on orders of his area commander, so my man says. We have no independent confirmation.'

'Isn't it better to just pass this on to MI?' I'd still not been keen to get involved in this.

Intelligence gathering was not our province anyway.

'No!' Kiriella had said firmly. 'No. I think we'll attend to this ourselves for the present. We can bring MI in to it if it looks promising.'

I couldn't argue with that.

I had never liked the bastard and he didn't like me. It might have been because he is a Kandyan and I am from the south. Maybe it's because he had risen from the ranks and I'd been recruited as a second lieutenant on the strength of my university degree. Perhaps he was just resentful that the troops liked and trusted me. But there is no denying Kiriella was a competent officer. I thought his problem was presumptuous ambition and he probably perceived me as a threat. He would take any risk if it helped further his career. Most often those risks involved his subordinates.

'How do you want this handled ... Sir?'

'The woman does not want to approach the army directly ... for fear of reprisals against her family,' Kiriella had explained. 'The arrangement is for her to be detained at a checkpoint near her home and taken in for questioning.'

He loved these little games:

'Her name is Kamala Velaithan. Her mother lives near Pallai so she must be staying there at the moment. She will come to the checkpoint at Pallai tomorrow evening at 16.00,' Kiriella went on. 'You had best take a woman soldier with you and pick her up.'

'Do you want her brought back here?'

'No. I think you'd better take her to Jaffna. I'll meet you there,' he had said. 'If her information is solid we'll have to fly her down to Colombo.'

*

It was getting late. I thought I would give her 15 minutes, then go back and advise Kiriella to drop the project. Although the peninsula was under our control during the day, it was never a good idea to move outside the fortified areas after dark.

The LTTE, they called themselves Tigers, had grown from a ragged band of youthful rebels in the mid eighties, to what is now recognized as one of the most powerful and ruthless terrorist organizations in the world. But I still believe we can beat them, if only the politicians would give us the weapons we need and left military decisions in our hands.

They never would, of course.

But there was no denying the Tigers' audacity and determination. Their cadres, especially the women, had perfected the art, or science, of suicide bombing. They hated us, the Sinhala majority, with a ferocity that I would not have comprehended had I not seen and experienced it in the battlefield. And I hated them back with equal intensity. But my loathing was for the Tigers, not the ordinary Tamil villagers. I even had some sympathy for the poor bastards who had lived in a war zone for nearly two decades, and been duly terrorized by both sides.

It was not a villager I expected to meet today.

Would one of these fanatics really turn against their cause?

I saw her then, a tall slim woman, with a young boy by her side. They came onto the main road from a footpath some distance from the barrier and walked slowly towards it. I moved back into the shadow of the hut and watched them come up.

She was wearing a brown cotton skirt that reached her ankles and a loose white blouse. Cheap, black rubber slippers. She had straight black hair, parted in the middle and pulled into a braid at the back. Widely spaced eyes set in an oval face. No ring, bangles or chain, just tiny gold ear studs. She walked confidently, holding herself erect like an athlete. She looked to be in her mid twenties. The boy might have been nine or ten years old, dark and serious.

I felt a rising antipathy as I watched her.

She gave her papers to the soldier at the barrier and turned around to talk to the boy. The soldier in turn handed the ID to the woman soldier I had brought with me. She glanced at the papers and signalled to the woman to step inside.

The soldiers at the barrier were not aware of any special arrangement. I had to show them, and the little boy who would take the information back to her family, that a genuine detection and arrest had taken place. I began a routine line of questioning, name, age, occupation, parents' occupation, domicile and so on. She stood very straight and answered correctly. She stared confidently at me as she spoke, unafraid. Her eyes had an expression I had seen before. Defiance mixed with a good measure of contempt.

I like my Tamils deferential.

I wanted to take her to the back of the hut and slap some respect into her. Sadly we were not allowed to do that anymore. We had strict orders to respect their human rights.

Human rights for terrorists!

'Do you speak English?'

'Yes.'

'It is necessary for you to be searched,' I told her gruffly. 'This woman officer will carry out the search in the cubicle at the back.'

'You have no right to do that.'

'We have every right,' I snarled. 'You will be searched, by force if necessary.'

She studied me calmly for a moment then shrugged her shoulders in acceptance. She turned and followed the soldier to the little cubicle, the front of which was covered with a crude screen of black plastic sheet.

An argument ensued behind the screen before the woman soldier emerged holding a crumpled document. It was, as arranged, an ID issued by the LTTE to people living in 'uncleared' areas administered by them.

It was enough.

'I am afraid I shall have to detain you for questioning,' I told her formally. 'You may send a message to your family that you are being taken to army headquarters at Jaffna.'

She stared at me insolently as I spoke, then walked over to the boy and spoke to him in Tamil. I saw his eyes widen in shock as he listened to her. He seemed close to tears. He tried to argue with her but was finally persuaded to leave. He went reluctantly, stopping several times to look back.

I turned to my driver, Piyasena, and signalled to him to bring up the vehicle. There was no chance now of getting to Jaffna, a good twenty five miles from where we were, before dark. We had to risk it anyway. A minute later Piyasena was standing in front of me, looking embarrassed. He was a short, round faced youth destined to be, well, no more than a driver for the rest of his career.

'Sir, we have a flat tyre.'

He had been standing near the vehicle for the last two hours and had only noticed the deflated tyre when we were ready to leave. I controlled my irritation with an effort and said: 'Well, change it then … and hurry up.'

'Sir,' the man muttered, looking down. 'We have no jack.'

I could have strangled the stupid lout.

'Let's try and lift that end up and prop it up with rocks,' I said impatiently. 'I hope you have a spare wheel.'

'I have the spare, sir,' the wretched bastard blurted. 'But, sir, we …. we have no wheel brace.'

I waved the driver away, not trusting myself to speak. The Tamil woman walked up to me followed, at a distance, by the woman soldier. For the first time since she came to the barrier she looked concerned. Up close I realized, in a remote section of my consciousness, that the skin of her face was flawless. She might have been attractive too, if not for her sullen expression and angry eyes.

She spoke softly, making sure she could not be

overheard.

'What is the delay, Captain?'

'We have a flat tyre … and no jack.'

'We cannot stay here, we must leave immediately.'

There was a note of urgency in her voice that made me look sharply at her, wanting to question her further. But my irritation got the better of me.

'You caused the delay yourself,' I told her angrily, "You should have been here at 16.00.'

'My mother was ill,' she replied calmly, as if that explained everything. 'But this delay could have been avoided with a little competence.'

The temptation to thump the arrogant bitch was becoming irresistible.

I was still trying to control myself when I heard the drone of a heavy truck coming up the road from Elephant Pass. With some relief I remembered that the men at the barrier were to be evacuated for the night.

Fortunately they had a multi-socket wheel brace in the truck. There was no shortage of helpers either, all anxious to be rid of us so that they could get back to the safety of their camp. Still it was nearly dark when the tyre was changed. The truck turned around with a roar and headed back to Elephant Pass, a distance of some six miles.

Piyasena, his confidence and good humour now restored, drove up to where I stood. We climbed in, the two women at the back, I in front. Piyasena turned the vehicle and we headed down the deserted road towards Jaffna, our headlights slicing sharply through the gloom.

They blew a culvert near Mirusuvil when we were a couple of hundred yards from it. We saw a bright flash directly ahead and felt the shock of the explosion. The vehicle swerved all over the road as Piyasena stood on his brakes.

'We are too late, the road is cut!' the Tamil woman said. 'We'll be under fire in a moment.'

She was seated directly behind me, on the transverse seat. Her voice was measured, but still conveyed the urgency of the moment.

'We have to turn back,' she announced calmly.

I made a circling motion with my finger and Piyasena didn't need any further urging. He swung the vehicle in an arc, careful still to stay on the tarmac. The gears crashed again and again before he had the vehicle turned around. I heard another loud explosion and a burst of small arms fire behind us as we roared away.

The woman spoke again.

'This whole stretch of road will be under attack tonight,' she said. 'We must turn off at Pallai … go towards the lagoon.'

She seemed to be the only one who had any idea at all of what was happening. I wondered for a moment if it could be some kind of trap but dismissed the thought. I was not important enough to justify the elaboration.

I told Piyasena to turn right as we passed the deserted barrier at Pallai. His eyes were wide as he hunched over the steering wheel, gripping it tightly with both hands. We turned on to the narrow road that led to the lagoon. The road had been macadamized in some bygone era but was badly neglected now. The groves of coconut gave way to Palmyrah palms and then scrub as we neared the lagoon. The road ended abruptly in a 'T' junction.

I could see the water in our headlights, black and still.

'Turn left at the top,' I ordered the driver. 'Let's get to the camp till things settle down.'

The barrier at Pallai was on the A9, the trunk road that also served as the main supply route connecting Elephant Pass to Jaffna. The secondary road we had now reached, hardly more than a cart track really, ran along the edge of the lagoon, parallel to the A9.

'Captain, we can't go to the camp,' the woman said sharply. There was an edge in her voice.

'Why not? It's much closer.'

She leaned over and said in a harsh whisper.

'There will be a … major attack on Elephant Pass tonight. The camp is already surrounded. We will not be able to get through.'

'Why the hell didn't you tell me this earlier?'

She ignored the question and said: 'Turn towards Jaffna. We might get through, if we are fast enough."

'What do you mean by fast enough?'

'There will be landings on this beach tonight … from across the lagoon!'

'When?'

'Anytime now!'

The entire region across the lagoon was in rebel hands; had been in their hands for many years now. They were able to launch attacks across the lagoon, or along the shallow reef bound coastline, using small boats. Our heavy naval gunboats are not able to operate safely in these waters.

Shit. What had I got myself into?

I was shaken by the speed at which my position had deteriorated. I told the driver to turn right, in the direction of Chavakachcheri and Jaffna. We bounced painfully in and out of potholes as he picked up speed. The headlights dipped at one moment, illuminating the broken road immediately ahead, then climbed up to show the crowns of the palm trees in the next.

We passed through a fishing village. Small boats were lined up on the beach to our left. The huts, to the right of the road, were well screened by the ubiquitous palmyrah leaf fences. There was no light showing, and no one outside to see us pass. These villagers knew only too well what the explosions must mean and what the following days and weeks would be like. And they had to pray their flimsy shelters would protect them!

Piyasena was driving fast, too fast for the narrow, broken road. He swung the heavy vehicle from side to side to avoid the worst of the potholes. As we bumped and swayed, I braced myself against the side of the vehicle, keeping a sharp look out for movement on the water.

Nothing. It was too dark to see very much anyway.

Suddenly the white beam of a spotlight flashed from close inshore. I heard the soldier at the back shout a wordless warning. The windscreen shattered into white lacework and the familiar drumming of machine gun fire filled my world.

I yelled at Piyasena to get us off the road, but I was a day too late. In the glare of the searchlight I saw him slumped across the steering wheel with his faced turned away and the top of his head missing. There was blood spattered everywhere and still the spotlight held us, as though impaled on a board. The woman soldier was shouting again, her voice now shrill with fear.

Gunfire raked the vehicle again and the screaming

stopped. I threw myself at the wheel pushing it to the right, away from me. The vehicle swung abruptly off the road and, still at speed, lurched nose first into a hidden dip in the sand. We went careening down the short slope till the left front wheel hit something, a rock or tree stump, lifting it up sharply. The impact tipped the vehicle on its side with a resounding crash. My head crunched into something and the door flew open.

I felt myself thrown clear, rolling over and over.

2

I was curled up on the sand by the side of the vehicle, stunned and feeling extremely ill. I must have blacked out, if only for an instant. I couldn't be sure. My head hurt abominably and when I touched it I knew I had a cut on my scalp, from front to back. I felt the sticky wetness of blood dripping down my face.

How long had I been unconscious?

I had to get away from the vehicle before the boats landed and they came after us. I could hear the babble of voices, shrill over the rumble of the outboard engines.

I got to my knees and crawled to the back of the Defender, now lying on its side. The rear door wouldn't open at first. I tugged frantically till it came unstuck with a bang. The Tamil woman was trying to pull herself up and out of the vehicle. She looked dazed but apparently uninjured.

I asked after the other woman.

'She's dead,' she said flatly. 'You cannot help her.'

I didn't believe her and crawled inside to check, struggling awkwardly to ease my bulk through the narrow door. The reflected glow of the headlights gave just enough light to see. She was sprawled across the backrest of the transverse seat, her head thrown back. A heavy bullet had torn open her neck. The Tamil woman crawled into the vehicle again and put her hand in the dead woman's tunic pocket. I was about to ask her what the hell she was playing at when I realized she was looking for her ID.

She found it at last, turned and crawled out again.

They must have been landing on the beach. The throaty buzz of outboard engines was muted now but seemed very near. The searchlight probed the road, just over my head.

I scrambled out of the vehicle and started running towards the scrub. My head seemed disconnected from my body. Flashes of pain shot through me with every jolting stride. The loose sand sucked at my boots, making every step a separate effort. I heard the woman behind me but didn't turn to look at her. My chest was heaving by the time I reached the bushes. I threw myself on the ground and heard her come down close by.

Moments later a light flashed from the road followed immediately by a burst of automatic gunfire. I ducked by instinct but they were shooting at the vehicle, raking it from end to end. The cone of the searchlight began to sweep over the bushes. It stopped for a moment over us and then moved on. We crawled cautiously away from them, deeper into the scrub.

I stopped and squatted on the ground, feeling nausea well up inside me.

'We can't stay here,' the woman whispered urgently. 'They will be moving inland. We should go back, towards the village.'

I clenched my teeth and stood up, taking a moment to allow the dizziness to pass. As soon as she thought I was ready she turned and led the way, picking her way through the scrub. She kept under cover of the bushes and worked her way parallel to the road, towards the village we had passed.

I kept up with her, trying to ignore the pain. My head was pounding and every step I took was an added torture. I stopped finally, feeling dizzy and bilious, unable to carry on. I yearned to lie down.

Were they close behind? Our footprints would be clearly visible in the sand. They could catch us. Easily.

She seemed to read my thoughts.

'I don't think they will follow us,' she said shortly. 'They will have their own mission for the night.'

I threw up, retching again and again. I hated the weakness of it, especially in front of an enemy. Especially in front of a woman!

I knelt on the ground and felt better. Slightly.

'Elephant Pass is our best chance,' I told her. 'We'll have to find a way through your lines.'

'It is too late, Captain,' she said evenly. 'The attack has already started.'

I only heard it then, the unmistakable boom of 152 mm cannon, and the rattle of small arms.

Bugger it!

I was thoroughly fed up with all of this. I wanted to suggest that we split up and find our own way back to safety. I would try to reach Jaffna and she, well, wherever she wanted to go. I was confident I could get back on my own.

There was just one unresolved problem.

'I need to know something about the information you offered to give us.'

'I did not offer to give you anything,' she answered curtly. 'I offered to trade some vital information, for … something I want.'

'I need to know what it is,' I said impatiently, 'so I can decide what to do next.'

'You mean, is the information worth the trouble of taking me along or are you better off on your own?' The derisive note was back in her voice.

Of course I do, you stupid bitch. Do you think I enjoy your company?

'Yes.'

'I know where my *thalaivar* will be, the date and the time. I know the location and precise co-ordinates of the building,' she said this softly, as though the trees around us could overhear. 'And they don't know that I know!'

Thalaivar means leader.

I just sat there, trying to take it in.

If true, this was an once-in-a-lifetime chance to bring an end to this war. The fighting had, so far, taken some sixty thousand lives and caused untold misery to tens of thousands of innocents. Over six hundred thousand people were 'internally displaced', living in refugee camps. The leader of the rebels, Velupillai Prabakaran, is a ruthless and despotic tyrant. He has not only killed off most of the moderate Tamil leaders but also his own deputies who may have posed a threat to his leadership. My government believes that if he were eliminated, the LTTE would disintegrate and a political settlement with more moderate leaders would be possible.

But Prabakaran is a wily and elusive target. The vast Wanni jungle is his domain. Our forces have tried long and hard to locate him but have never even come close. He always works in secret, is always on the move. To identify his precise location at a given date and time is intelligence of the highest value. The information, if properly used, could well change the history of my country.

'How sure are you?' I tried to keep my voice casual.

'Sure enough to risk my life!' she snapped. 'I am the one who initiated this.'

'So why are you doing this?' I asked. 'I need to know.'

'Betray my cause?' She laughed unpleasantly. 'My reasons are personal.'

'Is it because of your brother?'

'I will not discuss it'

'And what do you want in return?'

'I will negotiate that with the person … able to give me what I want.'

If you are trying one on, woman, you'll come to an unpleasant end.

We were silent for a time, busy with our own thoughts. Given the significance of her information I felt that, in a subtle way, the initiative had shifted to her.

'So what options are open to us?' I hated having to ask, but she had more local knowledge than I did. 'Try to reach Elephant Pass or lie low and find our way to Jaffna tomorrow?'

'Listen to me. Your camp at Elephant Pass is finished. Our boys have already cut off their fresh water from Iyakachchi. The supply routes from Jaffna will be closed soon. The camp will be overrun in a few days.'

She spoke with a calm certainty that I found very disquieting.

'Then they will turn on Jaffna! Our cannon need to be moved only a few miles more to control the airstrip at Palali. When air supply is cut, … Jaffna will be forced to surrender!'

Oh fuck off!

'Even if what you say is true, all of that will take days, if not weeks,' I said evenly. 'We can still get to Jaffna and fly out with your information.'

'You still haven't grasped the situation, Captain. By dawn this whole area will be under our control, then every hand will be against you,' she said. 'You will not move a mile from where you are seated now.'

'I asked you what the options were.'

'We have to cross the lagoon, get to the Wanni!'

Are you out of your mind? Do you think we can cross 75 miles of rebel territory?

My head was beginning to throb again. I couldn't concentrate.

'We'll be walking into a trap.'

'Do you really think all this is to capture one army Captain?' she asked scornfully.

I ignored the gibe. I would settle with her later.

'When is it your leader will be at this place?'

'Wednesday the sixth of April,' she said quietly. 'Ten days time!'

I tried to think and wished my head would stop aching.

This could be a chance that will not come our way again. My duty is to get that information to HQ. But cross the Wanni with this crazy woman? Come on!

My mind was racing but the gears wouldn't engage.

'How do we cross the lagoon?'

'There were fishing boats on the beach … near the village,' she said. 'We will have to take one!'

'What about your gunboats?' I asked. 'They'll blow us out of the water.'

'No. Those boats will be leaving from near the old ferry, further west. It is shorter across from there. I think we will be alright if we go south from here.'

'Suppose we do find a boat and get across without being drowned or shot, then what?'

'Find some shelter for tonight. I know what to do … afterwards.'

She had her head down. I could see the top of her head in the gloom.

She asked: 'How much money do you have?'

'I'm not sure, about three hundred rupees and change.'

'That won't get us very far,' she said abruptly and stood up. 'Let's look for a boat.'

I can't remember agreeing to the mad enterprise. I just hadn't the strength to say 'no'.

My head began to hurt again when I stood up to follow her. She worked her way cautiously just inside the tree line. I could hear the pounding of cannon fire in the distance.

Was it becoming more intense?

We reached the edge of the village. The fences of dry palmyrah fronds made a distinctive rustling noise in the wind. We crept up to the road, using the fences as cover, and scurried across to where the boats were beached. There were no cries of alarm. With the sound of battle in their ears, the villagers wouldn't come out to ask who was moving about.

They were all small boats, good enough I supposed, for fishing the calm waters of the lagoon. The woman selected a tiny canoe carved out of a single log with an even frailer looking outrigger. The wood was torn and cracked along the upper edges and I had no way of knowing if it was sea, or at least, lagoon worthy.

'This will have to do,' she whispered. 'Let's see if we can find something to paddle with.'

There was indeed a paddle of sorts, crudely carved out of the branch of a coconut palm. I was past caring by now.

She turned to me.

'You must put away anything that can identify you as an army officer or even as a Sinhalese,' she said. 'You do understand the need for this?'

Wordlessly I took off my camouflage jacket, boots, belt and holster. I felt naked without my 9mm side arm but knew it had to go. I took all the money out of my wallet, leaving my military and civilian ID in it. I threw it on to the pile of discards. I hated throwing my wristwatch away but I knew that alone could cost me my life. Peasants from Jaffna don't own expensive watches.

I was left barefoot, in a singlet and trousers. The pants would give me away but I'd be even more conspicuous if I took them off. The woman used the paddle to scoop out a hole in the sand, well back from the water line. I put all my kit in and helped to push the sand back and smooth it over.

Am I really doing this? I am committing myself now.

We pushed our fragile little craft into the lagoon and climbed in. We couldn't actually sit inside the dugout. It was much too narrow. There were planks tied across the top for sitting with just enough space in the hollow section to place our feet. The outrigger gave us stability although it creaked and moved alarmingly in the tiny swell.

3

It was a long haul but not as difficult as I had expected. The water was still, with hardly a ripple. There was a faint breeze behind, and to the left, of us and this must have helped because the little craft sliced through the water with surprising ease. But I had spells of dizziness making the horizon swing crazily from side to side. I felt the bile rise in me again.

I was sick over the side of the boat, retching painfully and feeling awful. I wished I could lie down.

The sounds of battle behind us, explosions, the crump of cannon shell and the rattle of small arms, were much louder over the water. The moon was, thankfully, just a sliver, much like a saucer of milk. But that, combined with the starlight, was enough to make me feel naked and exposed. We would surely be spotted if a Tiger gunboat went by. Our single advantage was that the tiny craft was so low in the water.

We could only steer by paddling either on the right or left side of the boat. Finding south was easy with a clear sky, for the three bright stars that make up Orion's Belt were almost directly overhead. A line of fainter stars, passing through the centre of the 'belt' to form the 'sword', pointed due south.

We took turns to row. When it was her turn, I scooped up some water in my hands to wash the blood off my face and rinse my mouth. The lagoon water was bitter with salt but even that was preferable to the sour aftertaste of vomit.

The woman sat at the front of the boat with her back to me. I could see, in the faint light, the long braid of her hair falling behind her, almost reaching the cross piece she was sitting on. She suddenly sat up straighter and leaned forward. She turned and signalled to me to swing left. I heard it then, the drone of diesel engines to our right, getting louder gradually. Instinctively we bent over, keeping our heads down. I stopped rowing and let the boat drift.

The throaty growl of the outboard engines grew louder and then we could see them, gray shapes in the distance, racing at full throttle.

Surely they would see us. They would have to!

I tensed up as the boats drew nearer. I found myself waiting for the searchlight to reach out and pin us down, for the gunfire that would inevitably follow. Long seconds ticked by as they came abreast and then passed us, the roar of the engines receding into the distance. I waited awhile for my breathing to settle down and started rowing again. The woman didn't say anything or even turn around.

We took turns to row and I lost track of time. The sounds of battle on the peninsula behind us diminished as the night wore on and we got further away.

At last I saw the palm trees rise up ahead and, much closer, on my right. We were entering a bay facing east. A short while later we reached a muddy beach with a dark tree line beyond. By my reckoning we were midway between Pooneryn and Paranthan on the mainland. It hit me then that I had placed myself squarely in the Tiger's lair.

The last bit was the worst.

If there had been a guard post hidden in the trees, they would have had us in their sights for some time now. What would I have done in their place? Wait till the intruders had beached the boat and stepped out on to the sand! They'd be easy targets then. We let the shallow craft ease on to the packed sand and stepped off. I had the jitters, waiting again for the burst of automatic fire that would obliterate me.

Once again the dreadful seconds ticked by and nothing happened. Just as I felt the tension drain away, I had a new worry!

'Will this beach be mined?'

Putting down mines is a routine to which I had not given a second thought. Mines are meant to blow up the enemy. The anti-personnel mines we used were designed to take off a foot neatly at the ankle. But the Tigers had lately become masters at this. So much so that they had produced their own version of a landmine. It was so powerful it took a soldier's leg right off, up to his hipbone.

It wasn't quite so much fun when you had to walk through a minefield yourself.

The woman said: 'We will soon find out.'

Yeah. Right!

She stepped out of the boat and signalled to me to help pull it up, away from the waters edge. We walked towards the trees. I took care to walk right behind her, just in case. There was no point in being furtive either. If anyone had been watching, we would have been long dead.

When we reached the relative safety of the scrub and palmyrah palms, the woman stopped and turned to me.

'We are in a bay near the old saltpans,' she said. 'We need to find some shelter.'

She didn't wait for a reply but turned and walked

through the trees, keeping to the shoreline. My head began to ache again when I started walking.

We passed a small village, dark and silent in a clearing set well back from the shore. We must have walked for about fifteen minutes when we came upon an abandoned hut. A single room with part of the thatched roof left intact. No door, but the walls were standing and the tamped mud floor was dry. I cleaned out a corner with my foot and sat down gratefully, my back to the wall. I felt drained and empty.

And lost.

'I'll try to pick up some things. Will you stay here?' she asked abruptly. 'If you are forced to move, go into the trees at the back and watch the hut.'

A shadow passed across the entrance and she was gone.

I sat there staring at the gray space where the door used to be. Enemy though she was, I felt oddly uncomfortable after she left, very much alone in a hostile land.

I put my head on my knees and tried to get some sleep. My thoughts drifted to my home in Akmeemana, a village near Galle, in the south of the country. I thought of my mother, how old and feeble she had become. She had struggled against hopeless odds to give me a chance to become someone, to find a rung on the ladder. By the standards of my village, I'd found it too and now she and my two younger sisters lived in reasonable comfort, and hope, thanks to the money I sent them. What would become of them if I didn't survive this crazy journey?

I must have dozed off.

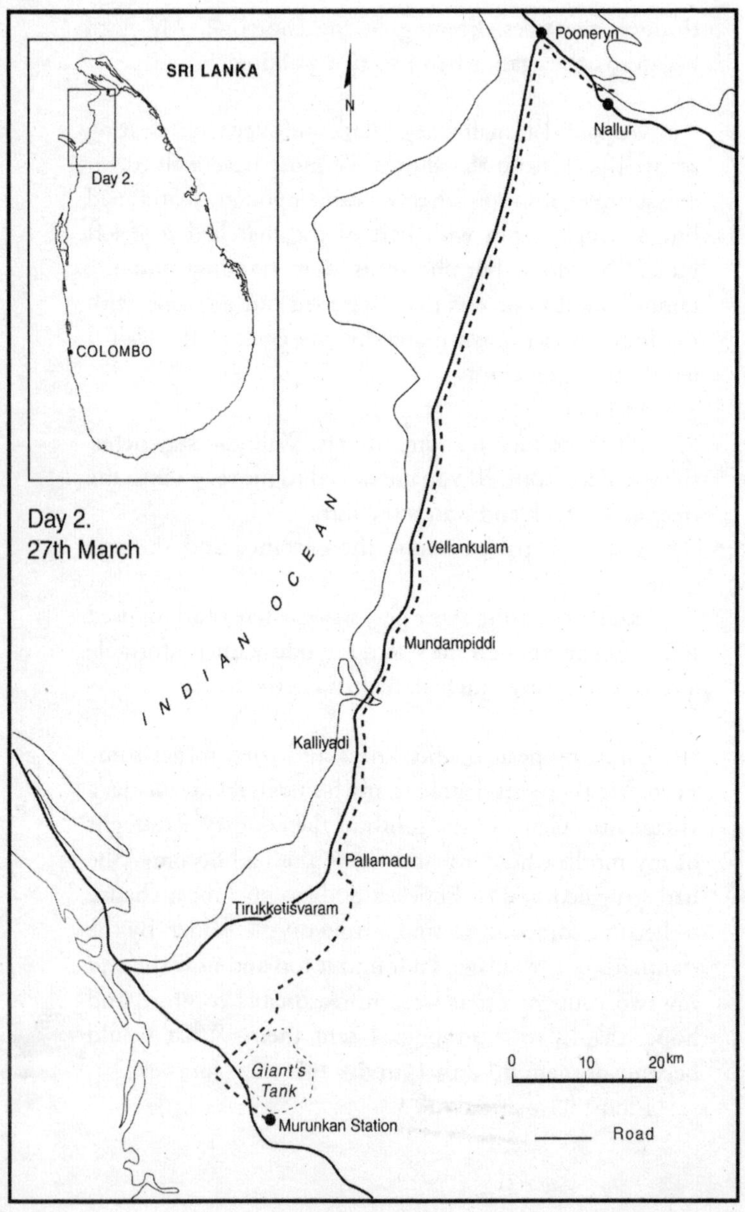
SRI LANKA
Day 2.
COLOMBO
N
Pooneryn
Nallur
Day 2.
27th March
INDIAN OCEAN
Vellankulam
Mundampiddi
Kalliyadi
Pallamadu
Tirukketisvaram
Giant's Tank
Murunkan Station
0
10
20km
Road

4

27th March 2000

I woke up with a start, groggy and disoriented. It was getting light, just after dawn. The sound of splashing water somewhere made me struggle to my feet. As I went towards the door I stumbled over a bundle of clothes on the floor. It turned out to be a pair of ragged black pants and a white shirt. She must have stolen some clothes from the village.

I went round to the back of the hut, relieved to find that my headache had subsided.

The woman had found a shallow well some way behind the hut. She had bathed in the clothes she'd been wearing. She was soaking wet with her hair loose on her shoulders, dripping water. She wasn't happy to see me and marched off without a word.

There was a rotting palmyrah trunk across one edge of the well. A rusty tin tied with a short length of coir rope had served to draw out the water. I stripped off quickly and poured bucket after bucket over my face and shoulders, taking good care not to wet my head wound. It was cold but wonderfully refreshing. I tried drinking some of it but found it too brackish.

I tried on my new pants. The owner must have been a short, fat man. It was loose around the waist but stopped well short of my ankles. I had to use a bit of the rope as a makeshift belt and fold the bottoms further, up to my knees. A collarless shirt with a torn and crudely darned pocket completed my new wardrobe.

The light had improved by the time the woman came up. She had changed into a shapeless, knee length dress that looked like a maternity smock. I noticed that she had found some school child's haversack. She washed her clothes and stuffed them in her bag.

I buried my army pants in a shallow hole.

'There will be security checks along the way,' Velaithan said. 'They normally require travel permits. We have to say that we were caught up in the fighting.'

Do you have a plan at all? Should I just hide out for the day and try to get back across the lagoon tonight?

Once again she seemed to read my thoughts.

'They will search this area when they find the boat,' she said. 'We have to move before that happens.'

I hadn't thought of that. Maybe they had found it already!

'Let's go then.' I was now in a hurry. 'What is our story?'

She stared at me for a moment.

'You will have to pass for my brother.' She looked as if she had bitten something sour.

Oh, thanks.

'Our home was near Iyakachchi. Last night our house was destroyed by cannon fire from Elephant Pass. You were injured by a falling rafter. You are concussed and disoriented, unable to speak. Since we have nowhere to stay, I am taking you to my uncle at Kalliyadi to seek treatment.'

'Where is Kalliyadi?'

'A village under our control, but near Mannar.'

'What about my papers?'

'All our belongings were lost. We couldn't find your papers when we ran to escape the shells.'

'Will they believe I'm so badly injured that I can't speak?'

'We have to make it look like that,' she answered calmly. 'I want to take some strips of cloth from this and bandage your head.'

She had what looked like some woman's ragged underskirt. I didn't want to know where that had come from.

'I need some blood to seep through the bandage ... to make it look real!'

She bit through the hem of the skirt and began to tear it into bandage-sized strips. As if on cue, my head started to throb again. I was trapped in my own machismo. I did not want to look a weakling, especially in the eyes of an enemy.

She didn't wait for me to agree. She held my head steady with one hand and raked over my wound with something sharp she had concealed in the other.

My head exploded in pain.

In all my life I have never actually thumped a woman but I came very, very close to it that morning. While I sat there almost fainting in agony, she calmly leaned over me, wrapping my head with strips of cloth until she had a rough, blood soaked, bandage in place. She fished out a safety pin from somewhere and pinned it in place. I just sat there holding my head, thinking how much I would enjoy strangling the damned woman.

She was trying to ask me something.

'Captain, what's your name?'

'What?'

'What-is-your-name?'

'Uh, Wasantha Ratnayake,' I said through gritted teeth.

'Your name is now Wasu. Wasu Velaithan. You must answer to that,' she said arrogantly. 'Will you remember?'

Fuck off!

I tried to nod and regretted it.

'It is important to look unthreatening. Walk with your head down. Stagger a little. Show some difficulty in keeping your balance.'

She spoke slowly, as if to a child.

'Allow me to help you to climb in and out of vehicles. Sit down whenever you have a chance, even if it is on the side of the road. Mumble to yourself. Can you do all of this?'

'Yes.'

'If someone speaks to you, even at a checkpoint, just say the words *enda thala nokudu.* That means ....'

'Yeah, I know. My head hurts.'

'Do you speak Tamil?' She sounded surprised.

'Just a little.'

'Just keep repeating those words and looking blank. Even an army officer should be able to manage that.'

Don't push it!

'None of this would be needed if you had come to the barrier on time,' I snarled.

'Or if you had made sure your vehicle had a tool kit!' she flashed back.

I was getting pretty tired of all this, and of her. Especially of her! I promised myself I'd dump her at the very first opportunity.

We walked, in strained silence, along the footpath that meandered past the saltpans. It curved gently to the left and finally ended in the main road that led from Paranthan to Pooneryn. The sun had cleared the trees behind us and was already signalling a scorching day. The sky was an arc of intense blue without a trace of cloud. This area had been under rebel control for nearly two decades and the road was more like a jungle track. The macadam had disappeared and the surface was deeply eroded, with ruts and potholes everywhere. The trees on either side of the road were covered with a layer of brown dust.

The woman sat on her haunches by the side of the road and gestured to me to do the same. She took off her stolen haversack and placed it on the ground.

'Give me some money, about a hundred in small notes, if you have it'.

I gave it to her and asked: 'Where can we buy some food?'

I was really starving now, parched as well.

'We have to wait till we get to Pooneryn,' she said. 'It's a few miles up the road'.

I heard a vehicle approaching, but it was going in the other direction. An ancient Leyland truck raised a choking cloud of dust as it rattled past us. I noticed that the vehicles had their own registration numbers starting with the Tamil letter 'tha.' I also remembered that most vehicles operating in Tiger territory were modified to run on kerosene. The back of the truck was full of people all jammed together like a deck of cards.

Two men came the other way, riding ancient bicycles having little racks at the back for carrying goods. Or passengers!

There were lots of birds about.

One of them, with a brilliant reddish breast and yellow head, soaking up the sunshine on leafless branch across the road I knew was a crimson-breasted barbet. A slight movement under the scrub allowed me to spot an Indian pitta, busily turning over fallen leaves in its hunt for insects. At any other time I would have been thrilled to see this lively little bird, with its blue-green plumage and yellow breast. I knew it was a migrant that would be gone as soon as spring came to the Himalayas. I saw sunbirds, ioras and bulbuls flitting from tree to tree.

The birds made me think of Mr. Karl. I could just picture him sitting in the sun and tugging at his beard as he watched them. He had taught me to love the outdoors, to identify birds and animals and learn their habits. Especially birds.

I missed him now, more than ever.

I first heard, and then saw, a tractor in the distance hauling an open trailer. It disappeared for a while behind some trees and then came bumping round a corner, accompanied by a billowing halo of dust. When it was closer I could see passengers crouched in the back, holding on grimly to their belongings.

Velaithan gestured to me to remain where I was, stood up and raised her hand. The driver, a tiny man with thinning gray hair and a deeply lined monkey face, brought the vehicle to a halt close to her. She went up and spoke to him, argued awhile, then paid him some money. He gestured to the back.

I played my role by remaining on my haunches, looking down at the ground, until she came and helped me to my feet. I swayed a bit as I walked to the back of the trailer. Standing suddenly did make me dizzy, so it was not all put on. She called to one of the men at the back who reached down and gave her a hand. She then helped to haul me up. Her arm was surprisingly strong for such a slimly built woman. The passengers appeared to be mostly farmers, both men and women, taking some meagre bundles of produce to town. They moved willingly to make some room for us to crouch on the floor of the trailer. If they took note of my gory bandage and strange behaviour, they made no sign and asked no questions.

In their situation, perhaps it was best not to know.

Sitting in a trailer being hauled over a broken road is not something I would recommend for a man with a crack on his skull. My head began to throb again and I wasn't acting when I held it with both hands and kept my eyes firmly closed.

I realized we had stopped only when the driver switched off his engine.

We had come to a checkpoint at the outskirts of Pooneryn. Through my fingers I saw two men in jungle fatigues walk slowly along the side of the trailer. Both men carried automatic weapons slung over their shoulders. One of them was an older man, hair neatly brushed back and wearing an untidy moustache almost invisible against his jet-black skin. The other was a skinny youth, possibly in his teens, with a face badly scarred with acne.

The older man said softly in Tamil: *'Errangu.'*

Get off.

The passengers scrambled to the back of the trailer and jumped down. They stood in a line without being asked to. I joined the line but squatted on my heels, not only to play my part, but also to conceal the fact that I was a good deal bigger than the rest of the passengers.

The older guard began checking papers and questioning each of the passengers, moving slowly along the line. I wondered if the boat had been found. There were no telephones here but the rebels use motorcycles to carry military information, quite effectively too.

I was getting a bad feeling about this. Busy with my thoughts, I didn't notice that the young guard had walked up and was standing in front of me.

'Elum bungo,' he barked suddenly.

Stand up.

I mumbled my formula:

'Enda thala nokudu.'

My head hurts.

I had been keeping my eyes on the ground so I was caught completely by surprise when he grabbed my hair, bandage and all, and yanked upwards, trying to force me to my feet.

The sudden stab of pain nearly made me lose control. I wanted to grab the vicious little thug and break him across my knee. I couldn't suppress a wordless yell as I struggled to get up and ease the pain.

'Nil.' The older man's voice was like a whiplash.

Nil. Stop.

The boy let go and stood to attention. The man said something rapidly, spitting out the words. He seemed very angry. The boy's face turned to stone. He turned and walked away, his shoulders stiff in protest.

The young guard's impetuosity may have saved us, because the older man seemed distracted after that. The Tigers are very particular about discipline in their ranks. They are capable of unspeakable cruelties so it was not so much what the boy had done, but his doing it without permission, that must have upset the older man.

His checking became perfunctory, merely glancing at the papers thrust at him. When it was her turn, Velaithan gave her ID and went into her story, speaking too rapidly for me to follow. He glanced at me casually, then nodded and moved on.

We were soon on our way, bouncing the short distance to Pooneryn.

From my briefings before I was posted to Jaffna, I remembered that Pooneryn had once been an important junction. An army base, with a naval detachment, had been set up there in 1991. The Tigers had launched a massive attack on the camp in November 1993 but the camp had survived till it was shut down in 1995.

Pooneryn was supposed to have a well-preserved Dutch fort. Four roads led from the town. The road to Paranthan was the one we had traveled. Besides that, two roads led north towards the lagoon, one the Nagatevanturai Jetty and the other to Sangupiddy jetty. Boat services had once been in operation to get people across to the peninsula. These services had long been abandoned. The fourth road led south, along the western coast of the country, towards Mannar.

That was the road we had to take.

The tractor took us to the junction and everyone got off, taking their belongings and produce with them. Velaithan jumped down and, once again, went through the pretense of helping me. Many buildings appeared to have been damaged by aerial bombardment. Some, on either side of the road, were completely destroyed. Others only had the remains of their walls left standing. Our boys had certainly left their mark on the town.

We passed small kiosks selling basic supplies like rice, pulses and bananas. Every kiosk had bottles of kerosene prominently displayed for sale. We went past at least two bicycle repair shops. People were moving about, attending to their daily chores.

Velaithan led me to the side of the road, signalled to me to sit on the ground by the wall of an abandoned roadside building, and then she was gone.

As I sat there with my bandaged head and beggar's clothing, I realized that by luck or good management, we had stumbled on an adequate cover story. In that unfortunate part of the country that had known nothing but war for eighteen years, being disabled and incapacitated helped make one invisible. Perhaps it was the norm. An able bodied young man who had not taken up arms for the cause would have been immediately suspect.

I saw, through half closed eyes, armed men in small groups, some in fatigues, some in plain clothes. They moved with urgency, coming and going. Villagers went about their business in relative silence. There was little of the noise and banter of a market.

No one gave me a second glance.

Velaithan was back, thankfully, with food and water. She had a loaf of bread, cut into four chunks and a small plastic bag filled with what looked like a fried onion 'sambol'. She simply sat by my side, scooped out the fried onions onto the bread with her fingers and began to eat. She left the food on a strip of newspaper in the gutter between us for me to pick up, if I wanted to.

I wanted to.

The bread was hard and stale. I saw small black dots

in it that must have been weevils from the flour, now nicely baked. I didn't want to inspect it too closely or the evil looking onion fry, which was sharp and dripping with rancid oil. We ate in silence, washed our fingers and drank from a plastic bottle she had picked up and filled with water from a well.

She spoke in a low voice, looking straight ahead and moving her lips as little as possible.

'It is about fifty miles from here to Mannar. There are trucks that go part of the way and will take passengers, if they pay,' she said quietly. 'No one is sure when the next vehicle will start off. We have to go to the market and wait. I only need to refill this bottle before we leave.'

'How much do they charge?'

I knew vehicle owners fleeced passengers mercilessly and I hoped my money was enough to see us through.

'Three hundred each,' she said and turned away, avoiding my next question.

I opened my mouth, and shut it again when I saw that her ear studs were gone.

She stood up and adjusted her haversack, then stretched out her hand to make a show of helping me up. Cold hands, like a mortician's. I followed her meekly, head down and mumbling to myself.

It was an old truck, smelling foully of dried fish. It had a timber half body with a ragged tarpaulin, supported by rusty metal hoops, over the top. The truck rattled and creaked as the driver swerved from side to side to avoid an unending series of ruts and potholes on the road. It carried a cargo of onions packed in wicker baskets and, mercifully, only three other passengers, an elderly couple and a sickly looking younger man. They kept to themselves, sitting on the far side of the truck.

'We're lucky,' Velaithan said. 'This truck is going up to Pallamadu, but there may be security checks on the way.'

She was right, of course. So far we had concentrated on getting as far as possible from Jaffna. I had no idea of what to expect on the way, just a conviction that we were going to need a lot of luck.

The Wanni is ruled by the LTTE. Apart from their armed cadres, they have their own civil administration, a justice system and a separate police force. They have their laws, and kangaroo courts dispense justice after their own fashion. They tax every activity that takes place in their territory.

The direct route from Jaffna to Colombo runs straight down the centre of the island from Elephant Pass through Paranthan, Mankulam and then finally to Vavuniya. The entire extent from Elephant Pass to Vavuniya is firmly in rebel hands. No one is allowed to cross their territory from one side to the other. Any person living in a rebel controlled area, and wishing to leave needs an 'exit visa' from the LTTE, which is purchased at some cost. 'Exit visas' are given only to those having valid reasons and, moreover, families are required to keep a hostage under Tiger control as a guarantee that the traveler will return as promised.

The 'exit visa' gets travelers past the last LTTE checkpoint on the road. They cross a neutral stretch and then face a series of checkpoints on the government side. As to the documents a traveler needs on the Government side, you don't want to know about that!

There was no way we could have got through that way, so the circuitous road along the western coast towards Mannar was a far safer route, up to a point.

I remembered from my lessons in school that Mannar, then called Mahatittha, was one of the earliest ports in the country. It had been a great trading post for Arab and other merchants in ancient and even medieval times. It is also the closest point to India. There had been a regular ferry service to India from Mannar before our civil war started.

Mannar once had a thriving economy. A high percentage of the population had been Moslems. Today the population has been greatly reduced and a limited amount of fishing is the only income generating occupation available. I knew the area fairly well having had a six-month posting there. It was a garrison town, with camps not only on the island but also on the mainland beyond the causeway. There was a large and well fortified camp near the Thiruketheeswaram temple. That is about four miles from Mannar, on the road we planned to travel.

'We must get to the camp in Mannar and radio Colombo from there,' I told Velaithan, anxious to be relieved of my responsibility. 'They will arrange an escort to get you to Colombo.'

She was silent for a while, thinking about it.

'No,' she said firmly. 'I think the risk is too great.'

She spoke as if the authority she had now assumed would remain after we had left rebel territory.

'I will give my information only to your Director of Intelligence,' she continued. 'The commandant at Mannar might have … other ideas.'

'I can make sure that doesn't happen,' I said confidently, trying to reassure her.

'I don't think you will have the power to guarantee that, and anyway there is another reason,' she went on quietly. 'We have informants in your camp. Our people will know, within hours, that I am there.'

'So what?' I asked. 'We can protect you.'

Her smile was scornful.

'They won't let you take me to Colombo,' she said softly. 'It will be easier for them to … eliminate the risk I represent, than rescue me.'

She might have been discussing a visit to the dentist. Her calm acceptance that her associates would kill her, rather than risk a leak of information, shook me for a moment. I looked at her but she was staring at the arid countryside flashing past the back of the truck.

What other options did I have?

I still thought Mannar was the best choice, for me at any rate. I wanted to be done with her and free to rejoin my men at Elephant Pass.

'Let's get out of the Wanni first,' I temporized. 'We'll discuss the next step then.'

She didn't say anything.

'Where did you say this truck will take us?'

'Pellamadu,' she replied. 'It's about twelve miles from Mannar.'

'I know the army camp on this road is near the Thiruketheeswaram Temple. That's about four miles from Mannar. So between these two points, there will be the LTTE checkpoint. We need to know where that is.'

'There are two causeways, one just before and one about two miles beyond Pellamadu. I think the second causeway is the logical place.'

'Can we find a way round it?'

'I don't think policing in that sector is very strict. I heard that villagers have ways of getting through, to buy provisions,' she said quietly. 'Yes, I think we can get around it but it will need a lot of walking.'

'Right!' I said breezily. 'Lets get past the checkpoint first, then we'll work on the next stage'.

She looked sceptical but said nothing.

5

We sat in silence, forced to look through the dust at the harsh landscape falling away behind us. We had left Poonery at about 10.30. At the rate we were crawling along, it would take at least three hours to reach Pallamadu, if the wretched truck did not break down before that!

The land on either side of the road was very sandy and dry, covered with scrub jungle. Dusty villages appeared on the roadside from time to time but we saw little of the people that lived there. Perhaps they were sheltering from the scorching heat of the sun. We did pass people on the road now and then, most of them on bicycles. It was almost unbearably hot in the truck.

I wanted to continue our conversation, just to pass the time, but then thought better of it. Velaithan seemed lost in her own thoughts, staring impassively at the passing scene. I tried to get some sleep but it was impossible with the heat and constant bouncing.

We entered a small town only different from the villages we had passed by having more screened houses, some of which were covered with rusty roofing sheets. I saw a sign in Tamil on the side of the road. The vehicle slowed down and creaked to a halt soon afterwards.

The driver climbed down and stretched himself. He was a short, but immensely broad, box shaped man dressed is a stained white shirt. His green batik sarong was tucked up and tied in an untidy knot below his belly, which drooped obscenely over it.

'Sappardu! Pathu nimisham,' he yelled.

Food. Ten minutes.

Velaithan helped the old couple down first. She spoke

to them and they courteously waited for us. I crouched on the tailgate and let myself down, leaning heavily on her. It was well that I did. Watching us from across the narrow street, in the shade of a building, were two armed cadres. I kept my head down and let Velaithan lead me away.

The old couple came with us, talking animatedly. The woman was past middle age, with thinning gray hair pulled into a bun behind her head. A smile transformed her thin, careworn face when she spoke to Velaithan. Her husband was a morose man who listened to the conversation between the women but never said a word. We must have looked like a family group.

It wasn't a real checkpoint anyway. The men stared at us for a while and then looked away. Velaithan told me later that this was Vellankulam. It was not a place of any significance except for a track that led inland from there, through the heart of the Wanni, and ended at the Vavuniya road.

The eating-house was little more than a hovel, a gloomy structure with mud-wattle walls and a tamped clay floor. The roof was a thick mass of dried palmyrah leaves resting on a frame of rough timber. The covering was held down by more brushwood piled haphazardly on top. The room smelt of wood smoke and stale food. But it was surprisingly cool inside, and the water stored in an earthenware pot was wonderfully sweet and refreshing. A toothless old crone, crippled with arthritis, hobbled out to talk to the visitors. Food was duly produced from a soot-blackened cavern at the back of the hut.

We sat on crude wooden benches and ate, balancing battered tin plates with one hand and scooping up food with the other. We had flat pancakes that looked like chapatis, but tasted a little different, served with a curry made from dried fish. We ate our fill, not knowing when we would have another chance.

The driver belched loudly and stood up. That was the signal for us to pay up and climb into the truck again. The sickly young man had not eaten with us and didn't rejoin the vehicle. The old lady was pathetically pleased to have someone to talk to and chattered away with Velaithan, who was surprisingly patient with her, answering all her questions with a quiet smile. The sullen look she always assumed when she spoke with me was not so apparent now.

The armed men, still lounging in the shade, took no notice of us.

The truck was like an oven, and the smell of onions and dried fish nearly overpowering. We climbed in with some difficulty and the driver started off with a jerk. The glare of the sun, reflected from the desert-like terrain, was making my eyes swim. All the sundry discomforts made me realize that my head wound was not as painful, or debilitating, as it had been earlier in the day.

The elderly couple got off near the marketplace at the next town. The old woman held Velaithan's hand and talked earnestly to her before walking away. But we had new passengers. Three men carrying cardboard boxes, probably traders, and a fat woman with three small children.

We tried sitting on the tailgate of the truck and found it a fraction cooler than the interior. We were passing through the arid zone of the country, the driest part of the dry zone. The heat was brutal and my nasal passages seemed to burn when I inhaled. The palms and the thorn bushes shimmered in the haze.

I'd been told that this was a wonderful part of the country for shooting grey partridge. Or had been, anyway, till the Tigers took control of it. To relieve the boredom, I kept my eyes on the scrub as we drove past, as I'd never seen a partridge in the wild. I knew that the birds, which foraged for insects on the ground, would fly a short distance when disturbed.

No luck.

We drove into another town, a bigger one. As we came to the bazaar area the vehicle slowed down with a series of jerks. Peering round the edge of the tarpaulin I saw a barrier across the road and an armed man holding his hand up. When we came to a stop another man walked up to the back of the vehicle, inspecting it carefully. He told us politely to get down and have our travel documents stamped.

The driver, who knew the procedure, collected some documents from under the sun visor in his cab and signalled to us to follow him. A prominent new signboard carried the Tiger emblem and some tamil lettering. Below that, proudly in English – POLICE STATION KALLIYADI. An opening in the fence near the barrier led to a lime washed building with a narrow varanda. It looked, and smelt, like a police post anywhere.

I have never liked policemen, not since my university days.

Velaithan was by my side, holding my arm as we followed the other passengers. I just hoped distaste would not show on her face, or on mine. A uniformed cadre stood near the entrance and pointed to a long wooden bench inside. The children stood looking around curiously as the passengers sat down to wait. We were in a surprisingly well-ventilated room with a high ceiling. It was bare of all furniture except for our bench and a desk at the far end of the room. A flattering photograph of the Tiger leader, Prabakaran, adorned the wall above the desk.

A man was seated at the desk, his grey closely cropped head bent over some papers. He didn't look up when we came in. I noticed a pair of crutches leaning on the wall behind him. It was very quiet.

The man at the desk finally closed what seemed to be a bulky file and put it away in a drawer. He was a slender man with a deeply creased, clean-shaven face. He studied us for a moment, shrewd black eyes looking over the reading glasses perched on his nose. He gestured with his hand for the first person, the driver, to come up.

The man studied the papers and asked a few questions. There were no chairs before the desk so the driver stood there awkwardly, shifting his weight from foot to foot. Grey hair finally picked up a seal and stamped the paper with a loud 'thonk'.

The fat woman was next and then, one by one, the others had their papers stamped and went outside. It was our turn.

Velaithan walked up to the man at the desk and handed over her Eelam ID. She spoke at some length, turning and nodding in my direction at one point. The man listened to her impassively, till she was done. He shook his head with an air of finality.

No.

Now what? Would they just turn us back or would they hold us for questioning?

My hands and face were damp with sweat.

Velaithan spoke again. I couldn't make out what she was saying but she was politely pressing her point. The man stared at her for a while, as if trying to make up his mind. He told her to wait and reached for the crutches leaning on the wall behind him. When he stood up I saw that he had lost his left leg at the knee. He hauled himself to the door leading to the back of the premises, knocked and entered an inner room.

He came back in a minute, leaving the door open. He jerked his head at Velaithan and limped back to his desk. He didn't look at her when she went through the door and closed it behind her.

The minutes ticked by. The driver came in and spoke to the man at the desk who was busy once again with his file. I guessed he wanted to leave us and be on his way. Grey hair just looked at him over the rim of his glasses. No word, no expression, just a look! The driver backed away hurriedly, his hand at his brow in a gesture of supplication. I didn't dare look up for fear grey hair would summon me. I concentrated on watching a column of tiny black ants trying valiantly to drag a dead moth across the floor.

The door opened and Velaithan came out, a sheet of paper in her hand. She gave it to grey hair without a word. If he was surprised he hid it well. He just stamped the paper and handed it back to her. I saw him watching her when she turned and came to help me up. I couldn't read the expression on his face. The last minute reprieve made me lightheaded.

How the hell did you pull that off?

The driver looked relieved when we emerged at last and climbed into the back. Velaithan sat in the truck without speaking for a while, lost again in her thoughts. I wanted to ask her what had happened, how she had managed it but somehow her expression didn't invite the question.

She sat very still and straight, with her head thrown back. There was an air of calmness about her, a forbidding self-sufficiency. For the first time since I got caught up in this mad enterprise, I began to have some hope that we'd make it through to safety.

One of the children, the oldest boy by the look of him, crawled over the back of the truck. He stood there, holding the chain that supported the tailboard, blithely ignoring his mother's pleas to get back. He was a sausage shaped little fellow in a pair of blue shorts and a cream shirt several sizes too big for him. He was more fascinated by the gory bandage on my head than by the passing scenery.

For some reason, I have always got on well with children. They are uncomplicated and I like that. Most kids respond to me in the same way.

I prodded him in the tummy and earned myself a grin from the kid and a frown from Velaithan. It saddened me to think that, a few years from now, the Tigers would conscript this kid, wash his brains out, put a gun in his hand and send him out against us. I, or someone like me, would be forced to kill the little bastard.

Velaithan spoke, still looking at the road falling away behind us:

'We'll be at Pallamadu soon. It is a junction with a track leading to some villages in the interior,' she said. 'Our best chance is to walk down that track for about a mile, turn south, cross the waterway that I think is called Nay-Aru, and rejoin the road further down. That should get us past the last checkpoint. After that .... I don't know!'

After that we would be in government territory.

Abruptly she asked: 'Are you planning to hand me over to the army at Mannar?'

I'd meant to break it to her gently.

'It would be the logical thing,' I said quietly. 'I will see to it that you are taken to Colombo safely.'

'It will only get me killed,' she replied. 'You really have no control over that.'

'The other option is to take the main road to Anuradhapura,' I said reasonably, 'but there will be security checkpoints along the way. They will certainly detain us.'

'No. That will not do either.'

I didn't say anything.

What the hell do you want me to do?

'Captain, this is a real chance to end the war,' she said gravely. 'Do you want to be known as the man who fouled it up?'

No, damn you!

'Isn't there another way?'

'I suppose we could go south,' I heard myself say. 'We could go through Wilpattu.'

I can't believe I said that.

Wilpattu had been the largest wild life reserve in the country, and probably the most popular one. It is spread over a huge expanse of land, some three hundred and twenty five thousand acres in extent, to the south of Mannar. The park has been abandoned for many years by the wildlife authorities because of terrorist activity. It is now a completely lawless region, frequented by poachers, illicit loggers, smugglers and the like. Gangs of army deserters use it as a safe haven. The Tigers also use it for mounting terror attacks on civilian targets in the south.

Wilpattu means the land, or plain, of lakes. The grassy plains that intersperse the thick and almost impenetrable forest and scrub are an unusual, perhaps unique, feature of Wilpattu. There are vast basins of water in the centre of these glades. Some of these are natural lakes, some are remnants of ancient irrigation works. Fortunately the park authorities had created rough tracks to connect the villus, since they are the best places to see our wild fauna. The area teems with game of all kinds including elephant, leopard, buffalo and bear.

Only a crazy man would volunteer to walk unarmed through Wilpattu.

I found her looking at me speculatively.

'Can we really go that way?' she asked softly.

Some deep-seated impulse had made me suggest it. I love the forest and, at the same time, feel challenged by it.

'Yes,' I told her. ' Yes, we can get across.'

She just nodded and looked away.

But we had to get there first.

There was the rebel checkpoint somewhere ahead of us, and then our army lines to negotiate. We needed shelter for the night, then clothes, food and a plan for tomorrow.

Velaithan seemed to have a disconcerting knack of parallel thinking.

'What will we do after we cross the Nay Aru?' she

asked.

'There is a road that branches off from this one, going towards Giant's Tank,' I said. 'We should try to get to that.'

'Do you know this area?'

'Yes. I've served in Mannar.'

Giant's Tank is an enormous irrigation reservoir some five thousand acres in extent. The swamp at the back, or eastern, side of the tank used to be a famous bird sanctuary. The bund of the reservoir is shaped like a crescent facing Mannar.

'It is about 13.00 now and we should reach Pallamadu soon. Say we will take two hours to avoid the roadblock and get back on the road, that's 15.00. From there it will be eight or nine miles to the place I want to reach before dark. It is much too far to walk.'

I knew she was looking at me, frowning. I pretended not to notice, enjoying the fact that control had shifted back to me.

'So where is it you plan to spend the night?'

'The road by the bund will be guarded. If we keep heading south on the by-roads, avoiding the bund, we will cross the rail track,' I went on. 'Since the trains don't run anymore, no one will be guarding the track.'

'So?'

'If we walk along the track we will come to Murunkan station, just below the bund of the tank. There should be some abandoned building we could use.'

'Why Murunkan?'

'The road south to Wilpattu starts from Murunkan.'

She is quiet for a while, digesting this. If she was impressed she gave no sign.

'So all we need is some transportation to get us close

to the railway?'

'Yes. Motor bike, tractor, anything.'

Moments later we entered another small town. The truck pulled up near the junction. The driver jumped down and yelled at us to get off. We had arrived at Pallamadu. There may well be a checkpoint on the causeway beyond the town, but there appeared to be another one right there in Pallamadu.

By sheer habit we had repeated our little act of Velaithan helping me off the truck. One of the guards shouted something in Tamil. Velaithan held my elbow to guide me as we walked over slowly. A short, stocky man with thinning hair and decayed yellow teeth seemed to be in charge. Behind him stood two much younger boys. The man, who had an ugly scar running down the side of his face, was dressed in a blue shirt and dark trousers. On his feet were black rubber slippers. The boys wore T-shirts and sarongs and were bare footed. All were armed.

Scarface barked at Velaithan, asking her where we were was going and demanding our papers. She spoke rapidly for several minutes, too fast and colloquial for me to follow. He examined our travel permit with care but didn't seem happy.

Velaithan spoke again, confidently and at length. The man was visibly undecided. He hesitated for what seemed like an eternity, staring at me. Finally he nodded, handed the papers to her and turned his back on us.

We walked slowly up the cart track leading inland, Velaithan holding my elbow solicitously. Then we were round a bend, and I was able to breathe again.

'What was that about?'

'Our permit was for travel up to Pallamadu only. I

told him we wanted to go to a village called Periamadu up this track. I said my uncle lived there,' she said. 'I don't think he was convinced but had no easy means of checking.'

'How did you remember the name of the village?'

'I talked to the old woman in the truck,' she explained. 'I just asked where this track went. The name stuck in my mind'.

The sun was really blazing down. There was little shade, except for an occasional palmyrah palm by the roadside. I saw a baobab tree with its huge, misshapen trunk and spindly little branches. The gravel burnt my bare feet. Men on ancient bicycles creaked past us without speaking. A party of women and small children went by, all of them carrying bundles of dry sticks and fuel wood collected from the forest. Some of them looked at me with curiosity but didn't speak to us.

We passed a tiny village, no more than a cluster of hovels. Most of the walls and roofs were made of palmyrah or coconut fronds, tied to a framework of sticks. Some had plastic sheets thrown over the roof, and held down by more sticks, to keep the weather out. Children were playing in a well-swept yard between the houses.

We must have walked well over a mile when we came to a footpath leading off to the right.

Velaithan gestured towards it and said:

'I think this may lead to a ford in the river.'

I was still jumpy.

'Let's sit in the shade for a bit,' I said, 'I'd like to be sure that bastard hasn't sent one of the boys to check on us.'

She nodded and we sat in the shade of a tree for a few

minutes. We needed the rest anyway. A man rode past on a squeaking bicycle, another man walked by, holding a little boy by the hand. Then there was no other movement for a while.

We drank the last of our water and set off cautiously along the footpath. We were committed now. If we ran into a patrol, we had no explanation to offer. I think the time of day helped us. It was about 14.00 hours with the sun almost directly overhead. There was little shade as the path wound in and out of the thorny scrub. We had to be getting close to the stream.

A sudden thought made me go cold.

'Hold on,' I said 'This is too easy!'

Velaithan knew immediately what I'd meant. They won't leave an unguarded footpath bypassing the checkpoints ... on either side.

'Guards or snipers,' I said quietly. 'Or mines!'

We turned away from the path immediately, pushing our way through the scrub and looking for open patches that would take us further downstream, away from the causeway. Progress was doubly difficult from there.

It was another thirty minutes before I thought it safe enough to turn towards the stream. When we reached it eventually we found it to be, in this season, little more than a muddy channel.

We sat under a small tree to rest and work out our directions.

'Beyond the causeway the main road curves right, towards the coast. The road to the bund branches off to the left. If we walk roughly south, we should get to the road well past the checkpoint.'

She looked very tired now, the skin pulled taut over the bones of her face. She had probably not had any sleep last night. We were entering Government controlled territory where she had to rely on me for protection, and that must have weighed on her mind as well.

I wasn't ready to feel sorry for the woman. I did take the haversack from her, though. There was no longer any need for me to play the walking wounded either, so I stripped off and discarded my soiled bandage.

In the rainy season we would probably have needed a boat to cross the stream. Now the stream bed was dry, the mud caked and cracked. There was a channel of green slow moving water in the middle. I walked in front, feeling my way gingerly through the murky water. It was only knee deep though and we were soon safely across.

The cross-country walk, without the benefit of a path, was brutal. We had finished our water and the sun burned down on us with fearsome force. We tried to orient ourselves by the sun but found we could not push through thorn bushes that blocked our way and had to go round them in wide detours. It was impossible to keep a steady direction even if we knew what that direction was. I tried to set a course perpendicular to the sun's shadows but it was very difficult to be sure. An added complication was that if we turned west too early, we could run straight into an army checkpoint. If we headed south too long, we would be traveling parallel to the road and have to walk a very long way indeed.

Velaithan looked so exhausted I was afraid she would collapse. My head had begun to throb painfully again. We walked and rested, walked and rested. I was the one to decide when to stop, and when to start again. The woman followed me doggedly, never saying a word. Only our walks were getting shorter and the rests longer.

I must have miscalculated badly.

It must have been close to 17.00, judging by the sun, when we came to a small patch of cultivated land with a hut in the middle of it. More plots could be seen further on. A narrow footpath ran between the live fences separating them.

We followed the footpath as it snaked its way through the cultivation and then between the houses of a small village till, eventually, it connected with a rough cart track. There, blessedly, on the side of the track was a common well with a low protective wall around it. An old woman, clad in a ragged yellow sari, with one end wrapped around her upper body, was filling a clay pot with water.

I was ready to hug the old crow in exchange for a drink of water.

Velaithan took out the empty bottle and held it out wordlessly. The old woman's eyes were bright with curiosity but she asked no questions. She poured water into the bottle and into our cupped hands as we drank and drank and then washed our faces. We smiled and nodded our thanks, not daring to speak, and walked away quickly.

6

We came to a tarred road soon afterwards. We turned left, in the direction I thought Giants Tank must be. We found ourselves in the middle of another village, houses once again neatly fenced for privacy with dried palmyrah leaf. And there, leaning against a fence, very near the gap that served as an entrance, was a bicycle. I looked towards the house in the compound as I walked past.

A ramshackle hut that looked abandoned!

Veleithan stood to one side of the entrance while I checked if the bicycle was locked. It wasn't. I wheeled it onto the road and was about to climb on when I heard a roar of anger behind me. I turned to see a man in a sleeveless vest and tucked up sarong come charging furiously through the gap in the fence and grab the back of the bicycle. He was shouting incoherently, so angry that I was sprayed with his spittle. I guessed that he had retired behind the fence to answer a call of nature.

He was not amused by what he saw when he came back.

He was a big man, and a bicycle is a valuable possession in this impoverished part of the country. I was going to have to disable him to make him let go, and shut him up as well. I let the bicycle go and wound up to belt him.

Velaithan had sneaked up behind the man. She grabbed his sarong, which was tied around his waist in a loose knot, and jerked it down in one motion, leaving him naked from the waist down. The man's eyes went wide with shock, his mouth in a soundless 'O'. He released his grip on the bicycle and reached down for his sarong, now in a pile around his ankles. He still tried to run after me, holding his sarong with one hand, but tripped and went sprawling on the ground.

I mounted the bike on the run and pedalled furiously. Velaithan ran up and, as I lifted my left arm, made a practised sideways leap to land on the crossbar. Cycling is an art form in Jaffna and she seemed expert at 'doubling'. We were round a bend and on our way before the fat man recovered his wits. We heard his roars of anger fading behind us.

I saw her shoulders shake for a moment and wondered if she was laughing. Probably not. I'm told the Tigers iron out humour in their recruits during basic training. When she turned to look back her face was set in its usual expressionless mask.

I don't like you, woman, but you have a good touch in a crisis!

We were now passing through more populated areas. Fortunately the bicycle was the commonest means of transport, often carrying two, and sometimes three, persons. We did not appear unusual in any way. I knew we had to head south to reach the railway. In a confusing grid work of minor roads, every junction became a puzzle. I selected roads that kept the red glow of the sunset at my right shoulder.

Till we ran into the cops, that is. Government cops this time!

Two policemen, armed with automatic weapons, were standing at the junction under the awning of a small building. I didn't even see them till one of them yelled at me in Sinhala.

'Aeii, meheta wareng.'

You. Come here! Only the tone said, 'Come here, arsehole.'

This was trouble. Without papers we were sure to be detained for questioning. If we were to be detained at all, I'd hoped it would be at an army checkpoint. I could always talk my way out, even if it took more time than we could afford. But there was often bad blood between the police and the army. They would never believe I was a captain in the army. Even if they did, especially if they did, they'd lock me up for a while just to piss me off.

I turned the bicycle and rode right up to them. I put my foot down for balance while Velaithan remained on the cross bar, looking down modestly.

Both cops were young men. The man who had called us over could only be described as the hairy one. He had a thick head of hair growing low on his forehead, bushy eyebrows and copious tufts coming out of his ears and nostrils as well as the hairiest forearms I have seen on a human being. The other man was a slender fellow, fair skinned with a wisp of a moustache on his upper lip. I wondered why we had been singled out for special attention. There were many other cyclists and pedestrians about, so why pick on us?

Perhaps it was my head wound, evident even from across the street.

'Koheda yanney?'

Where are you going?

I thought my best chance was to pretend to be a Moslem. Mannar is full of Moslems anyway and Velaithan couldn't pass for a Sinhalese. The Moslems speak Tamil fluently and Sinhala with an accent we think weird and wonderful. I'd spoken with a pseudo Moslem accent often enough, when relating funny stories, to be able to give a reasonable performance.

'Ralahamy,' I said, *'Magey leliva hadissi gamanak geniyanawa. Ledak dānne epā, mage gäni māva marai.'*

Officer, I'm taking my sister-in-law on an urgent mission. Please don't make an issue of it, my wife will kill me!

Both cops were leering at Velaithan.

'Ko umbey ID?' The hairy cop demanded gruffly.

Where is your ID?

'Mama haddissiye āvey. Genna amathaka wunā.'

I left in such a hurry, I forgot to bring it.

'Oluwata mokada wuney?'

What happened to your head?

'Gahaking wätuna.'

I fell off a tree.

It was touch and go, but finally the thought that something illicit was going on distracted them. They were grinning. The thin cop gestured to me to go. As I turned I heard the hairy one say:

'Thambiya lelita wädak denna yanawa wagey!'

Looks like the Moslem is going to bonk his sister-in-law. The word he used for 'Moslem' was an offensive one.

'Eka issalath ahuwenna äthi,' the other cop said nastily. *'Gäni mol gaheng oluwata deela thiyenney.'*

The bastard must have been caught at it before. His wife has already cracked his head with a rice pounder!

I pedalled off before they could think of anything else. We were soon round a corner and out of sight. It was getting dark now and fewer people were about.

We came to a kiosk by the side of the road that seemed to be selling food and dry goods. A Petromax lantern hanging from a rafter threw a pool of light on the road. Two women were standing at the wooden counter placed across the door, waiting to be served. A man was seated on a crude bench outside, drinking something out of a tumbler.

Velaithan jumped off as soon as I stopped.

'What did you tell those policemen?' she demanded angrily.

'I said you were my sister-in-law,' I told her cautiously, 'that I had to take you somewhere urgently.'

'So why were they staring at me and grinning?'

'I don't know,' I said airily.

'You do know!' she shot back.

I thought for a moment she'd stamp her foot. She knew something nasty had been said about her and wouldn't let it rest.

'What did they say when we were leaving?'

These Tamils are a straight-laced lot. I'm told the Tigers are particularly puritanical on matters relating to sex and morals. She would have been outraged if she knew what the cop had said.

I was tempted to tell her, but then thought better of it. She might add those two idiots to her list of people to be killed off someday.

'You don't want to know,' I said. 'Trust me!'

She didn't trust me one bit. She stood and sizzled for a while, staring at me.

'We'd better buy some provisions,' I said trying to change the subject.

She calmed herself down with an effort. It taught me something about her that I noted for future use.

'What do we need?' she asked.

'Food for tonight, and for tomorrow morning. Even biscuits will do. A couple of candles and matches and some old newspapers to sleep on.'

'I need some soap,' Velaithan said.

I gave her the balance cash I had with me, two hundred rupees. I didn't know how much she had left after pawning her ear studs. We'd have to find more money to buy the provisions we would need for Wilpattu.

She waited till the women had moved off and went up to the counter. Another woman with two little girls walked by. She was berating them about something. A man on a bicycle pedalled past and then a cart filled with woven coconut fronds, hauled by an old white bull.

She came back with a shopping bag of purchases and a folded newspaper in her hand. It was quite dark now. Fifteen minutes later we came to the rail track. There was a narrow footpath by the side of the track and we turned left in the direction that, hopefully, would take us to Murunkan station. Velaithan went ahead to show the way. I followed her, wheeling the bicycle and feeling a bone deep weariness creep over me once again.

It had been a very long day.

We were passing houses now shuttered for the night. The houses faced the road that ran parallel to the rail track and had their backs to us. At one of these, Velaithan signalled to me to stop and slipped away, pushing through the live fence that bordered the track. She came back minutes later carrying a shapeless bundle.

Some householder was going to miss his washing tomorrow morning.

When I thought we could walk no further we finally came to the raised platform that had once been a small wayside railway station. There were two rooms on the platform, thankfully unoccupied. Only the walls were left standing. The roof was gone and, with it, the doors and windows. But it had a cemented floor and the walls would at least shelter us from the wind. I lifted the bicycle up on the platform and we wearily carried our belongings inside. We cleared out two corners to sleep in and shared the newspaper to spread on the ground. Velaithan selected the corner furthest from the one I had selected, but still stayed in the same room.

'Can we find water?' Velaithan asked. 'I want to bathe before we eat'.

My only thought had been to eat something and stretch out. Luckily I remembered that one of the streams that fed the Giants Tank passed just across from the station, on the far side of the road that ran by it. We were both filthy with grime and perspiration so, when I thought about it, a bath was not a bad idea at all.

'There is a stream on the far side of the road,' I said. 'Crossing is a risk, we will have to be careful'.

From her purchases, she fished out a candle and matches. She lit the candle and stuck it on the floor in a neutral corner. She then spread the bundle of clothes she had stolen. I noticed she had found a shalwar kameez for herself. This is a dress that originated in Pakistan but is now popular in the country, especially among young Tamils. The top is a kind of long sleeved gown that extends down to the knees and has two slits at the sides. The bottom was a baggy pair of pants tapering to a tight circle at the ankle. It is the kind of dress that would please any missionary.

She had remembered to buy soap.

She held out something to me and I was surprised, and delighted, to see it was a sarong. I had been wondering if there was any point in bathing if I had to get back in the filthy clothes I had worn all day.

I wanted to say thanks but she had already turned away. She blew out the candle, to save it, and followed me out of the building. We had to cross the rail track and the platform on the far side, then through a gap in a dilapidated fence, the main road. We crouched in the deep shadow of a tree for several minutes while we examined the area for sentries or patrols. There was no movement or sound except for the drone of the cicadas in the trees and the faint murmur of flowing water ahead of us.

The stream was shallow, and the water still warm from the sun. Velaithan moved off to bathe in privacy while I just lay in the water with only my nose above the surface. If my head wound was to get infected, so be it. I was past caring. It was the best moment of a day filled with hardship and tension.

I changed into my new sarong and washed the filth off my clothes. I sat on a rock, listening to the night sounds and trying not to worry about tomorrow. There was no traffic on the road and no sound of human activity, just the frogs and the infrequent squawk of a night heron.

Velaithan took her time but emerged eventually, wading through the shallows. We crossed the road with care and got back to our refuge. We spread the washing on the station platform and went inside. This time I surrounded the candle with bits of rubble so that it gave a little light inside the room but kept the glow from showing outside.

'I bought some roti and fish curry, tank fish,' Velaithan said without apology. 'That was all they had left.'

Sri Lanka being an island, we are accustomed to eating saltwater fish. Spanish mackerel and tuna, called thora and kelawalla, are local favourites freely available in the south. The navy had severely restricted fishing in the north for security reasons, so fresh water fish had become an important part of the diet in these parts. These fish tend to have thick, slimy skins and taste muddy to my palate. I wouldn't have touched it if I had a choice.

'That's fine by me,' I said. 'Let's eat and get some sleep'

We sat on the newspapers on my side of the room, our backs to the wall. Velaithan placed the parcels of food and the bottle of water between us. Roti is a paper-thin pancake made from wheat flour, cooked on a hot metal grid and folded into a little square. Not having plates, we just opened the roti, pushed a bit of the curry inside and folded it over like a stuffed bun. It didn't taste too bad, except for the bones we had to keep spitting out.

Velaithan ate sparingly and sat staring at the light, lost again in her thoughts. The gaunt look had diminished and she seemed to have recovered some of her poise. Her hair was loose, spread over her shoulders, still dripping water. She had got herself a cheap plastic comb and held her hair in front of her with one hand as she gently untangled the knots with the comb held in the other.

She turned to speak to me.

'What about tomorrow?'

'There is a junction near here. We need to take the road south to Silavattura,' I explained. 'It is about thirty miles from here to the Modaragam Aru. That is the park boundary. It is much too far for a bicycle. We have to find some transport.'

'Is there any public transport?'

'Very little and too risky.'

'That means a motorcycle, doesn't it?'

'Yes.'

'You have a plan.'

It was a statement, not a question.

'The main road near here is well populated but the forest begins again about two miles down the road. We need to leave here very early, before the army send their morning patrol to open the road to traffic. Then we must find exactly the right spot, and get under cover.'

'And then?'

'Wait for a single rider and … no other vehicles on the road.'

She turned and looked at me questioningly so I told her what I had in mind. She thought about it quietly for a while, staring at me. She nodded and set about putting away the remaining food.

She went to her side of the room and I blew out the candle, now down to a little stump. I stretched out on the newspapers feeling the uneven floor under my back.

'At Kalliyadi,' I asked casually, 'how did you manage to get that travel pass for us?'

Velaithan answered from across the room.

'I told the officer that the army fired mortars at our village last night,' she said. 'I told him they destroyed all the houses, and killed many of the villagers, because they suspected that there were snipers hiding there.'

'Surely he'd know we don't do that kind of thing,' I said, surprised. 'Not any more anyway.'

'Captain,' she said quietly. 'You mustn't believe your own propaganda.'

'Our troops have strict orders not to attack civilian targets.'

'So how do you account for the atrocities committed your soldiers?' she asked icily. 'How is it they still burn down villages in reprisal attacks?'

I had to make an effort to match her tone, to stay objective about a subject that always got me angry.

'If it happens at all now, it must be very rare,' I said cautiously. 'Under-trained soldiers sometimes get carried away in the heat of battle.'

'Are you saying the authorities have prohibited it but sometimes soldiers disobey orders. Is that what you mean?'

'Yes.'

'I am sorry to say that I can't believe you,' she said coldly.

Do you think I give a fuck about that?

'I think you are quite mistaken,' I said reasonably, ignoring the provocation. 'We do have strict orders about retaliatory attacks. There is a lot of pressure on the government from the media and NGO's. But we know that at the back of all that is your propaganda machine blowing up minor incidents out of proportion and out of context. The international community gets taken in very easily. There is no one to tell the soldier's side of it'.

'My uncle was killed in a reprisal attack recently,' she said angrily. 'What is the soldier's side of that?'

'I'm sorry to hear about it,' I said defensively. 'I still maintain it is very rare now.'

'And you, Captain?' she asked, ignoring my argument. 'Do you think even one such incident should be tolerated?'

'I have some.... personal views on that,' I said. 'They are not the views of my government.'

'Do you mean you condone reprisal attacks on innocent villagers?'

She hadn't raised her voice but the tone had changed.

'We are at war with an enemy who use their own people as a human shield,' I said wearily. 'A sniper can shoot and kill a soldier from a village hut but we are not allowed to shoot back for fear of hurting some civilian. When a claymore mine is planted near a village and the explosion kills a couple of soldiers, when a few others lose their limbs and eyes, we are expected to smile and say ... oh, these are innocent villagers. But the villagers are not so innocent. They damn well know about these things in advance. Because they do nothing, our men are maimed and killed. They must pay a price for that.'

'Surely you understand their fear?' She was outraged. 'If they inform the army, our people would punish them severely.'

Now I was beginning to get irritated. I fought to keep it under control.

'It amazes me that the media and public, so many people, are unable, or unwilling, to see the absurdity of it. Call them what you like, your group are terrorists. When they shoot at a patrol from a village hut, they are inviting retaliation. They are the direct cause of civilians getting hurt. Our men are dying out there, they have to defend themselves.'

'What are you trying to say?'

Was there a new steeliness in her voice? I didn't care.

'Again it's just my personal opinion, but I think it is the only way to fight this thing. If a terrorist fired at me from the cover of the village, I'd want to fire back with maximum force. Once that policy is known, the villagers themselves are not going to take kindly to having their own 'boys' use them as shields. If my patrol hits a mine near a village, I'd burn the village down. Once the villagers know that there will be no mercy, they will start being more careful. They will either get their 'boys' to go further afield to lay their ambushes, or they will sneak the info to us. It is our pity for the villager that the terrorist takes advantage of. I think that is a mistake and it puts our men at risk.'

'Have you actually put your theories into practice?' she asked icily. 'How many villages have you destroyed in your campaign?'

'I once burnt down a village after a mine took out one of my vehicles. They lost their possessions true enough, but I lost two men and another man was crippled. I was nearly cashiered for it though. Our generals are more afraid of the ICRC and the NGOs than they are of the terrorists.'

'You really surprise me, Captain. You seem to be an educated man, yet your instincts are primitive,' she said sanctimoniously. 'Don't you see it is this attitude that makes your army so hated? These are your own citizens. Have you no consideration for them?'

'I can see you are missing a point here. I do feel sorry for these people. Most of them are truly innocent and have suffered greatly for a long time, too long. But I will not let your thugs derive a tactical advantage from any civilized instincts I may have. In the long run, I think this policy will help the villagers as well.'

'I'm sure those who are dead and maimed from your gunfire, those who have lost their homes and possessions, will be truly grateful that you have their greater good at heart.'

Sarcasm suited her.

'Your people started this,' I said, surprised at my own calm. 'They are the ones who put civilians at risk. Why don't you ask your leaders to change their tactics? Why have a double standard, civilized norms for us and any available tactic for them? If it means anything, I would probably … probably do the same thing if the villagers were Moslems or even Sinhala.'

'It is easy to say that, I suppose, when there is little chance you will have to act on it.'

I was getting bored with this.

'Why don't you give it a rest?' I said wearily. 'We have a long day tomorrow.'

I stared at the cloudless brilliance of the night sky above me and thought of the speed at which I had been caught up in this chain of events. It was only yesterday that I'd set out on a routine mission to pick up an informant. Today Jaffna was in flames and I was now committed to cross the entire length of the country, illegally too, with this strange and unpredictable woman.

I would be foolish to trust her. She would support me only so long as our objectives were the same. If they should diverge, I had no doubt that she would slit my throat with the same detached unconcern with which she had handled every other situation.

She knew my objective was to get her to army headquarters as quickly as possible. What was her real goal?

7

28th March 2000

The sound of rustling newspaper woke me from an exhausted sleep. There was just enough light to see Velaithan gather her clothes and leave the room. I knew she had gone down to the stream and wouldn't want me around. I dozed off and woke again when she returned.

We packed our belongings, dressed in our dry 'day' clothes and left. I had no idea of the time but could see a faint glow over the trees in the eastern sky. It was probably a half hour before dawn. On the main road we started cycling towards Medawachchiya, doubling up as we had the day before. We were completely vulnerable at this time because the road was officially closed at night and only opened for traffic at a specific time in the morning. If we were stopped on the road now we would, at the very least, be taken in for questioning.

But there was no one about. The road had been macadamized recently and was in surprisingly good condition. There was just enough light to see our way. Velaithan sat on the bar, with her haversack strapped to her back, and we made good time. We left the habitations and buildings behind and soon came to a thickly forested area. This jungle would run in an unbroken stretch up to Medawachchiya, some forty miles away.

My plan called for a straight stretch of road, perhaps a quarter mile in length, with bends at either end so that it was not visible at a great distance. Given that this road cut through virgin forest and was dead straight for most of its length, the ideal spot was not easy to come by. As I

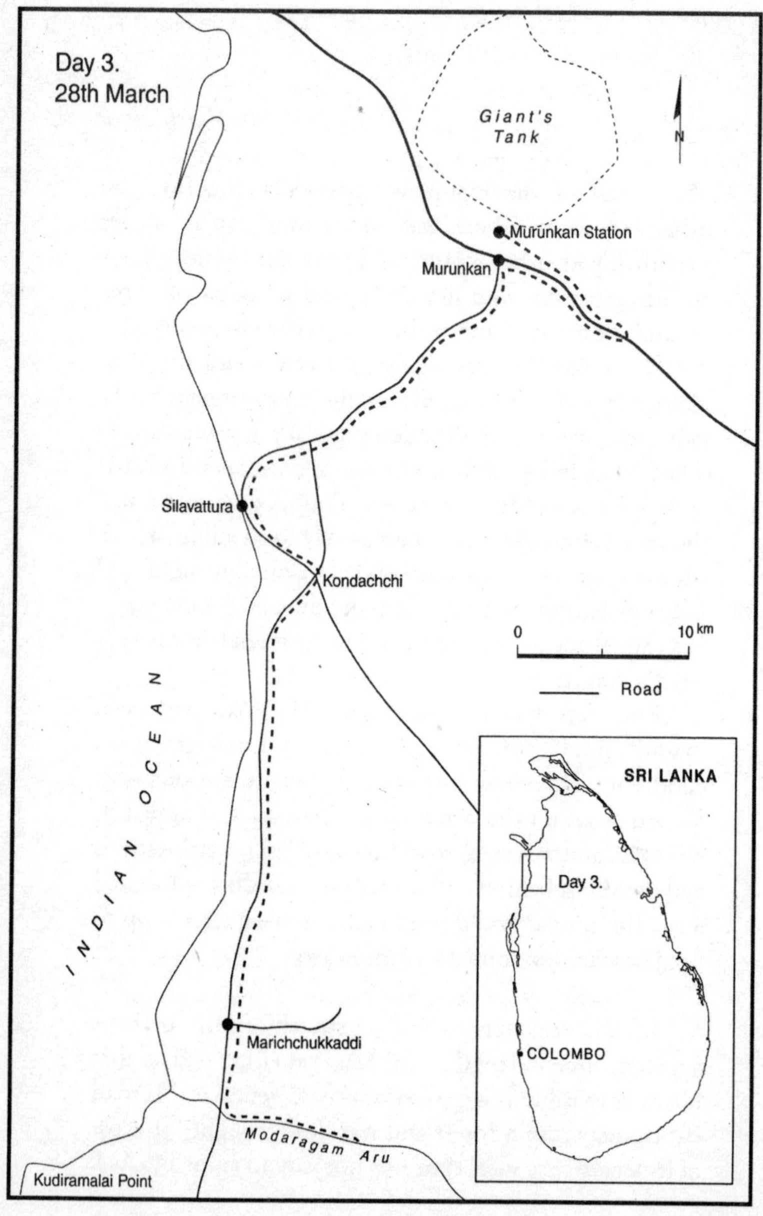
Day 3.
28th March
Giant's
Tank
N
Murunkan Station
Murunkan
Silavattura
Kondachchi
0
10 km
Road
INDIAN OCEAN
SRI LANKA
Day 3.
COLOMBO
Marichchukkaddi
Modaragam Aru
Kudiramalai Point

rode along, I was alert for the sound of a vehicle, ready to dash into the forest at a moments notice.

I had expected to find a suitable spot for my ambush without too much difficulty, but there was always something wrong, some missing essential. One particular stretch satisfied all my requirements except that the scrub by the roadside didn't give us enough cover. The sun was peeping over the trees ahead of us and I was getting a bit worried when we came to a stretch of road with thick cover on either side. The straight section was shorter than I would have liked and gave us no margin of safety.

We would have to be very quick .... and very lucky.

We hid the bicycle in the shrubbery and found a fallen tree to sit on. Velaithan had saved the remains of our dinner but I could not face another meal of rubbery roti and tank fish. I ate soggy crackers from a packet she had bought the previous evening while she quietly finished the rest of the roti. The people of Jaffna are, after all, known for their frugality.

It was a long and tiresome vigil.

The first vehicles to come by were a convoy of army trucks that roared past at about 07.00 soon after the sun cleared the trees. They were being driven at very high, almost reckless, speed down the open road. It has always amused me to realize that everyone, including myself, driving in a dangerous stretch of road, believes that there was safety in excessive speed whereas the opposite is probably true.

No vehicles came by for a while after that until a tractor rattled past, hauling a trailer loaded with firewood. I knew that the road from Medawachchiya would have been opened at the same time, but traffic from there would take some time to reach this spot. Most of the vehicles would be coming from the Mannar end and that suited me quite well.

It was getting warm. Birds were out in flocks, calling and whistling in the trees all around us. Faint rustles and chirrups in the undergrowth signalled the presence of ground feeders as well. I wished I had time to check them out.

The next vehicle was a military Land Rover with the canvas on one side loose and flapping wildly in the wind. Some minutes later we heard the unmistakable whine of a small motor bicycle. Velaithan stood up immediately and we took our pre-planned positions. It came quite slowly round the corner but, to my disappointment, carried two men talking loudly to each other.

Another tractor and a truck went past and then the first vehicle from the direction of Medawachchiya. I had hoped to get our hijacking over and done with before vehicles started coming from that direction, for that would double our chances of getting caught.

Velaithan sat some distance from me and did not speak at all.

I was getting just a bit worried when we heard the throb of a bigger engine. We were at our appointed stations in a moment. He came round the bend, a broad shouldered man hunched over the handlebars of a motor bicycle. Bareheaded too!

Her timing was just right.

When the rider was about fifteen yards away from her, she stepped out of cover and onto the road. She smiled brightly and raised her hand. A woman, young and pretty, standing there in the morning sun. When he went past the tree I was hiding behind, he was already slowing down. He braked sharply and drew up by her.

'Enna vernum?' I heard him ask in a gruff voice.

What do you want?

He didn't see me at all. At the very last moment, he must have sensed something was wrong, for he started to turn. The length of deadwood in my hand was heavy and I hit him on the back of his head with more force than I had intended. He collapsed across the handlebar in a limp heap. I caught him by his collar while Velaithan held onto the handlebar to keep the bike from tipping over. This was the critical moment. I had to get the man and his bike under cover before the next vehicle came along.

We heard it at the same moment, the roar of a heavy vehicle just around the bend behind us. Desperation must have given me strength because he was a heavy man, slumped over like a sack of rice. I grabbed his belt in my right hand and his neck in my left, lifted him bodily off the bike, pivoted and flung him into the bushes by the side of the road. He went through the shrubbery like a cannon ball. I heard him land with a thud.

I turned back in time to see Velaithan, still holding the handlebars, push the bike to build momentum and vault on to the seat, pointing it straight at the bushes. It plunged through the undergrowth and I heard the crash as it fell over. I scrambled behind the same tree I had used for cover from the rider.

We made it … just!

A truck full of troops roared past without glance in our direction.

I watched them out of sight and hurried into the bushes to assess the situation. The rider was lying on his face, his body twisted awkwardly, just as he had landed. I hoped he was not dead but didn't stop to check. I pushed my way to where Velaithan was trying, unsuccessfully, to lift the bike up. Thankfully, the only visible damage was a cracked headlight. I noticed that Velaithan was limping and the sleeve of her kameez was torn.

'Are you hurt?'

She stared at me as if I had made an indecent proposal and shook her head angrily. I suppose LTTE cadres are not allowed to feel pain or maybe they simply shoot their wounded. I was sorry I had asked.

We set the bike on its stand and went over to the unfortunate man who had so recently owned it. We dragged him further into the bushes and examined him. I was relieved to find him still breathing, if only in grunts and snorts. When turned on his back, I saw that he was a solidly built, dark man with a heavy belly that protruded above him, even as he lay flat on his back. He had a luxuriant moustache and short, curly hair brushed back from his forehead. He had on a black T-shirt and beige 'cargo pants', unusual for this part of the world. He was wearing a pair of sneakers, no socks.

I wanted his clothes the way a blind man wants to see. I was pretty uncomfortable in my oversized black pants and the improvised, coir rope belt. I would have settled for anything. But cargo pants on the Mannar road? I hoped his sneakers would fit.

I had him stripped him to his undergarments in seconds. We removed all the contents of his many pockets and heaped them on the ground. I retired behind the bushes and changed. Even these pants were a trifle loose around the waist and short at the ankle but I didn't care. The T-shirt was just right. Sadly the sneakers were a shade too small but I took them along anyway.

It is amazing how a few stitches of clothing improve

a man's attitude and confidence. I was almost whistling when I got back to see how Velaithan was doing.

'He's an EPDP bastard,' she said contemptuously as if that explained everything.

It did, actually.

EPDP is one of a host of Tamil groups that had taken up arms against the government. The LTTE, wanting to be the sole representative of the Tamils, had killed their leaders and decimated their cadres. Now EPDP and the others had aligned themselves with the government as an anti-LTTE Tamil group. Their cadres helped the army to interrogate suspects and identify LTTE sympathizers, especially at the crossing points between rebel and government sectors. Unfortunately many of these cadres had succumbed to the endemic corruption of this work and preyed shamelessly on the miserable civilians who passed through their hands.

We went through his belongings. A dirty handkerchief, an EPDP photo ID describing him as 'Captain Dinesh Shanthikumar', a national ID, some loose papers and a wallet with currency notes. I counted two thousand three hundred and thirty rupees.

Business must be good.

He was still unconscious when I took him by his legs and dragged him another thirty or so yards deeper into the scrub. I sat him up with his back to a small tree and used strips of cloth torn from my discarded shirt to tie his hands at the back of the tree behind him. I yanked his underpants off before I tied his feet together with more cloth binding. It would not hold him for long, but long enough, hopefully, to give us a head start. I reasoned that a naked man would take just a little longer to get organized than one who had clothes on. Everything helped. Five minutes wasted looking for a loincloth could mean the difference between life and death to us.

We took his money. His wristwatch was smashed and useless. We buried it some distance away with the rest of his stuff and my discarded clothes. I took my pedal cycle across the road and hid it carefully behind some bushes.

I wasn't planning to make life any easier for our EPDP pal.

8

Thankfully the motorbike started easily, but a check of the fuel tank showed only a modest amount of petrol at the bottom of the tank. Fuel is severely restricted in these border areas with civilians owning motor bicycles being issued some fifteen litres for the month. The EPDP man must have had a more generous allowance but the balance in the tank did not seem at all enough to get us to our destination. I decided to worry about that later.

We climbed on and set off towards Murunkan junction once again. Velaithan placed her rucksack between us and sat at the extreme edge of the seat behind me.

We passed two trucks on the road but reached the junction without further incident. I turned off the main road and stopped as we passed the few dilapidated shops, all that remained of what had once been a bustling little township. Velaithan stepped off almost before I had come to a standstill. There were people moving about, talking desultorily, stepping in and out of the shops, many of them carrying plastic shopping bags. A two-wheel tractor went past hauling some produce and people in a trailer.

'We need a lot of stuff,' I said. 'This is probably the last chance to get it'

'Is it safe to stop here?' She didn't appear nervous, just curious.

'I think, with reasonable luck, we have about an hour before our friend raises the alarm. Anyhow he'll think we've gone towards Medawachchiya. I don't think he will look for us on this road.'

She thought about it for a moment, staring at me in her inscrutable way.

'I'll get paper and a pencil,' she said, then turned and walked away.

She came back moments later with a cheap ballpoint and an exercise book. We sat in the shade of a tamarind tree to make a list.

'We will need at least four days to get across. Lets budget for that and for one extra day to be safe. All right?'

'I don't know,' she said. 'Let's assume that's right and go ahead'

'OK. Rice will be our staple. A kilo of rice will feed six persons. Three kg should see us through.'

She wrote:
Rice 3 kg
Dhal 500 gm
Dry fish 500 gm
Coconut oil 2 litres
Manioc
Salt 100 gm
Pepper 50 gm
Curry Powder & Chillie Powder 100 gm each
Lime 250g
Onions 500g

Aluminum Pans 2
Tin plates 2
Tin cups 2
Coconut Shell spoon
Citronella Oil – 1 bottle
Polythene rolls or sheets (black or dull colour) – 2
Coir rope
Matches – 6 boxes

Candles – 6
Kathi
Knife
Sling bag or Rucksack
Safety pins – 2 pkts
Needle & thread
Mineral Water bottles (empty) 2
Hats
Bread and curry to eat on the way.

Velaithan held her hand out. It was stolen money anyway, so I gave her ten grubby hundreds from the EPDP man's bundle.

I sat in the shade and waited.

Velaithan took her time, going from shop to shop, the bundles in her hands growing larger each time she stepped back on to the road. She was back after a while to say she had most of what we wanted except for the plastic sheets, hats and kathi. She had bought a sling bag of about the right size with two small carrying handles. The time we had spent there was making me nervous so Velaithan balanced the bags of provisions on her lap as I took off. Silavattura, on the coast, was about twelve miles from where we were. From there we would turn south towards Wilpattu, about eighteen miles further.

The thatched huts became less frequent and gradually disappeared altogether. The tarred road ceased to exist, except for short, potholed stretches. The road was bordered by patches of thorny bushes interspersed with sandy wastes that glistened whitely in the sun. Stubby baobab trees stood by the road like fat traffic policemen.

We crossed a causeway with only a trickle of water flowing in the river below. We looked too conspicuous with the pile of shopping bags between us so I stopped under a small copse of trees partly hidden from the road. We divided the provisions and utensils and packed them, as best we could, into the rucksack and sling bag. The food wasn't enough to see us through but we couldn't carry much more.

We'd have to live off the land.

The glare from the sand was searing and hurt my eyes. I felt hot air boiling up slowly around me, like water in a heated cauldron. It was just bearable in the shade, so I sat with my back to a tree and gestured to Velaithan to sit as well. She hesitated and finally folded herself cross-legged in the sand.

'Crossing Wilpattu on foot will be … very strenuous. We can find water along the way but we can't carry all the food we will need,' I explained. 'Any injury or illness to either one will be fatal. You do understand this, don't you?'

'Yes'.

No expression, just calm acceptance.

'It will also be dangerous,' I continued. 'We'll need a lot of luck to get through.'

'From animals?'

'Mm, animals can be a threat, yes,' I said carefully. 'The real danger is from men … with guns. Poachers and army deserters are active there. There could also be … groups of your people.'

'Have you been there?' she asked. 'Do you know the area at all?'

'I've been around, during my service in Mannar,' I said, selecting my words. 'I know the tracks and water holes.'

'You couldn't have been there on patrol, surely,' she remarked. 'What made you go down there?'

'Poaching'.

Did her lips tighten in disapproval?

'We need some rolls of plastic sheeting to use as a ground sheet and for cover at night,' I continued, ignoring her. 'We must find something on the way. We also need a kathi and the hats. Is there anything else we may have forgotten?'

'I got some bar soap and a couple of toothbrushes. No tooth paste though,' she said. 'I also brought some food for the afternoon.'

I found that the sling bag she had bought was capacious enough but inconvenient to carry over any distance. Something would have to be done about that. I picked up a twig and drew our route in the sand, as much to clear my own thoughts as for her benefit.

'This road goes to Silavattura on the coast. It should be about ten miles, say twenty minutes. From there we go down the coast road for about eighteen miles. The Modaragam Aru is the border of the sanctuary. It will be quite shallow at this time. If we ford the river we will be on what was called the north road in British times,' I explained carefully. 'There never was a road, just a track in the jungle plain. No sign of it now'.

'Is that the route we will take?'

'No,' I said. 'We won't go that way. It is mostly open plain with little cover. Fresh water is also more difficult to come by. My real worry is that we can be seen at a distance and easily ambushed'.

'What is the other route?'

'Lets get to the river, we can discuss it then.'

We got back on the road and headed west, towards the coast. We passed through a plantation of cashew trees, probably abandoned now, scattered settlements and more scrub jungle. This whole area was a kind of neutral zone where the army and the rebels were present but did not really confront each other. I had heard that the LTTE leader for the area was based somewhere near the town. Army patrols moved about in daylight without hindrance, but retired to their fortified camps at night. The night belonged to the rebels.

We were entering the outskirts of Silavattura. The buildings in the village were run down and dilapidated, but still far more solid than the mud huts I had seen in the Wanni. There was a tea kiosk and a banana shop, thereafter a couple of stalls selling vegetables. I saw a man in an open doorway, working on an ancient pedal activated sewing machine.

I stopped immediately.

'Could you ask that man to sew two straps onto my bag?' I asked Velaithan. 'I want to carry it like a rucksack.'

She just nodded, picked up the sling bag and walked into what was, hopefully, the village tailor-shop. She got the job done faster than I had expected. The short handles had been cut off. The tailor had, with some ingenuity, made two multi-coloured straps with bits of waste cloth. The straps went around the bag and provided loops I could slip my arms through. Across the centre were a strap and a buckle to secure the loops against my chest. The bag was shaped all wrong, being thin and long, but when I tried it on it seemed comfortable enough.

I smiled my thanks but she had looked away.

The road ended in a 'T' junction with the sea, now a very vivid turquoise, glittering in the background. A broad beach of fine white sand separated the road from the water. Some dilapidated fishing boats were lined up on the sand. Two men were sitting in the shade of a stunted tree, mending a net. Several small boys were playing in the surf, throwing wet sand at each other and yelling.

I stopped under a small grove of palmyrah palms and parked the bike. My heart sank when I opened the fuel tank. A puff of fumes escaped with a loud hiss when I loosened the cap but the tank was almost dry. We would not get much further without fuel.

The town was a dreary place with rows of tiny houses on the land side. The few shops were distinct from the houses only by having a wider front door of the type that is shut by inserting a series of vertical planks. The shops were open but had few customers at that time. A cart creaked past with an old man seated at the back of the yoke, whacking the bull with a thin stick. Some men rode by on bicycles, one of then with a skate tied to his carrier rack, its long whip like tail almost touching the road.

The first shop selling hardware items had what I most needed, a kathi. This is a type of axe with a blade shaped like a slice of watermelon, fitted to a rough wooden handle about two and a half feet long and two inches in diameter. Our villagers, especially those who live close to the forest, rely on the kathi for a multitude of uses including personal defence. No villager would venture into the forest without it. The kathi I bought for a hundred and fifty rupees was crudely made but the blade was sharp and fitted snugly on the handle. It would do very nicely.

We now needed the plastic sheets and hats. And petrol.

No, there was no polythene or canvas for sale but we did get two crude straw hats of the type fishermen wear when out at sea. Velaithan also bought six eggs, wrapping each one with newspaper before placing them carefully in a shopping bag. I was pleased to find the shopkeeper stocked some fishing gear. I picked up six of the smallest hooks he had together with twenty metres of thin nylon fishing line, wound on a bit of stick.

Petrol was the real problem. It is severely rationed in the area to prevent fuel reaching the LTTE. The trouble is the rebels have plenty of fuel but civilians have to go through hell to get a bit of it. There is a thriving black market, of course, and it is no secret that most of fuel for that business comes from the army itself.

Velaithan made some guarded inquiries from the shopkeeper.

He was an old man with skinny arms sticking out of his sleeveless vest. He was completely bald but compensated for this with a splendid white beard. His eyes were young though, bright and sharp as he studied us from behind his counter.

'Uncle, we need some petrol for our motor bicycle,' Velaithan asked diffidently. 'Would you perhaps have a friend who might have a little to spare?'

'I do not sell petrol,' he answered gruffly. 'There is no petrol available here.'

'Of course I know that, uncle,' Velaithan could smile winningly when it suited her. 'But perhaps you know someone who has not used his quota and might have a bit to spare? We are prepared to pay well for just two litres.'

The old man stared at us for a moment. He turned and shouted towards the back of his shop. The rear area appeared to be his home, separated by an opening covered with a filthy curtain hanging from a wire.

A small boy appeared, bare bodied except for a wisp

of sarong. The old man spoke rapidly and handed the boy a small plastic can from the shelf behind him. The man turned back to us.

'I will send my grandson to see if my nephew can spare some petrol. He has very little for his own needs so will charge a hundred and twenty per litre. You can pay me now and bring your bicycle to the back of the shop.'

The bastard was robbing us. The price of petrol in Colombo was fifty rupees a litre and only a few cents more in the countryside. I didn't care though. I blessed the EPDP man and paid for two liters straight away.

There was a narrow passage between the shop and the next building. We wheeled the bike through this to the back and put it on its stand. We stood in the shade offered by the low eave of the house. Although the road frontage was narrow, the old man's property extended some distance at the back. We were standing outside his kitchen. There was a masonry water trough with a rough rack made of sticks tied together with coir rope. A number of clay and aluminum cooking utensils were inverted on the rack. The fenced yard extended for some distance. There was an enclosure, surrounded by wire mesh, housing some scraggy hens.

His eggs, at least, were fresh.

The little boy returned after awhile, can in hand. I examined the contents carefully to make sure we were not buying kerosene, but it seemed genuine. The two precious litres went into the tank and the problem of fuel was resolved.

I started up and wheeled the bike in a circle to get back in the alley when Velaithan, sitting behind me, tapped my shoulder and pointed. I saw it then … and couldn't believe my eyes. The roof at the back sloped down to an eave at head height. It was covered with local clay tiles laid in parallel rows down the slope of the roof. These tiles were obviously old and black with fungus.

The roof must have been leaking badly, for laid over it, and held down by bits of timber, were several lengths of black polythene sheet. Each sheet was about eight feet across and twelve feet in length.

We went back inside and Velaithan opened the negotiations.

'Uncle, could you see your way to giving us two of the old plastic sheets from your roof?'

'I can't sell them,' he said. 'You can see I need them to keep my house dry.'

The old man was quite firm but added as an afterthought:

'I am sorry.'

'But uncle, it is now the dry season and no rain is expected for some time. You can surely get some new sheets to replace them before the rains start again?'

They argued back and forth for some time.

Greed won in the end and for an outrageous three hundred rupees, two of the sheets were ours.

The roof did not look strong enough to hold my weight so I hoisted the little boy up. He scrambled about with the agility of a monkey and soon had two lengths of sheeting rolled up and handed down. I ignored Velaithan's frown and slipped him ten rupees, earning a delighted smile in return.

I rolled the two sheets together into a tight tube and tied it, with the kathi, to the side of the bike below the seat. We had a cautious peep at the road as we came out of the alley but saw only two carts coming slowly down the road towards us. We set off on the last leg of the journey towards the Modaragam river, and the wilderness beyond it.

9

We traveled in silence for about twenty minutes. The road had deteriorated into a veritable cart track with whole sections badly washed away. What was left was corrugated in little hills and gullies that made progress slow and painful. We were passing through thorny scrub jungle with patches of open sandy areas that glittered and danced in the glare. It was getting very hot, even the wind in my face felt as if it came out of a hair dryer.

In the distance I saw a cloud of dust stirred up by an approaching vehicle, traveling fast. As it drew nearer I realized that it was a Land Rover Defender. It had to be an army vehicle. As it flashed past, I saw the soldiers glance curiously at us. Motor bicycles must be a rarity in the area.

'They have stopped,' Velaithan whispered urgently in my ear. 'They are turning to follow us'.

I immediately turned off the road into the scrub on the left. The sand was loose and the bike kept slipping and sliding but I kept her going roughly perpendicular to the road we had left. Over the noise of my own engine I could hear the whine of Defender in low gear, crashing through the bushes. I knew they had left the road and were following our tracks that must have been clearly visible in the sand.

I kept going directly away from the road for about half a mile. It was hard to judge the distance. I then swung in a wide semicircle to the right and then turned back towards the road. I could hear the Defender grinding away but we were well screened by the shrubbery and I didn't think they could hear the noise of our much quieter engine.

I hit a patch of really soft sand and the wheels sank up to the hubs. Velaithan was off in a flash, balancing my bag on the seat and pushing with all her strength. I could hear her gasping with the effort. Behind us the roar of the Defender got steadily louder. I stood up as well, straddling the bike and straining against the handles, rocking it from side to side. It came free at last and we started off again. When we came to the track, I rode straight across and then through the bushes on the far side. Once I was sure we were under cover, I killed the engine and waited.

I could hear the engine of the Defender clearly, getting louder.

'What made them follow us?' Kamala asked thoughtfully. 'Did we make some mistake?'

'I think it was the bike. There can't be many around and this road doesn't lead anywhere.'

'Will they really follow through now, do you think?'

'No,' I said with more confidence than I felt. 'My guess is they followed us on a sudden impulse. If we were really Tigers from the area, we might have ambushed them or led them into a minefield. They must have thought of that by now.'

Through the screen of bushes we saw the Defender come on to the road. They had followed our tracks all the way and emerged from the scrub with a roar. They stopped the vehicle with its nose to the road and the engine pointed directly at us. They were arguing, undecided.

Don't get down!

If they got down they would see our tracks in the sand on the far side of the road. We stood still as stone carvings, not at all sure now if the screen of bushes was solid enough.

In the end they thought better of it and turned to their right, towards Silavattura. We got off the bike and crept to the edge of the road to watch them disappear in another dust storm.

We passed through Marichchukuddi without incident and reached the river soon afterwards. The road ended at the ford with an indistinct track leading to the wilderness on the far side. A narrow footpath branched off on the near side, following the course of the river. The path to the right would lead towards the river delta and the sea.

I turned left.

The path was tortuous, winding around kumbuk trees, roots and rocks. Bushes and branches brushed against us on either side. After traveling about a mile I saw a game track to the right, heading towards the river. I manoeuvred the bike slowly towards the water, as far as we could safely ride. I could glimpse the river, a rocky stream at this time of the year, through the trees.

'Lets rest a bit and have some food,' I announced. 'We need to discuss the next stage'.

As usual Velaithan didn't say a word. She just dismounted, carried both bags and climbed down to the water's edge. I checked the fuel in the tank and could see just a bit of movement in the bottom of the tank. We had less than a half-litre left. I turned the bike around, resting it against a tree, and went down to join her. From the position of the sun, I guessed it was about 15.00 hours.

By any standard, it was an idyllic spot.

The steep, eroded banks showed that the Modaragam must have a strong flood of water in the rainy season but now, in the drought, the flow was placid. The water trickled through, and over, a jumble of rocks, gin clear and thigh deep in the pools. Huge, water loving, kumbuk trees lined the sides of the stream and provided a shady canopy.

Velaithan selected a flat bit of rock to sit on. We cleared it of leaves and debris and she began unpacking our bags. I sat down, then lay flat on my back and stared at the leafy mantle above me. We had made it to the river and, importantly, no one was chasing us.

I must have dozed off. I heard her calling, as if from a great distance.

'Captain. You'd better eat something.'

She had cut the loaf of bread into thick slices and had made rough sandwiches with a dry curry stuffing.

'What's in this?' I asked.

I didn't really care. In my condition, I would have eaten pickled dog.

'The man said it was mutton.'

It could well have been true. Goats are the only animals that thrive in this area.

And dogs.

We ate without speaking. The bread was a bit stale and crumbly but the curry was just right for a sandwich, nearly dry but with enough gravy to soften the bread. The mutton, if it was mutton, was delicious.

Something in the tree behind me attracted Velaithan's attention.

I turned to look. Perched on a horizontal branch leaning over the water was a large brown and white raptor with yellow eyes and a heavy, curved beak. It kept turning its head from time to time to survey the water below. A tuft of brown feathers rose majestically from the centre of its head, like the headdress of an Indian chieftain. The faint breeze coming downriver ruffled its crest from time to time.

'That's called a hawk eagle,' I announced, showing off a bit.

'Yes, I know,' she said softly. 'I have never seen one before. Isn't it magnificent?'

It was the first time I'd seen some animation in her face and it presented an entirely unsuspected side of her character. I looked at her with some curiosity.

'Yes, it does look rather regal,' I agreed. 'How did you know what it is, if you have never seen one?'

Her face froze up as if a curtain had been pulled down over it.

'From a book. Henry's *Birds of Ceylon*,' she said very quietly. 'I remember the … colour plate.'

Just then the eagle slid off its perch in a splendid sweep of its wings. It glided over our heads and, as we turned to watch, disappeared round the curve of the river.

The brief moment of shared interest withered and died with it.

'Where will we camp for the night?' Velaithan asked abruptly, all business again. 'Here?'

'No,' I said. 'I'd like to go further upstream.'

'And tomorrow?'

'I want to follow the jeep tracks that park visitors used in the old days. They will be overgrown now but should be quite easy to follow.'

'What is special about that route?'

'The tracks run through thick cover and connect up the villus, waterholes that is. It is the safest route.'

'Much longer, isn't it?' she asked abruptly. 'How long will it take?'

'I'd say four days. Five on the outside.'

'And if we take the north road and really push it?'

'It will be very dangerous,' I said cautiously. 'Water is scarce as well.'

'How many days, Captain?' she persisted.

'Two days, three at the most.'

She sat quietly for a few minutes.

'Captain, I think your route takes too much time. We might be too late, then my information will be useless,' she paused, then said firmly. 'We must take the north road.'

'Without weapons, we won't get through,' I said, trying to control my irritation. 'My route should get us to Colombo by the third or fourth. That's enough time to put the operation in place."

'You don't seem to understand how critical this is, Captain.' Her voice was sharp now, uncompromising. 'You will never get this chance again. We must be in Colombo with enough time to spare.'

'This is the safest …'

'Captain, safety is a luxury we cannot afford,' she said harshly. 'We must take the direct route, travel at night if necessary. There is no time to waste.'

I felt anger erupting in me. I hated it when someone argued tactics with me. Especially subordinates. Especially enemies. Especially women.

You stupid fucking cow, you don't know what we are up against. There are men out there who'd kill us just for the clothes on our backs or … just for fun!

'I'm running this mission,' I grated through clenched teeth. 'We'll do it my way or not at all. If you don't like it, I'll take you back to Mannar.'

She was very angry. She stared at me with blazing

eyes, lips set in a harsh thin line. I just ignored her. She got tired of it after a while and set about repacking the bags.

Time to leave.

I checked the fuel once again. The tank was almost dry. I wanted to get as far up the track as we could because it would make our trek tomorrow that much shorter. The track was no more than a footpath that wound in and around the large trees that grew near the river. Giant roots across the path needed careful handling, wasting both time and fuel. We had struggled through about two miles, perhaps less, when the engine coughed and stopped, then caught again. I saw what seemed to be a game trail leading off to the right and turned the bike into it. We had to duck our heads to avoid low branches and had managed to travel about thirty yards when the engine stopped. I tried several times to coax it to life again but it was of no use. That was it.

The bike had served us well. We unloaded all our gear and I pushed it off the path and into the middle of a dense thicket. It was well concealed and I didn't think it would be found for a couple of days at least, if ever. It was a short walk, and slide down a steep bank, to the edge of the river.

'Where do we camp?' It was the first time Velaithan had spoken after our spat.

The forest was very dense along the banks. Kumbuk and palu trees reached over the water from all angles and the undergrowth was tangled and gloomy, even in daylight. The area didn't look at all promising.

'Lets wade up the river till we find a suitable spot.'

The river was filled with boulders of varying sizes interspersed with patches of sand. The high water mark left by floodwaters on the banks again showed that the river must be a gushing torrent in the rainy season. The drought in March had left it knee deep in most places but the wet rocks were slippery as glass and we had to move with the greatest care. A broken ankle would end our project right there.

It was desperately slow going. Tiring too. I knew we needed at least an hour of daylight to secure ourselves for the night and time was running out. The sun was on our backs, almost directly behind us. The length of our shadows on the water seemed to get longer with each step. Despite all my training and fitness, I felt the strength and resolve draining out of me. Velaithan followed me doggedly, her face once again taut with strain.

She was giving me the silent treatment and I couldn't have wished for a greater blessing.

The river curved to the left and I saw, on the opposite bank, a stretch of brown-white sand about twenty feet across. It would have to do. We waded across and sat thankfully on a tree trunk that had washed up at one end of it.

10

'Is this it?' Velaithan asked.

I was tempted to say 'No', just for the hell of it, but I couldn't summon up the energy.

'Yes, we'll camp here,' I announced. 'Wait here while I check out the surroundings.'

She stood up immediately.

'I'll come with you,' she said. 'Tell me what to look for.'

She was not going to sit around and let me play the dominant male.

'We must make sure there are no game trails coming onto the sandbank,' I told her. 'We don't want animals stumbling on us in the night.'

She just looked at me. She wasn't overjoyed by the prospect but didn't say anything.

We surveyed the sandbank carefully. There were plenty of animal tracks, dainty footprints of spotted deer and the heavy cloven hoof marks of buffalo. Thankfully there were no elephant footprints or dung and no distinct sign of a game trail leading to it from the forest. Relieved, I selected a spot with two overhanging kumbuk branches, about ten feet apart. We cleared away bits of driftwood, leaves and other debris from the area. I used the kathi to cut two bushy branches to use as brooms and we smoothed the sand out as best we could.

The next step was to tie the thicker rope across the two branches and then sling one of the plastic sheets over it. I pulled the edges on either side as far as they would go and used bits of rock and driftwood to hold the edges down. I used the other length of plastic as a ground sheet.

Our 'tent' was only about four feet high at the centre and was wide open at either end, but it would shelter us from the damp and dew and give, at least, the illusion of security.

Our next priority was fire.

We needed two, one facing the forest and the other facing the river that we would also use as a cooking fire. There was an abundance of driftwood around, dry too, and we soon had two decent fires going. The fires gave me an immediate lift. I knew fire would keep the animals away from the camp but it would also reveal our presence if there was anyone about. I thought that was unlikely, though, given the dense cover on either side of the river.

It was dusk when we finished. Velaithan collected her stuff and went off upriver to bathe. I was itching to just lie in the water but wanted to try something first. In Velaithan's rucksack I found the remnants of our lunch, a crusty edge of bread. I took one of my fishhooks and tied it to the monofilament. Just downstream from our camp I found a gap between two boulders through which the water was cascading in a rush. Just below this, and to a side of the channel, was a pool of quiet, deeper water. I sat on one of the boulders bordering the pool and crumbling the bread to little bits, threw it in the channel of water going past the pool. From under the rock on which I was sitting a shoal of little fish, some of them nearly five inches long, darted out to feed on the bits of bread floating past.

I prepared more breadcrumbs, this time squeezed into tiny balls. I inserted my little hook into one of them, took the lot in my hand and deposited them in the current. Once again the shoal rushed out and, in a moment, I had a small fish dangling at the end of my line, the hook neatly embedded in the side of its mouth.

It took me about fifteen minutes to collect nine little fish, each four to five inches long. I went back to the camp quite pleased with my catch. I gutted them as best I could, rubbed a bit of salt and left them for later.

Velaithan came back to the camp dressed in her blouse and ankle length skirt, her washed clothes over her arm. Her hair hung down in an arc over her shoulders. She spread her wet clothes carefully over a low branch and set about unpacking our food supplies. She made no comment about my fish. I hoped she wouldn't, in her present mood, just chuck them back in the river.

I walked downriver till I found a pool with a sandy bottom. I stripped my filthy T-shirt and pants off and put them in the water to soak. I used my cupped hands to splash water over my face and my head. A healthy scab must have formed over my wound because I felt no pain or sting.

I sat down in the water, resting my head against a sloping rock. I closed my eyes and let the strain of the day wash away. I could have lain there forever but it was dark now and I was hungry. I washed my clothes, whacking the heavy pants against a rock. I wore the stolen sarong and went back to the camp wondering if the woman was on strike.

Thankfully she wasn't.

She had boiled a pan of rice and was stirring something that looked like lentils in the small pan. I cut a green twig off a bush nearby and, sharpening one end of it, speared my slippery little fish with it. I then placed two small rocks near the edge of the fire and balanced my kebab so that it was over the glowing embers and not exposed to the direct fire. I turned it over from time to time till the fish were brown and crisp.

I brought the ground sheet and spread it out so we could sit near the fire in some comfort. I also found the little bottle of citronella oil and we both used it liberally because the sand flies were getting to be a nuisance.

We ate our meal in silence. The simple fare of rice, dhal and fish looked poor but tasted fine, as meals always do when you are famished. I must admit my fish were not a great success, full of thin bones and tasting faintly muddy. Still Velaithan made no comment. She washed up and set a pan of water on to boil for our journey tomorrow. I scraped a narrow trench around the edge of the tent with my kathi. I collected ash from the campfire and spread a trail of it in the trench. Mr. Karl had taught me how this little trick kept the crawlers, ants, centipedes and such, away from our sleeping quarters. I also collected more driftwood for the fires, enough to keep them going till the early hours.

I stretched out on the ground sheet and stared at the sky. I could see the stars through the branches and, even without moonlight, there was just enough light to see the tops of the trees stretching out along the bank. I began to notice the jungle sounds, frogs and crickets mostly, over the tinkle and splash of the river, then the sudden 'quark quark' of a night heron somewhere close by.

Velaithan sat on the far edge of the groundsheet hugging her knees, staring at the fire.

Southerners like myself are given to sudden, volcanic rages. Our quick tempers, coupled with a heavy use of illicit hooch in our villages, unfortunately lead to countless violent conflicts. My earlier flash of irritation had subsided completely leaving me, as it often did, faintly ashamed. I tried to think of some neutral subject with which to break the ice.

'How did you get interested in birds?' I asked finally. 'Did someone teach you?'

'My father was very keen,' she answered readily. 'He taught me.'

'Is your father in Jaffna?'

My boss had only mentioned a mother.

She continued to stare at the fire. I thought she hadn't heard me.

'He's dead,' she said it so softly, I barely heard her.

'I'm sorry,' I said automatically. 'Tell me about him, about your family.'

I really don't know why I asked. Just idle curiosity I suppose.

She turned her head and stared at me for a while, then turned back to the fire. She spoke very softly.

'My appa was a teacher. He taught Biology at St. Peter's College in Colombo. We lived in a rented house, at Ramakrishna Road. I was eight years old at the time, my brother was three. I suppose with his teaching and his private tuition, appa made a fair living. We led a simple, Christian life. Appa treasured his collection of books on Ceylon birds. He told me later that many of them were quite valuable, first editions of Phillips, Henry, Wait and others.

'There was another teacher, Uncle Bernard, who was also a keen birdwatcher. Once every month, on a Sunday, the two of them would plan a field trip to the Attidiya swamp, or the Bolgoda lake, just to watch birds. They went by bus early in the morning. They took some food with them, sandwiches mostly, and spent the whole day out. They would write up detailed notes of what they had seen. It was appa's greatest pleasure.'

She was silent for a while, still staring at the flames.

I walked into it then.

'So what happened?' I asked innocently. 'Why did you move to Jaffna?'

'July 1983. The Sinhala mobs came to our home.'

Oh fuck! I should have guessed.

July 1983 was a black day in our history. Organized mobs, supported by powerful politicians, attacked the Tamils living in the south of the country. Thousands of people lost their homes and property. Many were killed. That was the real beginning of the war that still rages in our country, seventeen years later.

'The mobs came along the railway track. Appa was not at home,' Velaithan spoke in a dull monotone, as if to herself. 'They knew exactly where the Tamils lived because they came directly to our home.

'They were all young men carrying clubs and iron rods. They ordered my mother out of the house. She was carrying my little brother Ram. We had two tiny rooms on the first floor of our house. I was playing up there when they came. I hid when they started shouting at my mother.

'They did not steal anything. They simply collected all our possessions, clothes, TV and furniture and piled them in the centre of our hall. They threw all appa's books on top of the pile – and then they set fire to it all.

'My mother had thought it was better for me to stay hidden, that they would take our possessions and go. When she saw the fire she started screaming and tried to rush inside to get me but they wouldn't let her. They held her back till they were sure the fire was well established, that nothing could be saved. Then they … went away!

'The rooms were full of smoke and I couldn't breathe. I heard my mother screaming for me, so I crept to the window and looked out. The mob was gone and my mother was alone. No one came to help us. She told me that the stairs were on fire and to climb down from the window. I remember how terrified I was, it seemed such a long way down. When the smoke made it difficult for me to breathe, I jumped and luckily fell into a flowerbed. I hurt my ankle.

'By the time our neighbors came, it was too late. We had no home, no possessions – only the clothes we wore. We just sat in the garden, frozen in shock, and watched our home turn to ashes.

'But I still thought everything would be put right when my appa came home.

'Appa came. Someone brought him home in a three wheeler. He was unconscious, bleeding from wounds on his head. He had been walking along Galle Road when the mob caught him. They had beaten him with clubs and kicked him when he fell – they then threw him in a roadside gutter to die.

'My kind, gentle, appa who never harmed anyone in his life.'

She was hugging her knees, still speaking to the fire. She seemed to have forgotten I was there, lost in her memories and her pain.

'They took appa away to hospital. We were taken to Saraswathi Hall in Bambalapitiya. It had been converted to a refugee camp. It was crowded with people like us, people who had lost everything. We found a little space in a corner, just enough for the three of us to sit down. We had nothing to do but sit and wait. We were desperately worried about my appa but could get no news about him.

I could not walk because I had hurt my ankle. I remember people helping me to go to the bathroom. We existed like beggars there, waiting without hope.

'My appa's Sinhala friends came to see us later. Uncle Bernard too. They brought us news of appa. He had several broken ribs and was severely concussed by a blow on his head. He had been hit with an iron bar. They told us he would be all right. They lied. He lived, but never became all right.

'They brought us food and clothes, and were desperately sorry for us. But they would not take us to their homes. They were afraid.'

She rested her head on her knees and sat there, spent.

I got up quietly and tended the fires. I got some longer pieces of driftwood and laid them roughly upwind. That way they would burn slowly and, hopefully, last till morning. I put away our pan of boiled water to cool. The plastic bags containing our provisions, I hung from the rope that ran through the centre of our tent. When Velaithan got up and went down to the water, I dusted the ground sheet and smoothed it out in the sleeping area inside the tent.

It had been a long, long day and tomorrow we would be challenged in a completely new environment. Velaithan came back. Without a word she crawled to one side of the tent and stretched out. We both rolled up our empty rucksacks to use as pillows.

The sand was uneven and full of bumps. Despite the citronella, and the smoke, the mosquitoes troubled us greatly. But I was tired and long past caring. I drifted off to sleep. I woke up once to the noise of a heavy animal crashing through the undergrowth. By the time I grabbed the kathi and got to my feet I realized the noise was receding. I guessed it was a sambhur that had wandered onto the sandbank and panicked when it saw the fire or got wind of us.

I drifted off again.

11

29th March 2000

It was still dark, but close to dawn, when I heard Velaithan get up and leave the tent. Despite my training I hated to get up in the mornings, especially before daybreak. I just lay there with my eyes shut and listened to the tinkling flow of the river. The birds were active already, calling from their roosts. I could hear the raucous honking of the Malabar hornbills, high in the kumbuk trees, drowning the softer melodies of the songbirds. Day was breaking by the time I heard the woman pottering around the fire.

It was early light when I collected my clothes and new toothbrush and walked downstream for my ablutions. We had no toothpaste but a soft piece of charcoal from the fire, chewed into a paste, worked just as well. Better, in fact. It might be abrasive on the enamel but it certainly cleans one's teeth to a brilliant white. As I walked downriver, I startled a small herd of deer that had come to the river to drink. Further away I saw a rare adjutant stork, standing in the shallows, slouched over in its usual untidy fashion. This is said to be the largest bird in the country. Its bony skull and feather-free, yellow neck must make it one of the ugliest birds as well. It just stood there with its neck folded in and head resting on its shoulders. Why they have given this slovenly creature a military sobriquet is something I have never understood.

When I got back Velaithan had the water bottles filled and was using the pan to boil the manioc yams we had brought with us. I set about dismantling our camp and packing away the provisions and gear. I found the eggs all cracked and dripping so badly I couldn't scrape

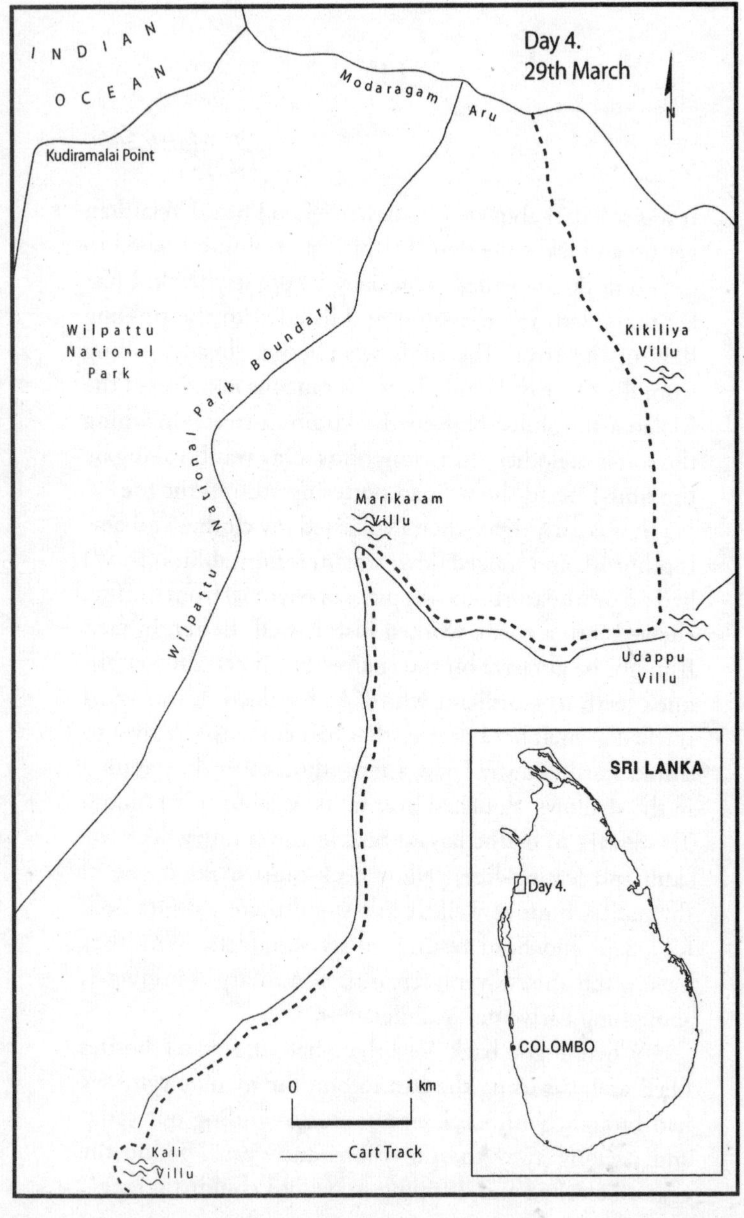

Day 4.
29th March
N
INDIAN
OCEAN
Kudiramalai Point
Modaragam
Aru
Wilpattu
National
Park
Wilpattu National Park Boundary
Kikiliya
Villu
Marikaram
Villu
Udappu
Villu
SRI LANKA
Day 4.
COLOMBO
0
1 km
Kali
Villu
Cart Track

up enough to cook. I hated having to throw them away.

We sat on the log to eat boiled manioc, spiced with a sprinkling of powdered chili and coarse salt. It was filling, if nothing else. I packed our two bags carefully, balancing the loads so the straps would not chafe the skin of our shoulders. I had managed barefoot since I discarded my army boots, but I knew I would soon be crippled in the forest. I tried on the canvas shoes I had taken from the EPDP man but was disappointed to find them too small. Fortunately I discovered that, if I cut a hole in each for my big toe to stick through, I could manage with reasonable comfort.

Velaithan had not spoken a word since last night. I thought the best way to ease the strain was to discuss the route plan with her. I used a stick to sketch it in the sand.

'There used to be a holiday bungalow called Kokmotai upriver from here. The road from there to Kalivillu runs roughly southwest. Our best bet is to find a game track from here that heads as close to due south as possible. If we can head southwards, we should meet up with the road at some point. That's not easy because game tracks go all over the place. My idea is to walk as far as we can in the early morning. When it gets too hot, we must find some shade and rest till evening. Then we'll walk again in the evening till we find a campsite. I'd like to get to Kalivillu for the night. Once we find Kalivillu, I have a rough idea of the tracks and water holes we might head for thereafter. Are you OK with this?'

She nodded without interest.

I tied my shoes to my backpack and rolled up my trousers for wading. Velaithan also stuffed her slippers into her bag but allowed her shalwar pants to get soaked. We walked upstream slowly, staying in the sandy stretches as much as possible, scrambling over boulders when no other route was possible. Velaithan was pretty agile but I still had to help her over some of the steeper rocks. I felt she disliked the physical contact but, in many places, had no choice but to let me help.

We must have struggled for several hundred yards when I saw a well-used game track leading off to our right. Animal tracks could be clearly seen on the bank and there was a path leading through the undergrowth, into the forest. I was getting a bit tired of scratching around the river anyway and was glad to leave it.

The undergrowth was thick and luxuriant for the first fifty yards and then thinned out into typical dry zone scrub jungle. The track seemed to meander in all directions, swinging in wide arcs to avoid fallen trees or dense thickets. Now and then it was joined by other tracks and it was hard to decide which would take us in the direction we wanted. I kept it simple by assuming that the shadows cast by the morning sun were pointing due west. If we kept the sun on our left shoulder as much as possible, we would be heading south. It was rough going because the path often tunnelled through thickets of thorn bush that caught at our clothing and skin. To negotiate these stretches, we were then forced to walk in an uncomfortable crouch till we reached open space again.

Game was either very scarce, or very shy. We surprised a small herd of spotted deer, several does and one fine stag. One alarm call and they went crashing through the scrub. We finally came to a small muddy hollow and saw, on the far side, an overgrown and badly neglected track that had to be the park road to Kalivillu.

We sat down with our backs to a tree to rest and drink some water. Velaithan had been like a zombie all morning, withdrawn and remote. Perhaps she was still haunted by the memories I had unwittingly stirred up last night. I didn't really care about her problems and thought it best to stick to business.

'I don't know how far it is to Kalivillu from here. My guess is five or six miles,' I told her. 'Lets go as far as we can and find a place to rest through the heat of the day. We must get to Kalivillu before dark.'

'Do you really know all this or is it just guesswork?' she asked nastily.

'I have a recollection of cruising along these tracks, looking for some animal to shoot. I know most of the waterholes and tracks,' I replied carefully. 'But it is one thing to drive around in a vehicle. Everything looks a bit different when you are on foot.'

She shrugged and looked away.

We shouldered our bags and started off again. The trees in this section of the forest all appeared to be of nearly uniform size, ten to twelve feet high. They formed a dense canopy that leaned over the track in the form of an arch. This gave us some shade and relief as we walked on in the increasing heat of the late morning.

I will freely admit that the thought of meeting a bear frightened me to an abnormal degree. Mr. Karl taught me that the sloth bear has poor eyesight, and is normally so preoccupied that it does not hear or see you approach. If you are unlucky enough to get too close, there is a great chance the animal could panic and attack you. Bear attack is quick and savage and pretty hard to turn. I have seen a villager who had one eye, and most of his face, removed by an angry bear. He had been a lot more proficient with a kathi than I would ever be, but it hadn't helped him all that much.

I presented a brave front though, and led the way. I did slow down at each bend and twist of the track to make sure the way was clear. I noticed birds flitting through the trees and one, in particular, kept up a haunting melody.

'That's a shama,' I said, knowing she had probably never seen that species before. Although she didn't say anything, I had the impression she was pleased.

I had discovered one way to snap her out of a foul mood. And we did, at least, agree that birds are interesting creatures.

It was getting very hot. The heavy undergrowth prevented any breeze from reaching us, so the heat was oppressive and remorseless. I saw through the trees on the right, a small water hole surrounded by relatively greener trees leaning over it. It seemed a fair spot to spend the rest of the afternoon. There was no path, so we pushed our way to it through the undergrowth. We came round a tree to the edge of the water when we were startled by a loud squelching noise ahead of us and very close by. Standing, with mud and water pouring down its sides, was a large bull buffalo. It had obviously been wallowing in the mud, as buffalo often do, chewing the cud. Our arrival had disturbed, and clearly, annoyed it.

Buffalo, especially lone bulls, are another species to keep clear of, when on foot. Velaithan was not happy.

'This place seems to be occupied,' she said warily. 'We'd better move on.'

'No. I'm tired of walking'.

I had been around buffalo, tame ones anyway, since I

was a child. I picked up a stone and flung it at the animal emitting a loud 'HAAAAR' at the same time. The rock missed the animal but made a satisfactory splash. To my surprise, and relief, the bull turned and galloped clumsily into the forest scattering mud and water in all directions. A number of water birds had been feeding along the edge of the pond. They now rose up in a body, with squawks of alarm and a flutter of white wings. In a moment we had the water hole to ourselves.

We made our way carefully to the far side, away from the road. The vegetation just around the waterhole was different from the rest of the forest, the trees being much taller and with a more luxuriant canopy. I selected a tree with good shade on high ground slightly away from the water's edge. We cleared an area of dead leaves and debris using, once again, branches as makeshift brooms. We spread the ground sheet to keep our things on and started collecting deadwood and twigs for a fire.

I noticed Velaithan tug casually at a rotten log, trying to disentangle it from creepers that had grown over it.

'You need to watch for scorpions and centipedes when you do that,' I warned her. 'You might even find a snake or two underneath'.

She dropped the log as if it had scalded her.

'You'd better collect the firewood,' she announced calmly. 'I'll prepare the food'.

I built a fire in the lee of the tree, using only bits of the driest wood I could find. Damp or green wood would give off more black smoke. I was anxious not to disclose our presence and location to anyone. I selected a piece of soft, dry wood and shaved tiny slivers of kindling off it. I arranged the shavings upright in a tiny wigwam and covered it with dry leaves. One match underneath was enough to get this little pile alight. After that it was only a matter of adding bigger twigs, and blowing, to encourage it. I was pleased to see that there was very little smoke from the fire, and even that was dispersed by the thick canopy.

Velaithan boiled some rice and we made a curry of dried fish. It was a plain meal but our stores were limited and we had to stretch what we had as much as possible. I knew that, however careful we were, we would still have to scavenge for food if we were to survive this journey.

We ate seated on the ground sheet with our backs to the tree. I insisted on washing up, and packing everything away, soon after we had eaten. I wanted to be able to make a quick exit if the need arose.

It was still and hot, even in the deep shade of our tree. We had many hours to kill before it cooled down enough for us to resume our journey. I saw some thin, bamboo-like reeds on the far side of the water. I went over and cut a few shoots of the stuff, wondering if I could devise a trap to catch some small animal. I like my food and I like some variety in it. An exclusive diet of rice and dried fish would drive me mad.

I cut the reeds into even lengths and split of them in four. I tied them into a bundle and put them away in my rucksack for later use.

The waders had returned to the pond and were patrolling the shallows. Some were seated on overhanging branches and preening. I saw egrets, pond herons and cormorants. A solitary darter was sitting on a dead branch with its wings spread, a snake attached to a bird's body. There was one open-bill stork with that funny gap between its mandibles. It always seemed to me like a pair of scissors that had been twisted out of shape, after being used as a can opener. They were all interesting enough but lacked dramatic appeal. They seemed to spend most of their time frozen in one place, waiting for some unwary fish or frog to come within reach.

Velaithan pointed.

A small black and white kingfisher was flapping its wings vigorously to stay in one spot over the water, like a helicopter. The little bird had its head bent over, peering intently at the murky brown water below. Suddenly it dropped like a stone, down through the surface of the water and back up to where it had been, without anything to show for it.

I glanced at Velaithan and was again surprised by the animation in her face. She watched intently as the bird dived again and again till, finally, it was rewarded with a catch, a tiny fish that wriggled in its beak. It flew to a tree near us and began to bash the fish against the branch it was resting on.

'Pied kingfisher,' Velaithan announced.

Once the fish was properly concussed, the kingfisher kept tossing it up, catching it nearer the head each time. It maneuvered the fish till its head was pointing downwards. It then proceeded to swallow the fish, jerking its head up and down to ease the passage. I marvelled at the cleverness of its technique. When the fish went down head first, the gills and fins all folded back neatly to allow a smooth passage down the throat. Swallowing it the other way would have certainly choked the bird.

Watching the kingfisher had put her in a better mood. After the bird flew off, she turned to me.

'How did you get interested in birds?' she asked. 'Did they teach you in school?'

She must have thought it a strange interest for an army officer.

'No,' I said. ' No, they didn't teach that kind of stuff at school.'

That was pretty funny, considering the type of village school I had attended.

'Then?'

'It was my scholarship monitor. Mr. Karl. He taught me.'

'Scholarship? I thought …' she seemed surprised but didn't continue.

'Did you think I had a privileged background?' I found that quite amusing as well.

'Well, yes!' she said seriously. 'Everyone living in the south is privileged, I suppose, compared with us. But you, more than most!'

'Well, you're mistaken there,' I said idly. 'Nothing could be further from the truth. My family is from a village called Akmeemana near Galle. We were very poor. Poorer than you will believe!'

She didn't say anything for a while, staring at the water. I thought she had dropped the subject when she surprised me.

'Tell me about your family,' she said.

I lay on the ground sheet, staring at the leafy canopy above me, my thoughts going back to the wretchedness of my early years and then to my first meeting with Mr. Karl. I had never talked about it before, not to any of my mates in university or in the army. It had been too painful and too private.

It seemed different now, in some strange way. Perhaps it was because Velaithan was an alien, not from my world. Or maybe it was the forest. Emotional baggage doesn't count for very much there.

'My father was a labourer. He would go to town each morning and work for the shopkeepers and transporters in the bazaar. When he collected his wages in the evening he'd visit all the illicit booze joints on the way home. He was a big, powerful man, and he was very … violent when he was drunk.'

Once I had begun, it all came gushing out.

'We were terrified of him, my sisters and I. He was capable of anything in his drunken rages. From the moment he came home in the evening, till he finally passed out, we were likely to get beaten at any moment, on any pretext. We hid ourselves, so my mother took the brunt of it. Something would always set him off. Often it was the food, too much salt or not enough, the rice being too cold or the vegetables being the wrong sort. He'd fly into a rage and smash up the kitchen and slap my mother around as well.

'Once, when I was about twelve, I tried to stop him hitting my mother. I wasn't strong enough at the time,' I went on bitterly. 'He broke two of my ribs.'

'I don't think he ever once gave my mother any money. When he hadn't been to work, he beat her till she gave him what little she had saved away. My mother had to feed, clothe and school the three of us by her own efforts with whatever little money she kept hidden from him.

'She grew manioc and bananas in our garden. We had a breadfruit tree and a few coconut palms. We survived on garden produce, … and the few rupees my mother made, by getting up at four each morning, to make hoppers and string hoppers to sell to the eating-houses.'

Velaithan had been listening intently but made no comment.

'No, I'm not from a wealthy family,' I said wearily. 'What made you think that anyway?'

'I suppose it is the way you speak English.'

'Ah, I see,' I said. 'That was because of Mr. Karl.'

'Tell me about this Mr. Karl.'

'That's a long story,' I said. 'Too long.'

I thought that would shut her up but all she said was:

'We have time.'

I suppose we did.

'From the beginning, my mother's only ambition, her only expectation in life, was for me to have a good education. She saw to it somehow that I always had my school uniform and my books. I won a small government scholarship in Grade Five. That helped me to get up to my O Levels. I did rather well there.

'Our local school did not go beyond that, but I got a place at Mahinda College in Galle, to study for my A Levels. That was a good school and a great chance for me to get ahead, but the extra cost of bus fare and books was more than my mother could manage. I had decided to give up my studies and find a job.'

'What happened then?' Velaithan asked.

'A friend gave me a cutting of an advertisement he had seen in a newspaper. Some setup called the Paul Perera Scholarship Fund was offering financial assistance to needy students studying for their A Levels. I applied and was called for an interview in Colombo.'

I had fallen into a reverie, my thoughts going back to that fateful day.

'So?'

'I learnt that Paul Perera had been a famous teacher and social worker at a Catholic school in Colombo. The

Scholarship Fund had been set up by a group of his former students, to honour his memory.

'A panel of six people interviewed me, mainly about my financial circumstances. They were very kind. They even reimbursed the exact bus fare my mother and I would spend coming to Colombo and getting back home. They said they would let us know.

'Two weeks later, without warning, three of them turned up at our home, to check on us. They had no difficulty in seeing how poor we were. We didn't even have three chairs to offer them, so one of them sat on the front step of our house.'

'So you got the scholarship, did you?' she asked.

'Yes, I got selected. They were to pay me four hundred a month, a lot of money at the time. But then my mother got worried. She wanted me to turn it down.'

'Why was that?'

'She was sure that it was a front. She thought they would try to convert me to Christianity. I didn't really care but it scared my mother.'

Velaithan didn't say anything, so I continued:

'She need not have worried. There was never a hint of that, not in all the years that they helped me. They appointed one of their members as a personal monitor to each scholar. My monitor was Karl Dias.'

'Mr. Karl insisted that I meet him once a month in Colombo, to collect my money and report progress in my studies. He took a keen interest in my work and insisted that I learn English. I spoke very little English at that time. Mr. Karl gave me books to read, and spent time discussing the contents the next time I visited. I had to write to him in English. I hated it at the start because it was very difficult for me. I got better as we went along.'

'You were lucky to find someone like that.'

'Yes,' I said, amused at my own understatement. 'Yes, you could say that.'

'What happened when you finished your A levels?'

'I did fairly well and entered the Faculty of Agriculture at the Ruhuna University,' I went on. 'The Scholarship Fund continued to support me, and increased the monthly grant to a thousand.'

Velaithan looked at me in surprise.

'You've been to university?' she asked.

'Why, yes,' I said.

She must have thought only savages joined our army.

'Go on,' she said.

'Mr. Karl had volunteered to carry on as my monitor, so we kept in touch as before. He was a keen naturalist and had a great collection of books about birds and animals, of hunting and travels in old Ceylon. Those were the books he made me read, to improve my English with. Over the years I must have read most of his collection.

'Mr. Karl loved camping in the wilds. He had been a hunter in the old days but became very much of a conservationist later. He took me along on his camping trips, if I happened to be on vacation. I had to do all the rough work but I loved it and he taught me … a lot'.

'Did you enjoy university life?' Velaithan asked, changing tack suddenly.

'Mm yes,' I said, thinking back. 'I never had enough money, even with the scholarship, but most of my friends were poor as well. Yes, I'd say we had a good time although politics on campus was a nuisance.'

'Was it the JVP? Velaithan asked. 'I hear they are very strong on the campuses.'

The Janatha Vimukthi Peramuna is a Marxist political party with a very strong student wing. They have many activists even within the army. The JVP advocated a chauvinistic, anti-Tamil stance in regard to the ethnic problem. I figured Velaithan wanted to find out what my political affiliation was.

'Yes, they were very active on campus,' I said, thinking back. 'I found some of their positions very convincing, especially about changes needed to our social structure.'

'So did you join them?' she asked.

'Most of my friends joined up and worked for the party,' I told her. 'I very nearly did, but in the end, I didn't. It made me a bit unpopular, but I had to live with that.'

'So why didn't you join?'

'I'm not too sure.' I tried to put my finger on the real reason. 'I think there were many reasons, one of them being that I couldn't accept the obedience they demanded from the membership. But probably the most important reason was because Mr. Karl wouldn't have liked it.'

'He must be … quite a man, this Mr. Karl,' she said quietly.

It got me thinking about him. I had tried to avoid that.

Mr. Karl had never married. He lived in Dehiwela with his sister and her family. When I was introduced to him for the first time I was completely taken aback, disappointed even. The other members of the Scholarship Committee had been serious professionals or business people. I had expected one of them to be my monitor. Although he had qualified as an engineer, Mr. Karl was an excentric. He had sported a wild and untidy beard and had a habit of tugging at it when he spoke to anyone.

He never cared about flashy clothes and dressed like a ragman.

And he loved his booze.

I will never forget my first visit to his home. Mr. Karl was lying in an armchair in his varanda, fast asleep. He greeted me warmly once he woke up though, and promptly introduced me to his sister's family. I thought he was quite old but I later realized he had been about fifty at the time. The back of his house had been converted to a miniature zoo and he lost no time in showing me around, assuming immediately that I would share his interests.

Mr. Karl had been fascinated by snakes at the time and proudly showed me his collection. He kept them in cages, long green whip snakes, kraits and even a baby python. He had organized his nephews, and a bunch of kids in the neighborhood, to provide him with the lizards, geckos and frogs he needed to feed his pets. He had posted a table of rates on the kitchen wall for all to see. Five cents for a gecko, ten for a frog and so on.

Needless to say, he was never short of pet food.

I didn't realize it at the time, but I became a member of the family on the very first day. I started by helping him to clean his terrapin pond and then was invited to stay for lunch. That became a pattern whenever I visited him. His sister would ask me to stay and 'share our meal', whatever that happened to be. Sometimes just bread and curry.

As I got to know him I realized that his untidy exterior and eccentric habits concealed a fine analytical mind. He could have been successful in any field if he had truly wanted to. But he wasn't interested. He just didn't see the point of wasting his life trying to make money. And he was kind to me. Kinder than any person I had ever known.

'Yes,' I told her. 'Yes. He was quite a man.'

'Are you still in touch with him then?'

'Till last year,' I said miserably. 'He was killed in a motor accident. I was in Jaffna at the time. I didn't hear about it till later so I wasn't even able to attend his funeral'.

Velaithan didn't say anything.

I stared at the motionless leaves above me with unseeing eyes. I couldn't get over the pain and loss I had felt when I went to see Mr. Karl and was told he had been dead for nearly a month.

12

From the length of shadows I guessed it was after 16.00 and time to get moving. I wanted to reach Kalivillu at least an hour before dark and I wasn't sure how far we had to walk. We regained the track and walked with the setting sun on our right. The track was heading south now. The afternoon was stifling with no hint of a relieving breeze.

We must have walked through thick cover for about thirty minutes when we came to an open glade. The track turned to the right and meandered along the edge of the tree line in a lazy semicircle. The centre of the glade might have held water in the rainy season but now was a patch of chocolate ooze. I heard deer calling in alarm and thought they had been disturbed by our appearance.

Some slight movement on my left caught my attention. I turned casually and then stood rooted in shock. Velaithan's quick intake of breath told me she had seen it as well.

Hardly twenty feet from us, and just into the trees, was a spotted doe. The animal was lying on her side, with its legs pointed towards us. Its head was twisted at an odd angle, muzzle pointed to the sky. Holding it by the throat, and lying on the far side of it, was a large leopard. I could just see the leopard's face and the back of its shoulders, the rest of the animal was covered by its victim and the undergrowth.

The leopard's eyes were fixed on us, yellow and brimming with hostility.

The doe was still alive and it was its feet, jerking spasmodically as it was being asphyxiated, that had caught my eye. The spectacle of a leopard on a fresh kill was one I had never witnessed before, and one I would have dearly liked to observe from the safety of a parked vehicle. On foot, and defenceless except for a kathi, it was not quite so thrilling. I caught Velaithan by the arm and drew her back slowly, step by step, the way we had come. I stopped when we were about thirty yards away and out of sight. I dropped my bag under a tree and signalled to the woman to wait there.

She whispered harshly, 'What are you trying to do?'

'I am tired of dried fish.'

'You can't be serious.'

'I want a piece of venison before the leopard drags the kill away.'

'It will attack you.'

'The books say that a leopard will not defend its kill against a determined approach.'

'Really? Does this leopard know that?' she demanded. 'Don't be damned stupid'.

I didn't say anything, just picked up the kathi and turned away. I wasn't being consciously brave, just caught up in a blood rush of foolhardiness. I had only gone a short way when I heard footsteps behind me. Velaithan came up. She looked angry as well as determined. She had the big kitchen knife in her hand.

'Where do you think you are going?'

'Two people will look more intimidating than one,' she said reasonably. 'The leopard won't know I am a woman.'

There was no answer to that, and no time to argue.

We went round the next patch of shrub and there it was. The doe had slumped in death. The leopard had released its hold on her neck and was sitting on its haunches in full view, grooming itself. It seemed like a big male. When it saw us, it crouched immediately.

We had to back off now, or commit ourselves.

Oh shit! Was this really such a great idea?

Pride, not courage, made me keep going. We walked very slowly, one step and then another, each one a separate effort of will. Velaithan was at my side now and I was more thankful for her presence than I was prepared to admit. When we were about five yards away I could hear it, a low growl that sounded like a rumble of distant thunder. I could see the leopard's tail twitch behind it and that, I knew, was a bad sign.

I was sweating.

The growling was much louder now, continuous too, like rolling thunder from a fast approaching storm. The eyes of the animal were blazing with fury, its lips drawn back in a snarl.

Don't show me your teeth, you bastard.

We were hardly three yards away. Why didn't it move?

One more step, and the leopard seemed to gather itself for a sudden spring. The ears went back, flat against its skull, and it crouched lower, the muscles bunched up on its shoulders. If it charged, it would be very quick and very hard to turn. One swing of the kathi was all I'd have time for. I felt the rush of adrenalin as I balanced myself. I had to make this count.

I had just dredged up courage for one more hesitant step when suddenly the animal's nerve broke. It straightened up still snarling and, as we stood still not daring to breathe, began to back off. It turned at last and was lost in the undergrowth. The carcass was ours but I knew the leopard was nearby, watching through the screen of leaves.

It had not begun to feed, so I pointed to a rear leg. I kept watch while Velaithan began to saw at the haunch with her knife. Our spring blade knife was heavy, and sharp enough, but it was hard work. I heard her panting with effort and told her to stand watch while I had a go myself. My hand on the knife was slippery with sweat. A low growl from the undergrowth reminded us that the leopard had not gone far.

I had to chop at it with the kathi to sever the bone at the joint and finally, after ten minutes of real effort, had a leg of fresh venison in my hand. We retreated at once, and with heartfelt relief, to where we had left our gear. I was all right till I reached the tree but then the reaction hit me. My forehead was clammy with sweat and my knees felt weak. I let the kathi and venison slip to the ground and sat down, my back to a tree.

'You could have got us mauled, even killed,' Velaithan said furiously. 'Do men always have to behave like idiots?'

'Only when they are showing off to Tamil girls'.

The reaction was making me light-headed.

For just a millisecond, something changed in the back of her eyes. I would have missed it if I hadn't been looking at her when I said it. It was like a shutter of a camera, gone in a flash, to be replaced by her customary glare.

'We had better be going, if we want to find a campsite before dark,' she said gruffly.

'My knees aren't working properly yet.'

'You should have thought of that before you started this nonsense.'

'Wait till you taste my venison curry'.

I tied a shopping bag over the gory end of the leg to prevent the blood dripping all over me. I swung it on my shoulder and balanced it there by holding on to the hoof. We set off again, this time leaving the track to give the leopard a wider berth. There was no sign of the animal, though. It must have dragged the kill to thick cover to feed in peace.

We walked along the track skirting the glade. I was worried that we were completely in the open and visible from a distance. We had no choice because the leg of venison was too heavy, and too unwieldy, to carry in cover. Even staying on the track was a long hot slog in the heat of the late afternoon. The track entered the forest once again on the far side of the glade, passing through thick cover and giving some welcome shade from the sun.

I was wilting when we finally reached the open plain that I knew to be Kalivillu. I stopped just before the track turned into the plain, telling Velaithan to stay under cover. I moved into the undergrowth by the side of the track and tried to assess the risks.

Kalivillu is a relatively large plain, with a good expanse of water in the centre. With the onset of the dry season, the water had receded, leaving a wide grassy plain between the water and the surrounding trees. The park bungalow that had been used by visitors was on our left, close to the road that also circled the plain on that side. I saw no movement or signs of habitation, but there was no way to be sure. Herds of deer were grazing in the tall grass and slowly moving closer to the water. I saw a sounder of pig, some sows and about half a dozen striped piglets, rooting in the mud. A black blob on the far side of the water looked like a lone elephant.

Velaithan turned to me.

'If there's no one there, why not stay over in the bungalow?' she asked. 'It will be much more comfortable.'

It was tempting.

'If someone came by, it will be hard to get away quickly,' I said carefully. 'And it may be booby-trapped … by one lot or the other.'

'Where will we camp then?'

'To the right, I think. Can you see the high ground there?' I pointed. 'It looks like a good spot.'

I had seen a promontory about half a mile away, where the trees came almost to the water's edge. If we could get there without being seen and camp on the far side of it, we would be hidden from the bungalow and most of the road.

We had no choice but to work our way through the forest now, the risk of being seen by someone in the bungalow was simply too great. But it was hard. Walking through the grass, away from the track, was difficult enough with hidden hazards under our feet. Walking inside the tree line, pushing our way past thorn bushes and brambles, was harder still. The leg of venison got heavier with each step.

We reached the headland eventually. The high ground thrust itself into the centre of the lake and was about fifty yards across. I found a flat area on the far side and decided to camp there. The trees would cover us from the park bungalow and from the track.

The sun was sinking behind the trees by the time we had the ground cleared and set up camp. I did not want to be too close to the trees so I cut two sturdy saplings to use as uprights. I anchored each one with two guy ropes secured on stakes hammered into the ground. I tied the rope between the two saplings and then swung our 'tent' over the rope. We used small rocks to keep the edges down, forming once again, a flattened 'A'. We collected deadwood and had two fires going just as full darkness set in. I built a small fire in the space between our tent and the trees. The larger cooking fire I established between the tent and the water.

Velaithan went off in the dark to bathe and wash her clothes. I found a flat rock near the fire and set about dressing my venison. Fresh venison tastes a bit 'green' and, in my poaching days, we would hang the meat till it ripened a bit. That always made a big difference. No chance of that when we had to keep on the move, so I skinned the thigh and cut the meat into thin strips. I then dug a shallow pit with the kathi and buried the bones and skin.

I piled the strips of meat in our big pan, sprinkled some salt on it and rubbed it in well. I added some water from my bottle and set the pan to boil. Velaithan came back just then. She peered at the pan and asked:

'Is it boiled venison for dinner then?'

'I thought I'd just boil the whole lot with a bit of salt. You can take some of it and make a curry for dinner,' I said cautiously. ' I'll smoke the rest later.'

'I thought you said, wait till you taste *my* curry.'

'Did I say that?' I asked innocently. 'I thought I said, wait till you taste *our* venison curry.'

She just looked at me. I grabbed the soap and made my escape.

The water in the villu was still warm from the sun. The thought of crocodiles kept me kneeling in the shallows, using the paint-tin bucket to bathe with. I thought of my wound for the first time that day, relieved to find it healing well. I took off all my clothes and washed them, soaping and bashing them on a rock in the custom of my village. I then wiped myself with my sarong and wore it, depending on the night air to dry it later.

When I got back Velaithan had nearly finished. The curry was done and the rice nearly ready. The smell of the venison made my stomach rumble. I hung my clothes to dry and spread the ground sheet for us to sit on. I tended the fire between the tent and the trees, adding more lengths of wood on the upwind side to make it burn slowly and last till morning. When the rice was ready we served ourselves. Velaithan ate sparingly, placing the rice neatly on one side and the curry on the other. She always finished what she had served for herself and never went for a second helping. I like to have a well-filled plate in my hand, especially at night. I always pile the rice in the middle of my plate and put the curry on top of it, right in the centre.

The Sinhalese love their rice and curry.

The venison did taste a little 'green' and the meat was tough and grainy. I wasn't complaining, though, and ate till I was bloated. After washing up, I made a small rack of green sticks over the glowing embers at the edge of the fire. I arranged the strips of boiled meat across the slats. I had never tried smoking meat before and hoped that my technique would work.

This was the best part of the day. A gentle breeze blew across the water and I could hear the night sounds of the forest. The alarm call of a deer across the water, rustles and scrabbling in the bushes near at hand, the high-pitched chant of the cicadas. Jungle creatures were on the move, the hunters and the hunted, but we were able to rest, secure in the dancing circle of firelight.

I stretched out on the sheet and looked up at the sky. Velaithan was packing away the remnants of our meal for the morning. We didn't want to waste time cooking again when we broke camp. She then set a pan of water to boil, to refill our bottles for tomorrow.

I saw something flit past the fire making a curious tuc-tuc-trrk sound.

'What was that?' I asked, testing her. ' It didn't look like a bat.'

'Nightjar,' she said shortly. 'They fly about after dark, feeding on moths.'

Not bad!

'Did your father teach you about birds?'

'Yes,' she said readily enough. 'He'd lost all his books but a friend gave him an old copy of Henry. I still have it.'

'Did you go together?' I wanted to get her talking. 'To watch birds, I mean?'

'No.'

She was quiet for a while.

Then she said: 'He told me to observe and take note of all the birds I saw whenever I went anywhere. I had to remember colour, shape and size, even imitate their calls. We would sit together when I got home and go through the book, looking at the plates and trying to identify the species. Sometimes my father would say that it was impossible, that the particular bird I had identified was a migrant or very rare and could not have been there at the time. We would argue about it for hours.'

'Where was this?'

'In Jaffna'.

'Why didn't your father come with you?'

'He never recovered fully from his head injuries. He suffered blackouts from time to time. He was not able to walk any great distance.'

'When did the family move to Jaffna?'

'When my father was fit enough to travel they sent us to Jaffna, by train. We were glad to go because we had no home in Colombo,' her voice had an edge of bitterness now. 'We also had no money because my father was not able to work. We went to stay with my mother's sister. We have been there since then.'

'Are your parents still alive?'

'My mother is. My father died seven years ago.'

'I'm sorry,' I said automatically.

'You should be. Your people killed my father,' she lashed out, suddenly angry. Her voice was harsh and bitter. 'He was a kind, decent man. To the end, he kept telling me that I must forget what had happened. That I must not fill my heart with hatread.'

She was staring at the fire and talking softly now, as if to herself.

'I'm not like him. I can't forget. The Sinhala have no right to peace after what they did to my family.'

Are you a bit deranged?

'How many times have your people bombed civilian targets in Colombo?' I reminded her gently. 'What about the families of the people killed and maimed in these attacks? If they also started personal vendettas, when will this war ever end?'

'I can't bring my father back. I can't give him back

the life they robbed,' she said in a cold, implacable tone. 'Someone must pay a price for that. Why should I care if the war never ends?'

'I don't understand you. You want to punish the Sinhala people for what happened to you in '83. Yet you came to us voluntarily with information that will damage your cause.'

She was silent for a time. I thought she was not going to answer.

'I have not given up the cause of my people. I will never give it up. The leadership is not the cause. My brother was only a boy. They said he … faltered under fire and executed him as an example to the others. My mother has not been … normal since then.' Her voice had a hard edge to it. 'The leadership must answer for that.'

'An eye for an eye?' I asked mockingly. 'Does your Christian faith permit this?'

'I have no faith. When my appa was alive, I went to church but that was only to please him,' she said in a dead voice. 'When he died … I gave it up.'

It was getting late.

Our next leg would be a long one, so I thought to turn in early. Once again I scraped a trench round the tent and filled it with wood ash and embers from the fire. I turned my strips of venison over and pushed more embers under the little lattice. I hoped the fire would keep jackals and other scavengers away.

I built up the fires with fresh wood and spread our ground sheet under the tent. I was amused to see Velaithan casually place some of our provisions and water bottles along the centreline of the tent, forming a kind of 'separate state'. She had nothing to worry about, really. I wasn't going to roll over to her side of the tent for anything in the world.

I didn't fall asleep for a long time. I lay on my back and listened to the jungle sounds around me, trying to identify each one. I heard an owl calling nearby, then the loud, cat-like call of a peafowl roosting on a tall tree. An elephant trumpeted again and again but that was very far away.

I was drifting off to sleep when I heard a sound like a carpenter sawing at a log. Two clear notes, one as if from the down stroke and the other from the return. It sounded menacing and it was close.

'What is that?' Velaithan asked.

She had been awake as well.

'That is the 'saw' of a leopard. Maybe it is the same one, come looking for its venison'.

'Are you serious?'

She didn't sound too happy.

'No, not really!' I said. 'Our leopard would have eaten its fill. This may be another animal. If it 'saws', it is not hunting, so we have nothing to worry about.'

'Well it has stopped 'sawing' now.'

'Humans are not the natural prey of leopards, unless we are dealing with a man-eater.'

'Really? That's comforting I suppose,' she said dryly. 'How do we know this isn't a man-eater?'

'We'll know in the morning,' I said. 'If we are both alive, it's not a man-eater.'

'That gives me a fifty percent chance of survival,' she said. 'And you are on the forest side.'

'It's interesting that in books written by hunters, most of the man-eaters' victims are women,' I told her. 'The man-eater creeps up when the woman is asleep, grabs her by the throat so she can't cry out, and then drags her away. The victim is then killed and eaten under cover of the bushes.'

She was silent.

I wondered if I had managed to make her a little nervous. Even if I had, she wasn't going to let me find out. I fell into a dreamless sleep soon afterwards.

13

30th March 2000

Our days were falling into a pattern. Velaithan's internal clock woke her well before dawn. She would gather her things and go down to the water. By an unspoken understanding I would go back to sleep until I heard her return and start messing around with our gear, normally after first light. This suited me fine because I hated getting up in the morning.

I lay there and listened to the voices of the forest. There was a chorus of birdcalls, many that I could not recognize. Jungle fowl were easy. The books described their call as sounding like 'George-Joyce'. That was silly, because to me it sounded more like 'Chruk-Chrruk'. The wail of a peacock echoed again across the jungle, coming from the tall trees by the water's edge. A magpie robin was whistling a cheerful melody, greeting the new day from the very summit of a tree.

I heard the rattle of pans as the woman put the remains of our supper back on the fire to heat up. I had a look at my venison and found the strips mostly browned off and dry. Some of them had fallen in the fire and been charred. I couldn't tell if the remainder had been smoked well enough to keep. Time would tell.

Velaithan had already bathed and changed into her 'day' kit. She always bathed before dawn, a practice that made me shudder. Her hair was now spread over her shoulders, dripping water. She ignored me. I wondered if she was still pissed off about my talk of man-eating leopards or whether it was another manifestation of her general disapproval of the Sinhala race.

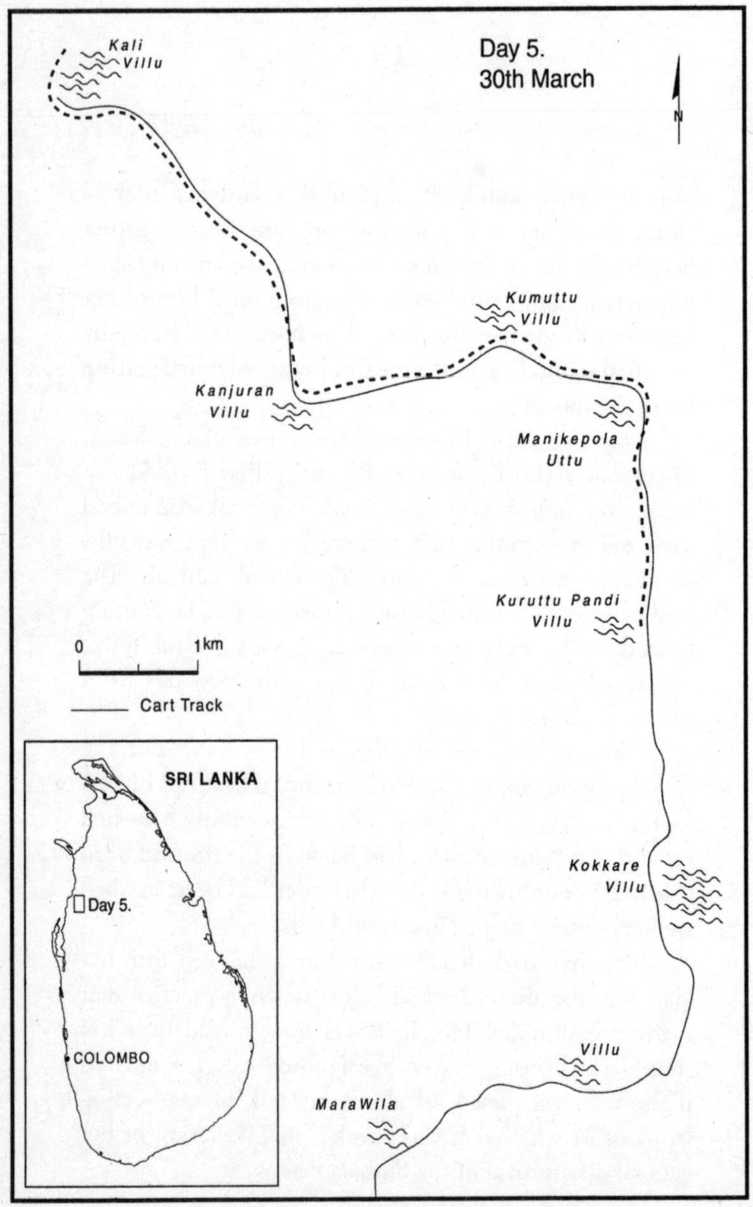
Day 5.
30th March
N
Kali
Villu
Kumuttu
Villu
Kanjuran
Villu
Manikepola
Uttu
Kuruttu Pandi
Villu
0
1km
Cart Track
SRI LANKA
Day 5.
COLOMBO
Kokkare
Villu
Villu
MaraWila

I collected my clothes, damp with morning dew, and walked down to the water.

Wilpattu literally means land of lakes and Kalivillu is one of its most picturesque. A special feature of this park is the thick, impenetrable forest that alternates with open plains and glades. The plains invariably have a basin of water in their centre, with waterlines that stretch and shrink depending on the rain. The villu, with its grassy perimeter, draws the herbivores from the surrounding forest. Deer, sambhur, buffalo, pig, even elephants, come to the plain when the sun goes down, to feed and to drink. For security as well, I daresay. They remain there all night and retreat to the forest only when the morning sun gets too hot for comfort.

A splendid vista opened before me when I came out of the trees and down to the water. The waders were out in force. Painted storks with their pink skinned heads, snow-white egrets proud in their breeding plumage, open-bill storks and a majestic grey heron were patrolling the shallows like guardsmen. A small flock of pelicans were swimming in formation further out, carefully herding a shoal of fish into the shallows. A couple of fishing eagles were perched on a tree overlooking the water, tilting their grey heads from side to side, trying to spot a fish coming to the surface. I could see herds of deer and buffalo on the far side of the villu. A small herd of elephants had their backs to me, feeding as they moved slowly towards the forest.

The water was icy and I had trouble working up the courage to plunge in. I was getting used to brushing my teeth with charcoal. You just need good teeth to chew it into a nice black paste first, easy enough after that. The heavy cargo pants were only partially dry but I climbed into them and put away my sarong.

Velaithan served the remaining food into our two plates and went down to wash the pans. I have a special fondness for rice and curries left over from the previous night's meal. In the village we call it 'heel buth', meaning literally cold rice. My mother often saved it for me to eat before I went off to school.

I found the curried venison even better after a night maturing in the pan. The 'green' flavour was definitely less pronounced. We had our meal, packed up quickly and broke camp. I rolled up the strips of half smoked venison and stored them away in my backpack.

We skirted the tree line and made our way to the far side of the villu. I hated this part of the journey, feeling horribly exposed once again. I wanted to get it over and done with as early as possible, before anyone else was up and about. In this case we had to walk a very long way till we came to the exit I wanted.

In all field operations, I make it a practice to explain my plans to the troops under me, so everyone would know what to do in an emergency. It had become a habit now.

'Kalivillu has several roads leading from it,' I told Velaithan. 'The first two we will come to, leading westwards, will take us to the north road. The one we want is the third track, heading east from the villu.'

'I thought the plan was to keep going south,' Velaithan observed, reasonably too.

'That road turns south after a while.'

I tried to sound confident, struggling to remember.

When we had loafed around in a Land Rover, looking for something to take a pot shot at, it never mattered if we took a wrong turn. Now, a wrong turn could mean disaster.

'We will pass a number of water holes today. If we make good time in the morning, we can rest up at Manikepola and get to another villu, further on, for the night.'

'They are all Tamil names,' Veliathan observed quietly. 'Kalivillu, Manikepola.'

'What about it?' I asked.

I knew where this was going.

The Tamils claim about one third of the land area of the country as their 'traditional homeland'. Some of the evidence they use to justify their claims, and to demarcate boundaries of the so-called homeland are, to my mind, dubious to the point of absurdity.

That is why we are at war.

She said: 'So maybe all this land was occupied by Tamil speaking people in ancient times.'

I'd heard this kind of argument before and it always made me angry. How could anyone say, 'My people were here a thousand years ago, so this land belongs us'? Someone else would have been there earlier anyway. Even if one race or tribe lived there in ancient times, what of it? They moved and someone else lived there later. Those who made these claims often produce 'evidence', based on selective research, to support their position. But I always came out poorly in these arguments, especially in my undergraduate days, because I didn't know my facts well enough and because I got angry as a result of that.

When I began to get the worst of it I would rely on some facetious remark to divert the discussion or else offer to push my opponent's face in. But that didn't mean my position was wrong, just that I was not familiar enough with the facts.

I stopped walking and turned to face her.

'There may be a Tamil word to describe the moon,' I said with unnecessary heat. 'It will take more than a name to claim title to it.'

'That's a frivolous argument.'

'You should expect that when you make a stupid statement,' I snarled, starting to lose control. 'This country belongs to all its people. We are not giving the Tamils any part of it for an exclusive homeland.'

'You don't have to give us anything, Captain,' she said calmly. 'The Tamils will take what is theirs.'

'No, they won't,' I growled hoarsely, getting carried away now. 'We'll kill them all first.'

'That's common knowledge,' she replied nastily. 'You have been killing Tamils for years now. You killed my father.'

'Piss off,' I roared. 'You Tamils try to steal our land and then complain when things get rough.'

Her eyes blazed with fury. I thought for a moment she would attack me. She controlled herself with a conscious effort and looked away, then walked off, leaving me to follow.

We continued to find our way round the villu. There were small herds of deer grazing in the wide expanse of grass between the trees and the water. Some dashed wildly into the trees, tiny fawns leaping in the air as they raced after their mothers. Others, further away, stared at us in fright, their alarm calls ringing out in the crisp morning air. A lone buffalo that was lying in the ooze at the water's edge stood up and stared malevolently at us, as buffalo are wont to do. We hurried past as quickly as the broken ground would permit.

It was a rough slog without the benefit of a track. The grass was tall and wet with dew, adding acutely to our discomfort. Velaithan was finding it difficult with her rubber slippers, slipping and stumbling from time to time. I was annoyed with her so I didn't offer to help with her rucksack. This war was being fought for land, most of it barren and desolate like this. Her claim of ownership, even if meant as a joke, had touched a raw nerve.

We finally came to a track leading directly west. I knew this was not our route, nor was the next exit, pointing south. Walking became easier though, as we were now on a rough track skirting the tree line. We finally came to a track leaving the villu in an easterly direction. It must have been an hour since we broke camp.

Assuming it was the right road, we still had a long trek ahead. From the point of re-entry to the forest I figured we had about seven or eight miles to go. I set a brisk pace.

The road was really two sandy tracks meant to accommodate the wheels of a vehicle, with an elevated, grassy centre, much like a 'W' in cross-section. We were heading almost directly east, with the sun in our faces. The dense growth of stunted trees on either side leaned over the track, seeking sunlight, and giving us a measure of shade.

My anger had subsided now and I would have liked to talk, but thought better of it.

I tend to fly into a blind rage in an instant. In my anger I am capable, unfortunately, of getting pretty violent. I'd cleaned up the common room at the campus once, nearly getting expelled for my effort. But I also cool down quickly and, most times, feel thoroughly ashamed of myself afterwards. I don't remember carrying a grudge for any length of time.

I figured that Velaithan and I were as different from each other as two people could be. She had cold-blooded control and concealed her feelings. I suspected that she was a good hater who would never forget an injury done to her. Or forgive one, either!

I must have heard it earlier, but was so lost in my musings that I was dreadfully slow to react. The thick undergrowth had masked the sound of the labouring diesel engine until it was just around the curve of the track. I caught Velaithan by the waist and threw her, and myself, towards a dense patch of bushes on the side of the track. I landed heavily, almost on top of her, and must have squashed her badly. I heard her gasping for breath but was afraid to move for fear of shaking the bush. Over my left shoulder, through the screen of leaves and branches, I saw the vehicle move slowly past us.

It was a short wheelbase Mitsubishi jeep, a bucket of rust. The canvas was in tatters and, standing at the back with his head sticking through the bare metal ribs, was a tall, bearded man. He had a gun of some sort resting on the hood. A driver and another man sat in front. Poachers for sure!

The man at the back shouted something and the vehicle stopped, not more than ten yards from where we were.

They've seen us!

If they saw movement in the bushes, likely as not, they'd take a shot into the middle of it hoping to bag something. Had they seen something suspicious?

I was relieved to see them get down without their guns. The driver was a short, powerfully built man with thinning gray hair. He was bandy legged and rolled from foot to foot as he walked. I didn't get a clear view of the third man. They had stopped to answer a call of nature. In my village it is said that if one Sinhala man announces his desire to urinate, every person within hearing distance develops a similar urge straight away. Two men stood facing the jungle on our side and the third, covered by the vehicle, on the far side. They chatted loudly as they eased themselves.

I tried to take my weight off the woman but was still afraid the movement would be seen. She was face down in the sand and I lay across her upper body, her head was under my chin. She must have hated the discomfort and the proximity.

Especially the latter!

'I lost a slipper,' she whispered. 'I think it's on the track.'

Bugger it.

There was nothing I could do, except hope it wouldn't be seen. I could see the third man now, a very thin, comparatively fair skinned, fellow with a boil on his neck. He was squatting on his heels, examining the sandy part of the track. The other two were smoking and chatting, leaning against the vehicle.

The thin man called out in Sinhala, pointing as he did so:

'Some people, at least two, have walked this way today.'

'We didn't see anyone.'

That was the bearded man.

If they walked down the track and saw the slipper, we were in trouble. We had to be ready to run into the forest and hope they would not see a benefit in chasing us. Or shooting.

The thin man remained where he was. Beard, evidently the leader, was not really interested. They finished their cigarettes and got back in their vehicle. A moment later I was able to roll off Velaithan and sit down to assess the damage. I had a bruised knee and a few scratches from the fall through the bushes. Velaithan looked shattered, recovering slowly from the fall with my weight on top of her. She had several scratches on her hands and arms, fortunately all of them superficial, even if they might have been painful. We pushed our way out of the wretched shrub.

Her slipper was there all right, black and in plain view at the edge of the track. By some stroke of luck, perhaps because they were not looking for anything unusual, the men had not seen it.

14

We started off again and soon came to another open glade with the water glistening in the distance. I thought I recognized this one as Kanjuran Villu. If I was right, we were on the right track after all. I avoided mentioning the name for fear that Velaithan would make another territorial claim.

Walking along the perimeter, following the track and feeling horribly exposed as usual, I was relieved to come to a fork in the trail. The road that led into the forest in an easterly direction was the one that would, I hoped, take us towards Manikepola Uttu.

Just before we re-entered the forest I saw something that struck a chord in my memory. In the open area, rising above the rough grass, were a few bushes about three feet in height. Close up, I saw that the leaves, nearly three inches in length, were light green in colour, soft and pulpy in texture. The edges were curiously serrated. I was sure that this was the shrub we called Podisinghomaran.

I quickly broke off a few leafy branches and hung the bundle on my haversack.

Velaithan looked curious. I noticed that she was more at ease with me soon after we had faced some common danger. Her natural resentments would then gradually surface and she would close up.

'The crushed pulp of these leaves are used to stop bleeding,' I explained. 'It also has antiseptic properties.'

'Really?' She didn't look too impressed.

'I can put some of it on those scratches on your arms, if you like,' I offered.

'No,' she said, looking away. 'They are not serious enough to deserve Sinhala folk medicine.'

But she said it lightly.

We turned into the forest.

'We're late today,' I said. 'I was hoping to get to Manikepola Uttu for the midday break. It's too far now, so we'll take a break at another villu that's close by.'

She didn't seem to care.

I went on anyway:

'I want to camp for the night at a place called Periya Pandi villu.'

'That's a funny name,' Velaithan said in her quiet way. 'It means big pig's waterhole.'

'Yes,' I said testily. 'I suppose you want to claim this one as well.'

'Of course!' Velaithan said. 'Once we have it, I'll tell everyone it was named after a certain Captain in the Sinhala army.'

I was so surprised I started laughing. She didn't actually laugh but for a millisecond her face split into a grin, on and off again. She looked away hurriedly, clearly regretting the thaw.

When I looked at her again, the stony mask was on.

Velaithan spotted a large raptor seated on a horizontal branch across the track. It had speckled brown feathers, yellow legs and a distinctive yellow circle round each eye. Serpent eagle. It held a small brown snake draped over the branch and was tearing strips of flesh off it with its beak.

I kept my ears open for the poacher's jeep. We reached another villu soon afterwards, a wide marshy stretch opening out on our left. It was very warm now and we were tiring.

'We had better rest up here,' I said. 'Manikepola is close by but it has an old bungalow. This place is safer.'

'How far is it from here to our night stop?'

'I'm not sure,' I said. 'My guess is about three miles.'

We left the track and walked along the edge of the trees looking for a good place to rest up. This villu was really a marsh covered with patches of tall reeds. Lotus and water lilies, resplendent with pink, white and blue flowers, dotted the waterscape. The ground we were traversing was soggy and covered with tall grass. We would need to find some high ground in which to camp.

It took time to find a good spot. We left the swamp and retreated into the forest, finding a small glade some distance from the water. I selected a tree with thick foliage and started a fire near its root mass. I used only the driest bits of deadwood and again, the canopy did a good job of dispersing the little smoke that did rise up. I checked it from all sides before I was satisfied.

Today's menu was again rice and dried fish curry. We wanted to save the venison for the night. While Velaithan started cutting up some dried fish, I walked back to the villu.

At first glance the swamp seemed devoid of life. I knew that birds of the swamp are shy creatures and the reason for their disappearance was the disturbance created by my presence. I sat on a log and waited patiently. I love watching the waders in open water but there is no denying that they get a bit boring after a while. In a reed-covered swamp there is little to see at first, but if you wait, the rewards are much greater.

The swamp grass and reeds grew in dense clusters, broken by stretches of open water. Scattered in the open water were masses of lotus and water lilies with multi-coloured flowers in full bloom.

As I waited and watched the swamp, suddenly, in a moment of magic, came to life.

The jacanas came out of cover first. Graceful, pigeon-sized birds with small white heads balanced delicately on long, slim necks. Their bodies were chocolate brown and white. Jacanas have long, beautifully curved tails and the longest toes I have ever seen on a bird.

When I stood up, the jacana disappeared as if I'd waved a magic wand. I rolled up my pants and waded into the water. I uprooted half a dozen lotus plants by simply grabbing a bunch of floating leaves and hauling them up. I washed the mud off the roots and examined them. They were not yams but a thickened stalk. I knew they were both edible and nourishing when cooked into a curry. I went back to camp ready to do battle with Velaithan about 'primitive Sinhala village dishes'.

She looked down her nose at my offering but made no comment.

I had the feeling, though, that she was tired of dried fish herself and welcomed anything to supplement it. We chopped up the nelum roots and made it into a curry of sorts by mixing in a bit of curry powder and then adding a capful of oil and a liberal dose of water. We then put the whole mess to boil. If I were ever to publish a cookery book, this particular dish would not be on the first page but it was a change, and it helped us fill our stomachs.

We washed up and I stretched myself on the ground sheet. Velaithan sat with her back to a tree, as far from me as the sheet would allow, busy with her thoughts.

I was still feeling a little guilty about my earlier outburst. My anger had also prevented me from presenting the point of view of my people, which I thought so undeniably reasonable. We had plenty of time and I was bored. On a sudden impulse, I decided to reopen the subject.

This time I was determined to control myself.

'Can you explain to me the logical basis on which the Tamils claim a 'traditional homeland?' I asked with exaggerated courtesy. 'How can 8 % of the population justify a demand for one third of the land area of this country?'

She glared at me, thinking that I was being facetious. I put on the most earnest expression I was capable of and waited. She looked at me doubtfully for a while and then appeared to be mollified. Partly.

'Our people have occupied these regions from antiquity. Population numbers today don't come into it.' She was making an effort to speak dispassionately. 'The Sinhala were brought to these parts only under colonization schemes. It is well documented that these schemes were introduced by Sinhala governments to take away our lands and dilute our political strength.'

'The Mahavansa and other chronicles provide evidence of a different kind,' I observed. 'This country was settled by Vijaya and his followers. They were Aryan stock. The waves of invasions that took place over the centuries thereafter brought the Dravidians who settled in the north and east.'

The Mahavansa is a history of our people, covering a period of some two thousand five hundred years, inscribed on ola leaf manuscript.

'Is it reasonable for these Tamil speaking people, the detritus of invasion, to claim a vast tract of country as their exclusive home, merely on the grounds that they had settled on it for a long time?' I asked.

Velaithan wasn't crushed by my logic.

'Your Mahavansa may provide an accurate religious history of the country,' she said with a matching measure of composure. 'Surely you will realize that the chronicle is heavily biased and unreliable when dealing with secular matters?'

I wasn't very happy with the direction of her argument.

She continued:

'For instance, your famous King Mahasena was depicted as a renegade during the first nine years of his reign, despite his other good works, because he supported another order of monks instead of the orthodox clergy of the Maha Vihara. A good king, according to the Mahawansa, was one who built great temples. Yet any economist will understand that building these monuments was a huge waste of resources.'

Facts! I was short of facts. Was she making all this up?

'In this context, you cannot rely on the Mahawansa to prove that the Tamil people did not occupy this land from ancient times,' Velaithan concluded grandly. 'It was not in their interest to admit it. You must find other evidence if you want to discredit our legitimate claims.'

'What about Prince Vijaya and his followers?' I was not ready to give up just yet. 'When they arrived the land was occupied by tribal people.'

'That is legend. The Mahawansa was written centuries after the event,' she said confidently. 'Even if the story of Vijaya was true, it does not prove there were no Dravidian people living in the north at the time.'

'So what are you trying to say?'

She was scoring too many points.

'Simply this: your written history is a religious text,' she went on. 'The Mahavansa alone is not sufficient to prove that your forefathers were the first settlers in this land.'

She seemed so sure!

'There is historical evidence in South India about invasions, and settlements of Dravidian people in Lanka, of similar antiquity,' Velaithan continued. 'Even if, for the sake of the argument, we accept that the Sinhala came here first, do you think they can now claim exclusive rights to the entirety of the land, after both races have lived here for over two thousand years? Do you realize that by that argument the land should belong exclusively to the tribal people your Vijaya displaced?'

'But the Sinhala do not claim exclusive rights to the entirety of this land,' I pointed out. 'What we say is that every citizen should have the right to live and work in any part of it. It is the Tamils who want to carve out a part of the land and say, 'This is exclusively ours'. Not just that. While keeping your part of the land exclusive to your own people, you still demand the right to live, work and own property in the rest of the island. So you're saying what's yours is ours, but what's mine is mine only. How can you possibly justify that position?'

'There are many, many justifications,' she sounded detached, as if reading a lesson. 'The history of violence and cruelty towards our people is the primary reason. This has been repeated time and time again – it is almost an instrument of government policy. We have the right to live without fear, to live in peace. We have the right to manage our own affairs, to use our own language and to preserve our culture. The Sinhala want to subjugate us and keep us as citizens of a lower class, a subservient race. That has been seen by the efforts of successive governments to colonize Tamil majority areas with Sinhala settlers.'

She paused and then continued:

'It is only by having a 'homeland', a place where our rights are both primary and unassailable, that our nation can live with dignity.'

'There is no dispute about your right to live without fear. What happened in 1983 was very bad, and a disgrace to our nation. But that was seventeen years ago. Since then there has not been a single instance of organized violence against the Tamils living in the south. This is despite the almost unbearable provocations and atrocities committed by LTTE.'

Why couldn't she understand this?

'You have bombed civilian targets in Colombo, killing and maiming hundreds of innocent people, yet there has been no backlash against Tamils living in the south,' I went on. 'I know you have suffered a terrible personal loss in '83, but Tamils have lived in the south since that time without any problem.'

'I'm sorry, Captain, but that is a typically patronizing argument.' Her tone was bitter now. 'You say, "There's been no violence against Tamils in seventeen years, so it is ok. Forget about the past, you can live here peacefully so long as you behave yourself". But that's not good enough.'

She was silent for a minute.

'We see it differently,' she continued quietly but her voice had an undercurrent of anger. 'We do not want security as a gift from the Sinhala, something that can be suddenly withdrawn at the whim of a Sinhala politician. We want it as a right that cannot, any day, be violated. Only our own state can guarantee that.'

'You are just eight percent of the population of this

country. There are countries like Malaysia where the Tamil population is much larger. There is open discrimination there against the Tamil and Chinese minorities, and in favour of the indigenous Malay. Yet the Tamils would not dream of asking for a separate state there.'

'We are not modelling our struggle after any other community, Tamil or otherwise. In any event, Tamils in Malaysia were not butchered in the way our people were. Even if they are willing to live with discrimination, it does not follow that we should be willing to do the same.'

'You can model your struggle in any way you want,' I said shortly. 'We are not ready to give a third of our land to satisfy eight percent of the population.'

'You don't have to give anything, Captain,' she said with menacing calm. 'We'll take it.'

Back to square one! Why did I start this?

It was still very hot but I thought we should start off a little earlier than I'd planned. It was a good way to cut short our argument and I had enough politics for one day. I started putting away our things and rolled up the ground sheet. We each had a half bottle of water to see us through till evening.

We walked in silence, seemingly separated by the irreconcilable differences of our two communities. I tried to concentrate, listening for the sound of a vehicle. We were approaching Manikepola Uttu, another large plain. I knew there was a bungalow by the side of it that we would have to get past without being seen.

I saw an open area ahead and the glint of water in the distance. As we approached the villu I heard it, the drone of an engine behind us. I had been half expecting it, so there was time for us to get off the track and take shelter in the shrubbery bordering the villu. I was keen to see if the vehicle would continue past the villu or stop at the bungalow.

It came into view then, groaning away in low gear. The tall man was still standing at the back, resting his gun on the ribs and torn canvas of the hood. We watched them drive slowly along the track that swung around the left of the villu. A small herd of deer that was feeding by the trees went crashing through the bushes long before the vehicle was in range. Some buffalo lying in the water all stood up in alarm, raising their heads to watch the vehicle pass by. We saw it turn off and disappear into the forest at the far end of the villu.

I gave it another five minutes and started off again. I could now see the old holiday bungalow across the water. If we kept to the track we would be in plain view but the going would be much easier. I had a long look at the dilapidated bungalow but saw nothing suspicious. Since we were not planning to camp anywhere nearby, I decided to take a chance and save us a long and tiresome hike through the forest. We made it without any surprises but I was relieved when we put the villu behind us and reached the shelter of the forest again.

We must have been walking for ten minutes after that when it happened.

I had no warning whatever till I heard branches snapping like pistol shots. Then an elephant squealed angrily and stepped onto the track, just ahead of us.

I do not suppose it was a particularly big animal, as elephants go. I had seen large elephants in the temples back home. I had also seen plenty of wild elephants from the relative safety of a vehicle. But I had never faced an angry wild elephant from a distance of about five yards, while on foot. It seemed to tower over us, eclipsing the sun.

It was a moment of pure terror.

The elephant raised its trunk and trumpeted loudly. I stood still, not daring to move. I heard Velaithan start to say something and choke it back. All activity seemed to evolve in slow motion. I had an impression of a single short tusk pointing at me from one side of the massive head. The other tusk had broken off short, leaving a jagged, yellow stump. And small staring eyes, mad with fury.

The elephant made a high pitched, squealing sound again and stamped its forefoot, raising a cloud of dust around us. It then curled its trunk into its mouth, lowered its head and charged.

We're dead!

We turned and ran but I knew in my heart it was no use. A trained athlete might outrun an elephant under ideal conditions, but even that is doubtful. We were loaded down with our bags and the ground was far from even. As if in a dream I remembered Mr. Karl telling me it is even more difficult to outrun an elephant in scrub jungle. The powerful animal could crash through the thorny undergrowth as though it were cobweb; we would be trapped in it like insects on a mosquito net.

Our only chance was to get under cover and hide. Elephants have poor eyesight so they can be fooled if you duck behind something. But this one was simply too close.

I saw an opening in the bushes on my right and plunged into it, leaving Velaithan to follow. In turning at almost right angles, I had a glimpse of the infuriated elephant for one terrifying instant. It was almost on us, a towering gray mass in a storm of sand and dust.

I had hoped the animal would break off the attack when we left the track. No chance of that! We ran into the forest, dodging and weaving to avoid thorn bushes and trees, unable to look back for fear of falling, staying just out of reach. The angry squeals and thudding footsteps were so close I expected to feel, at any moment, the trunk around my shoulders, the massive knee in my back. I ran myself to the edge of exhaustion, my breath coming in great heaving gasps. When I finally collapsed in the shelter of a large tree I could not have taken another step if my life depended on it. It was only then I realized that there was no sound of pursuit.

I turned to share my relief at our escape and – she wasn't there!

I couldn't grasp it for a moment. She had been right behind me when we ran into the shrubbery. Perhaps she was also under cover nearby. I called out to her. Softly at first, fearing the elephant was still around and then louder, with mounting concern. No answer, just an ominous, brooding silence.

I cautiously worked my way back towards the road. I knew the road was heading almost directly south and we had run eastwards. By walking into the evening sun, I knew I would eventually reach the road. I kept a sharp look out for the elephant and, every time I reached the shelter of a large tree, stopped and called out to her.

Nothing!

I finally reached the road, but not at the spot I had left it. I hid my bag under some bushes and cast around, trying to find where we had been attacked. I was disoriented. There were piles of fresh dung and elephant tracks everywhere. A herd must have been feeding in the area earlier. I walked southwards for some distance and then turned back. I had to keep telling myself that she was all right, just hiding.

I saw it finally, a black slipper with a loose rubber strap. It was off the track, lying in an opening between some bushes. This had to be the way we had run. Relieved, I entered the forest once again and called out to her, more boldly now, sure the elephant had wandered off. I realized that sound did not carry in this dense low forest. She would not hear me unless she was fairly near.

I found one area that looked as if it had been hit by a tornado. Small trees had been torn down and saplings uprooted. The undergrowth and thorn bush had been flattened and trampled into the ground. The elephant must have been on a rampage here, venting its fury on the vegetation. The extent of its savagery was frightening even now, after it had gone away.

Velaithan could not possibly have survived such a violent attack.

I looked around with dreadful foreboding, fearful of what I might find. But then, as I kept looking around, my spirits rose slightly when I found no sign of her. With increasing desperation I started casting round in circles. I slashed at branches with my kathi to mark my path. Half an hour of pushing my way through the undergrowth made me realize that this was not helping. I fought back my instinct to keep moving. I knew I had to think this out.

I went back to the track and sat by the side of it. I tried to put my thoughts in order, to plan something.

There was no sign of Velaithan, but there was some faint hope in that. Victims of elephant attack rarely escape with an injury. Either they escape intact or, if the elephant catches them, die quickly. I've never known an elephant to carry away its victim either. Since there was no sign of a body, there was a chance she had got away.

If Velaithan had somehow escaped unhurt but was lost in the forest, what would she do? How could I help her?

She was a highly intelligent woman. She knew that we were heading directly south and that we were not far from the villu at which we had planned to camp. If she managed to find the track, she only had to head south to find the villu. If she were lost, and unable to find the road, she would have to look for a game track heading in the same direction. All game tracks in this area would head towards, or away from, the villu. If she were alive, and uninjured, she would be able to find her way there. But the villu was a huge expanse of swamp, many miles in perimeter.

How would she find me?

I knew now what I had to do. I broke off several branches from the bushes by the side of the road, leaving an unmistakable mark to return to in the morning, just in case. I stuffed the slipper in my rucksack and walked away.

15

I had been living with death for some time now. I had seen my comrades suffer horrible, sometimes fatal, injuries. I had experienced unbearable sorrow and loss when a friend lost his life to a bullet or a landmine. Yet I had never experienced anything like the guilt that tortured me now. I had committed myself to the mission of getting this woman safely to Colombo so that the information she had could be put to use. Perhaps it would help to shorten, or even end, the war. Although she was really an enemy activist, she had also been a staunch and courageous ally in every crisis we had faced. Yet at the crunch, I had failed to save the mission and I had failed to save her life.

I tried to screen out my depression and focus on the positive. She might still be alive and I had to work on that premise. I had to play my part.

I soon reached the villu. It was more like a vast swamp, with broken stretches of open water here and there. The tree line was very irregular with many promontories of high ground covered with small trees and dense undergrowth. I had to find a good campsite not too far from the point where the track merged with the plain.

I turned to my left. We had run into the forest on that side of the track. If Velaithan found her way to the villu, she would come on the main road itself, or along some game path that led to the villu on that side of the track. The sun was touching the treetops on my right so I did not have much time, perhaps forty five minutes before darkness set in. I had a lot to do before then.

I found a secluded spot, not too far from the water, to set up camp. It was not ideal because the ground was not even and I had to hack away at small bushes to make a reasonable clearing. Fortunately the two rolls of plastic sheet were in my pack, as were the matches. I also had the pans and the balance of the smoked venison. The rest of our provisions had been in Velaithan's rucksack.

It took me most of the remaining daylight to set up the tent. I built the makings of two small fires on either side of it but did not set them alight. I baited a fishhook with a bit of venison and, wading in, selected a spot with waist deep water to position it. I tied the end of the line to a solid bit of driftwood.

I left the camp and hurried back to the point where track fell into the plain. I selected a spot near the water's edge, visible from the widest possible segment of the plain and started to build a fire. It was too dark to be careful about picking up deadwood. I just hauled all the small bits I could find and hacked away at sections of larger logs with my kathi. I was covered with sweat and desperately tired when I had collected enough fuel for a good bonfire.

I knew I was taking a risk. A large fire, on the edge of the water line, would be visible from any part of the villu and attract the attention of anyone in the area. I had no choice. If Velaithan were alive, and if she managed to find her way to the edge of the villu, I had to light a beacon for her, show her where I was.

I went through my routine of making a small pile of shavings and dried leaves and setting them alight, shielding the tiny blaze from the wind. I carefully fed in small dry twigs and deadwood until the fire picked up its own momentum and energy. I placed the larger logs downwind of it so that I eventually had a roaring fire that could not be missed by anyone coming on to the plain.

It was unnecessarily dangerous to sit by the fire.

I retreated to the protection of the trees a good thirty yards away. The forest here was very open with little undergrowth. One tree, I thought it was called gona-pana, had a very dense canopy and offered the deepest shadow. I cleared away the dead leaves on the ground, sat with my back to it and waited.

I had been working like a zombie, pushing myself from one task to another, closing my mind to the reality I was reluctant to face. But now that I had nothing to do but wait and hope, the thought kept returning to my mind like a persistent fly one keeps waving away - Velaithan was dead and my mission was over.

I sat in the dark and stared at the fire. I wondered if there was anything more I could do. I had to keep brushing away the thought that the time for decisive action had been when the elephant was about to crush the life out of her. I'd missed that chance. I felt utterly depressed and ashamed.

I have always loved elephants. They are normally gentle animals with a marvellously intricate social life. The herd leader is invariably a wise old female. Only other adult females, together with immature animals and babies, are tolerated in the herd. Mr. Karl had taught me to appreciate the wondrous nature of these creatures. We had spent hours and hours stalking them on foot and then observing their behaviour. Herd elephants are rarely aggressive to man, unless they feel their young are threatened.

Adult bulls only join the herd in the mating season. At other times they forage on their own, leading solitary lives. Even bull elephants are not normally aggressive, moving away when approached. False charges are common though. The elephant might charge a vehicle with its ears spread wide and trunk raised, trumpeting loudly. It is all just for show and the animal would always pull up short and move away.

When an elephant charges with its trunk curled into its mouth, and its massive forehead held low, it really means business.

Elephants wander over a wide area when feeding. They sometimes raid village gardens and that's when they get shot. An elephant nursing a painful injury is always dangerous but true 'rogue' elephants are extremely rare.

I suddenly remembered Pedris Mudalali's elephant. Pedris was a rich timber merchant who lived near my home. He had bought a baby elephant at an auction some forty years earlier, as one could in that era, and named him Rajah. Pedris brought up the elephant as a household pet and he was dead lucky in his buy. The baby grew into a magnificent tusker. Tuskers are quite rare in the wild today, having been hunted almost to extinction.

Rajah earned his keep by working at the timber yard, carrying heavy logs about, loading and unloading trucks. His mahout was Piyal, a thin wiry man, who became my friend. As a small boy, I would go to the yard on Saturdays to watch Rajah at work. Loading a customer's truck with logs was a special feature. Rajah was extraordinarily intelligent. He would select each log carefully, just the right size to fit into a gap between the others, so that no space was wasted.

Rajah became my pal too. I could approach him without fear and feed him some succulent titbit like a banana leaf. One day Rajah caught Piyal in his trunk, put him under his knee, and ground him into a paste. I ran to the yard when I heard that Rajah was on a rampage but found him standing quietly in his stable. But there was nothing left of Piyal, just some red and brown streaks in the gravel.

It was getting late and the mosquitoes were really bothering me. I had not bathed, as we usually did in the evening, and I think the dried perspiration on my skin and clothes was making me doubly attractive to them. There would be no respite, though. I had to keep the fire going through the night. If Velaithan did not turn up, I would have to go back in the morning and try to find some trace of her.

I must have dozed off. When I woke with a start I noticed that the fire was low. I stood up, half asleep, to tend it when I noticed moving pinpoints of light away to my right. Fireflies, I thought idly at first. Then I was wide-awake as if someone had jabbed a needle in my back. Those were flashlights. Some men, at least two of them, had seen my fire and were coming to investigate.

The lights disappeared then, raising my hopes. Perhaps they were hunters who had moved off into the forest. Minutes later the flashlights were back, and closer now. Much closer. The men must have been coming along the edge of the plain and been hidden for a time by a tree-filled promontory.

Decision time. I couldn't leave because this was the only spot at which Velaithan would be able to find me. She might have seen the fire already and be on her way. But there was no real cover close by, mostly trees without much undergrowth. It was good enough in the dark but a flashlight would show me up like a dancer on a stage.

I decided to give her as much time as possible. I'd

wait until the last possible moment and then move away. I just hoped these bastards wouldn't try something clever like having a man with a gun coming up ahead of the flashlights. I strained my eyes in the gloom. Sometimes it seemed as if there was some movement ahead of the lights but it might just have been my imagination, or a movement of a branch.

I watched them come closer until I could make out the silhouettes of three men, two with flashlights, one with a gun. It was time to fade away into the forest. I felt around for my kathi, casually at first and then in frantic haste.

It wasn't there!

I tried to recall when I had last handled it, forcing myself to remain calm. I remembered then I'd put it down by the fire.

The bastards will take it away and I'll be lost without it.

I got on my stomach and crawled. The ground was rough, covered with rocks and tussocks of grass. I had to pull myself along using my elbows and toes, not daring to get to my knees. As I got nearer the fire I began to feel more and more nervous. I kept my eyes on the men, who were now about fifty yards away. I expected, at any moment, to hear an excited shout or even a gunshot.

I was close to the fire now, on the edge of the circle of light, but on the far side from the men. I could feel the heat of the fire on my face whenever the wind shifted. Luckily I had not tended it for a while, since I had dosed off, so it wasn't as bright as it had been earlier. I looked around frantically for the kathi, trying to keep my head down at the same time.

It wasn't on my side of the fire.

I had to get to the other side and I hated doing it. I gritted my teeth and snaked my way in a semicircle, staying on my belly and keeping the forest at my back. I finally saw the damned axe, firelight glinting off the blade. But it was almost in a direct line between the men and the fire. There was no way I could pick it up without being seen.

The flashlights were getting awfully close and I couldn't leave it any longer. I tensed myself to take off like a sprinter and pick it up on the run, hoping the men would not shoot when they realized it was a man. Or would they? An excited shout made me stop at the last instant.

I'd left it too late! They've seen me.

Then I saw the flashlights swing away, towards the edge of the forest. I realized they had disturbed a hare feeding in the grass and the tiny animal was darting about, trying to avoid the twin beams of light. I scrambled into the firelight on all fours and was back in the sheltering darkness, kathi in hand, in the space of a heartbeat.

I stood up as I came to the sturdy trunk of the gona-pana tree, and someone was standing behind it.

Oh fuck. They'd sent a man ahead of the flashlights.

He must have a gun and have me covered, surely. Just the same my fingers tightened on the kathi for one despairing swing.

'I'm sorry,' Velaithan whispered.

It is hard for me to remember how I felt at that

moment, just a most overwhelming explosion of relief. I realized then that I had given her up for dead.

There was no time to make plans for the men had almost reached the fire. We had to find a place to hide and very quickly too. There was no cover at all under the trees.

'We have to hide in the tree,' I whispered urgently. 'I'll help you up.'

The lower part of the trunk was smooth and didn't offer much help. I hoisted her up and then scrambled up myself. A childhood spent stealing mangoes in the village had finally paid off. Once we reached the lower branches it was easy. We were soon in the thick canopy, uncomfortable but well concealed.

The men, three of them, had reached the fire. They were the hunters we'd seen in the Mitsubishi that morning. The tall bearded man was clearly identifiable, the barrel of his gun resting on his shoulder. The other two held the flashlights. They stood looking at the fire for a moment. The thin man walked around the fire, looking at the ground carefully.

'Eka minihekkge adi pāraval thiyanawa.' I could hear him clearly. *'Mokadda ekak vateta ädagena gihing.'*

There are footprints of one man. He has dragged something round the fire.

That man was dangerous. I wondered if my footmarks would show on the leaf mould under the trees.

The tall man just grunted and walked towards the trees, towards us. The other two followed him and I saw, in silhouette, that the bandy legged driver was carrying an axe in his left hand. They came to the trees, about ten yards from our hiding place, and began probing the forest with their flashlights.

Don't look up!

The tall man said: '*Yamu. Mekeng wädak nähä.*'

Let's go. This is useless!

I was relieved. They were hunters, not really interested in us. They turned and walked away, not back the way they had come but continuing around the villu. That would take them past the campsite. I had concealed the tent in the trees, but was it hidden well enough?

We had to follow them, keep them in view, to find out. I waited till they were about fifty yards away and climbed down, helping Velaithan over the last bit.

'I'm glad you are alright,' I said softly, my words sounded commonplace, inadequate. 'Are you hurt in any way?'

'Just some cuts and scratches, nothing serious,' she said apologetically. 'I lost the bag with the provisions. I'm sorry.'

From the way she spoke I felt she was on the verge of exhaustion.

'Don't worry about that,' I whispered softly. 'We can find it in the morning.'

'I was sitting under cover for nearly an hour, just over there.' She pointed to a spot not very far from where we were. 'I didn't want to show myself till I was sure whose fire it was.'

I wanted to laugh. I could have saved myself, and her, an hour's misery with the mosquitoes if I had only shown myself a little more. But then we may not have seen the hunters in time and they might have walked right into our camp.

Velaithan walked slowly, with a limp. Speed was not

important because the men were walking slowly too, waving the flashlights to flush out some game. We stayed within the tree line and followed them cautiously.

The men stopped abruptly and focused both flashlights at the edge of the water. They had disturbed a small sounder of pig rooting in the mud. The pigs, females and young together, were now racing towards the shelter of the trees, grunting in chorus. I saw the flame red of their eyes as the flashlights tried to follow them, but pigs are unbelievably quick on their feet. They don't stand mesmerized by the light, as some animals do. The man with the gun didn't risk a shot.

The hunters started off again and they were getting near the camp. I had pitched the tent in a small copse of trees. There was no fire to attract them but they'd see the tent if they really looked. They couldn't miss it!

I heard the distinctive alarm call of a deer. The flashlights immediately focused on one medium sized doe, blue–green eyes transfixed in the beam, and unable to move as the rest of the herd scampered away into the forest.

The bastards knew their trade.

The two men with the flashlights moved forward slowly, keeping the beams rock steady, while the man with the gun came up behind them. The hapless doe just stood there, shivering in the light, till they got close enough for the shotgun to be effective. The animal fell on its side at the shot, then scrambled up and tried to drag itself away. The squat man with the axe went running up and I heard the crunching thud as he dispatched the wretched animal.

They jabbered excitedly as they cut a sapling from the

forest, lopped off the branches and recovered a straight section long enough to sling across the shoulders of two of the men. They hung the carcass under the pole, tying the hoofs over it, and hoisted it up on their shoulders. I had expected them to go on, around the villu, but they turned and began walking towards us.

We crouched behind two trees, barely broad enough to conceal us but they went past, no longer interested in looking around. We watched them go past the fire and disappear around the first promontory.

I led Velaithan to the camp.

'I need to bathe. Is the water alright here?' I saw that she was drooping with weariness but making a valiant attempt to keep it casual.

'It's full of weeds and lotus, but we can clear a spot,' I said. 'Better to stay close to shore.'

I picked up my bar of soap and the old paint tin and led the way to the water's edge. Velaithan followed me till I got her to a suitable spot, a little less weed-infested than the rest, and then waited patiently till I left. I checked on my fishing line, hoping for a catch on this one day when we needed it most, but no luck. The bait was still on the hook so I threw it in again and went back to camp.

I spread the ground sheet and then pulled out the package of smoked venison. The rough strips I had cut now looked, and even smelled, like discarded shoe soles. It was all we had though, and grilled venison it had to be. The problem was the fire. If I lit another, it would be clearly visible from across the villu and give our position away. Even if I lit a fire on the forest side of the tent, the glow of it might well be seen from the other side.

I went back to my bonfire. The fire was low and the

larger logs were glowing brightly in a circle. I pulled them away and threw sand on the rest of the embers. I then went back to the camp and lit the fire I had already prepared on the forest side, behind the tent. I cut some branches to place around it, to screen it as much as possible. If those men did see the red glow reflected on the trees, they'd think it was the first fire.

I hoped so anyway.

I had just made another little rack of green sticks for the venison when Velaithan came back looking a little perkier, but sopping wet in her clothes. She dropped the paint tin 'bucket' and soap and sat down. The water gathered in a puddle around her. The gentle breeze coming across the water made her shiver from time to time.

'You will catch cold if you stay like that,' I said as offhandedly as I could. 'You'd better wear my sarong and hang your clothes up to dry.'

'No. My clothes will dry in a while,' she said evenly. 'Don't fuss.'

Despite her obvious discomfort, she was sitting on the edge of the ground sheet, as far from the fire as she could. I knew why, of course. She must have removed and washed her underclothes, hung them up to dry somewhere. Her flimsy shalwar, now ripped in several places, and wet to the bargain, was too revealing for her to be comfortable in the light of the fire.

'If you get ill, we won't be able to get through with this mission, not in time anyway,' I said firmly and threw the sarong at her. 'I'm sure I outrank you, so you can consider this an order. Go and change!'

'You can't know that since you don't know my rank,' she said, lightly now. 'What if I outrank you? Will I have control?'

'In a ragtag rebel army, everyone over fifteen is a Colonel,' I said. 'It doesn't count for much.'

'Every revolutionary army is called rabble - until they win.'

She'd keep this up forever and patience was never my strong point.

'Don't be a damned idiot,' I roared. 'Go and change.'

She must have been feeling cold and miserable because she got up with uncharacteristic meekness, picked up the sarong with two fingers, and went behind the tent to change. I called out to her to keep an eye on the venison and went down to the water to bathe.

I stripped off my clothes, washed them and slung them over a bit of driftwood nearby. I didn't realize how tired I was till I finally stepped into the water. It was dangerous to wade in too deep. I walked till the water reached my knees and cleared an area of its weeds and floating muck. Kneeling in the mud there I filled the tin with water and poured it over my head, over and over. The water was full of crud, streamers of weeds stuck to my head from time to time, and I tried to keep the thought of crocodiles out of my mind. Given all that, it was still a glorious bath. The day, so filled with mortal threats and near disasters, had ended well. Far better than I could possibly have expected.

I felt a high coming on.

I wore my wet pants again and carried the T-shirt in my hand. It was cold but I knew that a few minutes near the fire was all I needed. Velaithan was crouching over the fire, turning the strips of meat over. She stood up when she heard me. She had worn the sarong as a gown, tied in a firm knot over her breasts. It hung around her like a tent, reaching up to her knees. Her arms and shoulders were bare and I could see several ugly scratches and cuts on her upper arms.

She stared at me belligerently, as she always did when embarrassed, daring me to say something. I knew the best way to handle her was to pretend not to notice anything, so I ignored her stare and hung my T-shirt out to dry. I then collected some of the fleshy singhomaran leaves from the bundle tied to my pack. I put some of it in one of the tin plates and using the handle of the kathi, pounded it to a pulp.

By the time I had finished she was sitting near the fire, her feet tucked modestly under her. She looked at me suspiciously as I knelt down near her with the plate of olive green paste in my hand.

'I hope you are not planning to rub that muck on me.'

'Let me see your foot,' I said patiently. 'I saw you limping. You must have cut it.'

'It's nothing,' she said dismissively. 'It will be alright by tomorrow.'

She had her customary air of stubborn determination that I found so irritating, I had to fight an impulse to smack her on the head. I deliberately kept my voice calm and steady.

'Listen to me,' I said reasonably. 'We have at least three days of walking ahead of us, very long walks. If your foot gets infected, you will slow us down. We will not get to Colombo in time and our mission will fail. I know this herb is used to stop bleeding and arrest infection, it is the only medication we have.'

She hated giving in but, as with the sarong, she finally did with extreme reluctance. She leaned to one side and brought out her left foot. There was an ugly gash on the side of her ankle, long but fortunately, not very deep. The blood had congealed on the edges of the cut but the centre was still moist and oozing.

I held her foot and turned it sideways so that she was forced to lean further to keep the side of the ankle turned up. I noticed, for the first time, that her feet were nicely formed, slim and long, with a delicate arch. I had to use my fingers to apply the juicy green pulp directly on the wound. It stayed in place like a poultice.

'Do you have cuts on the other leg as well?'

'No.'

There was no way to tell if she were lying. She was not going to show me anything above the ankle anyway, even if it needed stitches.

'Let's have a look at that arm then,' I said gruffly, trying to sound like the family doctor.

She frowned with annoyance but stretched out her left arm. The upper arm had about four or five gashes that must have been painful but didn't look serious. I applied the rest of the paste on it anyway.

I had been dreading the moment but I knew it had to be said now.

'I feel … ashamed I left you back there.' My voice was strangled, coming from far away. 'What happened to you?'

'I lost one slipper on the road. Still I was right behind you when you dashed into the forest but the elephant was very close. Then I tripped and fell. I heard the elephant just behind me but it must have lost sight of me when

I fell. I was able to crawl out of the way, into a patch of bush before it went past.'

'I should have stopped for you. I thought you were following me.'

'We would both have been killed then,' she said gently. 'I think at the very moment I disappeared under the bush, the elephant lost sight of you as well and got very angry. It stopped just a few yards from me and went on a rampage. It kept trumpeting and tearing down all the trees and bushes around. It was so close, I could see its feet, stamping the ground and kicking up sand everywhere. It then started moving in my direction, flattening all the thorn bushes. When I tried to crawl away, my bag got stuck in the thorns and got torn off my shoulders. I had to slip out of it to get away. I was forced to crawl a good distance through the bushes before the elephant moved away. I then sat still for a long time, just to be sure it was safe.'

She paused for a while, reliving the moment.

'I tried to find my way back and got lost. I looked and looked but couldn't find the road. I found a game track but it kept winding in all directions. When I finally found the villu it was well after dark but then saw the fire. Only I wasn't sure it was yours.'

She was staring at the fire, as if it had a hypnotic quality.

She said softly: 'It was not very pleasant being lost in this bush after dark, especially after the elephant. I had to use all my … resources to keep from panicking. I kept telling myself the villu was not too far away if I kept going in the right direction and, when I got there, you would have left a signal for me.'

The strips of venison were well done and more,

charred almost. We were very hungry and it was barely enough for the two of us. Velaithan ate sparingly though, never too happy with flesh meals anyway, and I polished off most of the balance. Boiling water for the next day, making a trench round the tent, building up the fire and re-laying the ground sheet inside the tent. We went through the motions like robots, dead on our feet.

We crawled in and settled down to sleep. It had been Velaithan's habit to place some of our provisions in the middle of the tent to form a dividing line of sorts between her side and mine. Today she must have been just too tired to bother. Or perhaps, after the dangers we had faced, I had become a relatively less significant threat.

I couldn't sleep for a long time. I felt emotionally drained yet strangely content. Our mission was still on and we had a good chance of getting to Colombo in time. We needed to recover our lost provisions but, even if we couldn't, I felt we would be able to survive.

I was also thankful Velaithan was safe, thankful and strangely elated.

I listened to the jungle noises around me, an alarm call of a deer on the far side of the water and the belling of a sambhur. Now and then there was splash in the water, a grunt or a breaking branch in the forest, while the frogs and cicadas kept up an unending chorus. The denizens of the forest conducted most of their business at night and they were getting on with it.

By unspoken understanding I always slept on the 'forest' side of the tent and Velaithan took the side facing the water. It was hard to say which side was safer but the 'forest' side was a bit darker and gloomier, because of the trees. I watched the shadows thrown by the fire play on the trees and thought about going home. Perhaps I could get a few days leave when this mission was over. Much would depend on how the battle in Jaffna was progressing. I realized with a minor shock that I had not given it more than a passing thought since I escaped from the peninsula.

Was Velaithan's claim true? Could the Tigers seriously threaten the base at Elephant Pass? The base was strongly fortified and we had control of the air. I could not believe that an attack would succeed, that the camp would be overrun. Had I made the right decision to escape cross-country with her, instead of trying to rejoin my regiment?

I was still thinking about this when I fell asleep.

16

31st March 2000

I woke up just as the sky was showing the faintest pre-dawn glow. Velaithan had already left the tent. I lay there listening to the first tentative morning birdcalls. My body felt sore from the uneven ground and I hated mornings anyway. Velaithan must have woken up much earlier because I could hear her pottering about outside the tent. We had nothing left to eat except for two strips of charred venison left over from last night.

Velaithan always bathed in the morning before dawn. To go down to the villu before daybreak, and to bathe in the night-chilled water, was something I could never have steeled myself to do. I wondered idly if all Tamils were masochists. It occurred to me that, in the evenings, she always bathed in her 'day clothes', the much abused, stolen shalwar kit. She then changed into her 'night clothes', the blouse and long skirt she had first arrived in. She washed her day kit and hung it out to dry, ready for the next days' journey. In the mornings she bathed in her nightclothes, washed and stuffed the wet clothes into her rucksack. She dried her washing during the afternoon stopover.

Today she had bathed in my sarong and changed into her bedraggled day kit. She had washed the sarong and handed the soggy bundle to me with some mumbled words I took to be a vote of thanks.

We broke camp and I packed my bag with the remainder of our kit. I then hid the bag in a dense thicket near the track. We started out, with some trepidation, to

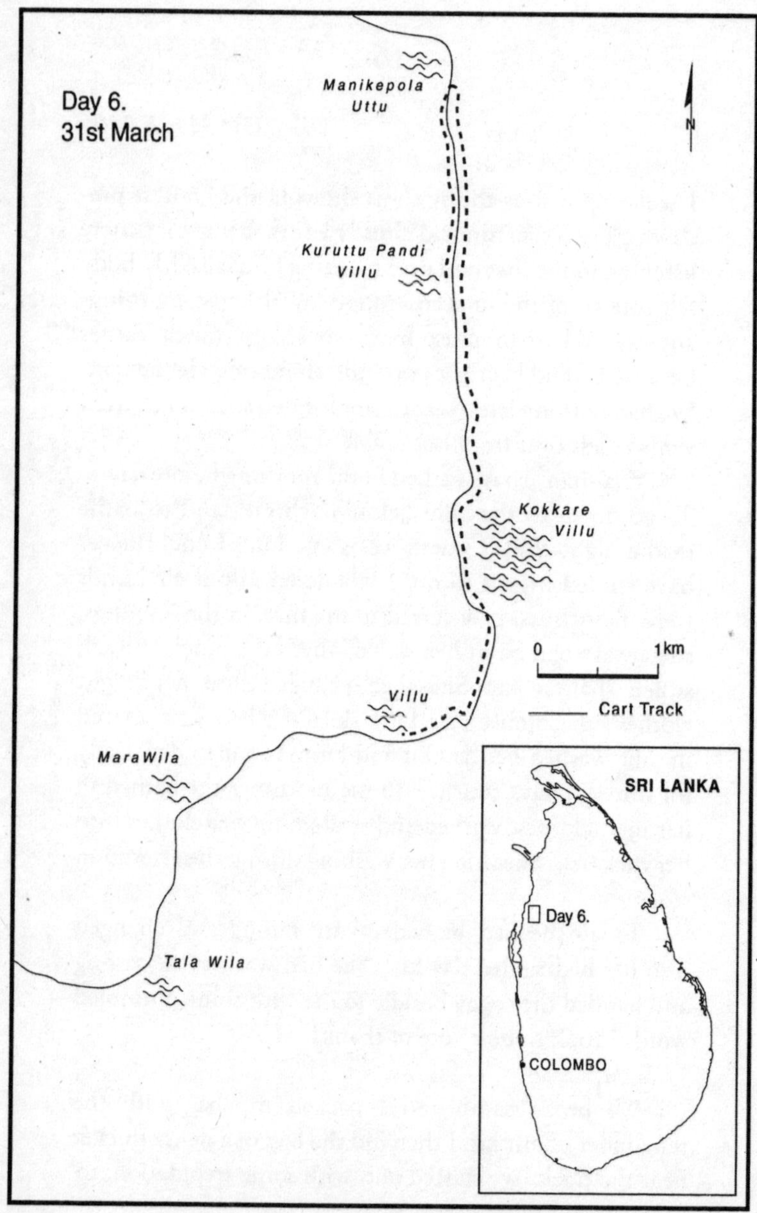
Day 6.
31st March
Manikepola
Uttu
N
Kuruttu Pandi
Villu
Kokkare
Villu
0
1km
Villu
Cart Track
MaraWila
SRI LANKA
Day 6.
COLOMBO
Tala Wila

look for the scene of yesterdays near-disaster. I noticed that Velaithan was not limping as badly as she had done on the previous evening.

I claimed a victory for Sinhala folk medicine and got some unladylike swear words in Tamil as a response.

My mind told me that there was no chance of meeting the same elephant today. Elephants travel great distances while feeding and don't hang about the same bit of forest. But the experience was fresh in our minds. Every shadow seemed threatening. By unspoken agreement, we walked slowly and kept a sharp lookout. I was also worried that I had not marked the spot clearly enough in my confusion last evening. If we missed it, we had no chance whatever of recovering our supplies.

As it happened we found it without difficulty. The elephant dung on the track alerted us and then the branches I had cut and left on the track were easy to spot.

'Where did you find the slipper?' Velaithan asked anxiously. 'Can you locate the spot?'

To walk barefoot in the jungle is never easy, even on the sandy track. Finding her other slipper was vital for us. She wouldn't be able to walk very far without them, especially when we were forced to leave the road.

'I think we ran off the track just about here.' I pointed to a small gap in the shrubbery. 'I cut a mark on a tree. Let's see if we can spot it.'

We entered the scrub, speaking in whispers and moving with extreme caution. We found the devastated area easily. A patch of forest, about the size of a basketball court, looked as if a bomb had been let off in it. I was glad I hadn't been around to see that performance.

Velaithan took over then and pointed at a dense patch

of scrub nearby.

'That must be it, I'm sure it is,' she said quietly, pointing to her left. 'My slipper and the knapsack must be somewhere in that patch.'

Once again it took time, but we found her slipper and, a little further in the same thicket, the rucksack, torn open at the centre with the rice and other provisions strewn about. The bag must have got caught on some thorns and been ripped off her as she scurried away. We collected what we could and repacked the bag but we had lost a good part of our rice and dhal.

We would have to find more food off the land to complete our journey.

We had only eaten a strip of venison in the morning. I was famished. Velaithan must have been hungry as well but she was happy enough to get her slipper back, repair it with a safety pin and put it back into service.

I had an inspiration.

'When the park was open, each of these bungalows had a cook and a helper. Since provisions were often short, they cultivated small home gardens to provide themselves with vegetables. Some of that might possibly have survived,' I told her. 'I want to go back to Manikepola and check it out.'

'What if the bungalow is occupied?' she asked.

I thought about that.

'It wasn't occupied when we came past yesterday. Even if it was occupied at night, I doubt anyone would spend the day there. We can check it out from cover,' I went on cautiously. 'It's worth a chance. We really need to pick up some vegetables and fruit, if we can.'

'How far is it to the bungalow?'

'More than a mile! Say thirty minutes.'

She didn't say anything more. She used some safety pins to repair the torn flap of her rucksack and slung it across her shoulders. We set off then, going back towards Manikepola villu we had passed through last afternoon.

The old holiday bungalow had been a comfortable building of stone and timber, with a wide, open verandah at the front of it. It had been located beside the open villu, commanding a great view of the water's edge.

We left the track as the villu came into sight, walking through the trees and scrub to approach the bungalow from the rear. It was not long before we were squatting behind some thorn bushes, quietly observing the silent building.

We could see what had once been the kitchen and storeroom. The staff must have lived in the outhouse that lay to our left. The roof of the outhouse had collapsed and grass and weeds had grown up around it. Clearly it had not been used for years. The main house was badly neglected but still looked habitable. I signalled to Velaithan to remain where she was and made a slow circuit on either side of it, first to the right and again to the left. There was no vehicle to be seen and no sign of any occupant. I told Velaithan to stay under cover and keep watch. I crawled into what must have once been the bungalow keepers' backyard and home garden.

I was delighted to see two papaya trees, both with clusters of green fruit. Some of the larger, orange tinged, fruits at the bottom of the clusters had been partly eaten by squirrels and birds. I would need a pole of some sort to dislodge the fruit. I decided to leave it for the end and pushed my way through the waist high weeds in search of vegetables.

It took time but I found, struggling bravely among the weeds, the slender green beans we called mäkaral, some bottle gourd and small green tomatoes. There was also a sickly citrus tree with curled yellow leaves. I was able to reach up and collect a few hard green limes. I pulled off my T-shirt and tied a knot at its bottom to form a rough bag. I collected whatever I could of the recognizable vegetables in it and went back to where Velaithan was.

She glanced at my makeshift bag and nodded. She smiled fleetingly and went back to her allotted task of keeping watch.

'There is no sign of anyone,' she whispered. 'I think the house is empty.'

'OK. Keep watching,' I said. 'I want to get some papaya.'

I found a dead branch that seemed long enough and went back to the papaya trees. Standing in the open I was an easy target, but there was no other way. It wasn't difficult to dislodge the fruit, not for an accomplished fruit thief like myself. A sharp prod to break off a single fruit at a time, and then one had to catch before it smashed to a pulp on the ground.

Back under cover I used the kathi to cut the papaya into slices. I had not realized how hungry I was until that moment. We sat together silently and ate and ate until we were sated. The fruit was nicely ripe and sweet from the sun. Velaithan, never a big eater, seemed content after a few slices but I took time to fill myself.

When we were done and about to leave, Velaithan pointed towards the side of the house and asked:

'Isn't that manioc? It will be useful if we could get some.'

How could I have missed it? Growing in a row,

and rising above the weeds and grass by the side of the bungalow, was the unmistakable leaves of manioc plants. The tubers growing from the roots of this plant can be boiled and eaten with almost anything. We had, my sisters and I, practically lived on it when my mother was short of money. It would be a neat substitute for the rice we had lost.

'It's pretty close to the house,' I observed cautiously. 'Do you think we should risk it?'

For once Velaithan had no doubts:

'We've lost most of our rice. We need as much as we can dig up.' She wasn't even keeping her voice down. 'Anyway I think the house is empty. We would have seen some movement if it was occupied.'

I left the rucksack, and the vegetables in my T-shirt, behind a tree. I picked up the kathi and went towards the house. Velaithan followed me. When I looked at her she said confidently:

'I think it is safe enough. It will be quicker if I help.'

I knew she was probably right but still went carefully to where the plants were. It was too close to the house for my comfort. I used my hands to pull out some of the weeds and clear the soil around the base of the plants. The axe-like kathi was an awkward tool for digging but the soil was sandy, so I loosened it and Velaithan used her hands to scoop it out. When the hole was about a foot deep we grasped the upright stem of the plant and pulled. I was relieved to find that the hair thin roots snapped easily and a nice carrot like tuber came out without too much trouble. But it took time and we were bathed in perspiration by the time we had seven stems, complete with tubers, all laid in a row.

I was just wondering if that was enough when a door

at the back of the house creaked open and a man walked out of the house. He hawked and spat as he went down the steps. He was bare bodied except for a filthy sarong that might have once been white. He was facing the other way but so close I could see the tufts of strong black hair growing at the back of his shoulders. He urinated at the base of the papaya tree I had stood under, just minutes before.

We were squatting on our heels, our heads clearly visible over the weeds. The man only needed to look over his shoulder and he'd see us. Worse, there was a window just above our heads with a shutter hanging down on a single hinge. We could be seen from inside the house, and there could well be others there. If there were, they'd have guns.

I signalled to Velaithan and we went down on our bellies. There was a good chance the rough grass would cover us when the man finished and turned around. I just hoped no one came to the window above us. The bastard took an eternity to finish, but he did finally. He turned back to the house, yawning and scratching himself, a dark, unshaven man with long greasy hair falling onto his face. I pressed myself down, the rough grass prickly against my bare chest.

We could see him clearly through the weeds. He'd see us if he looked in our direction, surely. If he saw us I knew my knee jerk reaction would be to charge down on him and disable him, then get away before the others could figure out what was going on. I gripped the kathi and readied myself, adrenalin pumping.

'Aiii, umbala nägitinne nädda?' he called out loudly in Sinhala, as he climbed the steps.

Aren't you buggers getting up?

Someone responded sleepily from inside, inviting him do something physically challenging. The man outside had used the word 'umbala', addressing more than one person. They must have been sleeping late after an all night hunt. The park seemed to be crawling with poachers. If we hung around till they got moving, we'd be seen for sure.

There was no purpose in waiting. As the man disappeared inside I just stood up, balanced the bundle of manioc plants on my left shoulder, took the kathi in my right hand, and walked away. Velaithan followed me silently but I stopped and made her go ahead. The back of the bungalow faced the forest and we'd left our provisions there. The front faced the villu. I walked away parallel to the forest, in clear view from the window, but relatively concealed from the back and front of the house, at least till we were some distance away. I counted off the first fifty paces without looking back, waiting tensely for a shout or gunshot.

Nothing happened.

At my signal, we turned and dashed off into the forest. Once under cover, we sat down to for a minute just to restore our nerves. I started laughing then, thinking how foolish I had been and how lucky. If that man had taken a leak just five minutes earlier he'd have walked straight into me trying to pluck those papayas.

'I should have checked the house first,' I admitted ruefully.

She was smiling. She looked … different when she smiled.

'If we did, we would have run away,' she said reasonably, 'then we wouldn't have collected all that stuff.'

I left her with the kathi to separate and clean the manioc tubers and went back to recover our bags. I made a careful detour and came up behind the house. It was well that I did, because two men were seated on the back steps of the house. One of them was cradling a tin mug in his hands, the other was cleaning a double-barrelled shotgun. A twelve bore by the looks of it.

There was no way I could get close enough to collect the rucksack and my T-shirt without being seen. I squatted behind a screen of lantana bushes to wait. We had lost too much time already and I was anxious to be on my way but the men seemed to be in no hurry, chatting idly as they sat there.

When I thought they would spend the rest of the morning there, I saw a movement on the side of the house. The man we'd seen in the morning appeared. He was walking casually round the house, towards the back. He stopped near the manioc patch and called out to the others.

'Mey ballapang. Kauda mangnokka tika uduragena.'

Look at this. Someone has pulled out the manioc.

'Uro wenna äthi,' the man with the gun said. *'Api methana hitiyanang unta denna thibuna.'*

Must have been pigs. We could have shot them if we stayed here last night.

'Uro nang gus thiyenna ona ney,' the first man said. *'Ävilla balapang.'*

If it were pig, the plants would be left. Come and look at this.

The first man was looking down at the holes we had dug. The other two stood up and went towards him. I waited till they were all standing together.

Now!

I had about twenty feet of open ground to cover and I did it on all fours, scrambling like a monkey. I didn't look up till I was back under cover with the rucksack and my sagging T-shirt.

Velaithan looked relieved when I got back. She had cut off the tubers and scraped the roots and soil off them. We filled her rucksack with vegetables and manioc and but I still had to use the T-shirt to carry the papaya. I was happy to walk bare bodied in order to save some of it for later. Slung over the shoulder, it wasn't too difficult a load. We retraced our steps, once again keeping to the trees, and were soon back on the track. It took us another half hour to get back to where we'd spent the previous night.

We rearranged our packs, now full and heavy, and headed south once again. It was late morning.

'We've lost too much time. I had planned to get to a place called Talawila for the night. We can't make it now,' I explained carefully. 'There is a large swamp called Kokkare Villu just ahead but that is too close.'

After yesterday's experience Velaithan listened attentively.

'Lets go as far as we can,' I said. 'We should be able to find a small villu along the way.'

Most days, especially in the heat of mid morning, the forest seems dead. One could walk for hours without seeing much more than occasional bird or butterfly flitting across one's path. Then there come those special days, when for some totally unknown reason, the forest seems to burst with life and action.

I should have been paranoid after yesterday's events, carefully peering round each tree for signs of danger. But I was high again. We had been phenomenally fortunate yesterday and this morning's raid had also gone well. Now the forest had come alive around me, matching my mood. There were birdcalls and whistles all around us, movements in the canopy and on the ground wherever we looked.

We had to adopt a leisurely pace on account of Velaithan's painful foot. She seemed surprisingly relaxed in spite of her limp, keeping her eyes on the trees, alert for signs of bird life. The forest was particularly rich in pigeons that morning and I saw bronze-wings darting swiftly across our path, their attractive brown and green wings glinting in the sunlight. Velaithan spotted a pair of very large pigeon-like birds with iridescent green wings and gray heads, sitting on a branch and cooing drowsily to each other. I recognized them to be imperial green pigeons. We saw another serpent eagle, perched on the summit of a dead tree, pitiless yellow eyes searching for prey on the forest floor.

We had one alarm when we stumbled on a herd of wild pig, several large females with some beautifully striped young. They were rooting around a little mud-filled hollow by the side of the road. It was hard to tell who was more frightened as they crashed off into the scrub.

I knew it was past noon and we were tiring. With no waterhole in sight, I spotted a banyan tree rising above the canopy and decided to sit out the afternoon in its shade. These mighty trees had held a special fascination for Mr. Karl. They teemed with life and he would never pass up an opportunity to have a close look at one of them.

We had to go round a dense patch of thorn bush to reach it but found the banyan tree itself on open ground. The area beyond it was a glade of short grass interspersed with small bushes. The tree seemed to have two main trunks, easily nine or ten feet in girth, and dozens of minor root-trunks.

The tree was in fruit and I could hear, as we got closer, birds squabbling in the canopy. There were lots of them about but the Malabar hornbills and the parakeets were the noisiest. The sandy area under the tree was covered with hoof marks.

We selected a spot overlooking the glade, on the side of the tree away from the road, to set up our camp. I cleaned an area of dried dung and rocks and spread the ground sheet. I lit a fire, quite sure that the dense green canopy would disperse the smoke. We chopped up some of the vegetables, tomatoes and beans and boiled them with a handful of rice. We had to use water from our bottles leaving just enough for drinking afterwards. The vegetable rice turned out well, except for some grit in the rice. We ate in silence and shared another Papaya afterwards.

I found a few more leaves of singhomaran in my pack, now shrivelled and dry. I crushed the leaves with a few drops of water.

Velaithan had been watching me, faintly amused.

'Let's have a look at that wound,' I said.

'There is no need for that stuff,' she replied mildly. 'I think it is healing well enough.'

I just stared at her and she just stared back stubbornly, no longer amused.

I didn't budge and finally she gave in with an exaggerated sigh. She had been sitting on the ground with her feet tucked in under her, as was her habit. She wasn't too pleased but finally brought her foot out for me to examine. The cut was still raw and red, but thankfully, without any sign of infection. I rubbed the paste carefully along the cut and, just to annoy her, slapped the remainder over her arm although the scratches were superficial and healing nicely.

We sat on the ground sheet in companionable silence to wait out the afternoon. The sun blazed down on the glade before us but it was wonderfully cool in the deep cathedral shade of the Banyan.

I remembered the strips of bamboo I had collected the previous day and fished the bundle out of my bag. Some of the aerial roots sent down by the Banyan seemed thin and pliant enough to use as twine. I cut some lengths off and set about making a trap.

Velaithan seemed amused by my efforts. After a while she asked:

'So what kind of animal are you hoping to trap, Captain?'

She had me there.

'I don't know,' I said sourly. 'A rock squirrel, maybe.'

'And if you catch one,' she continued guilelessly, ' how will you kill it?'

How the hell would I know, woman? Maybe I'll drown the bastard.

I looked up, ready to be nasty, and found her smiling. Not a big smile, mind, but just enough to show she was teasing me.

'Tell me, Captain,' she asked, changing the subject

abruptly. 'When you were hunting here, did you kill animals in the same way as those men?'

'Do you mean, did we shoot on foot?' I asked, pretending to misunderstand.

'Did you use a spotlight to mesmerize animals and then shoot them when they were helpless?' Her smile had faded.

'Well, no,' I said. 'We shot in daylight most times, and from the vehicle.'

'Was that how your guru taught you?' she asked, scornfully now. 'To use a rifle to shoot animals from a vehicle?'

'Mr. Karl was a conservationist. He taught me not to shoot,' I said mildly. 'And I didn't.'

'You said ...,' she began.

'My C.O. was very keen on shooting,' I explained finally. 'He didn't want to risk taking guides from the village. He took me along because I knew these tracks.'

She had a strange expression on her face.

'Are you saying that you've never shot an animal?'

'Pigs for the pot, a couple of times,' I told her. 'A peacock once. I regretted that ... later.'

I continued to struggle with my trap. The roots were not strong enough for proper knots and kept snapping just when I needed them to stay in place.

After watching my work for a while, Velaithan asked:

'Are you an intelligence officer?'

'No,' I was surprised by the question. 'I'm attached to an infantry brigade.'

'How was it you were sent to bring me in?'

Was she offended that a lowly infantry captain had been sent to escort her?

'My boss, Major Kiriella, had the contact. He wanted me to handle it,' I explained. 'It seemed simple enough, at the time.'

'So you've never handled intelligence work before?'

'In the early days, we didn't have enough intelligence personnel to go round,' I said innocently. 'At that time we had to cover intelligence work as well.'

'So you've interrogated suspects?' she persisted gently.

'Yes.'

Where the hell are you going with this?

'And if the suspects didn't co-operate?' she asked. 'What did you do then?'

'You mean did I respect their human rights?' I asked testily, getting defensive. 'What do you think?'

She looked at me gravely.

'Don't be angry, Captain. Since I will be interrogated as well, I want to know the procedure,' she said quietly. 'You are a man who doesn't shoot an animal. How would you interrogate an uncooperative suspect?'

Dangerous ground.

'You need to have a strong sense of justice,' I said slowly. 'If I were sure the suspect had guilty knowledge, and if lives were at stake, I believe persuasion is … justified.'

'You mean torture.'

'I suppose so,' I said. 'Yes.'

'And what about the suspect's human rights?' she asked quietly.

I had been waiting for that.

'These people are terrorists,' I said tightly, holding my temper for once. 'They want to tie us down with rules and conventions, then take cover behind those very rules to carry out terror attacks on civilian targets. I don't accept that.'

'These are civilized norms. Surely you can't justify torture in the name of security?'

I took a deep breath.

'Let me give you an example, then you tell me what is justifiable and what isn't,' I said mildly, surprised by my own self-control. 'Some months ago, on a tip off, we arrested a man suspected of planning a bomb attack. An intelligence officer was attached to our unit at the time, a young lieutenant called Ranjit. He was a conscientious officer and a trained interrogator. He wouldn't use any form of physical torture, he was just very clever and very patient. And he had the ability to keep going for long periods without a break, living on just cigarettes and coffee.

'He zonked the bastard's brains out. After two days of nonstop questioning the suspect admitted everything. They had planned to set off a large device in the market and the attack was planned for the next day. It was a pola day, when the villagers brought their produce to town. But he wouldn't, or couldn't, tell us where the explosives were hidden or the name of his accomplice.

'We were desperate. We couldn't close the market on a pola day. There was a good chance that the accomplice would set the device off and the civilian death toll would be … horrendous. Ranjit tried everything he knew but had to give up in the end. He told my boss there was nothing more he could do.

'My boss is not a man trained in the … niceties of interrogation. He had a truncheon and knew how to use it, how to maximize the pain. Ten minutes of that and the suspect was a bag of shapeless flesh on the floor, begging for a chance to tell us everything. We found the explosives all right, although the accomplice got away.'

'Both officers were guilty of cruel and degrading treatment of a prisoner,' Velaithan said primly. 'Surely you understand that it was totally wrong and immoral?'

'What morality are you talking about? The civilians we saved that day were Tamils, every one of them,' I told her. 'Don't innocent victims have rights as well? We had a duty to protect them. We saved their lives; all that bastard got was a few bruises.'

I had been working on my trap all the time and now had the base and two sides nicely spaced out and tied in place. I pulled gently on a knot but the rootlet snapped and the whole thing collapsed in a pile. I stared at it angrily for a moment, collected the lot and threw it away.

'Do you think beating up a few suspects will win this war for you?' Velaithan asked, changing tack and avoiding my question at the same time.

'Of course not,' I said gruffly. 'We won't win till the politicians leave us alone, to run the war.'

'You mean, if the military were given a free hand, they'd win the war?'

She didn't even try to keep the derision out of her voice.

'Yes, I mean just that.'

This was a subject I'd normally get a bit emotional and agitated over. If I could discuss it rationally, without actually assaulting her, I'd really be making progress.

'What would you change that would make a

difference?' she asked.

'Almost everything, but I'll touch on just a couple of important issues,' I told her. 'We get less than fifty percent of the value, or quality, of the armaments we spend billions on. Corruption in arms purchases is an open secret. That has to stop. Then all the strategic and sometimes, even tactical, decisions are taken by armchair generals and politicians in Colombo. If we could buy the weapons we need and had the freedom to decide strategy, then you will find the situation on the ground very … different.'

'If strategy were up to you, Captain, what would you do?'

I laughed bitterly.

'By the time I am in a position to decide strategy, the war will have ended.'

'But if you had the power today, Captain?' she persisted. 'What then?'

'My ideas are a bit extreme,' I said carefully. 'You don't want to hear them. '

'I'm sure they are,' she said dryly. 'Let's hear them anyway.'

'For a start I'd deny the Tigers their sanctuary,' I said slowly. 'They have the Wanni to themselves. They can attack when they want and then retreat to safety there. I'd want to put an end to that.'

'Carpet bombing?' she asked scornfully. 'That's been tried before, Captain. You'll just be aerating the forest.'

'No. I'd use commandos, Tamil speaking men, in teams of three. Dozens of teams! I'd infiltrate them into the Wanni. They'll live off the land and make life insupportable for those living there. Poison the water, mine the roads, booby trap everything,' I said grandly. 'They can even use GPS to call in air strikes on sensitive targets.'

'That would be a huge escalation, Captain,' she said quietly. 'Do you really think our people would accept that without retaliation?'

'Well, no,' I said warily. 'But what will they do that they are not doing already?'

'They can rain fire on your cities.' Her face seemed to harden as she spoke, her eyes changed in some way. 'You know they have explosives stashed in every major city in the south. And the people to set them off are in place. The only reason the south has been spared is the value our leader puts on the goodwill of western countries. If you adopted a scorched earth policy in the Wanni, the south will burn.'

'There again your tactics are based on taking advantage of the very freedoms that a democracy guarantees,' I countered. 'If it were up to me, I'd take away that freedom till the war is over.'

'And how exactly will you do that?' she demanded.

'Once an ethnic or religious group has taken arms against a government, then all members of that group must be treated as suspect. Whatever their personal feelings are, any one of them can be coerced into active insurgency. By your own admission, the Tigers have used the freedom of movement allowed to the Tamils, to smuggle explosives into our cities.'

'So?'

'So deny them that right.'

'Are you saying you would restrict the right of free movement to the Tamils?' she was outraged. 'You can't be serious.'

'Oh, I think we'd need to go even further than that,'

I said, now in full free flight. 'The Americans put all citizens of Japanese origin into camps for the duration of the world war. Did you know that?'

She didn't say anything.

'What if we place all Tamil citizens in camps for a period of one year?' I asked. 'We'd use that year to flush out and kill all the rebels hiding in the Wanni. You can't blow up our cities when your bombers are not allowed free access to economic and civilian targets, pretending to be innocents.'

'That idea is barbaric. It is only a short step from there to the gas chambers,' she said furiously and then brightened. 'But I like the idea. When you start on it, the whole world will condemn you. You will be a pariah state. It will help our cause in other ways as well. We'll have plenty of new recruits and funding from our expatriate community will increase immediately.'

'Oh, I understand that the idea is impractical but we don't have many options,' I said evenly. 'Do you remember Indira Gandhi and the Sikh problem? When the Sikhs were fighting the Indian Government, two of her bodyguards happened to be Sikhs. Mrs. Gandhi's advisors wanted to get rid of the men, but she refused. She had known those men for years and trusted them. More importantly, she believed that to move them out would, by itself, violate the principle, and concept, of a united India.'

'So?'

'So one day her trusted bodyguards shot and killed her,' I told her. 'They were Sikhs first and Indians second!'

'And your point is?'

'So long as the war goes on, any Tamil may willingly or unwillingly carry out a terrorist act or, at least, work against the state.'

I said slowly, sorting my thoughts as I spoke.

'But if we treat every Tamil as a suspect, they scream that they are being ill-treated and demand a separate state. If we treat them as free and equal citizens, they use that cover to wage war against us. Our security forces are in an impossible situation.'

'Oh yes,' she said mockingly now. 'I feel so sorry for your security forces.'

'You should, really,' I said seriously, faintly surprised that I wasn't getting mad. 'Look at the position of a soldier or policeman at a security checkpoint. If they really detect a suicide bomber, they get blown up immediately for their trouble. If they let the suspect through, the bomber will attack a sensitive target. What can those men do?'

'They've raped enough Tamil women at those checkpoints,' she said viciously. 'They all deserve to die and I hope they die suffering.'

'Be serious. How can they identify and arrest a suicide bomber, without getting killed themselves?'

'If I knew,' she asked acidly, 'do you really think I'd tell you?'

Then she was serious.

'Captain, there are no solutions to problems like this. You must see that this war will not come to an end by one side winning in a decisive way.'

She was lying on her back on the far side of the ground sheet, looking up at the canopy. Her voice was grave.

'You are a democratic state. You will never be allowed to take those measures you think are needed to isolate us. Why? Because you are a state!'

I didn't say anything. Velaithan continued:

'We are guerrillas and we use guerrilla tactics. If you

adopt draconian laws to control civilians, we will see to it you are crucified in the media. If you ease up and allow civil liberties, we will use those freedoms to infiltrate and destroy you. That is how this game will be played.'

I kept my mouth shut.

Where was all this leading?

She paused for a while, than continued: 'Any new weapons you may introduce only give you a short term tactical advantage, then we find a way to neutralize it. We know we cannot beat you in conventional battle, but we can exhaust you. You have to be alert all the time. You have to defend every city, every building and every economic target. We can plan in secret, focus all our resources and attack just one point. Do you realize that almost every one of our major operations has been successful beyond even our own expectations?'

Yes! But you've been lucky. You've not run into someone like me.

When I kept silent she continued:

'We will grind you down and destroy your economy. Your government will finally lose its will to fight.'

'That's good propaganda but it is not going to work out like that,' I said finally. 'Even if there are no clear winners, it will finally come down to manpower, and we have the population base. In a war of attrition, we have to win because of our numbers. We should be engaging you at all times, not waiting for you to select the battles.'

'You just reconfirmed what I have said,' she said composedly. 'When will your politicians and generals agree on a strategy of continuous engagement?"

There was no answer to that.

She waited awhile, then said:

'My way is much surer!'

'What do you mean?'

'My leader has asked his cadres to kill him if he ever gives up his call for Eelam, our homeland,' she said. 'If you want to settle for something short of that, he must be removed from the scene. Your best chance to do that is to go through with this mission.'

'Oh, I see. All this was to show me how important it is to complete this job,' I said. 'What about your personal agenda in this?'

'My personal agenda is not your business,' she said tartly. 'You should just focus on achieving your goal.'

She wouldn't be drawn further.

I let it go.

I lay back on the ground sheet staring at the deep green of the under canopy and the rare shafts of sunlight that came through it, like a laser swords from Star Wars. The birds were still at it, feeding and squabbling. Small flocks came fluttering in, calling excitedly to each other. They settled down to feed for a while and then, at some unseen signal, took wing to feed elsewhere. I tried counting the species, not always easy when all you had was the silhouette to go by. I saw Malabar hornbills, grey hornbills, brown-headed barbets, hanging parrots and rose-ringed parakeets.

'I've counted fourteen,' Velaithan announced suddenly. 'You?'

'Uh, twelve.'

'Did you spot the ioras?' she asked. 'A pair hopping about?'

The iora is a small, insectivorous bird. The male

has a bright yellow underside and black and white wing feathers. The upper parts of the female are a pale mud green. Now that she mentioned it, I remembered hearing the iora's very distinctive, 'drowsy afternoon', whistle.

'No,' I said. 'I didn't count them.'

She had counted a blue-faced malkoha.

I had to challenge that. The blue-face is a very attractive bird sporting a light green beak, a blue oval eye patch and white tips to its tail feathers. It is common enough in Wilpattu but I thought it was a scrub bird that wasn't often seen in the high canopy. How could she have identified a bird like that from underneath?

We argued about it, vehemently as only bird watchers are wont to, neither prepared to give an inch. More heat was generated than when we'd talked about the issues of the ethnic divide. Velaithan was convinced that the general shape of the bird and the distinctive white tips of the tail were unmistakable and was infuriated that I wouldn't take her word for it. She was probably right but I didn't want to give her the credit.

I had a good laugh. I tried to laugh inside my head but she knew what I was at and that pissed her off some more. She wouldn't talk to me afterwards and ignored my sallies.

I realized I was thirsty. I reached for my bottle and found it empty. Velaithan had used her water sparingly and had at least a half bottle left. I knew she was waiting for me to ask her for some so that she could make some nasty remark. That made me bite my tongue and hang on!

She had been watching me.

'Will we be able to find good water tonight, Captain?' she asked innocently. 'How will we manage if we don't?'

She knew damned well I would have to, but wanted to torment me a bit.

'Shouldn't be a problem,' I said offhandedly. 'If we don't find water, the army will commandeer all stocks in civilian hands.'

'I'm going to spit into my bottle,' she said childishly. 'You can commandeer it then.'

I ignored her and tried to sleep but the flies were a nuisance and kept me awake.

17

The sun was still blazing down when we set off again. Water was becoming a serious problem. Velaithan, in a better humour now, gave me a drink from her bottle before she consumed some herself. We had very little left. To add to our discomfort, the track was heading due west so we had no shade and the sun was directly in our eyes. The forest was also becoming a little less dense as we moved in the direction of Pomparippu.

Velaithan heard them first and tapped me on the arm. The sounds of snapping branches and blowing were unmistakable. A herd of elephants was feeding nearby. I realized how difficult it was to pinpoint sound in the bush, the noises seemed to be coming now from one direction and now from another. The animals were invisible but quite near. It seemed quite possible that a large herd was feeding on either side of the track.

I dreaded the thought of stumbling on them and having another traumatic experience.

I gestured to Velaithan to follow and cautiously crept behind a tree on the side of the track. I left my pack on the ground and scrambled up to a low fork and along a horizontal branch. Nothing. I climbed a little higher and suddenly the scene opened up before me, like turning the page of a book to an illustration, gray humps all over the place.

It was a herd of medium size. I counted some twenty adult animals but the young were difficult to spot from my vantage. They were feeding on both sides of the track and I was glad we'd decided to play safe. Herds with very young animals do not take kindly to potential threats and we would certainly have run into them if we had tried to sneak by. I didn't fancy another close encounter.

Velaithan looked questioningly at me when I jumped down.

I kept my voice down to a whisper. 'There is a herd feeding on both sides of the track. We will have to wait till they move off or go back and cut across the forest. What do you think?'

'What if they start moving towards us? Even otherwise it could take a long time for them to move a safe distance,' she reasoned. 'Why don't we go round them?'

I was not too happy to leave the track but it seemed to be the best option available. We cautiously shouldered our packs and retraced our steps for about a hundred and fifty yards. I took stock before leaving the track.

'Once we enter the forest it is pretty easy to get lost. This section of road is heading west,' I explained carefully. 'If we use the sun as a guide and walk three sides of a square, we should get back on the track. I hope.'

It sounded easy, in theory.

Velaithan just nodded and waited for me to lead the way. I tried to cut perpendicularly across the shadows and counted three hundred paces. It was not easy to move in a straight line due to the thorn bushes but we did our best, compensating when we made a detour, and hoping we'd got it right. We then turned towards the sun and counted another three hundred paces. I was ready to swing back to the track.

Velaithan asked quietly: 'What if the elephants have moved with us? We'll be walking straight into them.'

I should have thought of that. We were in low jungle now with no tall trees to climb. There was no way to check if the herd was still around.

'Lets walk another three hundred paces west and then cut back to the track,' I decided. 'They don't move quickly when they are feeding.'

We were passing through a dense thicket where visibility was poor. It made me edgy. There was a real chance of stumbling on the herd before we knew it. I tried to listen for the sounds of feeding but elephants can be awfully quiet at times.

Suddenly there was a loud crash on our right, a sound of branches snapping under the weight of a heavy animal. It was so close there was no time to react.

Oh shit, no. Not again!

We stood where we were, rooted to the spot, expecting to see an elephant charge down on us. It was only when I realized the sound was receding, and the animal was running away, that I was able to breathe again. A glimpse between the trees revealed a sambhur stag, with a magnificent set of antlers, in headlong flight. I needed to stand still for a minute to allow my bowels to settle.

I looked at Velaithan. She looked shaken too so I sat right there, with my back to a tree, gesturing to her to do the same. It was warm and still, a good opportunity to rest for a moment. We had just drunk the last of our water when Velaithan spotted a paradise flycather.

She was enthralled by it, and in her intent observation, she seemed to forget the recent shock she had just had. I found her enthusiasm infectious, and looked with fresh eyes at the perky little bird with the glossy white body, blue-black head and crest. Its long white tail curved down behind it as it sat on a branch quite near us, looking about for insect prey. As we watched, it flew from its perch and its tail moved in waves, like a long ribbon pinned to a kite. It snapped at an insect that was quite invisible to us, then returned to batter its victim against the branch before lifting its beak to swallow it.

The flycatcher darted away and was lost in the forest. We scrambled top our feet to continue our journey.

'I think we had better try to get back to the track. If we keep on like this we have a good chance of getting lost'.

Velaithan just nodded, hiding any doubts she may have had. We turned to our left and now tried to walk in a direction perpendicular, once again, to the shadows cast by the evening sun. In my simplistic reckoning, we should regain the track after three hundred paces, four hundred on the outside.

It didn't work out like that.

Sure, we couldn't move in a straight line due to the patches of impenetrable thorny scrub, but I knew we were moving south and should have reached the track by now. After some six hundred paces, and there was still no sign of it, I knew I had screwed it up.

We stopped to reassess our situation. I had expected Velaithan to say something nasty but she didn't. To be fair, she never did, when things went wrong. She just looked at me calmly and waited for instructions.

'I can think of only one explanation. The track was heading west when we left it. It might have turned away from us, to the southwest perhaps. That would make this leg much longer than I had expected. I think we should change direction, try to head southeast. We'll have a better chance then.'

'What about the elephants?' Velaithan asked. I didn't blame her. After her experience, she might prefer to be lost rather than run into another one.

'They could be anywhere but I think we have passed them. Lets just keep careful watch. If we stop and listen every few minutes we should hear them, if they are feeding nearby.'

It was not easy to figure out where the southeast was, but we tried. Fortunately we stumbled on the track soon after that. I was vindicated, for the track was now heading almost southwest.

And, thankfully, no sign of the herd!

There was well over an hour of daylight left when we came upon a small villu. The road skirted it, going to our left in a wide curve. I decided to camp there rather than try to cover more ground. We left the track and walked along the edge of the forest to the right, to the far side where I could see some boalders by the water. When we got there we found a jumble of rocks in the water just by the shore. The largest rose some twelve feet above the water and would screen us nicely from the track on the far side. There was a gap of some forty feet from the trees to the rocks, covered with coarse grass.

We could now put up our makeshift tent with practised ease. The plastic sheet was beginning to fray but still provided good service. I left Velaithan to sort our provisions and went to explore the rocks. My whole body was itching and I needed a good bath. My clothes needed washing as well.

Up close, I realized it was one relatively large rock surrounded by smaller outcroppings on the sides. The rock face sloped gently upwards from the landside but the angle was much sharper where it met the water. Fortunately there was one spot where the rock had opened into a crevice and here the slope was relatively less steep. I noticed that water birds, cormorants most likely, had used this part of the rock for perching and the surface was white with dried guano. Some birds were still resting there, bloated with fish from the villu. Little cormorants and Indian shags flapped clumsily away when I appeared on the skyline.

I got to a spot from where I could let down the old tin, now tied to a bit of coir rope, and draw water for my needs. It was so well screened from the camp that I took off all my clothes and began to wash them. The clothes were caked with mud and grime and needed pounding on the rocks in our traditional way.

I didn't know she was there till she spoke.

I was startled enough to half stand and take a step backwards, trying at the same time to cover my nakedness with my hands. I didn't allow for the rock surface that had provided a firm purchase when the guano was dry. Once wet, however, the guano had turned into a treacherous slime.

My feet slipped from beneath me and I fell, a tangle of arms and legs, into the water with a mighty splash, banging my back painfully on the rock as I went down. It was deep there, and murky, the water full of weeds and dead roots. I was terrified at the thought of crocodiles with one part of my mind and furiously angry with the other.

'What the hell do you want?'

We had an unspoken pact never to violate each other's privacy when bathing and the arrangement had worked well so far. Yet here she was, standing brazenly before me and looking faintly amused.

'There is a big buffalo near the camp and it won't go away,' she said calmly.

My first priority was to get out of the water. It was

turbid with mud and algae and I tried to keep the thought of crocodiles out of my mind. I might not, perhaps, have felt so jittery if I had been clothed. There is something about being naked, and immersed in murky water full of predators with sharp teeth, that made me shudder.

'Turn around so I can get out of here.'

Embarrassment put a rasp in my voice.

She laughed, the first time I had seen her really let go. It transformed her normally austere face and ordinarily I would have been pleased. Now it only increased my irritation.

'Don't mind me, just pretend I'm not here,' she said shamelessly. 'An army man won't be embarrassed, surely?'

'Stop fooling around. I thought girls from Jaffna were known for their modesty,' I said, torn between amusement and anger. 'You ought to be ashamed of yourself!'

'Section 14a of our training manual states that observing the discomfiture of a Sinhala army officer is a sacred duty for any activist and does not constitute immodesty.'

Oh, fuck off!

'Listen, this water is pretty deep and there may be crocs underneath.' I was splashing around to stay afloat. 'Just forget your bloody manual and turn the other way for a moment.'

She was still giggling but finally turned her face away.

I tried to scramble out of the water but, to my horror, found it impossible. The wet areas were so slimy, and the slope so acute, I could not get any grip for my fingers and slipped back repeatedly. Even the dry sections quickly turned into slime the moment my wet hand touched them.

I was trapped.

Velaithan turned and immediately understood what the problem was. She walked carefully to where my clothes were and picked up my half washed pants. She selected a dry spot and lay down, face towards me on the down slope. She rolled the pants into a makeshift rope and stretched it out to me. She appeared to have her eyes closed but her mouth twitched from time to time.

The bloody woman was enjoying this.

I noticed again how strong she was. She held on to her end firmly but I still slipped back several times before I finally managed to crawl out. I wasted no time in getting into my sarong and that improved my temper. Just a bit!

'So what's this buffalo doing?'

'You must have camped in its favourite spot,' she said, implying it was my fault. 'It won't go away.'

A lone buffalo, especially a large bull, can be pretty bad tempered. Mr. Karl had taught me to treat them with respect, never to get too close if I was on foot. I just hoped the blasted animal was not going to give us any trouble. I'd had enough emergencies for the day.

The buffalo was still there when we came over the crest of the rock. It was grazing on the tufts of coarse grass near the edge of the water. Our little tent was pitched just beyond. It saw us as we approached, lifted its head and stood still, staring at us balefully. A massive old bull with wide, curving horns. At close quarters it looked even larger than life and definitely unfriendly. I would have been more than a little nervous if not for our being on the rock. I doubted that the animal would try to climb its slippery slope.

Rocks.

I found some weathered bits of broken rock in a crevice and began to throw them at the buffalo. I missed with the first few shies. The thud of the rocks hitting the ground only made the animal swing its horns from side to side and snort angrily. One large chunk finally found its mark, hitting the bull's flank with a satisfying smack. The buffalo grunted loudly, swung round and galloped away.

Greatly emboldened, I ran down the slope shouting and threw a few more stones at the animal for good measure. It flashed through my mind how much braver one felt once the enemy has turned away and is in full retreat. My confidence would have evaporated if the animal had turned around and charged me. It didn't though, but went straight through a patch of scrub and out of sight.

'Do you think it will come back?' Velaithan didn't appear too comfortable at the thought.

'I suppose it might,' I said coldly, not having forgiven her yet. 'It will keep away once we have the fire going. Let's get that organized.'

Fortunately there was a fallen tree, uprooted by some storm, lying nearby. It was covered with creepers, and termites had attacked it on the sides. The rotten wood was easy to chop up and provided all the fuel wood we needed for the night. Velaithan, equally expert now, got the fire started and began feeding it till we had a cheerful blaze going. Boiling a pan of water had to be the first priority.

We were well screened from the track and it was now getting dark. We started the second, smaller fire on the far side, between the tent and the forest.

I had tried my luck with fishhooks and line whenever we camped near water. So far I had nothing much to show for it. I suspected it was due to my inability to get the baited hook to deep water as the villus sloped down very gently. This time it was different because I could cast the bait from the rock. I scraped a shallow hole in the soil near the waters edge and found a lively pink earthworm. It was a challenge to get the hook into the wriggling creature but I finally got the barb through its body. I found a spot where the rock fell away sharply into the water and suspended the baited hook about a yard below the surface. I tied the line securely to a little stunted tree growing in a crevice in the rock.

Velaithan had wandered over pretending to be interested in what I was doing. I suspected that she was still nervous about the buffalo. She looked faintly amused at my efforts but made no comment. She sat down on a bare patch of rock, hugged her knees and stared at the expanse of water before us. The sun had just set and the sky was a blaze of oranges and reds in the west. A faint breeze blew towards us and rippled the surface of the water. The shoreline running away from us was alive with birds. I could make out the bigger ones, pelicans, painted storks and a single adjutant stork, massive and ugly. A small flock of spoonbills were working in a line, their spatula like bills dipped in the mud, feeling for crustaceans. In ones and twos, the birds flew off to roost for the night. A white-bellied sea eagle was circling the water trying to catch one last meal before the light faded. It dived again and again, extending its massive claw through the surface as it flew past in a vain effort to scoop out a fish.

A small herd of spotted deer emerged from the trees.

A buck with a good spread of horn led the herd and kept gazing in all directions, alert for the slightest sign of danger. The hinds followed nervously behind. They came slowly towards the water, advancing in short spurts till they reached the edge and stooped to drink.

'Elephant,' Velaithan whispered, pointing at the trees.

At first it was hard to see the animal against the gloomy background of the trees. Then I could, as it moved into the open about fifty yards from our camp, just a little too close for comfort. I would have been nervous if we were without refuge but I felt safe on the rock. I was surprised it hadn't scented us but then realized that the wind was coming in towards us. I think our fire was concealed by a small rise in the ground.

One by one, more elephants became visible, a small herd comprising cows and young led by a large female. They fed on the long grass as they moved, grasping the coarse tufts with their trunks and then using their forefeet to kick up the roots. Once a tuft came loose, the animal would tap the roots against its foreleg to shake off the clinging earth, before consuming it. The very young animals, there were at least two of them, frolicked under the feet of the adults.

'They are very interesting, aren't they?' Velaithan observed. 'At least when they keep their distance.'

You can't watch anything else when there are elephants about, surely the most fascinating creatures on earth. We observed them as they moved slowly towards the water and noisily stooped to drink. Some of the animals lowered themselves into the shallows, wallowing and blowing water through their trunks. I knew the herd would remain there, bathing and resting, till late at night.

The young animals gambolled about with gay abandon, climbing over their recumbent mothers and tumbling into the water as they chased each other.

'Do you think they will stumble into our camp?' Velaithan asked doubtfully.

'No, I think there is very little chance of that,' I told her. 'A herd with very young animals will be cautious. They probably can't see our fire from where they are. They will stay well clear once they see it.'

It was getting dark now and the elephants turned into blurred gray humps in the water. I heard the loud cat call of a roosting peacock nearby and turned to see if I could spot its location. With the corner of my eye I noticed something moving on the rock near me. When I glanced down I realized that it was the little stunted tree I had used as an anchor for my line. It was jerking back and forth in the oddest way. I wondered idly what could cause it to sway like that, since the wind was hardly strong enough. It took a full second for me to realize that I had a strike, a good one too.

'I have something on, let's try to land it.' I scrambled over and wrapped the slack carefully round my hand before releasing the slipknot holding the line to the tree. The monofilament, as it tautened, cut painfully into my skin. Whatever I had on the line, it was strong and heavy and didn't want to come to dinner.

'How do you know it isn't a baby croc?'

Velaithan wasn't ready to give me credit for anything. I hoped like hell she was mistaken.

'Because crocs have to breathe,' I snarled. 'This one hasn't surfaced. It is a fish alright.'

'How are you going to land it?' she asked, getting into the spirit of it, for once. 'Can't you pull it out?'

She was more animated than was her wont. I wondered if it was the excitement of fishing, and not knowing what was at the end of the line, or just the prospect of a good dinner, that had got to her.

'The hook will open out if I try to lift the fish out of the water,' I said. 'I think our best chance is to work it gently towards the shallows and try to beach it.'

I walked slowly, one step at a time, down the rock and towards the camp, allowing more line when the fish gave a strong pull. I knew my hook was a very small one and the thought of losing this fish now was hard to contemplate.

I reached the edge at last and moved further away from the rock. I had Velaithan pick out a piece of driftwood and wrap the slack end of the line firmly around it. I then gently drew the fish closer, hand over hand, signalling Velaithan to walk backwards to keep the line taut. I knew the critical moment would be when the fish found itself grounded in the shallows. It would trash about then and, most likely, free itself.

I told Velaithan to stand still for a moment and ran to the camp. It took me anxious seconds to step into my pants. I had hung them up to dry and getting into a pair of wet pants, especially when you are in a hurry, is like getting toothpaste back in the tube. When I rushed back, sarong in hand, I was relieved to see the fish still on but the line swinging from side to side and jerking alarmingly.

'Keep it steady,' I told her urgently. 'Don't try to pull it in any further.'

Velaithan nodded nervously, relieved that I had got back. I moved to the left and waded into the water, trying circle the fish, to get between it and deep water. I couldn't see the fish but could see an area where the surface was being churned up as it wheeled from side to side.

I got into position. I held the sarong at the two ends and lowered it into the water so that, when I extended my arms, it billowed out like a net. I slowly moved closer, one step at a time, praying that the hook would hold for just one more minute. I called out to Velaithan to step forward slowly and allow the fish to come to me.

It was now so dark that I could barely follow the movement of the fish. I knew that, despite all my precautions, I would not be able to catch it if the hook came off. I saw some turbulence on the surface. I took one step forward and scooped the sarong under the fish. I was lucky, for when I lifted the sarong up I felt its solid weight inside, struggling madly.

I staggered to the shore, tripping over hidden stones and roots on the way. I tipped the catch onto the sand anxious to see what we had, to see if it was edible.

It was a long black fish, about as thick as my forearm, with an ugly, snake-like head. It writhed from side to side as it struggled to escape.

'What is this awful creature?' Velaithan was disgusted. 'Is it some kind of water snake?'

'It's an eel,' I said, mightily pleased with my catch. 'They make good eating!'

'I think I will be a vegetarian for today,' she said coldly. 'You can have it all.'

She dropped the line that she had been holding and went back to the camp.

I fetched the Kathi and used the blunt side of the blade to dispatch the fish. I then cut its head off and gutted it. I scraped clay-like mud from the edge of the water and covered the fish with a heavy layer, till it resembled a well-fed python. Velaithan watched curiously as I scooped a trench at the edge of our campfire. I placed my clay wrapped eel in the cavity and covered it with glowing embers.

I had never actually done a clay bake before, but another officer had taught me how. I fervently hoped it would work because I was ravenously hungry and I wanted to save as much of our provisions as possible.

My sarong was covered with a horrible slime and I spent the next half hour washing and scrubbing it. I was now condemned to spend another night in wet pants.

Velaithan had put some vegetables on to boil. We were used to our self allotted tasks and set about these in silence. I would make sure the tent was secure and would clear and level a place for setting down the ground sheet. I'd scrape the usual channel round the tent and fill it with ash. It must have been effective because crawling creatures had not bothered us so far on our journey. I stoked up the two fires and made sure that we had enough firewood for the night. Velaithan would cook the evening meal and store the rest of our provisions safely. She also filled our bottles with boiled water, ready for the next day's journey. She would go off to bathe once all her work was done.

It was time to check on the bake.

I scraped some of the embers off and inspected it. I saw that the clay was brown and the surface had cracks running all over it. I brushed off the ash and debris and carefully pulled off one segment of the burnt clay. Delightful! The clay covering came off easily, taking with it the slimy black skin of the eel. Underneath was the white flesh of the fish, succulent and aromatic.

The baked eel, with a sprinkling of salt and a few drops of lime juice, was delicious. I do not know if it was just that I was so hungry or that the catching and cooking was entirely my doing, but I could not remember tasting anything better. I was amused to see Velaithan, who had threatened to go vegetarian, serve herself a small portion.

We could only eat a part of the eel and left the rest, safely covered in a pan, for the morning. I hoped it would keep. We washed up and I stoked up the fires for the night.

'I want to sit on the rock for a while,' I announced. 'Do you want to come?'

She hesitated, then nodded and followed me.

The elephants had gone back into the forest but there was movement now and then in the grassy plain surrounding the water. There had to be herds of deer there, pig and buffalo as well, feeding and resting. The night sounds of the forest came to us, peaceful and unthreatening.

We went to the spot we had used earlier when the eel got hooked. Velaithan sat, Gandhi style, with her feet modestly tucked under her skirt. I stretched out on the rock, with my hands under my head, and stared at the sky. There were some fluffy bits of cloud in the west, still faintly yellow from the sunset, but otherwise the sky was completely clear. From horizon to horizon, it was filled with a surprising number of stars, galaxy upon galaxy, bright and glittering.

'There are billions of stars, aren't there?' Velaithan asked suddenly. 'Do you think there is intelligent life out there?'

This was a change from politics. Appropriate too, in this environment.

'Are you saying we have intelligent life on this

planet?'

That made her laugh and I marked a point for myself on my mental scorecard.

'From what we've been doing, I suppose not,' she said. 'But seriously, could there be other life forms some where?'

I tried to think of a good answer, dredging my mind for those half forgotten slivers of information I'd picked up here and there.

'Well, our sun is only a minor star in our galaxy, the Milky Way. The Milky Way has billions of stars and it is, itself, one of billions of galaxies. Earth is just a small planet in orbit around one minor star. There could easily be thousands, even millions, of planets, where conditions will support life as we know it.'

Was I getting this right? I could barely remember.

'So there could well be life out there but the chances are we will never find out.'

'Why?' she asked. 'Why do you say we won't know?'

'I suppose it has to do with the distance. The nearest star is several light years away. Most of them thousands of light years distant.'

'Light year?'

'Light travels at a constant speed of one hundred and eighty six thousand miles per second, that is something like six hundred and seventy million miles in one hour. A light year is the distance light can travel in one year. That's a mind-boggling distance. So if there is life on a star a hundred light years away, how will we get there or they get here?'

'What about space travel?' she asked, seeming to be genuinely interested. 'They might have advanced technologies, even if we don't. There have been so many reports of sightings, haven't there?'

'I don't know about the sightings. I think most of them have had rational explanations.' I was dredging my memory again. 'I think the problem has to do with natural laws. Einstein established that nothing could move faster than the speed of light. You cannot even approach that speed. So say you travel from another galaxy at say, half the speed of light, you'd take a couple of hundred, or a couple of thousand, years just to get here.'

She digested this for a while. I noticed she had also stretched herself out on the rock, her hands under her head.

'It's funny to think that even the stars we see now may not exist any more,' I continued, remembering another curious fact. 'What we see might well be an illusion.'

'What do you mean?'

'Well, lets say all those stars exploded and disappeared years ago. We would not see any change for years, maybe hundreds of years, because the light from the star takes that long to get here. We may be seeing stars that don't exist.'

'Did you study physics at the university?' she asked wistfully. 'Was it there you learnt all this?'

'No. I didn't study physics after the A levels.' Now I felt slightly embarrassed. 'It's just that I tend to read a lot. I think I picked up the habit from Mr. Karl. So I read old Time magazines in the common room, bits of newspaper, books of all kinds. Whatever came to hand really! As a result I retained bits of useless information on a wide range of subjects.'

'I wouldn't have called that useless,' she said seriously. 'How do you find the time to read now? In your job, I mean.'

'In the loo, mostly,' I blurted. 'It's the only place I'm

not disturbed.'

She laughed again. Laughing might become a habit if she didn't watch it.

She was silent for a while.

I stared up at the sky, brilliant with its shawl of stars. The sheer numbers and immensity of it was humbling. It made our long civil war now seem a petty, insignificant squabble. The glow in the east must be the old quarter moon climbing slowly into the night sky. There was no cloud at all, no movement except for an occasional silhouette of a passing bat. Some deer began calling in alarm, perhaps they had seen a prowling leopard. An elephant trumpeted on the far side of the villu.

'Tell me about your family,' Velaithan said. 'Is your father still alive?'

'Yes,' I said sourly. 'Yes. He is still alive.'

'Do you have any relationship with him?' she asked, probing.

I wished she would get off the subject. Even thinking about the old bugger made me squirm.

'No,' I said. 'Not now! Not ever.'

'Did you try? Surely you could have talked to him, once you were an adult?'

'When we were young we were very frightened of him. I told you he was violent when he was drunk, which was every evening.' I paused for a while, remembering. Did I want to dig up these memories?

'I hated him then,' I said slowly. 'I wanted to grow up fast so I could face up to him. To smash him up for the misery he caused, for my mother's sufferings.'

'And?'

Once she started to dig, she wouldn't let up.

'When I was big enough to handle him physically,

I realized he was just a broken old man. The illicit brew, kasippu, had rotted his liver. He was still violent at times, but now it's more pathetic than terrifying.'

'Does he still ... beat your mother?'

'Not any more,' I said. 'Not since I threatened to break his spine. He just smashes the clay pots in the kitchen from time to time. Seems to need doing that for some reason.'

The frogs were in mid season form, croaking in chorus from all parts of the tank. I heard the alarm call of deer somewhere behind me, not too far away. Then a pair of lapwings took it up. Their incessant 'did-he-do-it' and 'did-did-did-he-do-it' calls broke the stillness of the night. Some animal had disturbed them, come too near their nest. I hoped it was only an animal.

I rolled over and stared into the gloom. I finally made out a slow moving black mass and thought it was a solitary boar, or our friend the buffalo, walking towards the water. The lapwings settled down after a while and peace descended on the villu again.

'Are your sisters married?' Velaithan asked, continuing her inquisition.

'Yes,' I told her. 'They've married and gone away.'

'And you, Captain? Are you married?'

'No.'

'Are you planning to?' I saw a flash of teeth again. 'Do you have a girl friend?'

Nosy woman!

'You could say that,' I said.

'What do you mean?'

'Well my mother has made an ... arrangement.' I felt

slightly embarrassed discussing it. 'With a family from Baddegama, another village near my home.'

'Have you been to see the girl?'

'Yes.'

'Did you approve?'

'Mm …yes. Yes, I did.'

'Is she pretty?'

'Yes,' I said. 'Yes. Very.'

'What is her name?'

'Sriyani. She is a teacher.'

'Will you be married soon?'

'I expect so,' I said. 'My mother will decide when.'

She was silent for a time, digesting the information.

'What about you?' I asked, before she got started again. 'Are you married?'

'No.'

'Do you have a boyfriend?'

'No,' she said abruptly, and then. 'Well … yes.'

'Who is he?' I asked. 'Is he another … activist?'

'No. He is a lecturer in the university.'

'Do you plan to be married soon?' I asked innocently.

'No,' she said harshly. 'How can we think of marriage and children in that hellhole?'

No more questions from me.

She was sitting up now, hugging her knees and staring across the water, wrapped up in her thoughts. After a while she got up and went down to the tent. I stayed on, staring at the sky and thinking about my life. I wondered if I could wangle a few days leave after I delivered the woman to headquarters. I would like to see my mother, listen a while to her litany of aches and pains.

She was getting old now, old and frail.

Maybe I'd be able to visit Sriyani. I felt a tingle of excitement at the prospect. I'd only seen her twice. The first time was when I accompanied my mother and my older sister on a formal visit to see the girl. Her father, Simeon Mudalali, was a merchant. He was, by our standards, a wealthy man. He had built a house to match his status. A far cry from our own little shack, even though it was now much improved, thanks to the money I'd been able to send my mother.

Although we were of the same caste, and distantly related, an alliance between our families would not normally have been considered. It was my rank in the army that made me supremely eligible.

Simeon was a portly man, self made and very proud of it. He ran a hardware business in the town and, apparently, made a good living. He was rather full of himself, which quality did little to endear him to me.

But Sriyani was something else!

She had read for a degree in history at the Peradeniya University. She was now working as a teacher at a convent in Galle. She was small and fair, and devastatingly pretty. The prospect of marrying and bedding her made me dizzy with excitement.

An owl called from a tree near the tent and then took wing, silent as a falling leaf, intent on its hunt. I must have dozed off because when I woke up the quarter moon was almost overhead. The night wind coming over the water was damp and cold and I was chilled to the bone.

I went down to find shelter in the familiarity of the tent.

18

1st April 2001

Dawn was breaking when I came awake and I lay there lazily listening to the jungle wake up as well. A peafowl was calling again from a treetop roost and a jungle cock went 'Chruck- Chuck' in the bushes behind the tent. A small barbet was giving its imitation of a coppersmith.

Velaithan screamed.

I scrambled out of the tent, kathi in hand, and saw her running out of the shallows. She had been bathing. It was not like her to scream for help and I couldn't see any need to, yet when I got near I saw an expression of horror on her face.

She stared at me uncertainly for a moment and then, with extreme reluctance, lifted the edge of her skirt, now wet and clinging, to reveal the inside of her left thigh. Hanging there, black and shiny, was a large cattle leech. I felt a rush of relief, and a faint ripple of amusement I took good care to keep concealed.

'Sit here a moment,' I told her comfortingly. 'Don't try to pull it out.'

'Get it off,' Velaithan's eyes were wide. 'Quickly!'

We are a conservative people and the Tamils are perhaps the most reserved of the ethnic mix. Normally a Tamil girl would not even expose her ankle to a stranger, much less an enemy. Velaithan must have been mortified by the need to reveal a relatively intimate part of her body to me, yet she could not have got rid of the leech

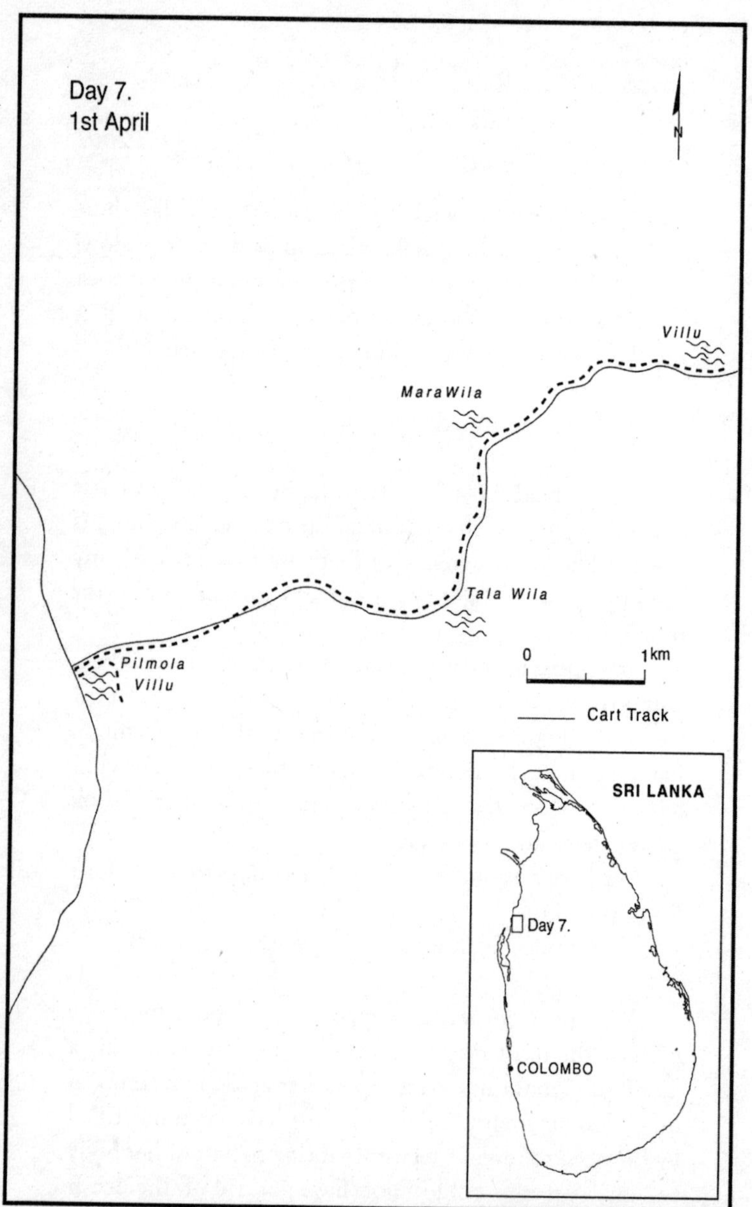
Day 7.
1st April
N
Villu
MaraWila
Tala Wila
Pilmola
Villu
0
1km
Cart Track
SRI LANKA
Day 7.
COLOMBO

without my help. The idea of allowing the leech to drink its fill of blood and drop off probably did not occur, or appeal, to her.

I knew that it was dangerous to pull the creature off because it would leave its mouthparts in the wound and that would get infected. I fetched a box of matches from the tent and lit a match. I held it briefly to the rear end of the leech. It immediately let go, curled into a ball, and fell off.

She was seated on the ground with her left leg stretched out and her foot turned outward to expose her inner thigh. The site of the leech bite was bleeding profusely because of the anti-coagulant present in the saliva of the insect. It looked like a serious wound but I knew it was trivial and would stop bleeding after a while.

I pretended to study the wound, just for the hell of it.

Her leg was well formed and smooth, the skin much fairer than her arms and face. I suddenly realized that her wet cotton dress was clinging to her body. Revealing too. I had an overwhelming and bizarre impulse to …

I looked up and caught her eyes just as the thought passed through my mind. She must have seen something in my expression because her eyes blazed with anger, white hot, like sunlight focused through a lens.

She jerked down the hem of her dress, stood up and stalked away.

I was laughing to myself as I went about the task of breaking camp. Velaithan came back soon afterwards, chastely dressed in her shalwar kameez day kit. She ignored me when I spoke to her. We warmed up and ate the rest of the fish for breakfast, then quickly packed our kit and left. I decided to circle the villu and rejoin the track on the far side.

The lapwings started having a go at us as soon as we stepped away from the rocks. A pair of them began to dive bomb us, plunging towards our heads as they circled us, pulling up at the last instant to go round again. They made an absolute cacophony with their hysterical 'did-he-do-its' repeated over and over.

There had to be a nest with eggs or chicks nearby to explain the frenzy of anxiety. I knew their nest would be just a scrape in the ground but the eggs would be beautifully camouflaged, almost impossible to spot. I noticed the slightest possible movement on the ground at the periphery of my vision, like a bit of dry grass bending in the wind. I fixed the point in relation to a small rock nearby and walked slowly towards it. If I blinked I knew I'd lose it.

I had to get really, really close to spot it. A lapwing chick crouched there with its head to the ground looking, to all the world, exactly like a lump of dried mud. It had been taught to freeze like that when the parent birds raised the alarm and the chick did not move even when I put out my hand and gently picked it up, a tiny, quivering ball of fluff, all head and legs.

Velaithan was still peeved with me but she was torn between her anger and her interest in the chick. Curiosity won. She touched the enchanting little creature with her finger, stroking its tiny head.

'There might be a couple of others,' I said lightly. 'We can boil them into our rice for lunch.'

She glared furiously at me and pointed imperiously at the ground till I put the chick down. She reminded me of a nursery school teacher I'd been terrified of.

I hate bossy women!

The parent birds kept up their appalling racket, diving at us and forcing us to duck and weave. We walked away quickly but it still took a while for the noisy bastards to settle down.

We continued to circle the villu and approached an extensive stretch of tall grass. We saw, ahead of us, some peahens stalking about, feeding on grass seeds and insects. As we came closer we saw the lone peacock, hidden earlier by a tussock of high grass. He was courting and the display was spectacular.

The morning sun was behind us and fell directly on the bird. It had erected its train in a semicircle and then, at the same time, spread and dropped its wings. It shimmered like a belly dancer, making the air hum with the splendor of its colouring, deep blue and an iridescent green. We had to stop and enjoy the spectacle.

I couldn't resist the opportunity to get a dig in.

'Did you notice that the male is so much more attractive than the females?' I asked innocently.

'Did you notice that the hens don't take a blind bit of notice of all that strutting about?' she shot back immediately.

That was true. The hens were going about their business, foraging in the grass, without even a glance at what must be one of the most magnificent courtship displays in the world.

'They have to be pretending, haven't they?' I responded gamely. 'Otherwise where do all the chicks come from?'

She couldn't come up with an answer to that so she just ignored it.

We came to the track soon afterwards and entered

the forest. It was a pleasant time for walking, with the sun still covered by the trees on our left. A small flock of jungle fowl was busily scratching around by the side of the road. They disappeared into the scrub when they saw us. A herd of buffalo must have crossed the road some days ago because the road, and the grass on the side of it, was covered with heaps of dried dung.

One of these dung heaps had been disturbed, and recently too. I stopped to have a look and didn't like what I saw. The dried buffalo pat, the size of a dinner plate, had been pushed aside and a shallow depression had been scraped in the sand where it had been. At the bottom of the hollow was a tiny hole, the size of a pencil. The claw marks around the tiny hole were distinctive, and very fresh.

A bear had been here not too long ago and had found termites under that particular dung heap!

Bears have a surprising ability to smell termites under logs or piles of dung. I kicked over a few of the other pats but there were no sign of the insects under any of them, just this one. But I was not thinking about their amazing abilities that morning.

Bears scare me shitless!

The sloth bear is not a big animal, some thirty inches at the shoulder when it shambles about on all fours. But a male animal could weigh in excess of two hundred pounds and is the most unpredictable and foul tempered animal in our forests. Bears love termites and spend hours with their noses buried in termite mounds. They have strong, curved claws some three inches long on their very muscular forefeet. They live on fruit, honey and even carrion but termites, or white ants as they were sometimes called, are their favourite food.

Strong claws were needed to scrape holes in the rock hard clay of a termite mound. Once it has made a tiny opening, the bear uses its lips like a suction cup to cover the hole and vacuum out the ants and the larvae.

That was the trouble. Once engrossed in white-anting, the bear will forget everything else and may not hear or see you till you get really close. When disturbed, its attack is fast and deadly. The bear will charge on all fours and then, when close in, rise up on its hind legs to slash at the head of the intruder with those terrible claws. The attack is short but devastating. Even a glancing blow can remove one side of a man's face. I thought again of the villager with only half a face, just a monstrous scar covering the rest of it. He had tried to stop a charging bear with a kathi.

'What is it?' Velaithan asked as I stood, staring down at the claw marks.

'A bear has fed on termites here,' I told her worriedly. 'Not long ago, because the sand in the hollow is still damp.'

'Is there any reason to think it is up ahead of us on the track?'

'No,' I had to admit. 'No. It could have wandered off anywhere.'

'No sense in waiting here then, is there?' she asked reasonably as I hesitated. 'We might as well press on.'

This was the only track we could take so I saw only two options. Hang around for an hour or so to give the animal time to move off or keep going in the expectation that the bear had ambled off into the forest.

Urgency overrode caution. We decided to keep going, but to walk slowly and keep a sharp lookout.

I hated that part of the journey. It is impossible to walk so slowly that one can check the forest on either side carefully enough to proceed. I'd heard of wayfarers who had already passed a feeding bear, being attacked from behind. The temptation to keep looking back was irresistible.

In the end we decided to walk abreast, Velaithan studying the forest on her side, I the other. We made better progress for a while. I was just beginning to relax when Velaithan stopped, pointing at the ground.

On a patch of loose sand was the footprint of an animal. The pad of the forepaw was clearly imprinted like a small human foot, flat and pointing outwards. Round it was a satanic semicircle of holes instead of toe-marks.

Claws!

This was what I had been afraid of. The bear was ahead of us on the road.

I quickly signalled to Velaithan to move back, get the hell out of there. As she turned, I saw a termite mound beyond her in the scrub, yellow and as tall as a man, rising up from a pile of small rocks. I was about to look away when a rock moved.

I heard a loud 'Whooff' as the bear whipped round and charged from a distance of about twenty yards. It came at us on all fours, ears pointed forward, making a sound between a bark and a roar, loud enough, and angry enough, to freeze my blood. The attack was so sudden, and the speed of the charge so great, there was no time to react. I had an impression of bared yellow fangs as it curled back its lips, and saliva drooling down the side of its mouth. Then it was on us!

I had one paramount thought whirling inside my head.

Don't let it stand up! Just don't!

I lifted the kathi high over my head, screamed at the top of my voice, and charged the bear. I realized later it was an act born of pure funk, combined with a desperate wish to prevent the animal standing up, to stop it from taking that dreadful swipe at my face.

They say the gods take special care of fools. My hysterical scream and sudden lunge surprised the animal and stopped the charge. The bear made another startled 'Whoof' sound, swerved to the right and made off at the same speed, its roar now changed to a plaintive whine, as though it were the injured party. It disappeared into the scrub.

I was still yelling.

Velaithan said: 'Captain, it's gone.'

I couldn't speak, so I just looked at her. I was dripping with sweat and still shaking from reaction.

'We'd better keep going.'

I nodded and we started off, glad to get away from that spot. We walked for some time, looking nervously over our shoulders. Velaithan took out her bottle of water and offered it to me. I sat on a rock at the edge of the road, a real rock this time, and drank.

I needed that.

'I nearly had a heart attack,' Velaithan said, smiling ruefully. 'What made you yell like that? It was worse than the bear!'

'I was scared,' I said without embarrassment. 'I've never been so scared in my life.'

She laughed, but I could see she was also shaken.

'Captain, if I knew it was going to be like this, I would have agreed to go to the camp at Mannar.'

'Now you tell me!'

I felt another high coming on. It had been a really close call, but we had survived it. Intact too!

I shouldered my backpack once again and we resumed our journey. The sun was warm on my back as I walked, not yet strong enough to be uncomfortable.

Surely nothing could go wrong now.

We trees were noticeably shorter now and were gradually giving way to dense patches of lantana and thorn bushes. We saw, from a distance, one copse of trees towering over the surrounding forest. The road took us close to it and I found a dank hollow filled with slimy green water. The trees bordering the pond were taller and more luxuriant than the surrounding forest. The dense canopy spread over the water, shutting out the sunlight.

I was about to say something when Velaithan gripped my arm. Having silenced me, she pointed with her other hand. She seemed to be highly excited. I looked up at the high canopy and finally saw what had attracted her attention.

Seated on a horizontal branch, and staring down at us, was a large owl with long, barred ear tufts that stuck out of its head like handlebars.

'Isn't that a forest eagle-owl?' Velaithan whispered breathlessly. 'I have never seen one before.'

'I haven't seen one either.'

The eagle–owl is quite rare and confined to deep forest. It is also nocturnal and spends the daylight hours concealed in thick foliage. It is the biggest owl in the country and one particularly difficult to spot because of its rarity and its habits. This one was a fine specimen and the light was just right to observe it.

Velaithan was glowing with excitement. She looked a completely different person. I thought fleetingly that, if not for the war and the personal traumas she had suffered, this might well have been her normal personality. In her excitement she forgot she was still holding my arm, fingernails digging painfully into my skin.

She realized what she had been doing and hurriedly took her hand away, flushing slightly at the same time. I made it easier for her by pretending that I hadn't noticed anything untoward.

'Did you know this is probably the devil-bird?' I asked her.

Mr. Karl had told me he heard the call of the devil bird once, while camping near Inginiyagala. It is a most dreadful noise and heard only late at night, a combination of shrieks, wails and howls, very much like the sound of a woman being strangled. Many hunters and naturalists had heard, and written about, a devil-bird in our forests. Villagers living close to jungle areas live in absolute dread of it, believing that, if one heard a devil-bird, someone in the village would die that very night.

Most experts agreed the guilty party was a bird and the chief suspect was our friend sitting on the branch above, brown eyes fixed solemnly on us.

'Yes,' Velaithan whispered. 'Henry seems to think it is only a mating call.'

'Not surprising then, is it, that its numbers are dwindling,' I observed facetiously.

'Have you heard the call?' she asked.

'No,' I said, trying to imagine what it was like. 'I've never heard it myself. Don't want to either.'

'Don't tell me it will scare you, Captain?' she asked, smiling mischievously.

'The unknown always scares me,' I said lightly. 'If I hear it at night I might jump to your side of the tent, out of fear, I mean.'

'I wouldn't advise it, Captain,' she said dryly. 'You'll meet the real devil-bird then.'

'Now that I believe,' I said.

The old owl spread its wings and floated away, disappearing through the trees.

We soon came to a large swamp, with stretches of open water in the distance. The track turned westward to skirt the grassy verge. The near edge was occupied by a large herd of buffalo. Some of them were wallowing in the water with only their heads above the surface, others were grazing in the tall grass. There were animals of all ages in the herd, calves with light brown hair and huge gray-black bulls. There was much snorting and grunting as they tossed their heads to drive off the flies that tormented them.

A flock of cattle egrets were at work, some on the ground stalking about the feet of the buffalo, others perched on the their backs. The egrets feed on the leeches and ticks that infest the buffalo hides and also the frogs and other insects the animals disturb when they feed on the grass. It is a fine example of a symbiotic relationship.

The egrets were in breeding plumage. A rich gold mantle of feathers, a far cry from the drab white one normally sees.

The space between the trees and the buffalo was not broad enough for us to get past safely. Some of the animals were grazing close to the road and the bulls in the herd were not to be trusted at the best of times. I'd had enough excitement for one day.

I drew Velaithan back to the shelter of the trees.

'This swamp is called Talawila,' I told her. 'We can't get past those buffalo on the road. We'll have to go through the trees.'

She nodded at first bur then observed:

'The shrub along the edge looks very dense. We might have to go in a wide circle to avoid it.'

I had been wondering about that. The ground around the villu was soggy and had resulted in a dense growth of small trees interspersed with shrub and tangled lianas. It was not going to be easy, or pleasant, to push our way through that lot, yet to avoid it we'd have to make a wide detour. That meant losing more time than we could afford and facing the added risk of getting lost.

I snatched some tips of grass from the ground and tossed them in the air.

'The wind is coming over the water, towards us,' I said slowly. 'We can try to creep along the edge of the trees and hope for the best.'

Velaithan stared at the herd for a while, weighing the options.

'I suppose we have no choice,' she said finally, but her tone was unhappy.

'Have you climbed trees?' I asked innocently and then couldn't help grinning when she snapped:

'Of course not.'

Young ladies in Jaffna wouldn't be permitted such immodesty.

'You'll have to learn fast, if the buff act up,' I told her.

She just looked at me and then smiled.

'I'm sure I will,' she said bravely. 'Let's go.'

I led the way. We left the track and walked along the

very edge of the scrub. The ground was soggy under our feet and made an unpleasant squelching sound. Velaithan found her slippers getting stuck in the mud and had to take them off and stuff them in her bag. She'd need both hands free if she had to do some quick climbing.

We made some progress without being noticed. Then came a point where an adult animal was grazing between the road and the trees. We had to pass by it at a distance of about six or seven yards. Much too close for my comfort!

I looked at the forest cover, hoping desperately for a game track or opening. It was as thick and tangled as ever, worse than it had appeared at a distance. I wondered how we'd reach a tree if the buffalo did get nasty. I looked back at Velaithan, to make sure she was ready, and then started off again.

I kept my eyes on the buffalo, which fortuitously, was facing the other way. We had almost edged past when I stepped on a twig that snapped like a pistol shot. The animal swung round with snort of surprise. Buffalo have a way of lifting their snouts and staring balefully at you over them that is quite intimidating. This one was big and black and had an impressive spread of horn.

I knew then I'd made a bad mistake. If the buffalo charged, we'd be caught against the tangled undergrowth, like flies under a swatter.

We didn't move. The buffalo suddenly tossed its head, snorted loudly and, just when I thought it was all over for us, turned and galloped off to join the herd. I looked again at Velaithan, who had a hand on her chest.

'Captain,' she said, summing it up. 'If I survive this journey, I'm going to join a convent.'

'Yeah,' I grinned. 'Me too.'

We were able to regain the road after that and then

walking became easier. The swamp was covered with reeds and tall grass and that gave way to a wide expanse covered with white and mauve lotus in bloom. Two small crocodiles were lying motionless on a patch of sand by the water. For some reason crocodiles keep their eyes shut, and their jaws gaping, when they bask in the sun. When we got nearer they sensed our presence, though, and slid smoothly into the water, like knives going through butter.

'There should be some buildings further along,' I told Velaithan. 'They must have been forest guard's quarters in the old days. I am pretty sure they are not occupied but … it might be safer to go around it.'

She nodded.

We continued along the track till the buildings came into view, crumbling and dilapidated, their doors and windows missing. There was no way to enter the forest though, so we stayed at the edge of the scrub and made a cautious approach. This time we had guessed right because the buildings were empty, and had been so for quite a while.

The forest began to change once we left Talawila behind us. The soil was more sandy and arid and the larger trees began to give way to scrub jungle with trees in scattered clumps. The sun beat down on us with wicked heat and there was very little shade on the track.

We were running out of food again. We had a few tubers of manioc and some scraps of dried fish left. I needed to find something off the land and tried to dredge up memories of my survival training. We had been shown several forest trees that carried edible fruit or leaves and had had several others described to us. It was quite hard to be sure when one was just passing by and I dreaded the thought of eating something that would make us ill. I remembered being told that it is dangerous to eat anything just because a bird eats it. Pigeons eat fruit that is poisonous to man. On the other hand, it is safe to eat anything that monkeys, or even rats, eat. How was I to stop and wait for these animals to turn up and lead me to a safe food source?

I knew that the bud of palm trees is edible but I'd have to cut the tree down to get at the bud and I wasn't yet hungry enough to make the effort! Animals or birds were my best bet but that meant building traps or snares and waiting patiently for something to happen.

Something moved in the periphery of my vision. When I stopped to look I could, at first, see nothing but some instinct made me stand and watch a while. I spotted the monitor lizard when it moved again.

I dropped my pack on the ground and ran after it.

This lizard, called thalagoya locally, has a curious, waddling gait that still covers the ground with amazing speed. The area was open so I was able to make a dash but found it difficult to close in. It would have got away easily if it had kept running, but it saw a termite mound and dived straight into an opening at the base. Its tail was just disappearing into the nest when I threw myself headlong on the ground and got my fingers round the tip of it.

I am a fairly powerful man with well above average strength. Yet pull as I did, jamming my feet against the rocklike mound, I could not yank the reptile out. We had reached a kind of stalemate when Velaithan came running up.

'Will you hang on to the tail while I try to dig him out?' I was scratched and dusty from my dive, but my hunter's blood was up.

'Are you sure that reptile is safe to eat?' Velaithan asked fastidiously. 'I thought these lizards are poisonous.'

She wasn't keen to touch it.

'Talagoya is edible,' I snarled. 'Just hold the damn tail.'

She knelt down finally and took hold of the tail, her face sour with distaste. I grabbed the kathi and started pounding the edges of the mound. The clay had set like rock and, initially, I only succeeded in chipping off bits of it. I finally managed to make a hole big enough to slip the blade of the kathi in, under the thalagoya. Using the handle as a lever, I finally loosened the grip of its claws long enough to haul it out.

The action started then. Velaithan was on her knees, hanging on to its tail. The wretched reptile was swinging from side to side in a desperate attempt to escape, its feet scrabbling on the ground. It avoided my blows with the kathi with surprising dexterity.

Velaithan was laughing again.

It only needed something that made me look foolish to put her in a good mood. One lucky swipe finally stunned the reptile and a second blow severed its head. Velaithan looked away in disgust when I hung the carcass at the end of the kathi.

The sun was almost directly overhead, and it was getting much too warm for walking, but we couldn't find water. It was Velaithan who spotted a rock some distance from the track that seemed to have distinctly greener trees on the far side of it. We wearily made our way towards it and, climbing up, found a hollow in the rock filled with weeds and green, algae choked water.

We were happy enough to find any kind of water and

made camp under the stunted trees that clung precariously to the rock on the far side of the waterhole.

We built a fire and Velaithan boiled a pan of water. We filtered it using a scrap of cloth. We then used the filtered water to boil the remains of our manioc yams. I went off to a secluded spot and used my knife to skin and dress the thalagoya. It yielded a good meaty residue, enough to keep us going for a couple of meals at least. I cut it into small squares and we boiled the lot with salt and the remaining scraps of vegetables.

I was covered with dust and grime so I had a bath of sorts, pouring the murky water over my head. It was marvellously refreshing, and even sitting in wet clothes afterwards was a relief from the stifling heat.

The meat of the thalagoya was as tough as leather but palatable, rather like country chicken. Even Velaithan supplemented the bland manioc with a bit of it. We put away the rest of the cooked meat for the night. It was the last of our supplies and we would need to find more food for the next day.

It was still and warm, the worst part of the afternoon. At this time most forest animals stand and doze in deep cover, waiting for the sun to settle in the west before venturing into the open again. Most birds enjoy their siesta as well, resting in the shade somewhere, waiting for evening.

'How far are we from the park boundary?' Velaithan asked.

'We are traveling due west now. This track should take us to the old road and that will take us to the Kalaoya,' I explained. 'The river is the boundary.'

'Are you planning to get to Puttalam tomorrow?'

'That's one option,' I agreed. 'It will depend on the time we reach the river. We have to find a way to get past the army camp that's about two miles down the road from the river.'

'If we get to Puttalam tomorrow night, we could take a night bus to Colombo, couldn't we?'

Velaithan was still anxious to get to Colombo as soon as possible.

'The problem for now is the distance from the river to Puttalam,' I said carefully. 'It's much too far to walk, so we will have hitch a ride in a truck or tractor. That won't be easy at night.'

'Maybe we could steal a vehicle.'

'Yes,' I said. 'It might come to that.'

Velaithan was silent for a minute.

'What is the other option, Captain?'

'Camp one more night at the Kalaoya,' I said. 'Get to the village early in the morning and try to get a ride. There should be some public transport going in to town at that time.'

'Today is the first isn't it?' She had been keeping count. 'That means we will be able to get out by the third. How much time will it take to get from Puttalam to Colombo?'

'If we take a bus, I'd say five or six hours,' I answered warily, knowing this was a sensitive area. 'We should be in Colombo on the night of the third.'

'Is that a good time to get there?' she was probing now, anxious. 'Will you be able to contact your superiors at that time?'

'I prefer to reach Colombo in the evening,' I told her. 'I have a friend who will put us up for the night.'

'Won't that waste more time?' she asked worriedly. 'Shouldn't we try to reach someone the same night?'

I looked at her with some surprise.

You are really anxious for this project to succeed, aren't you? Or maybe you need that success to get what you are bargaining for.

'No. I don't think so,' I explained carefully. 'I will call Brigade headquarters in the night and try to arrange a meeting with the Director of Intelligence for the next morning. That's the fourth. If we convince him, he has the rest of the day, and the fifth, to arrange for the operation on the sixth.'

She thought it over and nodded.

'Where do you plan to stay?' she asked. 'In Colombo, I mean.'

'My friend Upali has a house in the suburbs. He'll be happy to put us up,' I said quietly and then added. 'It will give us a chance to get some clothes and clean ourselves up.'

She nodded again, satisfied.

We packed our things and rose to go. The ground sheet was torn in several places but had served us well. I rolled it up and packed it away carefully. We had just skirted the hollow, hoping to climb down in the direction of the road when Velaithan spotted something on a tree that stopped her in her tracks.

'What are those?'

I followed her gaze. 'Weaver-bird nests.'

'I've never seen anything like it.'

We drew closer to the tree, which was festooned with nests, taking care not to disturb the sparrow-sized little brown and yellow birds at their domestic task of home building. Some of the pairs had nearly completed their nests while others were just getting started. As we stood watching, a bird came flying in with a long strand of grass in its beak, held carefully in the centre. Settling on a branch hanging low over the water, it draped the strand over the branch, with the loop on one side and the two loose ends on the other.

'Watch,' I said. 'Now it'll pull the two loose ends under the branch and through the loop, to make a knot. That's the foundation.'

Velaithan placed her bag on the ground, and sat down beside it, clasping her knees and staring across the water. I joined her, and wondered what she was thinking as she watched the birds fly back and forth until a dozen stalks of long grass, tied firmly to the branch, had given the nest stability and strength.

I wanted to ask what she was thinking about but thought better of it.

'Do you plan to get married soon?' I had asked her innocently, not so long ago.

'No,' she had replied harshly. 'How can we think of marriage and children in that hellhole?'

I was silent. Next to the nest that was being built before our eyes was another that had been completed. It was an extraordinarily elaborate affair, nearly four feet long, shaped like an inverted retort. It had a domed chamber that bulged at the side to accommodate the eggs; and later, a nestful of hatchlings.

'Each pair has a home of their own.' Velaithan's voice was so soft she might have been speaking to herself. 'And each home a unit in a peaceful village.'

'A perfect society?' I ventured.

'Not for people like me.'

She seemed to be in no hurry to leave. We handled one of the nests near the edge of the pool and found it surprisingly strong. The weave was so intricate that it would have been impossible to tear apart with my hands. Not that I tried.

'It's very beautiful,' she observed meditatively. 'Why do they need to build nests like that?'

'I think it's meant to keep snakes out,' I said. 'Other predators too.'

The far side of the rock was steeper than I had expected but we managed to get down without injury. It was still very hot and the sun beat down on us from directly ahead as we regained the track and trudged towards the western coast.

19

I was relieved to see that the track ahead of us led on to another road heading north–south. That had to be the old north road I had been looking for. We turned into it with relief, and without any premonition of disaster, and almost walked into them.

Five men at least, coming towards us. Some of them were carrying guns.

I knew at once that we were in mortal danger, for there were no friends in this forest. I cursed myself for my carelessness as I grabbed Velaithan by her hand ran into the scrub. I heard them shouting behind us but couldn't make out the words.

I tried to think who they could be. Most likely they were poachers from the villages across the river. They might also be army deserters, living rough. Whoever they were, they were bad news for us and our best chance was to get away into the forest.

Running in that sandy terrain was strenuous, hampered as we were with our bags and gear. It must have been much harder for Velaithan with her rubber slippers. I knew very well that if those men seriously wanted to catch us, we had little chance. Our tracks were clearly visible in the sand and they would be able to run much faster. Only a suspicion that we were also armed might persuade them to approach us cautiously. That could work for us, for a while anyway.

We would find out soon enough.

We were tiring. My breath was coming in heaving gasps and I could hear Velaithan's laboured breathing behind me. We could not keep going much longer. We burst through a patch of scrub and saw a great expanse of gently sloping black rock ahead of us. As we came into the clearing Velaithan tripped on something and went sprawling on the ground. When I helped her up her face was twisted in pain.

'Are you all right?'

I didn't know if they were after us, but if they were, they wouldn't be far behind. We had to keep going.

'I think I've twisted my ankle.' She calmly tested her foot and grimaced with pain. 'I can walk but I don't think I can run. I can hide somewhere. Why don't you lead them on and then circle back?'

'No. If they are hunters, they'll figure it out from the tracks,' I said, trying desperately to form some plan. 'Come on, let's get over this rock.'

I slung her bag over my shoulders and helped her up the sloping surface. It was a huge pile of weather worn rock with stunted trees and bushes growing in fissures and cracks. I half helped and half carried Velaithan up the face of it, rushing her and ignoring her gasps of pain. We were in the open, and easily seen, if they came into the clearing now. I was desperate to get over the crest and to the shelter of the far side.

We made it.

Once safely over, I lay on my stomach and using some small bushes as a screen, looked back at the way we had come. I saw nothing at first and was about to signal to Velaithan that we were in the clear when they came through the bushes. Two men, walking with their heads down, intently following our footprints in the sand.

They looked rough and unwashed. One was a short man with broad, heavy shoulders. He had his hair in a long ponytail, tied at the back with a bit of string. The other was taller with untidily cropped hair, wearing a dirty t-shirt and black trousers, rolled to the knee. The short man wore a sleeveless vest exposing his massive, wrestler's arms, and a brown, tucked up, sarong. The tall man carried a shotgun on his shoulder. Ponytail had a kathi, much like mine.

Although I had run away, I had hoped that my fears were unfounded, that the men would get on with whatever they were doing and not really follow through. From the way they carried themselves I decided they were probably deserters from the army, hiding out and living rough. They could not have imagined that we had anything worth robbing. Why then this ruthless determination to track us down?

Deep in my mind, I knew the reason. In the brief moment when they saw us, they must have realized that one of us was a young woman. They wanted her. I glanced at Velaithan and saw in her eyes the anger, and despair, of the perennial victim.

She knew!

The men came up to where our footprints reached the rock. They stood there looking up at the rock, undecided. If they came directly up the rock we were dead. They talked to each other softly, pony tail waving his hands from time to time. I held my breath. They must have finally agreed to circle the rock and find the spot where we left it because they turned and continued along the edge of it, going away to our right.

We crawled the other way. I helped Velaithan up only when we were safely below the skyline. I had to think fast. Velaithan could walk with some discomfort but moving quickly was out of the question. There was no escape in running. In any event, our tracks would show clearly in the sand and these men had a disturbing air of competence about them.

'Can we ambush them?' she asked calmly. 'Set a trap?'

She didn't need to be told what would happen if they caught us. They'd kill me out of hand but they'd keep her alive, for a long time. It wouldn't be … pleasant.

I thought about it seriously. I knew I could rely on her to do her part.

'No. They are too close and they look competent. So the trap will have to be good,' I whispered hurriedly. 'We don't have the time to prepare. Come on'.

I made sure the men were out of sight and went back along the rock, parallel to the direction in which we had come. I found a dense patch of eramaniya thorn scrub growing on the edge of the rock. We had passed close to it when we approached the rock. I parted the bushes as best I could for Velaithan to crawl through and followed her, allowing the branches to swing back after me. The thorns grabbed painfully at our clothes and skin. I felt no discomfort at that time, such was my anxiety to find a hiding place before those men returned.

The cover was good and we had reached it without leaving any tracks in the sand. It was horribly hot and uncomfortable though, crouching there without being able to move freely, insects of all types crawling over us.

We waited.

They took their time. Just when I thought they had taken another route to rejoin their companions, they came round the curve of the rock. They stopped once again at the point where our footprints reached the rock, talking softly. They climbed the rock at that point and stood at the ridge for a while, scanning the surroundings. They finally came down the rock, retracing their path. They went past the scrub we were hiding under, crossed the clearing and disappeared into the forest beyond.

They had been gone for several minutes now and I thought it safe to come out of cover. Velaithan looked at me questioningly, waiting for my signal. But something made me hold back, a little niggling worry in the back of my mind. I shook my head and waited.

I sensed movement behind me and, on turning, saw that a small troop of monkeys had moved on to the rock. The troop must have numbered about twenty animals, many adults, and some so young that they clung to their mothers' bellies. The adults had lush gray fur on their heads and bodies. They held their long, slender tails aloft as they walked. Grey langurs. They were feeding in the grass and some of the younger animals were playing, chasing each other, on the rock. One large adult climbed a tree, scanning the forest for danger.

The bastards had been hiding!

They came out of the bushes at a fast trot, deadly and silent. The man with the gun held it low against his hip, pointing at the rock. They had guessed we were hiding nearby and had waited for us to show ourselves. They must have seen some movement on the rock and thought they had us. They stopped abruptly when they saw the monkeys scampering into the trees in fear at their sudden appearance. Ponytail uttered an obscenity in Sinhala and spat in disgust.

The old langur in the tree had uttered an alarm call as soon as it spotted the men. The other animals had scrambled to safety in the trees the instant they heard the alarm. The look out, an old female, kept calling at regular intervals, its eyes fixed on the intruders. T h e men stood silently for a while, searching the rock for any other movement. The tall man then looked at the langur that bobbed its head up and down and called again. The man said something to his companion. I thought I knew what he said. If the old monkey had seen us, it would have given away our position.

They shouldered their weapons and disappeared into the bushes.

Were they really leaving or were they planning to hide in the bushes again? I kept my eyes on the langur. From its vantage point, high in the tree, the animal could see the men. It kept calling, turning its head slowly to follow their movements. The calls gradually reduced in frequency and finally stopped altogether.

My muscles were screaming in protest from crouching and remaining still. Velaithan's face was drawn in distress. She looked questioningly at me but I knew we could not move out of cover. Not just yet. The old langur had been our friend up to now. Not only had it marked their movements for us but must also have helped to convince them that we were not anywhere nearby. Had it seen us earlier, it would have kept turning its head to keep both potential enemies in view. Those men, obviously hunters, would have known that.

But now the langur was a threat to us. If we moved, it was certain to spot us. Its renewed alarm calls would be heard a long way and bring the hunters back in a rush. We had to wait till the troop moved away.

They did eventually, moving slowly from tree to tree, feeding as they went. They moved out of sight at last.

It was with infinite relief that I scrambled out and held the branches apart for Velaithan. The hooked eramaniya thorns were brutal, worse coming out than they had been when we crept in. The back of my hands and shoulders was a mass of tiny scratches, now beginning to sting as the perspiration reached them.

The sun was setting in a great orange bonfire in the west. We had run away from it in an easterly, or perhaps southeasterly, direction. There was no way to be sure.

'Are you all right? Can you walk?' I looked anxiously at Velaithan. If she couldn't walk, we were in real trouble.

'It is a bit painful but I can walk,' she answered quietly. 'Which way do we go?'

I am getting to know you. You'll grit your teeth and keep going, won't you, even on two stumps?

'The track we want to reach is due west from here. Once we reach it, it will go south to the river,' I told her. 'Our friends will know that. Our best chance is to move south now and find a place to camp for the night. We can plan our next step in the morning. We must find a safe place before it gets too dark'.

I set the direction from the sunset, keeping the brightness on my right shoulder. Velaithan wanted to carry her own bag, not wanting to show any weakness. I simply yanked it out of her hands and pointed the way. I expected her to be offended but she smiled and took it with what was, by her standards, good grace.

'Could they have been villagers from nearby, do you think?'

I had the impression she was more concerned than she wanted to admit.

'I can't be sure. From their appearance they seem to

have been living in the jungle for some time. The way they handled themselves, I'd say they've had some training,' I explained. 'I'm pretty sure they are army deserters. There are lots of them around.'

I thought about the thousands of young men who jostled each other to join the army, lured by the lush benefits and prestige of its uniform. The army was often the only employer who would give them a second glance. But after a couple of years in the front lines with little training and poor leaders, many of them lose their stomach for battle.

Deserting is easy. Get home on leave and just fail to report back. The problems only start after that, for deserters have nowhere to go. They are marked men in their villages and employers in urban areas know better than to hire someone without a thorough background check. A life of crime is their only recourse.

'We should have found a way to kill them.' Velaithan's tone was matter of fact.

Sitting under that bush, I had wished for a firearm. I would have killed them both if I'd had the means.

'No chance of that now,' I said reasonably. 'Let's find a place to camp.'

The sun had set now and the bright shades of orange were fading into yellows and ochre. The transition from day to night is very fast in the forest, a fleeting twilight, and then, complete darkness. We had to find a campsite fast.

We came round a dense copse of small trees and saw before us the strangest of sights. It was an immense dune of sand, rising some thirty feet above the floor of the forest. Except for an occasional clump of cactus, the dune was bare of vegetation. It was nearly dark now so I decided to climb to the top of it to see if there was any shelter to be found on the far side.

Climbing through the loose sand was exhausting, especially after our earlier exertions. I had to help Velaithan, who struggled bravely but obviously found each step acutely painful. Nearing the top, I made sure we kept our heads down to avoid being seen against the skyline. We crawled over the crest on our bellies. On the far side was another dune, and beyond that another. But nestling in the valley between the dunes was a small copse of palmyrah palms. The trees were unusual, not being natural forest trees. Perhaps a traveller in some bygone era and left some seeds to germinate in this desolate spot. I decided to camp there for the night.

'Is there any chance of finding water?'

For Velaithan, that was the prime requirement. If she had a chance to bathe and freshen up, she would be reasonably content with her lot. This was the first time we had camped without access to water.

'No chance,' I told her shortly. 'How much drinking water do you have left in your bottle?'

Despite our exertions, we had used our water sparingly. But it was not going to be enough.

'Half a bottle,' she said, 'It will not last long.'

'Lets get the tarp up before it's fully dark,' I said. 'We should avoid lighting a fire tonight. I don't think any large animals will bother to climb over these dunes.'

Our hardy plastic sheet was beginning to fray and tear at the edges. It still served its purpose though, sheltering us from the dew. I tied a rope across two of the palmyrah trunks and threw the sheet over it. We then placed a row of small rocks to hold down the edges. We spread the ground sheet outside to sit on while we ate.

It was a bit eerie without a fire. We had got used to it and it added a cheery homeliness to the camp. Something was bothering me and I realized what it was with a shudder.

Snakes.

We had not seen a single snake during our journey in the forest. However this sandy terrain was typical snake country and the preferred habitat of the viper family. I didn't know too much about vipers except that they are sluggish creatures often too slow to move out of your way. That meant we could easily step on one of the bastards in the dark.

I almost fell over myself in my hurry to gather fuel for the fire.

The palmyrah palm has a green, leathery leaf with a serrated edge. The leaves are about two feet in diameter, and fan out around the crest of the palm, like a crown. The withered leaves fall off the trunk leaving the dried branch along the main trunk of the tree. It was an easy task to cut off dead branches for the fire.

'I thought you said we would not risk a fire tonight.'

She sounded relieved just the same.

She would have been even happier, if she had thought of the risk of snakes. I'd got past the stage of getting a kick out of frightening her.

'Ye-e-s, it is a risk,' I said carefully. 'But we are down in this valley and it will not be visible unless someone tracks us here.'

She helped me start a small fire and we sat on the ground sheet, reluctant still to eat the last of our boiled talagoya meat and get to sleep. The fire gave out a cheerful light, and I felt better immediately, less threatened.

A random thought kept flitting through the back of my mind, something I knew would help us. It kept eluding me till Velaithan said:

'There are dunes like this in Manalkattu, miles and miles of them, my aunt told me. People would go there on a Sunday to sea bathe, before the troubles started.'

Dunes.

Then I remembered my survival training. Dune water. These were probably the wrong type of sand dune but it was worth a try. I went to the base of the slope and used my hands to excavate a shallow hole. Velaithan came over with burning palmyrah branch, held like a torch, to see what I was up to. When the hole was about a foot deep I felt, rather than saw, water slowly trickling in. I remembered, also from my training, to stop digging as soon as the water started to collect in the hollow.

It took time, and we could only get a cup at a time. But we were able to collect enough water to wash ourselves and then to refill our bottles. The water was sweet and clean. I was feeling much better when we sat down to eat. The talagoya meat was still tough but tasted better than it had in the afternoon. There was barely enough for the two of us so I just drank more water to distend my belly.

'Do you think we should keep watch tonight?' she asked, still concerned about the gang.

I thought about it.

'I don't think they will try to track us in the night,' I said finally. 'They'd need to be really expert to do that, using flashlights.'

'Do you think they'll give up then?'

'No,' I admitted. 'No. I think they will try to pick up our tracks in the morning.'

'So?'

'We should get some rest and leave here very early. If we can reach the river, we can hide our tracks.'

Velaithan was silent for a while, staring at the fire. I had the impression she was reluctant to call it a day.

'How did you know those men were hiding behind the bushes, waiting for us to show ourselves?' she asked.

'I wasn't sure, but I thought they gave up too easily,' I said. 'It wasn't a logical thought, just a feeling for what I would have done in their place.'

'And the old monkey?' she continued. 'What was it doing?'

'While the rest of the troop feeds, one adult keeps watch. It warns the troop when it spots any potential enemy.'

'But it didn't see us, only those men.'

'We were very lucky there! We were under cover when the monkeys came to the rock. If the monkey had seen us in the bush, it would have kept switching its gaze from the men to us, and back again. But it didn't and those men, being experienced hunters, knew that.'

'So?'

'So they'd have two possibilities to consider. One. We stayed by the rock and hid ourselves well enough to avoid being seen by the monkey. Two. We ran away from the rock before they came up to it, managing to cover our tracks.'

'And which one will they pick?' she asked

'The second possibility!' I said promptly. 'That's why I think they'll come back to the rock in the morning to search for our tracks.'

'But what if they were smart enough to pick the first possibility?' she went on probing. 'If it was you, Captain, what would you have done?'

'Then I'd pretend to go away, hide somewhere and watch the monkey,' I said slowly. 'I'd wait till the troop moved away and then come back to the rock. And ... look again for tracks.'

'They'd find our tracks then, won't they?'

She said it quietly but I could sense the tension in her. I felt sorry for her now. It wasn't pleasant to be hunted under any circumstances, but to be a woman being hunted for the purpose of sexual slavery, and worse, was a prospect I wouldn't have known how to deal with.

'Yes.'

'Then they'd be close behind us.'

A flat statement, full of despair!

Oh fuck! I'd taken my eye off the ball, hadn't I?

I picked up the kathi and scrambled up the dune, back the way we had come. Velaithan came after me, kitchen knife in hand. I stopped short of the crest and crawled up the last bit, cautiously poking my head over the edge.

The sand of the dune shone whitely in the dim starlight. I let my breath out slowly in relief as Velaithan crept alongside and had a look.

Nothing.

I scanned the scrub that began at the base of the dune and spread into the distance. It was dark and forbidding and I realized I wouldn't see them until they left the cover of the bush and stepped on to the base of the dune.

'Maybe they picked the second possibility,' I said after a while.

'Or maybe they are sitting in the bushes over there, waiting like us.'

I thought Velaithan was a little paranoid but who could blame her?

'Let's wait here for a while,' I said finally. 'If they followed our tracks, they'd have to come this way.'

The sand was still warm from the sun and I felt the heat spreading through my chest as I lay there. A faint breeze coming over the forest played on our faces. By force of habit I picked up a few grains of fine sand in my fingers and let them cascade back to the ground.

'Why do you do that?' she asked. 'I've seen you do that with sand and grass.'

'Checking the direction of the wind,' I explained. 'It's just a habit I've picked up.'

'But what's the point of knowing the wind direction?'

I had the impression she just wanted to keep a conversation going. If it helped get her mind off her problems, I didn't mind.

'In the forest, most animals have a very keen sense of smell. If the wind was blowing from behind us as we walked, all the animals ahead of us would get our scent at a great distance and move away.'

'Is that all?'

'No. There are lots of implications.'

I was surprised to find I enjoyed explaining this stuff to someone who was interested. Just as much, I suppose, as Mr. Karl had enjoyed teaching me, in the old days.

'Say we wanted to study the habits of elephants and wanted to get close to a herd. Naturally we'd have to stalk them, staying hidden under cover. But all that would be useless if we were upwind of them, because they'd scent us immediately.'

'So?'

'So we'd have to check the wind direction and start downwind of them,' I told her. 'Of course, the wind changes direction sometimes, then all your hard work goes to hell.'

White teeth flashed in the dark and I was oddly pleased.

I went on, showing off now:

'It's interesting that wild animals don't know that we have no sense of smell. They think we can smell them. Sometimes we can use that to our advantage.'

'Go on.'

'If you had to walk through a forest where, say, a man-eating leopard was operating, you could work out where the animal would be waiting for you, just by checking the wind.'

'Really?' I could tell she was interested. 'You're joking, aren't you?'

'No. Just think about it,' I explained. 'The leopard thinks that we can smell him, so he will be downwind of us, just as it would be to a deer or other animal.'

'So?' she asked again.

'So if I was going through a patch of jungle with the wind at my back, I'd know the leopard will be ahead of me, and will try to pounce on me as I pass it. I don't need to worry about my back. If the wind is coming from the right, the leopard will be on my left. If the wind is coming from the left, then the animal will be on my right.'

She was smiling broadly now.

'That's very clever,' she said. 'But what happens if

the wind is in your face? Then the animal will be behind you.'

'In that case the only safe way to go is by tacking, like a sailboat.'

'What do you mean?' Velaithan asked. 'What's tacking?'

'You go some distance to your left at forty-five degrees to the direction you want to go. At that time you keep a sharp lookout to your left. Then you turn at right angles and tack to the right, again at forty-five degrees to your selected direction. This time you keep a lookout on your right. You have to keep doing that. Do you follow?' I was enjoying this and she was a good listener. 'That's the only safe way.'

'It sounds awfully difficult,' she said. 'Are there man-eaters in our forests?'

'None have been declared in the recent past. That may be due to a lack of information,' I said. 'There have been cases of man-eating leopards in the past.'

Velaithan was silent. I scanned the dune and the jungle beyond it once again. The sliver of moon had cleared the trees now, so visibility was better.

Something dark and heavy came out of the scrub and moved on to the sand. All I could make out was a slow moving object against the whiteness of the dune.

I strained my eyes in the gloom.

Velaithan asked tensely: 'What is it? Is that a man?'

'No, the shape is wrong,' I told her finally, relaxing. 'It looks like a lone boar, just rooting around.'

After a little while she asked:

'Captain, when we were resting under that banyan tree yesterday, you showed me a track made by a snake.

Why were you peering at it so closely?'

Once again I had the impression she was trying to keep herself awake by dredging up things to talk about.

'I was trying to figure out the direction it had gone in, by looking at the pile,' I told her. 'Mr. Karl taught me about that. He'd read about it in a book.'

'What's pile?' she asked.

'If you look closely at dust and fine sand, the particles on the surface are not all flat. Some particles stand up at various angles. That's the pile.'

'Yes but how do you tell direction from that?'

'If you run a road roller through a paddy field, all the paddy plants will flatten out in the direction of the roller. It is the same with the pile. It will flatten in the direction the snake has gone.'

I loved explaining this stuff.

'So if you examine the track carefully, you can tell the direction in which the snake had gone.'

'Mm.'

'Mr. Karl believed he could pick up more information from the track,' I continued blithely. 'The girth of the snake and whether it was poisonous or non poisonous, for instance.'

'Really?' she asked skeptically. 'How did he do that?'

'He'd measure the track in five or six places, depending on the depth of the dust. The girth is four times the average width of the track.'

'And whether it is poisonous?' she asked, thoroughly bemused now. 'That's what interests me.'

'Non-poisonous snakes generally chase after their prey. They also need to escape from their own enemies. So they are equipped to travel very fast and their track will be nearly straight. The rat snake is a good example of this. The only exception I've heard of is the python. That track is much broader so you can tell.'

'And poisonous ones?' she prompted.

'They generally lie in wait for their prey, so they have no real need to travel fast. Slow travel results in excessive wriggling. That means the track will be in a series of arcs.'

'Not bad, Captain,' she said. 'Not bad at all.'

We talked desultorily for a while. It was getting late and I felt weariness, like a mist, creeping quietly over me.

'It looks like you were right, they did take the second choice,' Velaithan said finally.

'That means they'll be after us in the morning so we'll need to make a very early start.'

'Yes.'

'We'd better get some rest then.'

I knew she was still desperately worried but she hid her concern well.

You are quite a girl, Kamala Velaithan!

I had one final look around. A sambhur belled in the forest but there was no movement on the dune.

We went down to the camp.

20

2nd April 2000

There was a suffocating weight on my chest and a sharp pain in the side of my neck. My nostrils were filled with a foul, feral smell.

O God! Some large animal had me by the throat.

I forced myself to remain still while I assessed the situation.

I realized that it was a man, seated on my chest. He was holding my head down with one hand and had a sharp knife pressed against my neck, with the other. I felt the skin split open and blood drip down the side of my neck. I could see the silhouette of his head against the sky. Ponytail. He smelt like a big cat in the zoo, sour with stale sweat.

Kamala screamed something in Tamil.

I couldn't turn my head but could just see with a corner of my eye that she had been dragged out of the tent to the ground outside. A dark figure was straddling her. I could hear them struggling, then a loud slap followed by a cry of pain.

Ponytail was distracted by the sound. He had turned his head at the sound of the blow, intent on watching his friend raping the woman. He might also have been lulled by a lack of movement on my part, mistaking it for submission.

He should have killed me while he had the chance.

I grasped his knife hand in both of mine, turning

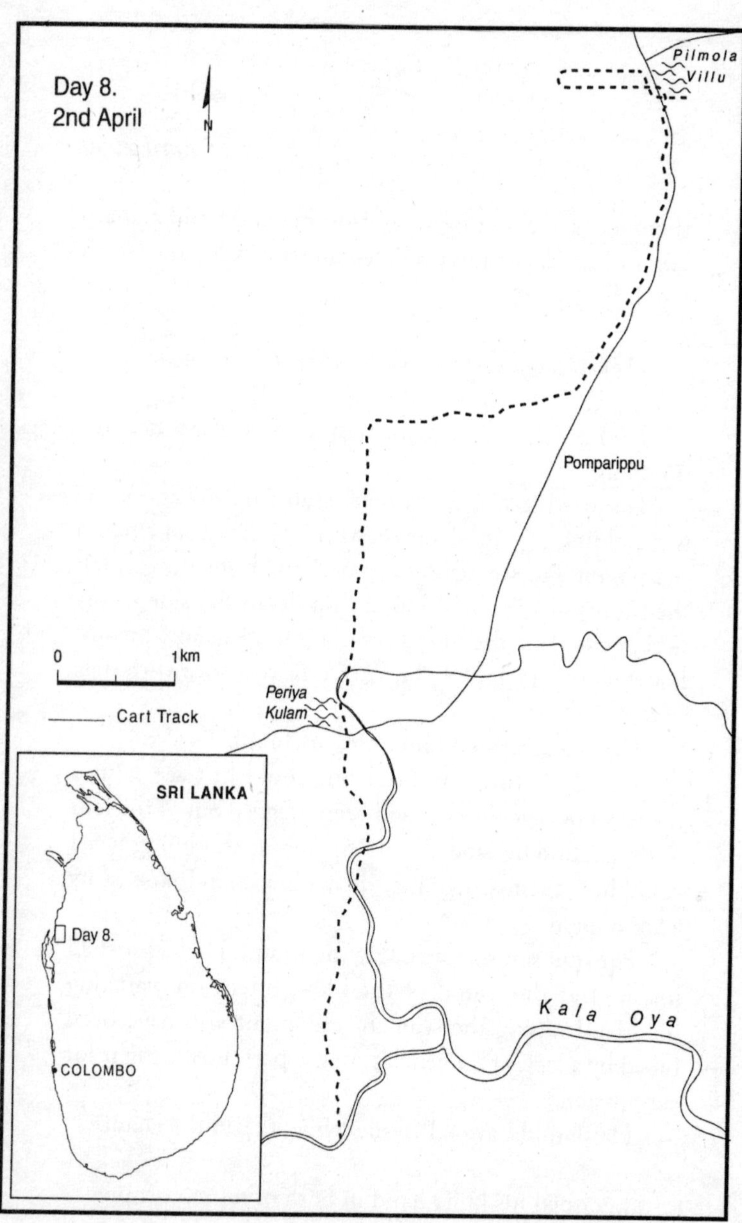
Day 8.
2nd April
N
Pilmola
Villu
Pomparippu
0
1km
Cart Track
Periya
Kulam
SRI LANKA
Day 8.
COLOMBO
Kala Oya

it away from my neck. I rolled over to my left twisting his wrist as I did so. He was strong and fought back ferociously, trying to turn the knife back on me. It wasn't any use though. I felt a rage exploding in me that could not be contained. I held down his knife hand with my left and hit him twice in the neck with my right fist. I heard his choking gasp and felt the strength go out of him. I reached over and picked up one of the rocks I had used to hold down the edge of the tent. I swung it against the side of his head.

It made a solid crunching sound and he went limp.

Kamala screamed again, a helpless, despairing wail. I heard the sound of another blow, a cry of pain, the sound of ripping cloth. I picked up the kathi and ran round the tent towards them, almost blind with the strength of my anger.

The man crouched over her. He held both her wrists in his left hand and was leaning his elbow on her chest, pinning her down. He was tugging at the cord of her trousers, trying to strip them off as she kicked and struggled. She twisted and jerked her lower body in desperation, like a stranded fish.

She called my name this time, but there was no hope in her voice now. The man had his right hand raised to strike her again. He must have heard me coming because he turned at the last moment, his mouth open in surprise. He lifted his arm further to protect his head as I swung the kathi with all my strength.

I'd held it wrong, with the cutting edge turned away, but the back of the axe blade still caught him near his elbow. I heard a clapping sound as the bone snapped. He screamed and rolled away, cradling the broken arm with his good hand.

He was kneeling, crouched over and hugging his elbow. He was making a keening sound at the back of his throat. I turned the blade forward and lifted the kathi high over my head for the killing blow. I wanted to cut him in half, to see his brains spill out into the sand.

I was out of control, filled with savage bloodlust to slaughter my enemy. Somewhere in the dim recesses of my mind I heard her scream.

'No, Wasu. Don't do it!'

It shouldn't have been possible for me to stop, not after I had started the downswing. Somehow I felt my muscles seize up and stop, rigid with tension. I stood over him, shaking, half of my mind still urging me to finish the job. Slowly my fury ebbed away and I was able to think rationally again.

I turned the kathi around and gripped the wooden shaft near the blade. I swung the handle in a short, sharp arc against the side of his head. It made a solid, thumping sound and he sprawled over. I kicked him in the ribs to make sure he really was unconscious.

Kamala was seated on the ground, her knees drawn up and her head resting on her forearms. She shuddered when I touched her shoulder. I felt her whole body shaking, as if in a high fever. I felt awkward, unable to find words to comfort her.

'Kamala, we can't stay here. The others may be nearby,' I said gently. 'Help me.'

I had touched the right button, for she was a professional. When she looked up I saw that her cheek was puffed and the rest of her face drawn in pain and stress. She controlled herself with a visible effort.

'What do we need to do?' Her voice was still shaky.

'We have to pack up and leave. Get as far away from here as we can,' I said and then asked gruffly. 'Are you ok? Did he hurt you?'

'I'm alright, really!' She was recovering fast. 'What about these men?'

She gestured towards them.

'Break camp and pack the bags,' I told her. 'I'll attend to them.'

I checked ponytail first. He was moaning softly but still seemed unconscious. The hair on the left side of his head was matted with blood, so the rock must have made an impression on him. I was glad.

I dragged him over to one of the smaller palmyrah trees and laid him out on his back, with his head at the base of the tree. I yanked his sarong off, nicked it with the knife and tore it into strips. I then took his arms around the tree and tied them together securely on the far side. I used some more of the rolled up strips of fabric to tie his feet together for good measure.

The other man was totally unconscious. I caught him by his legs and dragged him unceremoniously to another palmyrah tree. I turned him face down and pulled his legs around the tree, one on either side. I tied his ankles together on the far side. I then pulled his arms behind his back and tied them as well. His right arm was twisted at an awkward angle at the elbow and I knew the fracture would cause him a reasonable amount of discomfort when he became conscious again.

That would make the bastard think a bit!

Kamala had packed our tarps and other possessions in the two bags. We had no food left, just the bottles filled with dune water. We had only the light of a dying quarter moon to go by so we walked round the campsite to check if we had collected everything.

Kamala said: 'Captain, look at this.'

I should have thought of it. Placed carefully on the ground, near the base of another palm tree, was another kathi, a two-cell flashlight and a twelve bore shotgun. There was one cartridge in the breech.

I thought for a moment and went back to short hair, the man with the broken arm. It wasn't too difficult to search his pockets, face down as he was. There was just one more cartridge in his pocket. Not enough for a gun battle, but enough to give us some teeth. I buried ponytail's knife and axe, carefully smoothing the sand over the hole.

I handed my kathi to Kamala and shouldered the gun.

Kamala stood patiently, waiting for me to show the way. I hated the thought of moving about the forest at night. Just the same I knew we could not wait till morning, we had to get as far as possible from the camp before dawn.

21

'The road is due west of us. We will come to it sooner or later if we head that way. The real problem is that we can easily miss it in the dark and keep going.'

'How do we find the right direction?'

'That's Orion's Belt,' I said, pointing. 'Do you see a few fainter stars forming a line with the middle star? That's called Orion's sword. The direction of the sword, from the belt downwards, points due south. That means west is perpendicular to the direction of the sword and on the right.'

She didn't say anything.

We climbed the dune slowly. Kamala was having trouble with her ankle but wouldn't let me help her. Once at the top, I worked out the direction we needed. Fortunately the dunes seemed to be a local peculiarity and the forest spread out again on the far side of the third dune. The vegetation was sparse and that helped us to keep direction. It also reduced the risk of encountering a large animal.

'How is your ankle?' I asked. 'Will you able to keep going?'

Yesterday's incident seemed a long time ago. By now the ankle would have begun to stiffen and become more painful. If it gave out, we would be in trouble.

'It is a little better,' she said. 'I can keep walking so long as we don't have to climb too much.'

She wasn't going to admit she was in pain.

'What about our tracks?' she asked. 'They followed us once, won't they be able to find us again?'

'Those two men won't be able to free themselves for

some time. Even if they do, ponytail will first have to take the injured man back. The real danger is if the others come looking for them. Then they could split up and come after us.'

'Is it possible to hide our tracks?'

There was no fear in her voice but I couldn't blame her for worrying about it. If they caught us again they'd extract a heavy price.

'No. It's not worth the trouble, or the time,' I told her. 'These men are proffesionls. They will be able to track us, whatever we do.'

'They'll catch us then, won't they?'

I tried to work it out.

'The rest of that gang will not get anxious till morning. Let's assume they start looking for their friends after dawn. The only way to find them will be by following their tracks, or ours. That run around at the rock won't hold them up for long. Even with a good tracker, I can't see them getting to our campsite till late morning. That's the lead we have. We need to get as far as possible in the night and try to hide our tracks once we have some light to work with.'

'How did they find our camp so late in the night? Kamala asked. 'You said they wouldn't be able to track us in the night.'

'I made a stupid mistake,' I admitted ruefully. 'They did exactly what we had feared, followed us soon after the monkeys left. The trouble is, we thought of it quite late in the night and didn't allow for the time lag.'

'You mean, when we went racing up the dune to check, they were already hiding close by, watching us?'

'Yeah,' I said. 'I think they were over the second dune.

They just waited till we went to sleep.'

Kamala stopped and looked at me.

'We are a fine pair of fools, aren't we?' she observed ruefully.

'Yes,' I said. 'We were lucky to survive that mistake.'

Keeping to a set direction became harder as we went along. I couldn't keep looking up while walking and it was not always easy to spot the belt and the sword. I finally worked out a simpler scheme. I would check the direction first and try to find a taller tree or other landmark in the gloom and then work our way towards that, then check the direction again and find another landmark. We made some progress but more slowly than I would have liked. I tried not to think about stepping on snakes.

The small flashlight helped. The hunters had used some tape on the face of it, reducing the aperture. It gave enough light to check the darker spots when we had to find our way through small copses of trees. I used it sparingly to save the batteries.

We walked without speaking after that, stopping every so often to check direction. We thought we were traveling in a straight line towards the west but it's quite likely we moved in a crazy zigzag.

We found the road more easily than I had expected. We might still have missed it if not for the open plain, at least an absence of trees, suddenly spreading out before us. We then looked for, and found, the ruts of the track heading south. It had to be the old 'north road' that led to Puttalam. That track would lead us through Pomparippu to the Kala Oya, the river that was the boundary of the sanctuary. We just needed a safe passage down this road.

My relief at finding the track made me careless.

We walked blithely round a sharp bend in the track and straight into the poachers' camp. They were seated round a small fire on the side of the track, dark figures. We could clearly hear the rumble of conversation and a bark of laughter. They were not more than twenty yards from where we stood.

We retreated slowly, step by step, until we had regained the shelter of the trees. Someone must have detected movement because a beam from a powerful flashlight swept over the track where we had stood a moment earlier. We were safely under cover by then.

I had a choice. We could work our way through the trees and try to reach the track further down or cross the plain and trust the darkness to hide us. The quarter moon had disappeared behind a hazy cloud, so it would be harder to navigate through the trees. I was afraid of getting lost, and even if we found the track again, I was getting a bad feeling about it. There were too many people around. I signalled to Kamala that we'd go back along the track and swing out through the plain.

We moved away from the camp, keeping to the edge of the trees until I judged it safe enough. I counted two hundred paces.

'What is your plan, Captain?' Kamala had regained her composure now. She was whispering but her voice was steady. We stopped at the edge of the track, reluctant to commit ourselves.

'I think we will be better off crossing the plain,' I told her. 'If we go west for about a mile and then turn south, we have a good chance of avoiding contact. What do you think?'

'We'll be in the open, won't we? If they spot us, they will catch us easily. I can't run. Won't we be better off in the trees?'

'I'm worried about those clouds. It will be harder to keep direction in the trees and we may get lost,' I said. 'I also want to avoid this track. Too much chance of meeting people.'

I continued thoughtfully.

'If they try to follow our tracks tomorrow, they'll keep checking the road. They might find it harder to believe we crossed the open plain.'

'So we cross the plain safely, what then?' Kamala asked. 'What's beyond it?'

'When we head south we must finally reach the river, the Kala Oya. There are several streams & tributaries before that but they'll be mostly dry in this season. Anyway there will be a broad belt of trees that will mark the edge of the plain. We have to reach the trees before daylight.'

'Can we do it?' she asked. 'Do you know how far it is?'

'I don't know. We have no way of knowing.'

'We had better get going then, hadn't we?' she said decisively. 'Do you know what time it might be?'

'I don't know for sure,' I told her. 'I'd guess we have about five hours of darkness left.'

We set off then, looking warily at the camp, still hidden by the curve of the track. It came into sight soon after, the glow of the fire reflected on the trees. The ground was relatively flat, sand and rock covered with coarse, close-cropped grass. It was mostly open plain with thorn bushes and stunted trees breaking the skyline here and there.

We walked into a lapwings nest and the wretched birds rose into the air, their 'did-he-do-it' alarm calls ringing like fire sirens in the stillness of the night. The beam of a powerful flashlight cut through the darkness, sweeping over us from left to right. It passed us and came back, holding us like moths pinned to a board. I stood still, glancing at Kamala as I did so. She had been well trained. She was standing like a statue, one arm frozen in its swing.

I knew, at that distance, we would look like tree stumps provided we did not move. Dropping to the ground in a panic was far more likely to be observed. But that didn't work this time. The lapwings could be seen in the beam of light, diving at us and screaming their stupid heads off.

I heard confused shouting from the camp and more flashlights were switched on. I grabbed Kamala by the hand and ran, injured ankle and all, for a clump of bushes nearby. I dived behind it but the flashlights followed us easily, lighting up the shrub. It gave us some cover, though, and we used it to scramble away on all fours, staying in the protective shadow till we reached another thicket.

I stopped to see what they were doing, and to get my breath back. There were three flashlights now, but fanned out in a wide semicircle. The men in front of us were advancing deliberately but the light on my extreme right was bobbing up and down. That man was running.

I'd have done the same thing.

'Why is that man running?' Kamala asked, pointing.

'They know we want to go south, to reach the river,' I explained. 'They want to stop us doing that.'

'And then?'

'They are trying to drive us towards the sea,' I told her. 'It becomes very open as we get closer to the coast.

They want to trap us with our backs to the sea.'

'What can we do?' Despite the desperate danger we were in, her voice was steady.

And she didn't blame me for making a bad decision.

'We can't go south, because they've cut us off. If we go west, we'll be caught in the end. So…'

'So we have to go north?' she said quietly. 'Yes, I agree.'

'OK,' I said.

The flashlights were getting nearer and we were running out of time.

'Lets go a little further towards the sea then swing round towards the north.'

We moved in short spurts, dashing from one bit of cover to the other. Trying to move quickly over rough ground in a crouched position was incredibly tiring and uncomfortable, but there was no other way to do it. I don't know how Kamala managed it, but she kept pace and never complained. Fortunately we were able to make up some ground. The men in front of us were advancing slowly, checking every bit of cover, while the man on our flank was now almost parallel with us.

We stopped to rest.

Kamala asked: 'Won't they be able to track us?'

'I think it will be difficult in the dark. Anyway let's try to avoid the sandy bits. Stay on the grass and hard ground.'

'Captain?' For once her voice was hesitant. 'If they see us, and we have to run … you don't have to wait for me, it will only get you killed!'

'Shut up,' I snarled, unreasonably angry that she should suggest it. 'I'll kill them all or … I'll kill you. Will that be all right?'

'Yes,' she said seriously. 'Yes, Captain. That will be all

right.'

The lapwings started their cacophony. The neurotically anxious birds that were responsible for our present problems were now giving the poachers a workout. They called and dived, called and dived, till the men had passed through the nesting area.

We moved in an arc, keeping under cover but swinging towards the north and away from the sea. After about fifty yards of scattered scrub, we came to a relatively dense patch of bush that seemed to stretch away on either side. As there wasn't a gap I could spot, I went ahead and pushed my way through it.

The ground disappeared under my feet and I fell into space. I landed heavily on my shoulder and banged my head painfully against a rock. I rolled over and tried to get my breath back.

Kamala whispered from somewhere above me:

'Captain, where are you?'

'Down here.'

'Are you hurt?'

'No. It's ok,' I said doughtily. 'I think this is a dried up watercourse. I'll help you down'

The monsoon rain had carved out a channel through the plain that was about seven feet deep where I stood. I was lucky to get away with a glancing blow on the head for the streambed was strewn with boulders. The channel was completely dry now but was probably an impressive torrent in the wet season. The edge of the channel, which seemed to be about fifteen feet across, was lined on either side with a dense screen of bushes.

I left the gun and bag on the ground and climbed on

a rock to help Kamala down. She handed me the kathi and bag first and climbed down cautiously, careful not to aggravate the injury to her ankle.

'Shall we hide here?' she asked.

'Mmm. Yes,' I answered. 'It's a good place.'

But I was not happy.

'No,' I said finally. 'Let's go back some way.'

'You mean towards them?' she asked.

My instinct was also to get further away from them but I knew that was a mistake.

'They won't expect that.'

We collected our gear and picked our way carefully between the boulders. I tried to estimate the time it would take to cross the advancing line of men. Not much, we'd taken too much time moving laterally. We had covered about twenty-five yards when I saw an uneven jumble of boulders on the side of the gully, reaching almost to the top of the bank.

The watercourse, with the bushes that lined its banks, gave us a chance to walk upright, which was a blessing. But it ran quite straight and we would be easily seen, and caught like rats, if anyone thought to come to edge of the bank and run the beam of a flashlight up and down it. I had to get under cover and the bushes overhanging those rocks were as good a place as any.

The boulders were smooth and difficult to climb. I helped Kamala up. She had just wriggled under cover of a bush when a beam of light flashed along the scrub over our heads.

Someone was coming to check the gully.

There was no time to pass the bags and weapons to Kamala. I pushed them between two rocks at the base of the pile. I thought about the gun, undecided for just a fraction too long, and finally decided to hide it as well. I pulled myself up and crept into the space Kamala had left for me under a small leafy bush that leaned over the bank.

We just made it. The beam steadied over the scrub we were sheltering under and a man walked towards us.

Had he seen us?

The man pushed his way through the rim of bushes and came to the edge of the gully. He was no more than two yards from where we crouched, not daring to breathe. He was scanning the gully, up and down. I couldn't see his face but had the impression of a heavily built man, bare bodied except for a pair of dark pants. He was carrying a Chinese T 56 assault rifle on a canvas sling, going over his right shoulder. A cleverly devised clip, fitted on the side of the barrel, held his five-cell flashlight. He held the stock of the rifle in his right fist and swivelled it from side to side to scan the ravine.

I deserved to be shot for being such a stupid, stupid bastard.

If only I had carried the shotgun with me, I could have put the muzzle almost to his belly and blown him in half. With his assault rifle in my hands I would have fancied my chances to clean up the rest of those bastards, and anybody else we were likely to meet.

But my gun was hidden in a crevice at the bottom of the gully, six feet below me. It might as well have been in Brazil.

Don't point your flashlight downwards!

If he spotted our kit, I'd have to charge him, hoping to reach him before he could get his gun up. A doomed enterprise, if ever there was one. Luckily it wasn't easy to point the flashlight downwards, the way he'd rigged it on his gun and the man didn't really think we were close by. He had a cursory look up and down the gully and turned back.

'Jagath,' he called out loudly as walked away.

Another man answered from further away.

'Mang watura pāra dige yanawā. Mey aina tikak balapang,' the first man said.

I'm going down the watercourse. Watch this side of it.

Thankfully he didn't try to climb down the pile of rocks we were crouched on, he'd have stepped directly on us. I saw a dark figure jump down to the gully a little further downstream and walk slowly away from us, scanning the bushes on either side as he went.

'Will he see our footprints?' Kamala asked softly.

For fear of being overheard, she was forced to lean against my shoulder to whisper. Only days ago, she would have been revolted by the enforced proximity, now she took it in her stride. I was moved by her assumption of friendship and trust.

'The ground is quite rough. I don't think he'll see anything,' I said. 'If he does spot something, he'll turn around immediately.'

'You'd better fetch the gun then, hadn't you?'

Hell, yes.

I jumped down and quickly retrieved the gun. I collected the rest of our stuff as well and concealed the bags on the bank, in case we had to escape that way. I checked the cartridge in the breach and got back under cover again, more confident now.

'Why don't we sneak away now, towards the road?' Kamala asked.

Good question.

'That man is still too close. If he turns around and uses his flashlight, he'll spot us easily,' I said finally. 'Let's wait till he is out of sight.'

We watched his progress from the movement of the flashlight but he didn't go much further. We saw the dark figure turn and come back towards us.

Had he seen a footprint?

He walked unhurriedly, the flashlight gun swinging alternately from left to right and back again. I began to worry whether our cover was good enough. The bush beneath which we were sheltering offered a perfect screen from above but the cover was less dense when seen from below.

Challenging a man with an automatic rifle with nothing more than a shotgun was something only a comic book character would attempt. I knew I would have to take him unawares and drop him with a single shot. That meant that he had to come within ten yards and still not spot us.

If he spotted us from beyond that range, we were dead.

He was getting closer. I took note of a rock outcropping that stood out darkly at about the right distance. I used it as a marker, deciding to fire the moment he came up to it. But once again he surprised me by stopping about fifteen yards from it. He pointed the beam down the gully, studying it for a moment, then switched the flashlight off. We saw a dark figure climb the bank and disappear into the shrubbery.

'Jagath,' the man called out loudly, startling us.

'*Hoo,*' the answering call came from a distance.

'Mokuth däkkada?'

Did you see anything?

'Nä aiya.'

No brother.

'Meheta wareng ehenang. Senatath kiyapang torch eka arang enna kiyala.'

Come here. Tell Sena to come as well, and bring the flashlight with him.

We waited. We were too close to them to risk moving now. I wondered if the first man, Aiya, had seen a footprint and was gathering the gang to search the gully more thoroughly. That would mean big trouble for us.

Two other men came up, flashlights stabbing the dark. At least one of them had a gun.

Aiya continued in Sinhala. He sounded like the leader.

'Mokuth däkke nädda?'

Didn't you see anything?

One man said: *'Palaweni särey vitharai. Dennek hitiya.'*

Only the first time! There were two of them.

'Gäni hitiyada?'

Was the woman there?

'Ow.'

Yes.

'Damith geng kohoma berila äwada danney nähä.'

How did they escape from Damith and come here?

The other said: *'Unta berila yanna bähä. Kohehari hängila äthi.'*

They can't escape. Must be hiding somewhere.

There was some mumbled conversation we couldn't make out, then:

'Mekeng wädak nähä. Mey karuwaley hoyanne kohomada? the leader said finally. *'Api eli wunahama allagamu.'*

This is useless. How can we find them in the dark? We'll track them down in the morning.

To my intense relief, Aiya, having said this, turned abruptly and walked back in the direction of his camp. The other two followed him, ghostly silhouettes passing our refuge at a distance of about thirty feet. I left the shelter of the bush to follow their progress but they didn't turn on their flashlights again and were soon out of sight.

When I came back Kamala asked:

'Are they giving it up?'

'Looks like it,' I told her. 'They are going back to their camp.'

'So we can stay with the original plan then?' she asked. 'Go across the plain?'

'Yes,' I said, hesitating. 'Yes, I suppose so.'

We were squatting by the bushes, afraid to stand up yet. I felt her eyes on me.

'You are worried about something, aren't you?'

'Did you follow their conversation? In Sinhala?'

'Yes,' she said carefully. 'Some of it.'

'Do you remember the man who was running to outflank us?'

'Yes,' she said.

'When they called him back, the man called Aiya said

– tell him to bring the flashlight,' I said, trying to recollect the exact words. 'I wonder why he said it like that.'

'Why?' Kamala asked. 'What's strange about that?'

'Why would the man leave the flashlight behind?'

'Only if …' she stopped abruptly. 'Oh no.'

'Yes.'

'There was more than one man there. We only counted the flashlights.'

'So they brought one man back, with his flashlight, to make us think they had all gone away,' I said slowly. 'There is at least one armed man stationed out there, waiting for us to pass by.'

Kamala was silent, digesting the information.

Then she said: 'That is a big area for one man to cover. Surely we can sneak through if we are careful?'

'That isn't all,' I continued. 'They were speaking just a little too loudly when they were here. Maybe they knew we were somewhere close by and wanted us to overhear. Maybe some of them have gone round again, to cut us off from the south.'

'It sounds logical but it's still guesswork, isn't it?'

'Then there are the lapwings,' I added mysteriously.

'What do you mean?'

'Have you heard of Sherlock Holmes?'

'No,' she said, puzzled. 'Who is that?'

'He was a famous detective in crime fiction,' I explained. 'In one story, he calls the attention of a colleague to a curious incident of a dog in the night time. The colleague says, 'But the dog did nothing in the night'. Holmes then explains that that itself is the curious incident!'

'What are you going on about?' she asked in exasperation. 'Those wretched lapwings did nothing ….

oh.'

'Yes.'

'They didn't go back to their camp, did they?'

'No,' I said slowly. 'No. I think they are out there, waiting for us to walk into the trap.'

'Bastards,' she said bitterly. 'What do we do now?'

'These boys are smart,' I said. 'They might have stationed a man to cover this gully as well.'

'Where does that leave us?'

I had been thinking about it.

'We have to cross the gully and go north for some distance, then turn east, cross the road into the forest again,' I told her. 'We'll use the forest cover to get past their camp.'

'How long till dawn, do you think?'

'Three hours, four at most,' I said, hoping fervently I'd got that right.

We just had to get under cover before dawn.

22

I jumped down into the gully and then helped Kamala. She allowed me to hold her under the arms and lift her down. We took up our packs, scrambled up the far bank and walked away to the north, every step taking us further away from our destination.

'I hope we don't run into more lapwings.'

That would screw things up in style and I walked warily. The dense growth by the edge of the watercourse gave way to open country and we were able to make good progress. We didn't come across any game at all, understandable I suppose, with a poachers' camp so near. Thankfully there were no nervous lapwings either.

I set a northeasterly course using the stars again and noticed that scattered bits of cloud were again drifting across the sky. I hoped this was not going to become a problem later on. We reached the road soon afterwards, unmistakable because it skirted the tree line of the forest.

We turned back then but decided to stay in the trees, and keep a sharp lookout, as we approached the poachers' camp. Progress was slow but I felt much more comfortable walking under cover of the trees. Ten minutes of careful advance brought us to the camp. The fire had died down but threw enough light to show a rough canvas tarpaulin, strung between two trees.

The camp appeared to be empty.

I didn't intend to take any chances, though, and made a wider detour into the forest till we were well past the camp. Even as we did, I felt a knot of indignation grow in my belly. I was an officer in the army and represented the authority of my government. This woman was in my custody. Yet these scum had the temerity to hunt us, as though we were animals.

We reached the road again and turned south. Walking was much easier now and I thought to follow it for some distance before turning westwards again. I noticed Kamala limping again.

'How is your ankle?' I asked. 'Is it painful?'

'Slightly,' she said dismissively. 'I can manage.'

'Let me take your bag.'

'No, Captain,' she said brusquely. 'I can manage. Don't fuss.'

We walked in silence for a minute but something was bothering me. Something I had overlooked. I tapped Kamala, who was walking ahead, on the shoulder and drew her into the shadow of a tree.

'We saw that the camp was empty, didn't we?' I asked her, trying to arrange my thoughts. 'So we were right. They are out there, waiting for us.'

'Yes,' she said quietly, knowing this was important. 'So what's worrying you now?'

'If you were the leader, where would you position your men?'

'In a line, going westwards, towards the sea.'

'Would that be all?' I asked. 'Would you be satisfied with that?'

She was quiet for a minute, thinking about it.

'No,' she whispered finally. 'No. I'd want one man to cover the road.'

I didn't say anything.

Kamala continued: 'He has to be somewhere close by, hasn't he?'

'We can go deep into the forest and try to go around him, but that will take too much time. We might lose our way as well.'

'So what is the other option, Captain?' Kamala asked quietly. 'You always have another plan.'

'Are you feeling brave?' I asked.

'No,' she said, but I saw a flash of teeth. 'But what do you want me to do?'

She was game, despite an injured ankle and having been beaten up once already.

'Can you walk ahead?' I asked. 'I'll stalk you from the trees.'

'What if the man just shoots me?' She was only half jesting.

'I think, you know, they want you … alive.'

'Yes.' All the animation had drained from her voice. 'Yes, I'm sure they do.'

'Do you think you can manage it?'

'Yes.'

'OK,' I told her. 'Walk slowly and don't look back.'

'All right.' She turned to go.

'Kamala,' I said gently. 'I will be close behind.'

'Yes, Captain,' she said. 'I know you will be.'

I gave her ten yards.

I would have liked it to be more but it was too dark to spot movement at a greater distance. Kamala walked slowly in the middle of the track, her rucksack making a hump on her back and the kathi held in her right hand. I stayed well inside the trees and scrambled from tree to tree, using the inkiest shadows for cover. The trees gave way to a dense patch of thorn bush and I found my way completely blocked. Going round it meant making a wide detour and losing sight of Kamala. Getting on the road would give me away.

I paused for a moment to work out what to do. Suddenly there was a second shadow, moving very fast in the gloom, and I heard a stifled cry from Kamala. Then the shadows merged, struggling furiously from one side of the road to the other, and then fell to the ground.

I dropped my rucksack and ran, holding the gun across my chest. I came up behind them and saw Kamala flat on her face and a dark figure sitting astride her. He had her right hand twisted behind her and was pushing it up, towards her shoulder blades, forcing her face into the ground.

She cried out.

I held the shotgun by the stock and swung it in a full arc, like a golf club. The heavy barrel caught him on the side of his head with a dull thud, snapping it sideways. He catapulted off her, rolled over twice and was still.

I helped her to her feet.

'Are you hurt?'

She didn't say anything but kept massaging her right elbow and shoulder with her other hand. There was grass and sand on her face and down the front of her dress.

I left her and went over to the man. He was sprawled across the road, face down and hands outspread. A tall, thin man dressed in dark coloured pants and a shirt with the sleeves cut off. Even in the uncertain light I could see that the right side of his head had a great depression where the gun had struck him. I turned him over and put my finger on his carotid artery, just to be sure.

His poaching days were over.

I searched his pockets and found two more cartridges. I went and fetched my rucksack and took out the flashlight. I searched the side of the track, by the bushes, till I found his gun. Another ancient, single barrel, twelve bore shotgun with a cartridge in the breech. I dragged him over to the edge of the thicket, held him by the neck and the waistband of his pants, and heaved him into the middle of it.

'Is he dead?' Kamala asked.

'Yes,' I said brusquely.

I shouldered both guns and began walking down the track, towards the poachers' camp.

Kamala asked: 'Captain, where are you going?'

'Keep the bags and stay under cover,' I said grimly, so angry now I was hardly able to speak. 'I'll be back in a little while.'

'But what are you going to do?'

'Kill all of them,' I grated. 'Just as I said I would.'

'You said yourself that they were professionals. They are under cover and they have automatic weapons,' she said quietly. 'The odds are too great and it will be light soon.'

'I've been trained in this. I can take them out,' I said. 'These bastards don't know what they are up against.'

I could almost taste the froth of my fury. I started walking away.

She called after me quietly: 'Captain. I'm asking you not to go.'

Do you really think I can be controlled like that?

But my feet stopped!

I found, for some reason, my rage dwindling, like a pan of boiling water subsiding once the gas has been turned off. I knew she was right, of course. I took a deep breath and turned around.

'All right,' I said. 'Let's get out of here.'

She didn't say anything but I had the impression she was smiling.

'How is your arm?'

'My shoulder hurts,' she said. 'Nothing serious, though.'

She would say that even if the shoulder was dislocated.

'Let me have your bag,' I said gruffly.

'No, Captain,' she said lightly. 'I told you. I can cope!'

'I'm in the mood to whack someone. Don't let it be you!' I snarled. 'Give me the damned bag.'

'Oh, all right,' she said, slipping it off her shoulders and giving it to me. 'If you insist.'

I slung it over my left arm and picked up one gun. I left her with the kathi and the second gun. We started walking again, abreast now.

After awhile Kamala said:

'You know, Captain, in spite of being a Sinhalese, you are a good man!'

'Shut up.'

I'd been called many things in my life, but never 'good'.

But I felt better after that.

We tramped along the road for a while without speaking. We had been on the run for most of the night and I felt a deep weariness creeping over me. But we couldn't stop now. We had to get under cover, and hide our tracks, before dawn. How much time did we have?

Then I began to have a bad feeling about the road. I stopped to rest and drink some water.

'I think we should leave the road now,' I said. 'When

they find the man in the bushes, this is the way they will follow us.'

Kamala didn't say anything.

'And there may be other groups operating in the area,' I added. 'They will all use the road.'

'What do we do then?' Kamala asked quietly, waiting patiently for instructions.

'I'd like to go across the plain towards the sea for about a mile and then turn towards the river,' I said. 'Just as we had planned to earlier.'

'All right, Captain,' she said wearily. 'Let's do that.'

'It's very rough country,' I reminded her. 'Will your ankle hold up?'

'Don't worry about that, Captain,' she said firmly. 'I won't delay you.'

'All right then! Let's find some hard ground to leave the road on,' I said. 'It might hold them up for a little while.'

Fortunately it was still clear enough to see the stars, with only scattered bits of white cloud drifting slowly inland. I had to pause every hundred paces or so to recheck the direction and find fresh markers. Once, when a dense patch of cloud covered the section of sky I was using, I became disoriented and had to stop for a while till it cleared. More masses of cloud were building up in the west and the breeze was bringing these, slowly but surely, towards us. If we didn't make it to the shelter of the trees before the night sky was obliterated, we would be in some difficulty.

Although there was little vegetation, I found the ground rough and uneven. There were open stretches of sand interspersed with rocks and rotten tree stumps, tufts of coarse grass and bushes bristling with thorns. It might have been easy in daylight, but in the predawn darkness, it was difficult to move at a steady pace.

After we had covered about a mile I turned south, relying again on the stars. I marked yet another silhouette of a tree as a landmark and set off immediately. I could see that Kamala was limping badly and in some distress, but we couldn't stop to rest. We both knew we had to press on and find shelter before the sun came up.

It was a nightmare journey that never seemed to end. I kept stifling my doubts. Was I really heading south or out towards the sandy desert and the sea? How much further did we have to go? What time was it?

It must have been there for some time before I realized what it was, a horizon that was an irregular line with bumps in it. A line of trees! I had got the direction right. The trees were scattered at first and then increased in density. We were weary beyond measure when I decided we had come far enough. I found a level area under a tree, cleaned it out and spread the ground sheet. By then I was absolutely buggered.

'Let's rest here till daylight,' I said. 'It will be difficult to move through the trees in the dark.'

She wasn't listening.

She just lay down on the sheet, curled herself into a ball and went to sleep.

I sat with my back to a tree. I checked both guns and put them down, with the flashlight, beside me. My mind told me that they wouldn't be able to find us till well after daybreak. That wasn't enough though. After last night, I needed a more secure refuge before I could close my eyes again.

23

The forest was eerily silent. I heard the hoot of an owl and an occasional rustle in the undergrowth. I sipped some water from time to time, brushed away the mosquitoes and waited. I only realized that dawn was imminent when the birds started calling, but this jungle dawn brought me no joy. I was desperately tired and hungry, and there seemed to be a sprinkling of fine sand under my eyelids.

Kamala was asleep, still in the same foetal position. She was normally the early riser and it was very unlike her to sleep past dawn. The physical and emotional trauma of the last twenty-four hours must have told on her.

It was time to move out. I called her name and her eyes opened instantly, wide with alarm. She relaxed visibly, smiled even, when she realized that there was no emergency.

'I'm sorry, Captain,' she said. 'I should have shared the watch. I just … passed out.'

'It's all right,' I assured her. 'You did well.'

'Those men will come after us won't they?'

'Yes,' I said. 'It's bloody stupid, but I think they will.'

'How much time do we have?'

'There were three of them left … intact, four at most,' I said. 'They might all go looking for their first two friends, then start following our trail. If they do, we'd have a head start of three or four hours.'

'What would you have done?' Kamala asked.

She was seated now, hugging her knees. Her face was smudged with dirt and there was a scratch on her cheek.

'I'd send one man to check on the first two,' I said. 'I'd take up the trail with the rest.'

'That means there will be at least two men coming after us,' she observed. 'Will they be able to find us?'

'They will follow our tracks along the road till they disappear,' I said thoughtfully. 'But when we left the track, there was only one direction we could select. So they'll cast around till they find some sign. Yes, they'll be able to follow us.'

'How much time does that give us?'

'An hour and a half after dawn,' I said thoughtfully. 'We must assume that's the margin we'll have.'

'We'd better get moving then, hadn't we?'

'Yes,' I said.

She tried to get up but fell back, holding her shoulder.

'What's the matter? I asked.

'My shoulder is still sore,' she said quietly. 'I think there is a slight strain.'

When I looked anxious, she continued with a smile:

'Don't worry, Captain. It won't hold me up.'

The eastern sky had finally begun to brighten when I stood up and stretched myself. My back felt stiff and sore.

'How far is it to Puttalam?' Kamala asked. 'Do you think we can reach Colombo today?'

I was tempted to make a dash for it. Steal some vehicle to get us to Puttalam and then, a bus to Colombo. I was getting tired of this stinking forest.

'I thought about that,' I told her slowly. 'No, it's too risky. It will take us too long to cross the river and reach the village on the other side. We have to find a safe place to rest up and try to reach Colombo tomorrow.'

'We'll be cutting it very fine, won't we,' she asked anxiously.

Yes, it was getting tight. Today was the second. If we reached Colombo tomorrow evening, I could contact headquarters and arrange a meeting with DMI for the next morning. That would be the fourth. If he was in Colombo and if he agreed to see us! If DMI were convinced, he'd have to report to the Joint Operations Command through the Army Commander. The Air Force would then need to be properly briefed on the operation. Prabakaran was to be in the target area on the sixth.

I thought we had enough time. But yes, we'd be cutting it very, very fine.

'We have no other choice.' I was pretty sure it was the best plan. 'Let's get moving.'

The light had improved as we spoke. I folded the ground sheet and drank some water. We had no food left and I missed it badly. I could undergo hardship and discomfort but I hated going hungry. I picked up both bags and slung them over my shoulder.

'I can carry it, Captain,' Kamala insisted. 'Really!'

'Take one gun and the kathi!' I told her gruffly. 'I'll take the bag for the moment.'

'But …' She wouldn't let it rest.

'Both of us have to be ready with our guns,' I said. 'Can you manage one?'

'Of course.' She was slightly mollified.

I went back to the edge of the plain first and took some time to study the expanse before me. I saw some animals moving greyly in the distance, pig or buffalo. No men with guns.

I got back to the trees and led Kamala westwards,

towards the coast. I knew that any game trail we cut across would lead us to the river, the only source of water in the area. We soon came across a well-used game track that meandered through the trees, but generally leading south towards the river. It was still dark and gloomy under the trees but, thankfully, we didn't stumble on any animals.

The undergrowth on either side of the track became denser as we went along, the trees greener and taller. I was surprised because I had expected the river to be much further away. The track bisected a patch of thorn bush, and as we moved carefully through it, found ourselves on the steep bank of a dried-out stream, the muddy hollow at the centre of which was occupied by a small herd of buffalo.

The buffalo were all wallowing in the muddy ooze and didn't look aggressive. In fact they ignored us completely and went on placidly chewing the cud, nodding their heads from time to time to drive the flies away. The problem was the thorny undergrowth. It was so dense and tangled that we couldn't move sideways. The bank itself was steep and slippery and led directly to the hollow, now filled edge to edge with massive, muddy gray backs.

There was no help for it but to climb down the bank carefully without disturbing the animals, edge past them somehow, and get up the far side. The bushes were too full of thorns to hang onto so I unloaded Kamala's gun and had her hold firmly onto it while I lowered myself down. I looked around quickly as I did, but found the animals still lying down, only now with their eyes fastened suspiciously on me. They'd stopped chewing.

Reassured, I signaled to Kamala to brace herself against the end of the gun, which I now held, and climb down the bank. She took one step and her feet shot out from under her as if she'd stepped on a roller skate. She let out a startled yelp as she hit the ground with her butt.

I heard loud, squelching sounds behind me. A quick glance was enough to tell me that the whole herd was on its feet and, some of them at least, were looking distinctly peeved. We were so close, I could have reached out and touched the nearest animal, and they me! I grabbed Kamala by the hand, yanked her unceremoniously to her feet, and ran, dragging her behind me.

The sticky mix of mud and sand in the streambed was like treacle and after ten yards I was done. But one glance over my shoulder was enough to reassure me. The buffalo had not moved, except to turn their heads and stare after us. Kamala was glowering at me, furious at the indignity of her fall, treating it as though the fault was all mine. It didn't improve the situation when I saw the back of her dress, now covered with a circular patch of mud, and started laughing.

It did look pretty funny, as though she'd accidentally sat on a chocolate cake. For some unfathomable female reason, she refused to see the humour of it, even after I pointed it out!

There was no game track on the far side of the stream, so we had to walk downstream for some distance before I saw a break in the undergrowth wide enough for us to crawl out of the streambed. Kamala ignored my outstretched hand and pulled herself up with grim determination. She wouldn't walk in front of me either, pointedly waiting for me to go ahead.

The silent treatment came into operation.

The bush gave way to more open country as we

moved away from the stream. Dense thickets of thorn bush, groves of trees together and open glades spread with coarse grass. There was no game track to follow at first so I kept the sun, now rising over the trees, over my left shoulder and we were able to make steady progress. I came upon a faint track running through a copse of short trees. I decided to follow it even though it was taking us to the southeast.

I stopped to take a leak.

I'd normally warn Kamala in time. She would move away and pretend to look at birds till I was done. Since we didn't appear to be on talking terms, I just stopped, stepped away from the path and leaned the gun against a tree. When I fiddled pointedly with my zipper, Kamala walked past me and stopped on the other side of the footpath.

I'd just got started when I heard her running lightly towards me. Before I could turn my head around, she'd put one hand behind my neck and the other in the small of my back and pushed me forward violently, towards the bushes. Caught completely by surprise, I staggered a few steps, then stumbled and fell on my face. Kamala threw herself to the ground beside me and lay on her side, looking over her shoulder at the footpath.

I knew it was an emergency and stayed very still, and very quiet. We were well short of the bushes but, providentially, the grass was thigh high at that point. I could see the area around the footpath when I turned my head. Whether we could be seen from the footpath, only time would tell.

Voices first, speaking in Sinhala, then men in jungle

fatigues, armed with automatic rifles. I counted them as they filed past me, a five-man patrol headed by a corporal. I had left my gun leaning against a tree. If they saw that, or had a glimpse of us sprawled in the grass, they were likely to panic and start shooting.

Fortunately it seemed to be a routine patrol, and routine showed in their conduct. They were chatting desultorily, obviously bored. They filed past without a glance in our direction or at the gun. I fervently hoped they'd run into the poachers and shoot each other to pieces.

I waited for a couple of minutes and then stood up, as did Kamala. I had to turn away quickly and yank the zipper of my pants up to make myself decent. I felt the fabric sticking wetly to my legs. It was only when I looked down that I realized, with utter dismay, I had urine all over my pants and shoes!

'We've had an accident, have we, Captain?' Kamala asked innocently.

Her ill humour had vanished and her eyes were dancing. Anyone would think she'd won a lottery.

'Shut up,' I growled. 'You were the cause of it.'

'You can't blame me if the army doesn't toilet train its officers.'

She was having another one of her giggling fits, annoying the living shit out of me.

'SHUT UP!'

I picked up my gun and marched away, pulling at the wet pants that were sticking uncomfortably to my legs. You could say I was pissed off.

We passed through the grove of trees and came into park country again. I immediately set a course to the right figuring that, if the patrol came from the main army camp, we were a lot closer to it than I wanted to be. The sun was hot on our backs, winding itself up for another scorching day, and we had little cover.

We had to ford another small stream with a trickle of muddy water. Thankfully there were no buffalo this time but it was impossible to cross the sandy stretches without leaving our footprints.

Kamala said, 'We can collect some palmyrah nuts to eat'.

I saw a small copse of palmyrah trees on the side of the track. Palmyrah palms have tall, straight trunks much like the coconut. They are much easier to climb because the stubs of dead branches remain attached to the trunk and make convenient footholds.

'I didn't know you could eat them,' I spoke to her only because we were discussing food. 'There are plenty of fallen nuts around.'

'The immature nuts have a soft pulp ... like young coconut,' she said serenely. 'But you need to watch out for centipedes when you put your hand in the crown of the tree.'

She dropped the gun and kathi on the ground and nimbly climbed up the first tree.

'I thought you said you couldn't climb trees,' I reminded her sourly.

'These are Tamil trees,' she answered gaily.

She was still in high spirits.

I climbed up the next tree and had a close look at the palmyrah fruit, fibrous nuts like miniature coconuts, about the size of my fist. It was not difficult to select the young nuts by their lighter, greener colour. I had seen the giant centipedes that often infest the crowns of coconut palms. Nut-brown creatures as thick as my thumb! They have a venomous bite, the pain of which has to be experienced to be believed. I had once been bitten by one of its smaller cousins that had crawled on to my mat at home. I can still recall the agony that took almost a full day to abate.

I looked very carefully before I inserted my hand anywhere. I then hacked at the bunch till it came free and dropped to the ground. Green nuts were scarce. We collected an even dozen and stuffed them in our bags. Hungry though we were, I did not want to stop and eat. We would lose too much time.

We got near the river eventually. The trees became lush and green once again and the undergrowth turned into dense thickets. I scouted around till I found a clear game track through the tangled cover and followed it to the river. We stepped over the exposed roots of an enormous palu tree and there it was before us, a brown expanse of slow moving water. We had reached the Kala Oya. Some egrets and a painted stork, which had been stalking along the shallows, took off in alarm at our approach.

The Kala Oya is one of the perennial rivers on the western seaboard. The river commences near Kekirawa in the interior, first falls into the Rajangana reservoir, then continues westwards to form the southern boundary of the Wilpattu National Park. It falls into the sea at Dutch Bay near the mouth of the Puttalam lagoon.

'I think this must also be a ford,' I observed. 'That looks like a footpath on the other side.'

'Are you planning to camp on that side?' Kamala asked.

'No,' I said, having thought out the pros and cons. 'I want to stay on this side, downriver from here.'

'Shall we look for a site now?' She looked drawn and tired, beads of perspiration covering her forehead.

'No. I want to swim across and leave some tracks on the far side, just as a precaution.'

She thought about it for a while.

'Do you want me to come as well?' she asked with a marked lack of enthusiasm.

'No,' I said. 'I can handle it.'

I walked into the water with her, leaving clear footprints in the mud as we did so. Once in the water I turned upstream and waded till we reached the shelter of a tree that was leaning over the water at an acute angle, its branches offering some cover. I emptied my pockets into the rucksack and concealed it on the bank, along with my gun.

'Can you handle a shotgun?' I asked her.

'Yes.'

Affirmative. No qualifications.

'Stay behind the tree and cover the track. If they come, you'll have to wait till they're bunched up. Aim for the man with the assault rifle first.'

She just nodded and held out her hand for the extra cartridges. She inserted them between the fingers of her left hand, brass cover uppermost, ready as one could be for quick reloading. Holding the cartridges firmly, she lifted the stock of the gun with the palm of her left hand and rested it on the bole of the tree.

She knew how to handle a gun all right. I'd forgotten who she was!

'Let me have your slippers,' I told her.

I stuffed them in my pockets and waded slowly into

the river.

'You'll remember to give those pants a good scrub, won't you, Captain?' she called after me.

'Shut up.'

The tide was up because the river was high, but still flowing sluggishly towards the sea. The water rose gradually up to my waist and further till finally I was forced to swim. I aimed well upstream and allowed the current to bring me gently to my exit point, a small segment of muddy ground carved into the high bank. A steep path ran up the bank from there and disappeared into the bushes.

I waded gingerly out of the water, leaving a set of footprints in the mud. I pulled out Kamala's slippers and, bending over, pressed them as realistically as I could, into the mud. I repeated this at every step until I came to hard ground. I climbed the bank, walked a few yards then moved off the track stepping, as far as possible, on hard ground and tufts of grass. I circled back to the edge of the river.

I had seen an uprooted tree with its trunk on the bank and branches leaning over, and resting in, the river. I found it but had a hard time crawling through its tangled root mass, now spread out like a fishnet, to reach the trunk. I dived clumsily off the trunk and, once again aimed well upriver to allow the current to carry me to my target. What I had done was not very professional, and it wouldn't fool a competent tracker for long. It just gave us a slight edge and it had not taken too much time.

By now I was starting to get jumpy. If those men had really pushed it, and been lucky, they might be very close. The very last thing I wanted was to be caught in midstream when they turned up.

Kamala was waiting patiently under cover of her tree when I got there. I gave her slippers back and slung my bag over my dripping T-shirt. We had to cross the footpath to get downriver and that was when we'd be most exposed.

'We'd better be careful,' I said. 'I'll cover you while you cross over. Get to that clump of bamboos and cover me.'

She nodded, put away all but one of the extra cartridges, slung her bag over her shoulders and moved out. I stayed behind the tree and covered her but she crossed without any problem, as did I, when it was my turn.

Kamala led the way but wading along the edge was hard work. The bed of the river was uneven, muddy and rocky in turn and given to unexpected deep holes. The trees along the bank leaned over the river, some with branches almost brushing the water, forcing us to duck and creep.

The river curved gently to the right and at the bend, we came to a rock that formed part of the bank and sloped into the river, blocking our path. It seemed a good spot to leave the river because the sun, now like a blowtorch on our backs, would soon dry any footprints we would leave on it.

She didn't need coaching. She sat herself on the edge of the rock and first swished her feet around in the water to prevent mud or sand being carried on to the rock. I did the same thing. We climbed up and walked along the rock to find some hard ground to step on to. The rock was surrounded, on the landside, by trees and scrub but we found space to squeeze through by the bole of another kumbuk tree. We could not avoid leaving tracks on the sandy soil beyond it. If they tracked us this far we'd be in a bit of trouble.

It was nearly noon and I was knackered. Kamala looked worn out as well but she didn't say a word, just looked at me calmly for instructions.

'We must find a place to camp first,' I said, 'we can rest once we are under cover.'

'What are we looking for?'

'An open space, well screened by trees and bushes, but not too far from the water.' I tried to sound confident. We just had to keep looking till we found something suitable.

Fortunately the trees and undergrowth thinned out as we came away from the river. We must have moved about fifty paces from the bank when we saw a useful landmark, a tall trunk of a dead tree that may have been hit by lightning. It stood, like a sentinel, at the edge of an open glade covered with knee high grass.

'Why don't we split up and look for a spot?' Kamala asked. 'It'll double our chances.'

'Yes, maybe that's the best way.' I should have thought of it myself. 'Keep your bag here and use this tree as a landmark. Let's search a semicircle about hundred yards from this tree. Keep the tree in sight.'

She dropped her bag at the base of the tree and turned to go.

'Kamala,' I called after her. She stopped and turned. 'When you get back, stay by the tree. Don't come looking for me.'

She nodded and took off, moving downriver, towards the sea. I turned the other way and began to work my way through the trees. It was difficult to move in a straight line in the densely wooded forest but I counted out hundred good paces and then turned back, trying to cover the area in a wide zigzag.

It was hopeless. There were small glades, but they were too open for safety. The areas screened by bushes were completely overgrown and would take hours of work to clear. I tried to cover a wider area and nearly got lost. I had to climb a small tree to locate our landmark and find my way back. I returned to the dead tree tired and dispirited.

Kamala was seated near the tree, waiting patiently. She must have guessed, from my expression, that I had not had much success.

'I think I've found a place, Captain,' she announced calmly. 'You'd better have a look.'

She stood up and collected her gear. I was glad to pick my stuff up and follow her. We crossed the open glade, walking with our heads down to avoid stepping on piles of elephant and buffalo dung strewn around.

She led the way till we came to a dense thicket of screw pine and thorn bushes. On the far side of the thicket were some stunted trees with thick leathery leaves growing close together. It did not look at all promising from where I stood. Kamala squeezed through an unlikely gap between the trees without looking back. I got through with some difficulty and found myself in a small clearing, almost completely surrounded by scrubby thorn bushes and screw pine. It was well concealed and secure although I would have liked a little more shade. It would do.

It would do very well.

I quickly set up camp, rigging the tarp in the partial shade of one of the trees leaning into the clearing. I was desperately weary now, and very hungry. We had no food left except for the palmyrah fruit we had collected. I only wanted to eat something and then get some sleep.

'I need to bathe,' Kamala said quietly. 'I'm going down to the river.'

I should have known.

It was an unnecessary risk but I was too tired to argue. The river was some distance away and I couldn't let her go alone.

'I'll come with you.'

'There's no need, Captain,' she said coldly. 'I can manage on my own.'

'No.'

'I'll take the gun, Captain,' she insisted, 'and I'll be careful.'

'No,' I said equally firmly. 'It's too risky. We'll both go.'

She scowled and gave in with bad grace.

We collected the last sliver of soap and our change of clothes and went back to the river. Our faithful paint bucket had a hole in it, so we took our cooking pan along to fetch fresh water for the camp. We climbed onto the rock once again and slipped into the water downstream of it, away from the footpath. Once in the water, I was glad I had made the effort for the water was cold and refreshing. I sat on a submerged ledge in the rock and splashed water over my face and body. I felt a sharp sting as the water touched the cut on the side of my neck. Luckily it seemed only a superficial gash and hadn't given me much trouble.

Kamala waded downriver, around the bend, to bathe in privacy. The tide was still coming in so the water level was high and the current very slow and sluggish. The sun shone fiercely on the water but the bank of the river, and the rock I was seated on, was covered by the shadow of the kumbuk tree.

I was wondering what to do about drinking water. Our bottles were empty but we dared not light a fire till nightfall. The river water was brown with turbidity and didn't look at all inviting. I slipped off the rock and collected some loose sand from the bank. I put it in the pan and washed it several times till all the clay and mud was rinsed away. I then drained it, leaving the sand at the bottom of the pan, and refilled it with fresh river water.

Kamala came round the bend looking fresh and perky. Bathing always lifted her spirits. As I looked up I saw her eyes widen in alarm. She immediately crouched in the water, signalling urgently to me to get my head down. I slipped into the water, bending over and turning around as I did.

Three men were standing at the edge of the river, staring at the far bank. They appeared to be young men, all unshaven. One man, the tallest of the three, carried a T 56 assault rifle on a sling. He had to be the nameless leader we'd seen yesterday. The other two also carried firearms, shotguns of some sort. Even at a distance I could tell they were a hard, dangerous bunch.

Although I had taken all the precautions I could think of, in the back of my mind they were just that, precautions. I hadn't really expected the bastards to follow through. It didn't make sense! Three of their gang were dead, or badly injured, and they'd know we had at least two guns. They must also have realized by now that we were professionals. Logically, they should have decided to cut their losses and let it go. Yet here they were, hot on our trail.

They were about a hundred yards upriver from us, yet clearly visible as they stood in the sunlight. After some discussion, one of the men took his shirt off, gave his gun to one of the others, and waded into the water. He walked till the water came to his chest and then swam, as I had done, till he came to the landing by the footpath. We saw him walk carefully across the patch of sand and mud and study the ground for a while. He then turned and signalled to the others, pointing to the path going into the bush. I thought, hoped really, he was indicating that we had gone up the path.

'*Thiyala wareng,*' the tall man called out from this bank.

Leave it and come back.

I felt an enormous sense of relief. If he was a good tracker, and I had every reason to believe he was, he would have suspected something if he had followed our tracks further into the shrubbery. That would have turned their attention again to this bank, where we had gone to ground. But he didn't climb the bank, so he had no way of knowing!

The man turned around and swam back, using a clumsy breaststroke.

'Why didn't he go up the bank?' Kamala whispered. 'Why didn't they all cross the river?'

'They know we had a head start of about an hour and a half. That is enough for us to reach the village.'

'Yes, I suppose so,' Kamala said doubtfully.

'There's something else I should have thought of before,' I said slowly. 'There is a big army camp across the main track a couple of miles downstream, yet this footpath clearly bypasses it.'

'You mean there has to be a guard post somewhere?'

'Ye .. s,' I said. 'If these bastards are deserters, that might be another reason for their reluctance to cross the river.'

The swimmer was back, wading across the shallows, his hair plastered to his head and dripping water. The men clustered round and spoke animatedly for a minute. The tall man with the automatic weapon looked carefully, first down and then up the river, before turning and gesturing to the others.

They shouldered their weapons and walked back into the forest.

Kamala looked at me. Every indication was that they had finally given it up. It made sense, for they had injured men to look after and we had obviously escaped from their domain. But they were a tricky, tenacious bunch, so we'd have to remain on our guard.

We collected our stuff and moved away cautiously. We got back to the camp, trying hard to avoid leaving any tracks. It wasn't always possible. If they got this far, then they'd see some sign.

We had to sort out the water problem.

'It's too risky to light a fire,' I told Kamala. 'We'll have to manage with river water.'

Kamala just nodded.

I picked a large leaf from a bush, washed it thoroughly and made a crude funnel out of it. Then I took a bit of rag from Kamala's rucksack, placed it in the funnel and packed it with a handful of washed river sand from the pan.

Kamala held the bottles patiently while I tilted the pan to pour water through my makeshift filter. The water collecting in the bottle was still slightly turbid but that was the best we could do for the moment.

I drank some water and cut open a palmyrah nut. When I sliced off the top I could see three compartments containing a soft white kernel. Kamala cut two twigs and shaped them like ice cream scoops to help scrape the kernel out. It had a sweet, milky taste, much like the meat of a young coconut. The first lot were delicious, the second, palatable. By the time I cut open the last nut I was getting sick of it.

But I was still very hungry.

I drank some more water and stretched out on the ground sheet we had spread under another small tree at the edge of the clearing. I was desperately tired, my body weary beyond measure and my eyes filled with grit. But I couldn't drop off. Time and again I felt myself drifting away, on the verge of sleep. Each time the thought of those men stealing up on me, and taking me unawares, brought me awake with a jolt.

After the damage I'd inflicted on them, they'd show me no mercy.

'Get some rest, Captain,' Kamala said softly. 'I'll keep watch.'

She'd been watching me and, by some instinct, seemed to guess my problem.

She was seated cross-legged, at the far end of the sheet, leaning against a tree. The shotgun was across her lap with the cartridges, arranged neatly in a row, by her right hand.

'You need rest as well.'

'I got some sleep last night,' she said gravely. 'I can manage now.'

She did too, looking fresh and alert.

'You can let go, Captain,' she went on, smiling as she said it. 'I'll stay alert.'

'I don't like it when people read my mind.'

Her smile broadened, taking what I'd said as a compliment. Perhaps it was.

I drifted off to sleep soon after that.

24

I woke up in a bath of sweat, still dazed and groggy. Kamala was seated in the same place, holding her pose like a stone sculpture. Perspiration covered her forehead and some strands of hair were plastered across her face. She smiled when she realized I was awake.

The sun was still blazing down on the clearing but was now touching the tops of the stunted trees on the edge of it. I drank some water and splashed more of it on my face to clear the cobwebs in my head. I realized I was very hungry.

We had to find food.

I lay back and considered my options. I could find my way down to the sea and try to look for crabs or turtle eggs. That meant working in the open and revealing myself to any fishermen or soldiers who might be about. I could try for fish in the river but that was pretty uncertain. I looked towards Kamala and found her watching me.

'I think a recce is in order,' I announced. 'We need to find a safe way through the security posts for tomorrow morning.'

'Do you mean, cross the river and go into the village?' Kamala asked.

'Yes.'

Kamala was smiling.

'You want to buy food, don't you?' she asked gently.

'I've told you before,' I said peevishly. 'I hate it when you read my mind.'

'I'm getting to know you now, Captain,' she went on smiling disarmingly. 'So that can't be helped!'

'This army marches on its stomach.'

'I can vouch for that, Captain.'

Then she was serious.

'There is a problem, though,' she said. 'I can't swim.'

I looked at her in some surprise. She'd been so competent in everything else I had assumed she could swim as well.

'I could go down alone but you'll have to cross tomorrow morning anyway,' I said. 'We might as well work out the best way to get across safely.'

'All right.' She was a good soldier. 'Do you want to wait till after dark?'

I thought about it.

'I want enough light to spot the security post, but it must be dark when we get to the village,' I said, studying the angle of the sun. 'Let's leave in about an hour.'

'All right.'

There wasn't much I could do till then. I crept through the gap in the trees and had a careful look around, then circled the thicket that surrounded our campsite. I satisfied myself that no one could tunnel his way through that lot in a hurry. The only way in was through the trees and I had an idea I could close that off as well.

I came back stretched out on the ground sheet again, hands under my head.

'So what are you asking for?' I asked Kamala. 'What do you want in exchange for your … information?'

I wondered if she would freeze me off with one of her icy stares but, it seemed, times had changed.

'A new identity and passport,' she said without hesitation. 'A visa and a ticket to Canada and … safe custody till I leave.'

'Where will you go in Canada?'

'Vancouver Island,' she answered promptly.

That surprised me.

The LTTE never forgive a traitor. If she planned to hide from the long arm of the Tigers, she wouldn't want her own mother to know where she was. Unless she was lying, of course!

Somehow I didn't think she was.

'Do you have relatives there?' I asked.

'You know very well I won't be able to go near any relative,' she said, smiling gently. 'No. I have a friend who lives there that no one knows about.'

'A man?'

She had an infectious grin.

'No,' she said. 'No. A girl friend who married and settled there.'

'What about your boyfriend?' I asked, meaning to test her. 'Will you get him down as well?'

'You know very well they'll be waiting for that,' she said despondently. 'I can never see him again.'

We were quiet for a while. I started thinking about the next day.

'We must reach Colombo no later than tomorrow evening,' I said. 'We have used up all of our safety margin.'

'What do you plan to do?' she asked emotionlessly.

'We have to find transport to Puttalam, and we have to do it without creating too much of a disturbance,' I said. 'Let's check out the possibilities tonight.'

'And from Puttalam?'

'If we are not being chased by the cops, and we can buy some clean clothes, we can take a bus directly to Colombo.'

'God willing!' she murmured.

‘I thought you didn’t believe in God.’

‘I didn’t say that.’ Her voice had changed in a subtle way. ‘I said I was … disappointed in him.’

‘You can’t blame God for the viciousness of men.’

‘What do you know about it?’ she asked harshly. ‘You have no God.’

I knew I was treading on dangerous ground, but then, I fancied myself as a cool debater when there were no emotional issues involved. Emotionally sensitive to me, I mean.

‘Whether I believe in God or not is not the issue,’ I pointed out. ‘Your position is simply illogical.’

‘What do you mean?’

‘Just consider an example. Your people set off a massive bomb in the Pettah bus station. Dozens of people died and many hundreds were badly injured, left to live without arms, legs and eyes. That one bomb ruined the lives of hundreds of families, all of them innocents.’

I paused for a moment to gather my thoughts.

‘Should the affected persons blame God for the atrocity or blame the Tigers?’

She looked confused for a moment.

‘I take your point,’ she said finally. ‘But our people didn’t start this. The Sinhala attacked us first. We were reacting to atrocities committed on our people.’

‘Let’s take one issue at a time,’ I said firmly. ‘Would you agree that it is illogical to blame God, when clearly a group of people were responsible for the atrocity?’

She hesitated, then grudgingly:

‘I suppose so,’ she said. ‘But the Sinhala … ’

‘That brings me to my second point.’

‘What?’

‘Almost all such generalizations are wrong,’ I said. ‘Dangerously wrong sometimes.’

'What the hell are you talking about?'

'You say the Sinhala attacked your family,' I said as gently as I could, ' but it wasn't the Sinhala nation was it?'

'Who was it then?' she asked frostily.

'It was a gang of men who happened to be Sinhala.'

'What difference does it make if I said Sinhala gang rather than Sinhala nation?' she asked dismissively. 'And why is it dangerous?'

'It makes a great difference,' I said slowly. 'It has to do with confusing 'all' and 'some' in the minds of people. When you say the Sinhala are vicious murderers, you imply that ALL Sinhala are like that. Surely that's not true. So what you really mean is, SOME Sinhala are vicious murderers! Well SOME Tamils are vicious murderers too.'

'I still can't see what difference all this makes!'

'If I say that only some Tamils are criminals, I have no right or justification to attack all Tamils! I have to seek out the criminal element and punish them. In the same way, if only some Sinhala are the guilty ones, the Tamils cannot justify indiscriminate attacks on innocent civilians.'

'So when you burnt down a village in a reprisal attack you told me about that night at Murunkan, you were not observing your own principles?'

Trust her to dig that one up.

'No,' I admitted grudgingly. 'No. That was a criminal act. But remember, the Sinhala nation wasn't responsible for it, just me.'

'You are a strange man, Captain.'

'You called me a good man this morning,' I pointed out.

'Did I say that?' She feigned surprise. 'I'm sure you'd have misheard me. Strange describes you better.'

'Strange as in surprising?' I asked. 'Or strange as in peculiar?'

She laughed and said:

'Strange – peculiar is just perfect.'

It was baking hot in the clearing. I could feel the perspiration erupting all over, to form little rivulets and drip down the sides of my body. The shadows were lengthening but I judged it still too early for us to show up in the village. We might escape too much attention if it was dark enough but in broad daylight we'd raise a few eyebrows.

I heard a familiar 'tchik, tchik' call of a tailor-bird and saw a pair of them hopping about in the shrub above my feet. The noisy little buggers were easy to identify with their greenish bodies and brown caps and mostly by the incessant calls they used to keep in touch with each other.

'What will you do ... afterwards?' Kamala asked casually. 'Will you go home to visit your mother?

'Yes, I've been thinking of doing that,' I answered. 'If I can get a couple of days leave.'

'Will you go and visit your fiancée as well?'

'Uh ... I hadn't really thought about it,' I said. 'Maybe I will.'

'Is she a kind person?'

'What?'

'Is she ...'

'I heard you.'

'Well?'

'I don't ... know,' I said, taken aback by the question. 'I've only met her twice.'

'You should find out, Captain,' she said gravely. 'It is much more important than having a pretty face.'

'I suppose you are right, but how will I find out?' I asked, bemused by the direction of our conversation.

'You should see her more often, for a start. She'll be kind to you, of course, but that doesn't count,' she said seriously. 'See if she is kind to other people. That's a good indication.'

'Mm. I'll keep that in mind.'

'Do that, Captain.' She was smiling now. 'You won't regret it.'

After a few minutes of companionable silence I asked:

'Do you have any relatives in Colombo?'

'Only a distant cousin of my appa,' she said. 'I don't know them very well.'

'Do you want to contact them when we get there?'

'No,' she said abruptly.

'You mother. Won't she worry when you ... disappear?'

'No. She will not know,' she said mournfully. 'She suffered from fits of depression after my father passed away but it wasn't too serious. My brother Ram was the centre of her life. When he was killed she seemed to withdraw completely into herself. She doesn't speak to anyone. She spends all her time ... staring at the road.'

'Don't you have other relatives in Jaffna then?'

'No one close,' she said. 'My appa was an only child. There were three in my mother's family. We live in my aunt's house. My uncle lives in Germany, but has little contact with us.'

'You told me your uncle was killed by the army when they razed a village.'

'I lied, didn't I?' she said brazenly.

'Then?' I asked. 'Or now?'

'Let me see.' She pretended to think, smiling mischievously. 'Then, I'd say. Yes, definitely then.'

'I believed you then. I've half a mind to come over there and smack you one,' I said furiously.

'No. You won't,' she replied, smiling confidently. 'That Mr. Karl has civilized you too much.'

'Don't count on it,' I said sourly.

'What did he die of, Mr. Karl?' she asked after awhile.

'He'd been run over while crossing Galle Road,' I said. 'A bus knocked him down while he was on a pedestrian crossing. He died on the spot.'

'I'm sorry,' she said softly.

'I wanted to find the driver of the bus,' I told her, feeling once again the pain of my loss. 'The owner of the bus had already dismissed the man. He was being prosecuted but was out on bail. I finally traced him to a remote village in Akuressa.'

'You wanted to beat him up, did you?'

'I thought I'd break both his legs for a start.'

'Did you?'

'No.'

'What happened?'

'The man lived in a miserable mud hut with his wife and two small children. He had lost his job and the family was literally starving. He was facing the prospect of being sent to jail as well.'

'But he killed your friend.'

'Yes, I remember that. But while talking to him, I learnt something of the system. The bus owners demand a fixed sum from their employees every day. The driver and conductor only take home what remains of the day's collection, after paying the owner. If they drive carefully they make just about enough to pay off the owner. They have to really race the vehicle to fit in that one extra trip every day, so they'll have something to take home.'

'So you let it go?' Kamala asked.

'Yes.'

She looked at me quizzically for a moment.

'That's not all, is it, Captain?'

I didn't answer.

'You gave the man some money as well, didn't you?' she asked.

'Yes,' I admitted grudgingly.

She laughed and laughed till I started to get annoyed.

Shut up!

'I'll say it again, Captain, you are a strange man,' she said and then added, 'You should never have joined the army.'

'You talk a lot of crap, don't you?' I said roughly to cover my embarrassment. 'I like my job and I think I'm a good soldier.'

'You know very well I meant it as a compliment, Captain,' she said gently. 'Tell me, what would you have liked to do, if you hadn't joined the army?'

'Ahh. I don't really know,' I said. 'I haven't really thought about it.'

'You should have joined the Wild Life department. That would have been a better job for you,' she said seriously. 'Maybe it's not too late.'

'Why are you so keen to have me out of the army anyway?'

'I'll not tell you now.' She was smiling enigmatically. 'Maybe later.'

'And you?' I asked. 'What would you have liked to do?'

The smile vanished and she looked away.

After a long pause, she said: 'I would have liked to study further, go to Medical College maybe.'

'Dr. Kamala Velaithan,' I mocked her. 'Yeah. That has a nice ring to it.'

'In my next incarnation,' she said, smiling ruefully.

The shadows were getting longer and a slight breeze came in from the sea.

'It's time to go,' I announced, standing up and stretching.

'Must we do this?' Kamala asked.

I looked at her without speaking.

'Oh, yes,' she said with resignation. ' I forgot the army and its stomach.'

We would need dry clothes on the far side for what I had in mind. Our day clothes, stained and torn as they were, had been good enough for the forest. In the village, they would make us stand out like scarecrows. If our poacher friends had connections in the village, and had left word to watch out for us, we'd be spotted quite easily.

Kamala's skirt and blouse, the clothes she had on when she came to the checkpoint, had been used only for sleeping in. They were rumpled and untidy but clean enough and would have to do. My stolen pants were in a sad state, stained and ragged. I would have to use my sarong, ubiquitous in any rural community.

I collected a shopping bag we'd used for our provisions, and saved when the food ran out. I put our dry clothes and the T-shirt I was wearing in it, tying a secure knot at the top. I took a short bit of rope and, making a loop through the knot in the bag, slung it across my shoulder. I took one gun with a couple of cartridges.

We made our way past the glade to our landmark, the tall dead tree, and then down to the rock by the river. I was dismayed to find that, although the water was lower, the current was much stronger. The tide had turned. Kamala must have seen it too. She didn't make any comment but her expression was far from sunny.

'The tide's going out,' I said calmly. 'We'll have to wade upriver, well past the track, so we can allow the current to carry us across.'

We were crouched behind the rock, scanning the banks of the river. Had the poachers gone back to their camp? Or were they hiding patiently by the track for us to show ourselves?

'We'll be exposed when we are walking along the edge,' Kamala said. 'I'll go first. You could cover me.'

It made sense.

She climbed over the rock and slipped into the water. She walked slowly along the edge, staying in the open, while I crouched under cover of the rock. After she'd gone about twenty yards, she stopped and pretended she'd hurt her foot. While she stood on one foot, inspecting her heel, I crept up close to her, going along the very edge of the bank. Kamala took off again without a backward glance. If someone came out of the forest she would be directly in the line of fire. I knew, without having discussed it, that she'd throw herself down immediately so I could fire over her head.

We combine pretty well, don't we? Too bad we play for different teams!

She repeated the gambit once again and then she was at the point where the track emerged from the forest. This was it. Kamala stood still for a moment, facing the river and with her back to the forest.

Nothing happened.

Kamala made a leisurely turn, looked carefully up the track, and then waded past it, staying the shallows. I followed her soon after, going past the track cautiously, and found her waiting patiently by a dense clump of rattan, some thirty yards upstream of the tree we'd hidden behind earlier in the day.

I had to hide the gun where I could find it again in the dark. I pushed it into the base of the rattan and twisted a shoot over to mark the spot. I couldn't find a hiding place for the spare cartridge so I was forced to stuff it into the plastic bag with our dry clothes.

We were most vulnerable when we waded into the open. If they had been watching, and were real smart, this was their moment. Nothing happened. As that worry ebbed away, another took its place. The current seemed stronger now, swirling and foaming as it raced towards the sea.

I took my pants off and slung them across my shoulders. Kamala looked the other way, appearing to study the forest out the far bank. The shalwar kameez she wore was clearly unsuitable for swimming. I wanted to tell her that the sensible thing was to take it off, but that would only have earned me a venomous stare and another hour of attitude.

I signalled to Kamala to follow me and waded towards

the middle. She was clearly unhappy about the whole enterprise but followed me doggedly without a word of protest. The current tugged at us as the water got deeper and we struggled to hold our balance. I kept Kamala upstream of me, just in case. When the water came up to my waist I knew it was dangerous to wade further and we'd be better off swimming. We had to let the current do the work for us.

I stopped and tied two firm knots, one at the bottom of each pants leg. I then soaked the garment thoroughly, pulled the zip up and, holding the waist wide open, smacked it down on the surface. The air trapped inside the thick fabric made the two legs balloon out of the water.

I made Kamala turn around and face the bank we'd just left.

'You have to float on your back. Put your head as far back as possible and bring your legs up,' I told her. 'The pants will keep you afloat.'

I held the pants behind her shoulders and manoeuvred an inflated leg under each of her arms. The air-filled tubes came partly out of the water when she, with great reluctance, leaned back and allowed her head to touch the water.

Standing behind her, I placed my hands on either side of her head and slowly allowed the current to take hold. At first she struggled to lift her head up but I felt her relax when she realized she was floating easily. I used a kind of scissor kick to give us momentum and saw, with some satisfaction, the far shore receding slowly as we were swept downstream. My feet finally touched the ground and we were able to stand up. I found we had traveled a good distance beyond the fording point and now had to wade back to it.

Kamala struggled to her feet and turned around. She was smiling with a mixture of relief and exhilaration.

'Swimming is easy, isn't it?'

'You must try it on your own, on the way back,' I said dryly.

She just grinned.

'Let's climb out on to that dead tree,' I said, pointing to the log I had used to return to the river when I'd first got across. 'I don't want to leave any more footprints in the mud here.'

The log was slimy with moss and fungi, not quite as easy to climb on to, as it had been to jump off. We finally scrambled ashore and into the shelter of the scrub. Kamala took her dry clothes and went away to change. I stepped into my sarong and pulled the T-shirt over my head. When Kamala came back, I stuffed all our wet clothes into the bag and hid it carefully in a hollow under the log. I pushed the flashlight into the fold of the sarong around my waist and gave the money to Kamala.

It disappeared to wherever women, when they have no pockets to use, put things for safekeeping.

The sun had disappeared over the trees and the sky was a welter of orange and yellow streaks when we finally started down the track. We could only walk in single file so I told Kamala to walk ahead and spoke over her shoulder.

'The north road comes to a causeway about a mile, maybe two, upriver from here. As far as I remember, the road from Puttalam ends in one of our camps about two miles before the causeway.'

'This track, will it lead to the road and then to the camp?' Kamala asked. 'Or will it go round it?'

That thought had occurred to me as well.

'I simply don't know.' I was trying to work it out. 'The sunset will give us some directions for at least half an hour. If the footpath keeps roughly southwards, then it is probably heading for a village, bypassing the camp.'

'If they guard the main road with a big camp,' Kamala asked softly, 'they won't keep this footpath unguarded, will they?'

'No,' I said. 'There must be a security post overlooking this path, if it leads to the village, that is. It will also explain why those men didn't want to go up this track.'

'So?'

'It is likely to be a small post. Three or four men.' It was a guess but tried to keep my tone confident. 'Most likely they would have positioned it on the far side of a clearing, giving them a clear line of fire. We just need to watch for likely places.'

It was getting darker. The trees and scrub were thinning out as we moved away from the river, allowing the footpath to be relatively straight. The glow in the western sky was steadily on my right shoulder so we were still heading south, but it was getting hard to see the way forward in the deepening gloom.

We had a stroke of luck.

Cautious though we were when we came to a small clearing, we would probably have stumbled on them if the soldiers had stayed under cover. The post itself was hidden behind a pile of camouflaged sandbags, almost impossible to spot in the fading light. But the soldiers, three of them, were standing outside the bunker with their arms and backpacks. As we watched they began to walk away along another footpath to our left.

'It looks like they withdraw to the main camp at night,' I whispered.

I hated the thought that this information might one day be used against our troops, but then again, any terrorists operating in the area would know the pattern. If there is one quality that distinguishes our army, it is the predictability of its operations.

'Maybe they have just been relieved and the new lot are inside.'

Kamala was always the cautious one.

'I don't think that's likely,' I said. 'Let's get closer and check.'

'Why not just go round it, through the forest?'

Security posts were not popular with the residents of Jaffna.

'We have to come back this way later, and in the dark,' I reasoned. 'We could easily get lost trying to swing round it. If we make sure now, we can just stay on the path.'

It was dark under the trees now, so we had few problems in circling the clearing under cover, coming back to the track almost level with the bunker. The sandbags were higher where it faced the path we had come on. From where we stood, the post looked deserted, unless the soldiers were squatting inside. The door of the hut behind the bunker was shut.

I watched for a while and finally I tossed a small stone onto the corrugated tin roof of the shed. I missed with the first couple of throws. The third hit the roof but the noise was so insignificant, it would not have brought even an alert sentry out to investigate. I scrabbled around under the bush and picked up another stone, this one about the size of my clenched fist. Impatient now, I lobbed it over and it hit the roof with a huge crash, leaving a sizable dent in the middle of it. If there'd been a sentry there, and he hadn't died of a heart attack, he would have come out firing.

No reaction.

'My God, Captain. Are you trying to start a war?'

'I'm hungry,' I said. 'Let's go to the village and get some food.'

'Your stomach is serious business, isn't it, Captain?' she said. 'If they refuse to sell us food, I suppose you'll want to burn the village down?'

'No. I'll make a human sacrifice to propitiate the gods.'

'Well, don't look at me.'

I waited for a while and then stood up. It seemed safe to carry on and so it proved. The footpath soon fell onto a broader, deeply rutted, gravel track. I guessed that, when we turned to our left, this track would lead us to the main road. There was an abandoned shack with a partially collapsed roof across the road. I noted it as the landmark to help us find the footpath on our return.

We were soon walking past small houses, huts really, most of them set well back from the road. Two sarong clad men, talking softly, passed by without looking at us. Then came a woman carrying a small child, and balancing a bundle of sticks on her head.

'We have a choice about tomorrow,' I said as we strolled along. 'The easy way is to go to that camp in the morning and convince the Commanding Officer to provide us with transport to Colombo.'

'No.'

She kept her voice low but there was a note of finality in her tone.

'I will only give my information to the Head of Military Intelligence. I am not going to waste time trying to convince some low ranking field officer.'

She was probably right. Our story would have been improbable enough at Mannar, now it would strain the credulity of anyone. We had just one day to get to Colombo and going to the camp could easily cost us that day.

Two men on bicycles went past us. One of them had a huge bundle of fuel wood tied to his carrier rack.

Kamala waited till they were out of hearing and said firmly:

'So we find some transport to get us to Puttalam?'

'It's about twelve miles from here,' I explained again. 'There won't be many vehicles around here, but those who own them will have them parked near their houses. Let's try to spot some prospects.'

We walked in silence using the flashlight from time to time. We saw some figures coming towards us in the gloom. They turned out to be two women, their heads covered with the ends of their saris, accompanied by a little girl. Tamil speaking Moslem women, chatting loudly. They took no notice of us.

Kamala saw it first. When she stopped and pointed, I saw a white van parked in front of a small house. I tried to find some landmark to identify the spot and noticed a tall tree that looked like ironwood by the side of the road. We moved on and soon saw another prospect, a blue half-bodied truck, of the kind used for hauling bricks and building materials. It was parked beside what might have been a small warehouse. Later on we saw another white van parked in front of a small house.

We could see the junction where the gravel track fell on to a macadamized road. The army camp would be some distance along that road to our left. Opposite us, across the road, was a small boutique.

'Wait here,' I told her. 'I'll go and pick something up.'

'Captain, you haven't seen yourself lately,' Kamala said. 'You haven't shaved and that scar on your head is quite … prominent. Anyone looking at you will get suspicious.'

'What are you saying?'

She was standing close to me and speaking softly:

'I'll go.'

'How will you manage the language?' I asked, not convinced this was a good idea.

'I know enough Sinhala to pass for a Moslem.'

She sounded confident, so I didn't say anything.

'What do you want to eat?'

'Rice, if you can get it,' I said immediately.

We southerners love our plate of rice. Our motors are tuned on it from birth.

'If I can't get rice?'

'Bread, manioc, any damn thing that's edible,' I snarled impatiently.

I moved to the shelter of a tree by the side of the road watched her go. A covered van drove up and turned into the gravel track we had used. The headlights swept past me. If the occupants noticed anything unusual about me, they didn't stop to ask questions. Two men came along the main road, from the direction of the army camp and walked on, talking quietly.

She didn't take long. I saw her silhouette against the dim light spilling out of the boutique and she walked on to the road. She had a shopping bag in her hand.

Natural caution made me stay under cover, and it was well that I did. When she came close she didn't turn her head towards me but looked straight ahead. I could just see that her free hand held was awkwardly across her chest, open palm facing me with fingers pointed up. A stop signal, invisible from behind! She walked past me at a steady pace as I remained under cover.

I soon saw why.

A man came out of the boutique, stood there for a moment seeming to stare after her, then stalked across the road. When he came closer I saw he was a short man, sturdily built and wearing a sarong with a light coloured shirt outside it. He didn't see me behind the tree as he went past.

Shit.

This was the one complication I didn't want. If he was a villager just suspecting Kamala to be an infiltrator, he would either ignore it and mind his own business or run off to the army camp and let them handle it. He would not try to capture a Tiger cadre by himself; that would be suicidal. But he seemed to be following her. It made me suspect that he was connected to the poachers and knew what had happened last night.

I fell in about ten yards behind him, just able to see the blur of his white shirt ahead of me. I stayed on the verge to prevent, in case he turned around, my silhouette showing against the light behind me. I rapidly considered my options, not liking any of them.

There was no purpose in disabling him in order to

make our escape. He would raise the alarm and that would ruin any chance we had of coming through the village the next day. There was no practical way to keep him captive till we passed through, so that left me with only one option. I had to kill him and hide his body so it wouldn't be found for at least twenty four hours.

I thought we must now be close to the dilapidated hut that was our landmark. He was most likely to make his move when she turned off the road to enter the forest. I lengthened my stride and got closer. I could see some movement beyond him that must have been Kamala walking ahead. I was pretty confident that I could take him out if I could get close without alerting him. The best moment would be when he moved in to attack her.

He made a move all right, but not the one I had expected. He suddenly turned to the left and, stepping through a gap in a live fence, went towards a small house a few yards from the edge of the road. He walked into the pool of light spilling through the door and entered the house, shutting the door behind him.

False alarm!

I hurried after Kamala who was unaware of what had happened. I called softly when I got close and drew her into the deep shadow of some cashew trees by the side of the road.

She asked quietly: 'What happened to him?'

'He went into one of the houses,' I said. 'I don't think he is involved.'

'He stared very intently at me when I was in the shop. I thought he would follow me and … he did.'

I was immensely relieved.

'Maybe he was drunk,' I said lightly, 'and fancied you!'

I saw her teeth gleaming in the dark.

'Maybe he wasn't drunk.' Was all she said.

We came to the abandoned shack soon afterwards, unmistakable even in the faint moonlight. We turned into the forest track and found it much darker under the trees. I pulled the torch from my waist and switched it on. I had already pulled off the masking tape the hunters had used but the beam was still fairly dim. I led the way. We were just passing the security post when the light flickered, then came on again when I shook it.

Oh damn it. I've buggered this up!

In my anxiety to buy food, I had forgotten to get fresh batteries. If the flashlight gave out, it would be difficult to find our way back to camp. It also exposed us to another, and more serious, danger.

Our country has innumerable varieties of snakes but five species, including cobras, vipers and kraits, are really bad news. They are not really aggressive. However, being cold blooded, they have a tendency to lie in open spaces, like footpaths, that remain warmer in the early evening than the surrounding undergrowth. Not having ears, snakes pick up noise from faint vibrations in the ground. They would almost always move away if they pick up the signal of heavy footsteps approaching them.

Being barefoot posed a twofold problem for us. The vibrations from our footsteps would not be strong enough to drive the snakes away, not in time anyway. So there was a good chance we'd step on one of the bastards. Being barefoot also meant we had no protection against a bite.

For these very reasons, hundreds of our rural villagers suffer, and die, from snakebite every year. In combat boots I wouldn't have given snakes a second thought.

Kamala tapped me on my shoulder but I ignored her.

I remembered another chilling fact. A hungry snake had a full sac of venom ready for the day's business. One that has fed would probably have very much less to bless us with. Snakes come out to hunt for prey at dusk, just about now. Any poisonous snake I trod on at this time would be ready to whack me with a full dose.

The flashlight flickered again and went out. I shook it again but this time it didn't work.

Damn, damn, damn! We'd have to turn back.

Kamala said: 'I bought some batteries.'

I was not listening.

'I'm sorry. We will have to go ---' I said. 'What did you say?'

'I bought two batteries.'

I started laughing.

I would have hugged her if I thought she would stand for it. She didn't make a sound but she knew I was mightily pleased.

I loaded the new batteries and we started off again, moving much faster. We reached the river without further problems. The only snake I saw was a harmless olive green and yellow ratsnake, crossing the path in a flash, like a drop of mercury skidding across a plate.

The water was lower but the tide was beginning to come in now. We found our bag of clothes and Kamala disappeared into the bushes to change again into her wet kameez. I just had to step out of my sarong. I took time to tie a good, firm knot on the bag of provisions. I put it into our bag of dry clothes and tied another knot.

We were able to wade much closer to the centre of the river and I had to swim only a short distance. This time I made Kamala hold the bag, with its knot above water, while I ferried her across once again with the help of my inflated pants. The current was sluggish but, even then, swept us downstream of the footpath. I made Kamala wait and splashed my way upstream to collect the gun. I found it without difficulty and we waded slowly towards the rock marking our exit.

'I'm going to bathe,' Kamala announced. 'You'd better go on to the camp. I'll find my way.'

'I'll stay,' I said reasonably, sitting on the rock. 'We'll both need the flashlight to get back.'

'No,' she said stubbornly. 'Take the flashlight and go on. I can manage.'

'Listen carefully. You have survived for seven days without getting a good thumping from me, and it isn't as if I haven't been provoked,' I said in my most reasonable tone of voice. 'Do you really want to spoil your record on the last day?'

'Did you bully the other children, when you were in school?' she asked acidly. 'Just because you were stronger?'

'Only the stubborn idiots.'

She stood still for a while. I had the notion she was undecided whether to laugh or get mad. In the end she punched me on the shoulder with her clenched fist and turned away with her bag of clothes.

She waded along the shallows till she disappeared round the bend in the river.

25

I stepped into my sarong, sat quietly on the rock and listened to the gurgling of the rising tide. I saw some small bats flitting across the water as they hawked for insect prey. These micro bats use an incredibly sophisticated radar system to locate and capture small insects on the wing. Their radar is better than anything the military has, and the bats had it millions of years earlier.

Kamala came back and pulled herself on to the rock.

'Are you asleep, Captain?'

'I'm too hungry to sleep,' I said grumpily. 'Let's go.'

We stuffed all the wet clothes into one shopping bag. Kamala carried that and the provisions while I shouldered the gun and carried the flashlight in my left hand.

'What did you get for food?' I asked.

I suddenly felt good.

We had coped with all the deadly threats of the last twenty four hours with a mixture of action, guile and luck. We now had a safe campsite just ahead. The prospect of a filling meal and a good night's rest made me feel immensely content.

'They didn't have much. I bought bread and a tin of mackerel,' Kamala said apologetically. 'And a few onions and green chillies to mix it with. Is that ok?'

'That's fine.'

It was.

Most of my mates in the army hated canned mackerel. They were forced to eat it so often. I rather liked it, though. When I was young, my mother often prepared a curry of the stuff for some special occasion, like when my aunts came to visit. It was all she could afford. Now tinned fish made me think of festivities and the small gifts visitors always brought.

Even with the flashlight it was difficult to scramble through the scrub and the trees by the bank. I let Kamala go ahead at first and held the torch to her feet so she could see her way. That didn't work too well because the thorns kept catching at her dress and hair. It was easier as we left the river behind us and came near the grass field. We walked side by side so I could shine the light on the ground before us. I was still paranoid about snakes.

We made it up to the dead tree and stepped around it to the clearing beyond. I casually raised the flashlight to scan the clearing and nearly died of fright. The beam of light fell on the enormous rear end of a feeding elephant so close I could almost have reached out and stuffed the flashlight up its butt.

I can be very, very quick when I'm frightened.

I dropped the gun and switched off the flashlight in an instant. I grabbed Kamala round the waist, lifting her off her feet, and flung myself behind the tree. The animal had already been alerted by the light or by some sound I had made, for even as I was moving, there was a sharp explosion of breath, half trumpet half whistle, and it started to swing around.

I could see its little marble eyes glinting in the moonlight. It seemed to be looking directly at us. The animal slowly raised its trunk, trying to scent what was in the deep shadow behind the tree. The tip of its trunk, waving from side to side, was not more than five feet from where we stood with the animal towering over us, blacking out the sky.

Our luck had finally run out.

I suddenly realized that I was standing behind Kamala, my arm around her waist, holding her firmly against me. That realization, and the imminent threat, made me giddy. My chest began to pound so hard it hurt, but I couldn't get enough air into my lungs. When you know you are going to die, there is a sense of liberation, of not caring about mundane consequences any more.

I leaned over, moving my head with infinite slowness, and kissed the edge of her ear.

She reacted as if she had been electrocuted. I felt a tremor pass through her body. She didn't make a sound or move at all but with her one free hand she tried, with surprising strength, to remove my arm. She didn't have the leverage to move it but kept trying in silent fury, her fingernails digging painfully into my forearm.

Her hair was still wet from the river. I felt the damp against my face as I leaned over her shoulder and tried, as gently as I could, to touch her cheek with mine. When I kissed her cheek, a featherlike peck really, she turned her face away immediately, still pulling at my hand. That exposed her neck, which was even better.

I now think it was only the wind, blowing steadily inland from the sea, that saved us that night. The elephant couldn't scent us because we were downwind and its eyes were too weak to see us in the inky black shadow. The animal trumpeted suddenly and, a moment later, I heard it batter its way through the scrub to our right.

It is a true measure of my preoccupation that I didn't look up.

I had expected Kamala to struggle more violently once the threat of the elephant was removed. I was surprised, and mightily pleased, to find she didn't. She just stood there as I caressed her cheek. I dropped the flashlight to free my left hand and gently turned her around.

She offered no resistance when I kissed her eyes, the tip of her nose and finally her mouth. I'm sure I felt, for one ecstatic moment, her tongue touch mine. Then she pushed me away and stepped back.

'You must not do that,' she said hoarsely. 'Just don't.'

She had dropped the shopping bags and was bent over, hands across her chest, hugging herself. She wasn't angry, that much was clear. But she was in the grip of some strong emotion I didn't understand. I waited.

'I've lost my slippers,' she said in a small voice.

I found the flashlight by getting on my knees and feeling around gingerly in the grass. I checked the glade first, quickly recovering my gun and, after some scouting around, her slippers that had been flung off in the melee.

She turned and limped off, towards the camp. Utterly bemused, I had no choice but to pick up the rest of our gear and follow her. We reached the camp without further incident. We set about our evening routines as though nothing untoward had happened. I started a small fire with the deadwood I had collected before setting out. Kamala sat at the edge of the ground sheet slicing the onions and green peppers. I used the knife to smash open the tin of mackerel, almost destroying it in the process. I went back to the river, with some trepidation, to fetch more water.

Business as usual, except for the strained silence.

Kamala had the meal, such as it was, ready when I got back with the water. She served my plate, piling it high with mackerel salad and roughly sliced bread, and brought it over to me. Her eyes were shadowed so I couldn't read her expression. She served herself and sat at the other end of the ground sheet. We ate in silence.

Afterwards I set a pig trap.

I had seen, just outside our clearing, a small tree with a trunk that had divided into two branches close to the base. I cut it down just below the 'V' and then lopped the leaves and twigs off the top, leaving a giant catapult almost my height.

I inverted the 'V' and tied one arm to a tree on one side of the gap through which we had entered our clearing. I tied the knife to the end of the other arm and stretched it across the narrow passage to a tree on the other side. I set a trip rope, as I had been taught, that would release the arm of the catapult and the knife, with some considerable force.

If an intruder used a flashlight he would probably spot the trap. On the other hand, if he tried to creep up on us in the dark, and used the convenient gap in the trees, he was going to get a very nasty gash in his thigh or hip. I didn't really expect intruders because we had covered our tracks adequately and the camp itself was well hidden. It just gave me an added feeling of security.

And it gave me something to do.

By the time I had finished setting the trap Kamala had cleared up the food and washed up. I helped her to pull the ground sheet under our makeshift 'tent'. I made a pillow of my empty rucksack and stretched out in my usual place on the far side from the fire. She was sitting at the other edge, hugging her knees, staring at the fire. I could see her silhouette against the light of the fire. We hadn't spoken one word to each other.

'Will you come over here?' I asked.

My throat was dry and the words came out as a hoarse rasp.

She ignored me, sitting still as a statue.

I'd never been short of girls. As an undergraduate and especially later, as an army officer, I was considered pretty eligible on campus and in my village. Opportunities for casual sex were not common but gratefully accepted when they did come my way. The girls concerned had not meant anything to me, either before or after. Then I'd met Sriyani, and she had captivated my mind and filled my horizon.

Till now!

Some twist of fate had thrown me into the company of this strange, moody woman sitting on the far edge of the ground sheet. She was a trained militant and an enemy of my people. She had now chosen to betray her own leader. My job was to deliver her, and the information she was privy to, safely to my superiors in Colombo. Any involvement with her was an act of criminal folly that would have a disastrous impact on my career.

Yet I had killed one man, and grievously injured two others, because they had tried to molest her. I'd do it again too, gladly.

And I ached for her now!

She uncurled herself, crawled over to where I was and, without a word, lay down beside me. I could hear my heart thudding like a drum in a parade and each breath I took needed a separate effort of will. My instinct told me to be careful, as if I were gentling a wild doe. I knew it needed only one false move and she would be gone.

I turned towards her, careful still to avoid any physical contact.

I bent over and brushed my lips on her forehead. I then gently kissed her eyes, nose, ears and finally the edge of her mouth.

Kamala asked: 'Where did you learn to kiss like this?'

'Watching English movies on TV,' I blurted.

It was true enough.

She started giggling. It spoiled the whole mood but I think that was when the barriers between us finally came down.

'Captain, you disappoint me,' she said, still greatly amused. 'I thought I was in the hands of a practised lover.'

'Shut up.'

Still, I did my best to please her and her response was palpable.

I drowned in her.

As I lay on my side trying to get my breath back, Kamala sat up and tried to move away.

'Where are you going?'

'To my place,' she said calmly. 'Why, what's the problem?'

'Don't go,' I said urgently. 'Your place is … here.'

'I thought … afterwards, men needed their own space.'

Was there a tinge of bitterness in her voice?

'I don't know about other men,' I said evenly. 'I'd like you in my space.'

She sat still for a moment. Then, when I touched her shoulder, lay back with a sigh. She reached for her skirt, which I had flung away earlier, and tried to slip her feet into it.

'No. Leave it.'

'What do you mean, leave it?' She seemed slightly scandalized. 'Do you mean I have to stay like this all night?'

'Why not?' I asked. 'You can always cover yourself with it if you are cold.'

'But it's … it's indecent!'

I put my arm over her, and buried my face in the hollow of her neck, effectively ending the argument.

'Captain, do you realize you have violated all my human rights?' she said in resigned voice.

'What are you talking about?'

'I am under your protective custody. You have taken away my clothes. You have been, well, intimate with me and now you are depriving me of sleep.'

'But you are on my side of the tent,' I pointed out.

'Which side of the tent is that?' She had a nice laugh, a kind of gurgle. 'Do you really think any judge is going to believe that I consented to all this?'

'Well, if I am to be punished anyway, I might as well abuse your rights as much as possible.'

I ran my tongue along the side of her neck. She tasted slightly salty but nice. I began to lick her chest and shoulders.

'What the hell are you doing now?' Kamala demanded.

'Grooming,' I explained. 'All mammals do it. Haven't you seen this on Discovery Channel?'

'I am not a baboon to be groomed. All you are doing is rubbing spit all over me.' She was torn between amusement and disgust. ' Isn't there something else you've seen on TV that is more civilized?'

I had.

Plenty of things!

Much later she rested her head on my chest and I ran my fingers through her hair.

I asked gently: 'Does it still bother you that I am Sinhala?'

'Yes,' she said gravely. 'Yes, it does. In one part of my mind, I am appalled at what I have done.'

'And the other part?' I asked. 'I want to know what the other part thinks.'

'I am not going to tell you.'

'That means you liked it.'

'Shut up.'

Then she said seriously:

'You mustn't read more into it than … there is.'

'I won't,' I said, not quite sure what she meant.

'Tell me something, Captain,' Kamala asked lazily after a while. 'We've been so many nights in the forest, how was it you didn't come to … my side of the tent earlier?'

'If I had, would you have allowed me to stay?'

'No,' she said smugly. 'But I would have enjoyed chasing you off.'

'You really are a wicked woman,' I told her. 'Did you know that?'

'Of course,' she said with a chuckle. 'You'd better remember that for the future.'

I buried my face in her hair.

'I like the smell of you.'

'What smell is that?' She sounded pleased.

'Bar soap and Tamil girl.'

'Do you have a preference?'
'Well, the bar soap is pretty nice.'
She raked my chest with her fingernails.
'Actually the girl smell is quite nice too.'

I drifted off to sleep then, utterly content.

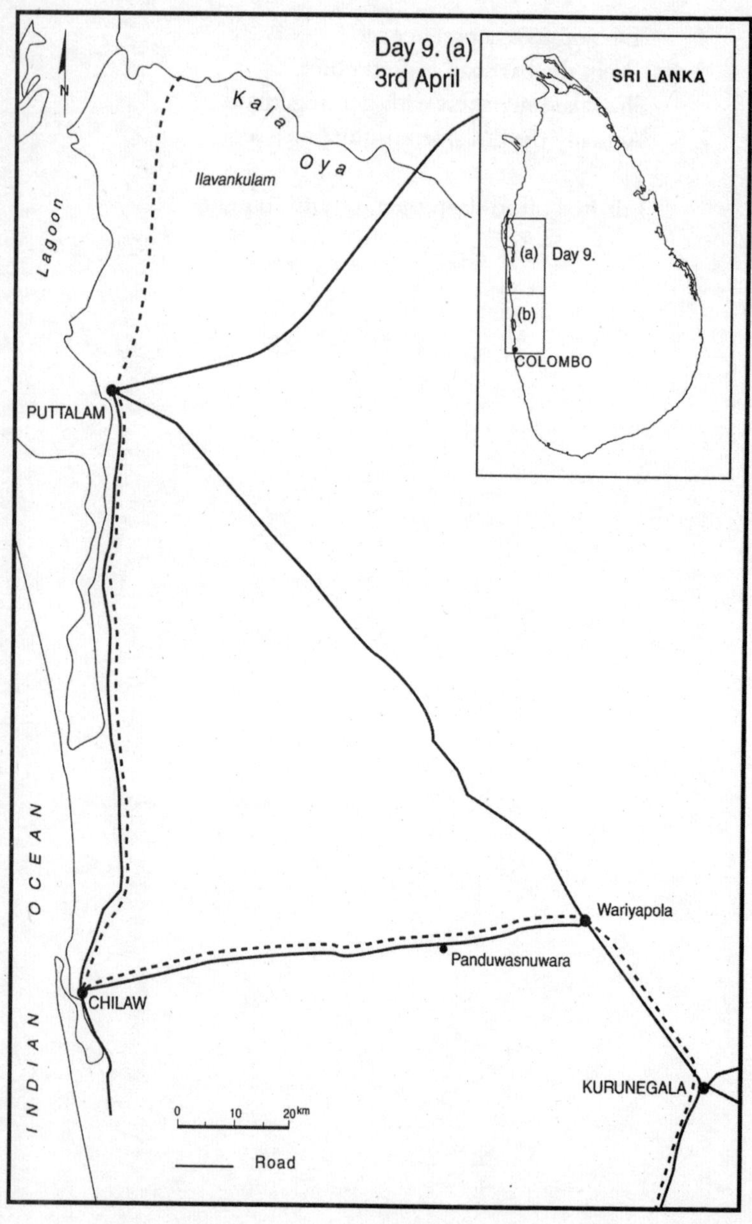

Day 9. (a)
3rd April
SRI LANKA
(a) Day 9.
(b)
COLOMBO
N
Kala Oya
Ilavankulam
Lagoon
PUTTALAM
INDIAN OCEAN
Wariyapola
Panduwasnuwara
CHILAW
KURUNEGALA
0 10 20km
Road

26

3rd April 2000

It was still dark when I woke up. I reached out for her and she wasn't there. I knew she must have gone down to the river.

The pig trap!

She had seen me set it up but, what with my preoccupation last night, I had forgotten to warn her properly. I was racked with anxiety as I scrambled out of the tent. It was too dark to see the trap and not the best idea to feel for it in the dark. I couldn't find the flashlight either but finally managed to dig out the matches in my bag. I felt a rush of relief when I saw that the trap had been sprung and the tip of the blade was safely embedded in the fixed arm of the catapult. Thankfully, there was no sign of blood.

I was still worried, and angry that she'd left without waking me. I hurried down to the river, cursing when I stumbled over roots and rocks in the dark.

Dawn was just breaking when I got there. I stood a while under cover of a tree, savouring a voyeuristic thrill in watching her bathe. She had modestly worn the shalvar top to bathe in and was kneeling in the shallows below the rock. She bent over and ducked her head again and again in the water, coming up only to catch her breath.

By some instinct she became aware of my presence. She turned and smiled at me briefly and continued with her ritual. The water looked too cold for bathing, so I used some of the charcoal she had brought to clean my teeth and then washed my face in the shallows. I sat on the edge of the rock with my feet in the water, waiting for her to finish.

She did, finally, wading towards the rock for her clothes.

'You will have to turn around while I change.'

'Come over here for a moment.'

'The arrangement was only for the night,' she said steadily. 'It's over now.'

She looked as if she meant it.

'You cheated me by sneaking off before dawn,' I told her. 'Come here.'

'Do you seduce all the Tamil women you arrest?'

'Not all,' I said. 'Only the really ugly ones.'

She was learning to laugh at my jokes, even the poor ones.

She stood in the water below me, her head level with my chest. Her hair was plastered to her head, dripping water. She looked very young at that moment. I placed my hands on either side of her head and felt her shiver. I looked down at her, as she stood between my knees, and felt a rush of unfamiliar tenderness.

And dread.

In the forest, despite all the dangers and threats we had faced, I felt I had control. I could, and did, protect her. Outside, I'd have to deal with the system, and I wasn't sure I could cope.

I said: 'Once we report to HQ, everything will be out of my hands.'

'So?' She was calm, unworried.

'They might refuse to believe you and treat you as a hostile captive. Even if they were to believe you, but somehow the operation went wrong, they will then assume you had set them up. In either case, they could be … brutal.'

'My information is solid,' she said. 'They will have to believe me.'

'I am not sure that is enough, Kamala,' I said gloomily. 'I am afraid for you.'

'What else can we do?' She was still calm and collected, looking up at me gravely. 'This is what I came for.'

At that moment I stepped over the edge.

'I could get you to Colombo and then let you go,' I said recklessly. 'I'll report that you were killed on the way.'

'What about the operation?'

'If you brief me, I could convey the details.'

She stared up at me for a while then looked down. She appeared to be turning it over in her mind.

'No, it will not work. They will never mount a major bombing raid unless they are convinced the information is really authentic,' she said finally. 'I will have to provide the details personally.'

'Forget the operation then. I will find a safe place for you in Colombo, and a passage to Canada.'

She moved closer and placed her hands on my shoulders.

'Wasu, you are a fine, resourceful soldier. No one else could have brought me safely through this forest. But there is a streak of goodness in your character and that makes you vulnerable in this game. I am afraid for you. Afraid it will get you killed or … ruined!'

She looked up into my eyes.

'That is why I wanted you to leave the army.'

'What are you going on about?' I asked in exasperation.

'This is not about me. It's about you, and your safety.'

'No. I am a professional. This is what I set out to do and I know the risks.' There was a note of finality in her voice. 'I must go through with it. That is not the problem. Really it isn't.'

'What, then?'

'I want you to handle the rest of the operation my way. Will you do this just to please me?' she asked earnestly. 'It really is important.'

'You'd better tell me what you want first.'

'Get me an interview with your Director of Intelligence,' she said earnestly. 'Then leave. Don't get involved.'

'No.'

'Listen to me,' she said very slowly, emphasizing each word. 'Forget last night. It – is – over. You are a soldier. You cannot afford any personal involvement with me.'

'No.'

'Don't be a fool, Wasu.' Her voice had an urgent appeal in it and I felt her fingers dig into the side of my neck. 'You must handle this like a professional. If you try to help me in any way, it will cause … complications.'

'No.'

There was enough light for me to see her eyes and the resigned, despairing expression in them. She bowed her head, resting her forehead on my chin.

'Who is the stubborn idiot now?' she asked in a small voice.

We stayed like that for a minute.

I said: 'It's time to go.'

We hurried back to camp and prepared to leave. I cut a rectangle of material from the ground sheet to wrap the gun in. I packed some twigs around the barrel to change its shape and tied the bundle with a bit of string. It was an odd looking package, but not obviously a gun.

We prepared for the river crossing as we had the previous night, carefully packing our dry clothes in a watertight shopping bag. I felt a pang of regret as I hid the plastic sheets, pans and kathi, together with the second gun, under some bushes. Our improvised equipment had served us well.

The anxieties of the day ahead kept us quiet.

The tide was coming in and the river was high. The current had slowed so swimming was easier although we had much further to go. Kamala, buoyed by my air filled pants and more confident now, had no difficulty in holding the gun and bag of clothes above water as I towed her across. On the far bank, Kamala disappeared into the shrubbery to change into her skirt and blouse and I, back to my sarong and threadbare T-shirt. Kamala still had her worn rubber slippers. I was barefoot.

Despite knowing that the sentry point was ahead, and watching for it, we nearly stumbled on it once again. The whole forest looked different in bright sunlight and the landmarks I had carefully noted in the night had changed in appearance. We couldn't see any soldiers but had to assume that the post would be manned by now.

I decided to circle the post by turning right, to the west. That way we would avoid the path to the main camp the soldiers going off duty had used the previous evening. But after just a few steps I began to have second thoughts.

Mines. Would they have mined the area to the west of the post? Surely not, with a village close by. What about trap guns or alarms?

'Let's turn back,' I whispered. 'I want to use the same route we used last evening.'

Kamala said quietly: 'We could run straight into the guards, if they happen to be late.'

'We have to take that risk.' I was adamant.

I'd rather handle any number of soldiers than risk stepping on a mine.

We crossed the path we'd left and made our way cautiously through the trees and shrubs on the other, eastern side of it. There was no way we could retrace the precise route we had followed last evening, but we tried. We came to the footpath the soldiers had used and crossed it safly. We then made a wide detour and regained the main path leaving the guard post behind us.

We reached the gravel road and turned on to it. There were people about, mostly children by themselves, or with adults, on their way to school. Kamala still looked faintly respectable but I must have been a curious sight with my dirty clothes, unshaven face and scarred scalp. Then there was the shapeless black bundle I carried on my shoulder.

Happily our villagers don't go out of their way to search for trouble. So, while we drew our share of curious looks, no one stopped or questioned us.

We came to the ironwood tree I had used as a marker for the first house with the van. The house was there, shuttered and closed, but no van. We were too late. Kamala just looked at me. I shrugged and moved on. The blue truck was next but, when we came to the spot, we saw two men carrying bags of cement out of the warehouse, loading it up. There may have been others inside. No chance there.

We couldn't remember where the next house with

a vehicle was, so we checked all of them. There were people about, sweeping gardens, coming and going. No vans. Then we were at the junction with the main road. I looked to my left and saw, not more than a quarter of a mile away, the barrier across the road. The army camp was closer than I had realized and I could see a bus parked on the side of the road, near the entrance to the camp.

'There must be buses or vans taking people towards the town,' she said. 'Why don't we just get on one of them?'

'There's a bus parked over there,' I said, pointing towards the camp. 'It will probably take off in a few minutes.'

'Do we get on it?'

I thought about that.

'There are checkpoints on the way,' I explained. 'The way we are dressed, they'd suspect us immediately.'

'So it's not just a vehicle, is it?' she asked quietly. 'We have to get into a house to get clothes as well.'

'Yes,' I said briefly, 'and money.'

We turned to the right, towards Puttalam and walked slowly down the road. A tractor roared past us hauling an empty trailer. Children of all ages, in school uniforms, stood waiting by the road. The bus must be due soon.

Kamala touched my arm. She was looking at a small house on our right. It was in a garden set well back from the road. A neat little building with whitewashed walls and a red tiled roof. Under a tiny porch covering the front door was a metallic blue motor bicycle leaning on its stand.

As I slowed down, wondering how best to approach it, the door opened and a woman stepped out calling out to someone behind her. She was a stout woman dressed in a sari with a shawl over her head. Behind her came two little girls dressed in neatly pressed white uniforms, their school bags slung over their shoulders. She ushered the girls out, fussing over them, and shut the door behind her.

We stood as though we too were waiting for the bus. We watched them come through the garden and cross the road towards us. The woman gave us a hard stare and then looked away.

Kamala nudged me again.

Two soldiers on bicycles, guns slung across their shoulders, were riding slowly towards us. I figured they were going back to the camp after a routine patrol. They were talking loudly to each other, and laughing at something, when one of them spotted us. In our tattered clothes we must have stood out like gypsies at a society wedding. The man on the right glanced behind, to check the road for other vehicles. I knew he was preparing to cross the road and question us.

How was I to explain the gun inside the bundle at my feet?

'Aiya, bus eka enava nette mokada?' Kamala called out loudly, in atrociously mispronounced Sinhala. *'Kedilada kiyala balanawada?'*

Brother, why isn't the bus coming? Can you check if it's broken down?

Village women would not, normally, have the effrontery to talk like that to soldiers, or ask them to run errands. The soldier was deeply offended. I expected him to react angrily but this was a Moslem village, and Kamala sounded like a Moslem woman, even if she was not dressed like one. And a sensible man doesn't get caught up in an incident involving a Moslem woman.

He hesitated but common sense won. He decided to drop it.

'*Pissu ganiyek*!' I heard him tell his companion, not bothering to keep his voice down.

Crazy woman!

Then they were past us, going on towards the camp.

I looked at Kamala and found her grinning smugly. She had taken a big chance and it had paid off.

'Your Sinhala is rotten,' I said softly.

'It's a useless language,' she answered cheekily. 'Not worth learning.'

I was getting worried that the owner of the motor bicycle would take off at any moment. I couldn't make any move till his wife got on the bus and the crowd thinned out. I wondered if she'd come out only to see the children safely on the bus. That would make our task more complicated. The minutes ticked away and then, to my relief, the bus parked near the camp came rattling up the road, stopping every fifty yards or so to pick up the clusters of school kids waiting by the road. I turned my back to it as it approached, so the driver ignored us and stopped a few yards further, to pick up the fat woman and her children. I knew the woman was looking suspiciously at us, wondering why we weren't boarding the bus.

We watched the bus start off, stop again further up the road and then disappear round the next bend.

The road was deserted after the bus left. I picked up the gun in its wrapping and we walked unhurriedly down the path to the house. When we were close to the front door I crouched behind some flowering bushes, making sure I could not be seen from the road, and ripped off the plastic wrapping. I loaded the gun with one of the two cartridges I had tucked in the waistband of my sarong.

I nodded to Kamala. We had not spoken, but I was sure she would know what to do.

'*Aiya, Aiya!*' She rapped sharply on the door, as she called out urgently. '*Bus eka häppila. Oyagey powlata thuwalai.*'

Brother. There has been an accident! Your wife is injured.

He came out in a rush, yanking the door open, his voice high with anxiety.

'*Mokakkada? Mokada wune?*'

What is it? What's happened?

I had the gun jammed in his belly, pushing him back into the house, before he could get his mouth shut. Kamala was right behind me and I heard the door slam. I pushed him against the wall and whispered in Sinhala:

'If you shout I will kill you.'

He was a scrawny, middle-aged man with thin arms, the makings of a potbelly and a bitter, bad tempered face. He was dressed in a neat, white shirt worn outside his blue checked sarong.

His eyes glittered venomously.

'Who else is in the house?' I spoke in Sinhala again, knowing that he would understand. He made no answer, simply continuing to stare at me, unafraid. He was a man of spirit!

I looked about.

The house was quite small. The room we had entered served as a sitting room with a small dining table at the far end. There was a loaf of bread and the remains of a meal on the table. He must have been eating his breakfast when we broke in. There were two rooms, with open doors, to my left. I gestured to the man to lead the way and, looking over his shoulder, quickly made sure they were empty before cautiously opening the door at the back. It led to an open veranda with a small kitchen at one end.

No servants.

There was a nylon cord slung across the veranda with household washing hanging up to dry. I looked at Kamala and again figured she knew what was needed. I hurried the old man to the bedroom and carried with me a stout armchair from his dining table. I'd just settled him in it when Kamala was there with a good length of the rope.

Our teamwork was getting really slick now!

We quickly tied him to the chair and then anchored the chair to the bed. I picked up a soiled serviette from the dining table and forced it into his mouth, tying a strip of cloth, torn from his bed-sheet, across his mouth to prevent him spitting it out. He never said a word. No threats and no struggle, yet his eyes were blazing. I would not have relished the prospect of being in his power, if by some twist of fate our roles were reversed.

We needed clothes and money. I searched the bedroom and dining room for his wallet. No luck.

I thought for a moment and finally unbuttoned his shirt. Sure enough, tucked into the waistband of his belted sarong was a fat leather wallet. One crisp thousand, three hundreds and some tens! I had hoped for a bit more to get us some decent clothes and bus fare to Colombo. He must surely have more money hidden away somewhere in the house, a man like him.

He looked a stubborn old bastard so he wouldn't tell if I

asked him nicely. I'd have to beat it out of him. I had already reached out to remove the gag when I realized I didn't have the stomach for it. And I didn't want Kamala to see me beat up a helpless old man.

We would manage with what we had!

I found his ID tucked into a little window in the wallet. Mohamed Sadiq was his name and his photograph, faded as it was with age and handling, still bore no resemblance to me. The first two numbers of his ID, 58, gave his year of birth. He was forty two, twelve years older than I was. I stuffed the money together with the few notes Kamala had left into the wallet and tucked it in my waist.

I found the keys to the motor bicycle on a table by the front door. I opened the front door and looked out. There were people on the road but no one seemed particularly interested in us. No sign of the woman yet.

Kamala said: 'I found a sarong for you. His shirts will be too small.'

'Did you find anything for yourself?' I thought a burqa would have been ideal.

'No. There are only saris,' she said. 'I found a shawl I can use.'

She held it up so I could see, a scarf with lace along the edges that Moslem women covered their heads with.

There was a basin, with a bucket of water beside it, in the rear varanda. I found soap and a much-used disposable razor on the table. I scraped away at my beard, nicking myself and suffering greatly before I was satisfied. A small mirror hanging from a nail near the basin gave me a more civilized appearance but for the scar on my scalp. I hurried to the bedroom and soon found what I needed. A circular cloth cap that Moslem men wear, especially when visiting the mosque for prayer.

It was perfect for covering my head wound. I'd need to buy a high collared shirt to cover the cut on my neck.

We were ready. I looked longingly at the bread and lentils on the table. Kamala smiled and shook her head. She was right, of course. I hid the gun in a pile of firewood behind the kitchen, then closed and locked the bedroom door. I threw the key into the bushes behind the house. I closed and locked the front door, throwing the key away as before. It was a mean thing to do but I hoped that it would buy us a little extra time while the woman fetched help to break the doors down.

Kamala had the shawl draped modestly over her head. The motorbike was a Honda 125 in good condition. It started at a touch and we were on our way. There were some pedestrians about but no one took any notice of us as we turned into the road.

I fervently hoped the fat woman had planned to do her marketing today or maybe talk to the teacher about her children. Anything, just so she'd delay enough for us to reach Puttalam and get rid of the bike.

'How many checkpoints before Puttalam?' Kamala had to lean forward to speak in my ear. She was resting her hands lightly on my shoulders.

'I can only remember one.'

I was trying to think back to the last time I had come up here. You tend not to notice these things when you are a uniformed officer.

'I'm pretty sure there's just one police barrier.'

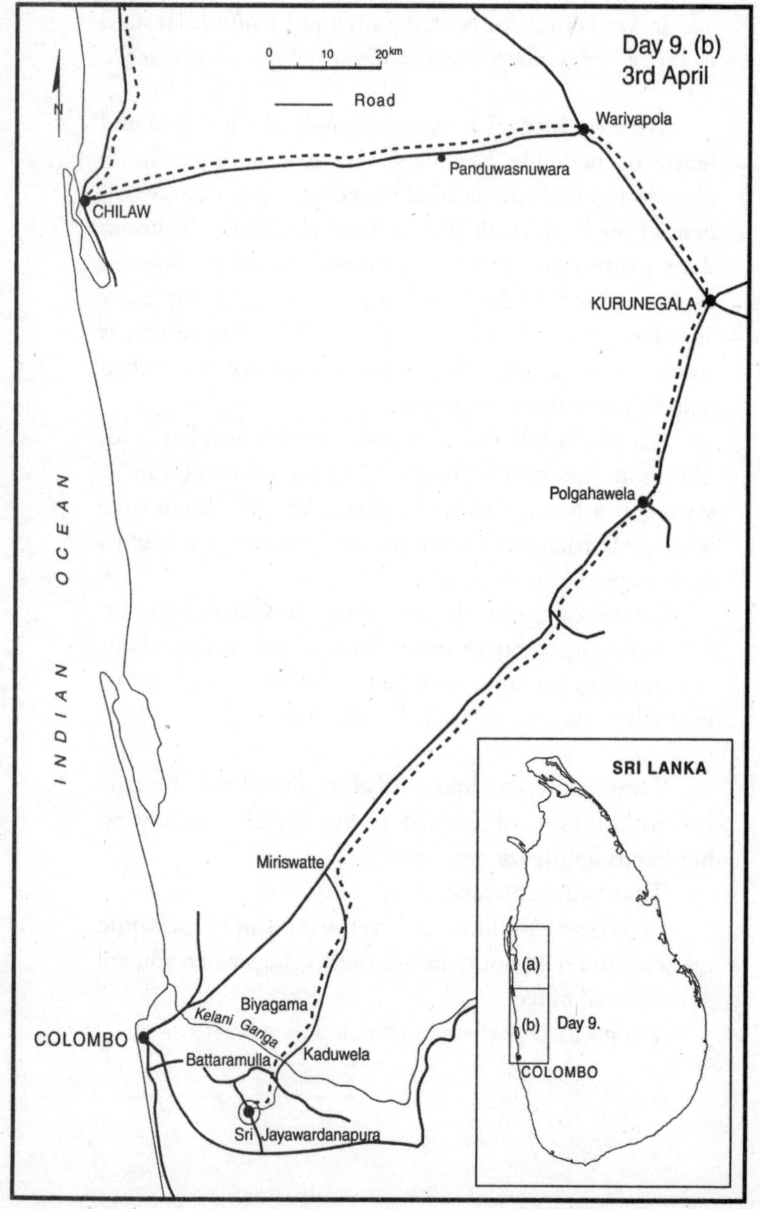
Day 9. (b)
3rd April
0 10 20km
Road
N
Wariyapola
Panduwasnuwara
CHILAW
KURUNEGALA
Polgahawela
INDIAN OCEAN
SRI LANKA
(a)
(b) Day 9.
COLOMBO
Miriswatte
Biyagama
Kelani Ganga
COLOMBO
Battaramulla
Kaduwela
Sri Jayawardanapura

27

Fortunately the road was, for most of the way, dead straight. I saw the sand-filled barrels across the road that forced motorists to drive a zigzag to get past. A guard standing at the front end would hold up a stop sign whenever he felt like it and the unlucky motorist had to pull up for questioning at the guardhouse further on. I did not want him to stop us, so I switched on the left signal, indicating that I was going to stop near him.

I slowed down and stopped, remaining seated on the bike. The guard was quite a young man, very dark with a round face and flattened nose. He stared at me suspiciously but didn't say anything.

'*Ayubowan.*' I spoke in Sinhala, offering the traditional greeting. 'Is there a shortcut from here to the Anuradhapura road?'

Our road went directly south to Puttalam. The main road from Puttalam to Anuradhapura lies in a northeasterly direction, and formed a V with the road we were on. It was a logical question and I could not think of anything else to ask.

'Where are you from?' he asked cautiously.

I was relieved that he had asked the right question, giving me a chance to explain.

'We are from Colombo. We are staying with our uncle at Vanativillu. I have to take my sister to place called Kalawa on the Anuradhapura road.'

'Yes, there are several rough tracks, but it is quite easy to lose your way.' He seemed reassured. 'It would be much better to go directly to Puttalam and take the main road.'

I heard a vehicle approaching the barrier behind me so I thanked him and took off. There were two other constables seated at the counter in the guardroom. They glanced at us and then looked away as we rode past. There were no more barriers and we reached the outskirts of Puttalam without incident. Houses clustered closer together but the land remained arid and desert-like. Palmyrah trees grew sturdily in scattered groves while other trees appeared stunted and brown. The huge Puttalam lagoon opened up on my right as we entered the town and I could see the fishing boats bobbing in the gentle swell.

A parking space by the side of the market seemed to have been reserved for motor bicycles. I got off and wheeled the bike into the centre of it, making sure the number plate was not clearly visible to a casual observer on the road. The market was open and people were bustling about. Fish, crab and giant prawns were piled up on the concrete shelves, as the vendors called out to would-be customers. I stood in the shade of a tree and looked carefully at the street and at the bus station across the road. There were two armed policemen standing at the corner but they looked bored and uninterested. There was no sign of an alert. Not yet.

'So we made it to civilization,' Kamala said.

'You did well with the soldier,' I told her. 'I thought he'd come over and belt you one.'

I could tell she was pleased.

'I'd have told him not to mess with me because my lover is a Captain in the army.'

'Oh, yes,' I said. 'That would have frightened him

off!'

She grinned again.

'So what do we do next?'

'We need to buy some clothes,' I told her. 'Pick up something simple and go over to the bus-stand. You can change in the public toilet. Let's meet over there in about fifteen minutes.'

I gave her five hundred rupee notes. She stopped before leaving and asked:

'Why not use the motorbike? Won't it be much quicker than a bus?'

'I thought about it.' I had indeed. 'But once a general alert is given, all the cops along the way will be on the look out for it. I think a bus is much safer.'

She nodded and walked away.

I went across to the far side of the bus station where some hawkers had set up stalls on the pavement. I soon bought a pair of cheap pants, a cream-coloured T-shirt and a pair of rubber slippers. My shopping cost me four hundred and thirty rupees, leaving me with about eight hundred for food and fares to Colombo. It would have to do.

The public toilet was not a place to linger in. I held my breath as I changed and washed my feet thoroughly at a leaking faucet outside the entrance. I rolled up my used clothes and dropped the bundle in a heap of rubbish. I retained the prayer cap.

Kamala was already standing near the bus shelter when I got there. She had selected her clothes wisely. A modest, ankle-length skirt in a pale cream and a brown long sleeved blouse. It was a fairly normal dress for a young Moslem woman and her shawl, now draped chastely over her head, completed her outfit.

I stopped before she saw me and had another careful

look around. The two policemen were chatting to a man on the road.

Kamala saw me and smiled. The whole bus station sparkled.

Where had the sullen, angry woman gone? I tried to picture her, as I had seen her on the first day, and found it hard. Had I changed too?

She held up a shopping bag.

'What have you got?'

'Fish buns, plantains and a bottle of water,' she said, pleased with her shopping.

'If I were a Moslem, I would find you very attractive,' I told her seriously.

'Really?'

'For a junior wife, maybe!' I added as an afterthought.

She said something unladylike, but her eyes were amused.

A small queue had formed to wait for the coach to Colombo. We joined it and an empty bus pulled in soon afterwards. I took Kamala right to the back of it, to a seat on the left hand side of the bus. Most of the other passengers sat on the other side, away from the morning sun. I figured the left seat gave us a better view of anyone signalling to the bus from the side of the road.

I thought the bus would take off immediately but it didn't. When I enquired, the conductor told me they were waiting for more passengers and would take off in about ten minutes.

I wasn't happy about that. If the police were alerted,

the first thing they'd do was to check passengers on the buses leaving for Colombo. And we'd be seated inside like chickens in a coop. I placed Kamala's shopping on the seat, asked the conductor to keep our places, grabbed Kamala by the hand and took her outside.

I led her to the shade of the bus shelter. It gave me a good view of the main road. If a posse of cops came to check the bus station, I'd see them first.

'We're jumpy this morning, aren't we?' Kamala observed, amused at my antics.

'We've come so far, I couldn't bear it if some stupid cop stumbled on us,' I said. 'Do you think I'm overreacting?'

'No, Captain! When it comes to field operations, I've never seen anyone better,' she said seriously. 'Remember I've worked with some really good men.'

Yeah. Butter me up.

Then she spoiled it by saying: 'Your flaw is your lack of ruthlessness.'

'Ahh, don't start on that again,' I said irritably. 'You just haven't seen that side of me.'

'No.'

She put her hand under my arm and briefly pressed the side of her face against my shoulder.

'No, you have no other side,' she murmured into my sleeve. 'I like you for that, but it worries me a lot.'

The conductor stuck his head out of the door, looking for us. I waved to him and stopped to take another look at the road. Two more armed policemen had come up and were talking to the first lot. They looked pretty relaxed, bored even. We climbed aboard and took our seats at the back.

The bus was still half empty when it took off. The conductor came up to collect our fare and issue tickets. I meant to say Colombo but changed my mind in the last moment and asked for two tickets to Chilaw. When the man had moved on I turned to Kamala and saw the question in her eyes.

'I got nervous again,' I explained. 'Taking a direct bus to Colombo just seems too predictable.'

'How far is it to Chilaw?'

'About thirty miles. Let's get off in Chilaw and well – check out the situation.'

Kamala just nodded, placidly accepting the plan, or lack of it. A pleasant breeze was coming in through the open window and with it, a sense of security, false though it was. Kamala was looking out through the window at the passing scenery. I looked at her profile with a mixture of feelings, serenity for the moment and apprehension for the future.

I wished there were some way in which I could protect her from what was to come.

She must have known that I was looking at her because she turned with a smile.

'Are you hungry?'

I had to laugh.

She knew how easily the prospect of food distracted me. She brought out the shopping bag from under the seat and we ate in companionable silence. The fish buns were surprisingly fresh, still warm from the bakery and delicious. By the time we finished the food and dusted off the crumbs I saw that we were in the outskirts of Chilaw. I noticed that some clouds had rolled up and the sun had disappeared. Chilaw is on the border of the dry zone so any rain was unusual at this time of the year.

We went over the new bridge spanning the Deduru Oya. This used to be a very popular picnic spot that I had visited several times during my student days. One could drive down a rough track by the old bridge and reach the bank of the river. The river is wide and shallow at this point, broken up by sandbanks and islets. Travellers would frequently stop here to bathe and to have a picnic meal.

We crossed the railway line and I knew the town was just ahead.

Driven by another sudden impulse, I stood up and rang the bell. Kamala looked surprised but followed me out of the bus as it pulled up abruptly.

'Do you think they will be checking the buses at the terminus?' Kamala had guessed the reason for my sudden move.

'They must have alerted the police in Chilaw by now. Checking passengers in the bus from Puttalam would be the obvious thing to do,' I said. 'Let's walk towards the junction. You go ahead. I'll be close behind'

'And at the junction?'

'Turn down the road to the left, walk about a hundred yards and then wait for me.'

Was I being too cautious, trying to do things the hard way?

Kamala asked: 'Where does that road go?'

'A town called Wariyapola and then on to Kurunegala,' I told her. 'I think they'll concentrate on the buses on the direct route to Colombo.'

This time my instincts had served me well.

As we walked towards the junction, the main bus station came into view. I saw a posse of policemen surrounding the bus we had been on. They had asked the passengers to get off and were checking their ID's, one by one. There was an excited chatter as pedestrians and idlers craned their necks to see what was going on.

Two more policemen were standing on duty at the junction. I saw one of them look intently at Kamala as she walked past. It worried me for a moment but I realized that his interest had nothing to do with suspicion of wrongdoing. Fortunately Chilaw also has a large Moslem population and no one else bothered to give us a second glance. Kamala turned down the Wariyapola road, walked some distance and stopped by a small kiosk.

We spent ten nervous minutes waiting for a bus. One rattled up eventually, a far cry from the fairly new and comfortable vehicle that plied the main route to Colombo. We got on board and moved to the back, as we had done before. There were only a handful of passengers on board but I found the bus stopping frequently to pick up others. I bought two tickets to the destination, Kurunegala.

'How far is it to Kurunegala?' Kamala asked. All these names and places were strange to her.

'My guess is about forty miles.' I was trying to work out time and distance. 'I think, the way this is going, we will take at least two hours to get there. By about 13.00, I'd say.'

She just smiled and nodded.

Her hands were resting on her lap. I reached out and ran my finger down her arm up to her wrist and fingers. She lifted my hand and placed it on her cheek, then turning towards me, buried her face in my chest. She let me hold her for a brief moment, then pushed me away and turned back to the window.

I was getting used to her mood swings now. In a perverse way, I found it adding to her aura of enchantment.

We passed through Bingiriya and then Hettipola. The landscape changed gradually from dusty aridity to lush green rice fields and coconut plantations. We came to Pandugasnuwara, a small town well known for its historic ruins. It is believed that Parakramabahu, one of Lanka's great rulers, built a fort and palace there in the twelfth century.

The checkpoint was on the outskirts of Wariayapola.

The sky was overcast now and a very light drizzle had started when we came up to it. This was not an ordinary check point, where only selected vehicles were stopped. There were two barriers about fifty yards apart. The bus stopped at the first one and an armed policeman ordered all the passengers to disembark and form a line. He then started a methodical search of the vehicle. Once he was satisfied, he signalled to the driver to move the bus to the far barrier and wait there for the passengers.

Two other cops were seated in a little guardroom with a counter at the roadside. Passengers were expected to come up to the counter one by one and hand over their ID. They also had to explain where they were coming from, where they were going and why. All this useless information was taken down in longhand by one cop while the other man sat there fingering his weapon and trying to look tough.

We were the last to get off so we were at the end of the queue.

'Say you are just eighteen,' I whispered. 'You have applied for your ID but haven't got it yet.'

She smiled and nodded, more at ease than I was.

If word of the robbery had reached this lot, the ID I had would give me away instantly. We would certainly be arrested. Even if I was able to establish my real identity, the police were not going to be sympathetic. We would be held long enough to ruin our mission.

The line got shorter but, meanwhile, the drizzle was slowly turning into a regular shower. The policemen, seated comfortably inside the shelter, took no notice at all. Some of the passengers unfurled their umbrellas. An old man, in the queue just ahead of us, invited Kamala to share his. She accepted readily with an amused glance at me.

It finally was our turn and the awning over the counter gave us some shelter. I tried not to drip water over the cop. I placed Mohamed Sadiq's ID on the counter before him. He picked up the card, looked at it and glanced up at me. The cop was a middle-aged man with a broad, clean-shaven face and decayed, betel-chewer's teeth.

Had he got word about the robbery?

I knew immediately that he had not been alerted and the light was so bad he couldn't see much of the photograph. He bent over his register to start writing when he noticed Kamala standing by my side.

We were expected to come up to the counter one by one.

'Meya kauda?' he asked gruffly.

Who is this?

'Mage duwa, ralahamy,' I answered humbly.

My daughter, officer.

'Ko ID?'

Where is her ID?

'Eyāgey vayasa daha atai,' I explained. *'ID ekata dāla thiyenney. Thawama labuney nähä.'*

She's eighteen. We've applied for her ID but haven't got it yet.

He bought it. It was no secret that the department responsible for issuing identity documents took a very long time to get the job done.

'Kohey indalada enney?'

Where are you coming from?

'Halawatha.'

Chilaw.

'Kohetada yanney?'

'Where are you going?'

'Kurunegala.'

The cop laboriously wrote all that rubbish down and then we were free to go. The rain had eased to a steady drizzle.

Kamala was having a fit of giggles.

'Captain,' she whispered as we walked away. 'If I can pass for your daughter, you are much too old for me.'

'Stop it,' I said anxiously. 'That cop will hear you.'

'I'm serious, Captain.' There was no stopping her in this mood. 'Can't you introduce me to someone a bit younger when we get to Colombo?'

'Shut up.'

I pushed her aboard and the bus took off immediately afterwards.

The bus stopped briefly at Wariyapola junction to drop some passengers off and pick up others. We then turned onto the main road heading towards Kurunegala. I knew Kamala was still on a high. She sat close to me, even though there was room to spare on the seat, and rested her hand lightly on my knee.

She started asking me about university life. Had I been in a hostel? Who had been my special friends? Had I had a girl friend there? What facilities had been provided? Had I enjoyed the life? What undergraduate escapades had I got involved in?

I could tell she had really yearned for that life. I told her what she wanted to hear, glossing over the ugly side, the politics and the jealousies. Some of the stories were funny and made her laugh.

Half an hour later we were in Kurunegala. The rain had stopped.

Kurunegala is a large and prosperous town that has grown around the foot of an enormous rock outcropping called Athagala or Elephant Rock. From some angles the likeness to an elephant is remarkable and Kamala looked at it with awe. The bus station and the shops around it were teeming with people. There was no sign of police activity. I was feeling hungry by now and yearning for a good Sinhala midday meal. I led Kamala to one of the eating-houses nearby. We ordered rice and curry. White rice, curried lentils and two other vegetables and a chunk of curried chicken! Fried dry fish and coconut sambol were extra.

I insisted they serve it in separate dishes so I could feast my eyes on it, the first proper meal I'd had since I'd left the camp at Elephant Pass about a decade ago. Kamala watched with amusement as I heaped rice on to my plate. There's absolutely nothing in this world to equal a big plate of steaming rice, nicely surrounded with hot, spice filled curries. I disdainfully put aside the fork and spoon provided by the waiter and used my fingers. I am firm in the belief that eating rice and curry with cutlery is like fondling my girl friend with surgical gloves on my hands. Kamala was, as usual, satisfied with a modest potion and looked on with amusement as I cleaned up the rest of the food spread out on the table. In the end I felt like a well-fed python, unable to move, but sated at last.

We boarded a bus to Colombo soon afterwards. The conductor told me they would get into the city by about 17.00 in the evening. The bus was crowded and we were lucky to get two seats. A number of passengers stood patiently in the aisle, hanging on grimly as the driver swung the big bus from side to side with one hand while using the other to hold down the horn button.

We were now well into the wet zone. The countryside was lush and green with stretches of rice fields interspersed with home gardens, dense with coconut palms and banana trees, very different from the arid landscape of Jaffna.

After a while Kamala turned away from the window. Her mood had changed and she seemed preoccupied.

'Will we go to your headquarters this evening?' she asked finally.

'No. I want to stay with the original plan,' I told her. 'My friend will put us up for the night. I'll call my brigade and arrange a meeting with the intelligence people for tomorrow morning.'

'Whom will I see?' Kamala had to speak into my ear to be heard. 'I have to get to someone with authority enough to call up an air strike.'

'The Director is Brigadier Kularatne. It won't be easy to get to him, but I will do my best.'

I knew this was critical if she was to negotiate some

concessions.

'It will depend on whom I can reach in my Division.'

'Where does your friend live?' Her voice was calm but remote.

'He has a house in Pelawatta, near the suburb of Battaramulla.' I was happy enough to talk of something else. 'He is from my village and we've been friends for years. He is now a businessman.'

'Can you trust him?'

'Yes.'

She nodded and turned to the window once again.

'I want to get off this bus at a junction called Miriswatte,' I said. 'We can get another bus from there that will pass fairly close to his house.'

That would also help us avoid the checkpoint on the Kelani Bridge.

'Are you sure your friend will put us up?'

'I'm sure he will,' I said. 'I just hope he is not out of town.'

I knew my friend Upali would welcome us but I wasn't so sure about his wife. Samanthi had been a fair, pretty girl when she married Upali some seven years ago. She comes from a wealthy family and it was her money that had enabled Pali to venture out on his own. They had been a handsome couple, and very happy, in those early days. But marriage had soured her. She had put on some weight and, at the same time, lost her sunny disposition. She tolerated me but generally disapproved of all Pali's friends.

We lapsed into silence for the rest of the journey.

Miriswatte is a small junction with a few boutiques

and shops. On leaving the main highway the road would swing through swamp and paddy lands to cross the Kelani river at a town called Kaduwela. From there it would be a short journey to the eastern boundary of Colombo, avoiding the city centre.

We joined a crowd of people waiting wearily for a bus. I put Kamala in the queue and went into a communication centre to call Pali's house. I knew he'd still be at work but I didn't know his number there. Perhaps Samanthi would tell me. The telephone rang and rang but no one answered.

A rattletrap bus appeared. We climbed in but all the seats had been taken by then. Having bought two tickets to Battaramulla, we had to stand in the aisle, hanging onto the backs of seats. I thought the bus was crowded at Miriswatte, where we started off. I was wrong. The driver stopped every fifty yards and they just kept picking up more passengers. Just when I thought there was absolutely no more space left, they'd stop again and two more bodies would be stuffed in. Kamala took it all in good grace, smiling up at me when I used my shoulder to protect her against the worst of the crush.

We passed a checkpoint on the road but the cops were busy chatting about affairs of state and ignored the bus. We reached Battaramulla soon afterwards. Getting off was another battle, pushing past women with shopping baskets, men with briefcases and loafers who wanted to rub themselves against Kamala. We finally reached the pavement, dishevelled but intact.

I bought a phone card and called Pali's home again from a call box. He wasn't there but, to my relief, his manservant answered and remembered me well enough to trust me with his mobile number. I reached Pali in his car, caught in the evening traffic on the way home.

'Wasantha!' He was yelling so loud I had to hold the phone away. 'Where the hell are you? I heard you were trapped in Elephant Pass.'

'No. I got away but that is a long story.' I hoped he was alone. 'I need a place to spend the night. Can you put me up?'

'Sure.'

I could almost picture his grin. He'd already be making plans for drinks in the garden. 'When will you get there?'

'Twenty minutes. I have a friend with me. Is that OK?'

'No problem,' he said cheerily as he rang off. 'I'll be there before you.'

My friend Pali lives his life to the full. He has made his money importing second hand cars and does not hesitate to spend it on whatever, or whoever, strikes his fancy at that moment. He is a passionate friend, who will go to any length to help someone he considers close. A good-looking man, he is a committed womanizer and his escapades were always a subject for amused discussion whenever his friends met. Samanthi was a strong willed girl who had been pleasant enough in the early days of their marriage, but her disposition had gradually turned vinegary. I have a feeling it was Pali's philandering that had caused her decline.

I gave the rest of the money to Kamala to buy toiletries for herself, keeping just enough to pay for the three-wheel taxi that deposited us at Pali's gate soon afterwards. He answered the door himself, a welcoming grin on his face.

'Hi Was .... ' He stopped, his eyes widening when he saw Kamala standing behind me. 'Hello,I'm Pali.'

He recovered quickly and politely ushered us into his sitting room.

'Pali, this is Kamala. She is a witness in an important matter. Where is Samanthi?'

'She's at her mother's house. The children are with her,' he said, smiling and relaxed. 'I'm alone except for old Banda.'

I was relieved. I had wondered how Samanthi would react to Kamala's presence.

'We've come a long way,' I told him. 'We'd like to shower and change. Can you find some clothes for us?'

He took us upstairs to a kind of family room with a TV and easy chairs. Four bedrooms opened onto it, two on either side. He went into his own bedroom and pulled out an armful of dresses from a wardrobe. He then took Kamala solicitously to one of the guest rooms and showed her where to find towels. He shut the door of the room and turned to me.

'WHO IS SHE?' His eyes were burning with curiosity. 'Come on, you can trust me.'

'Pali, she has some vital information that could impact the war effort. I have to get her safely to Headquarters tomorrow.'

He wasn't too concerned about the national interest.

'Do you have something going on with her?' he asked in a conspiratorial whisper, even though Kamala was safely in the bath.

'Of course not.' I tried to appear offended. 'She is an informant, nothing more.'

His voice had changed in a subtle way.

'There is something about her.' His smile had acquired a vulpine quality. 'Would you mind if I tried … , you know?'

I tried to say it lightly, but the words came out in a hoarse growl.

'If you so much as look at her,' I heard myself say, ' I will ...'

The words didn't come out but the intent hung in the air, like smoke from a firecracker. Pali was clearly startled. He recovered quickly though, holding his hands up, palms towards me, in mock surrender.

'Alright, alright.' He was grinning, not offended in the least. 'I asked you if you fancied her and you said no.'

I didn't want to pursue the point.

Instead I asked: 'Are you sure Samanthi won't turn up suddenly?'

'No chance of that.' He wasn't smiling any more. 'She's left me. For good she says.'

'Let me guess.' I wasn't really surprised. ' You got caught with one of your women?'

'Bloody girl from the office! She got jealous about some other woman I'd been seeing and sneaked to Samanthi. Said I'd been screwing her, promising to marry her after divorcing Samanthi.'

I couldn't help laughing.

He looked affronted for a moment but then started smiling ruefully. He punched me on the shoulder and turned away.

I had no doubt that the girl's story was true. He must have been screwing her. He made it a practice to screw all the girls in his office. I'd known that his philandering would catch up with him some day

'Let me get you a sarong and a towel.'

I enjoyed that leisurely hot shower and shampoo. The cut on my neck was still oozing so I found some sticking plaster to cover it. The sun had set by the time I went downstairs and Pali took me to the little gazebo at the bottom of his garden. The back of Pali's house slopes down to a swamp of tall grass and scrubland that is a designated 'green' area. Plenty of bird life is on display in the day but now all we could see were the hordes of giant fruit bats passing over, on the way to their feeding grounds.

'Is it really over between Samanthi and you?' I asked him. 'Any chance of patching things up?'

'I don't know, Wasantha,' he said sombrely. 'I miss the children. This place is like funeral house without them.'

'Would you like me to talk to her?' I offered. 'I'll probably be in Colombo for a couple of days.'

'Uh. Maybe,' he said hesitantly. 'I don't think it will help.'

'Let me sort out this matter and then we'll see,' I said gesturing towards the house and Kamala.

Pali brightened up immediately.

'Is she really an important witness or just a bird you are trying to prong?'

'She's a witness,' I said shortly.

'There's something about her … ,' Pali said thoughtfully. 'I can't quite put my finger on it.'

'I told you what I'd do if you put your finger on it.'

We shared a good laugh then.

'You've made it with her, haven't you?' he asked shrewdly. 'I can tell from the way she looked at you.'

'Shut up.'

Kamala came to the French windows, saw us in the garden, and came outside.

She was wearing a simple two-piece dress that suited her. She must have done some work with pins and stuff because Samanthi was a good bit broader at the waist than she, although they were about the same height. Pali jumped up and fussed over her, fetching a chair and a soft drink. She looked amused but accepted his attentions with good grace.

It was time to call headquarters.

I had been dreading this moment, putting it off as long as I could. Once I lifted that phone, I'd be crossing a line. There'd be no backing out if things went wrong. Pali pointed to where the phone was, in the dining room through the French windows. I left them chatting comfortably together and went inside.

The sergeant on duty who answered the phone was surprised when I identified myself.

'Sir, you were reported missing,' he said, sounding pleased that I was back.

'I need to reach the Colonel,' I told him shortly.

Colonel Hemal Perera was Kiriella's superior. He is a fine officer and a good man. I hoped I didn't have to go higher than that.

'Sir, Major Kiriella is also here. He had gone to Jaffna to wait for you and couldn't get back to Elephant Pass after the attack started.'

This was a bit of luck. Kiriella knew the background and would find it much easier to arrange a meeting at Intelligence HQ.

'Can you connect me?' It turned out that he could, and I was soon speaking to Kirella in his quarters.

'Captain, are you all right? Where are you?' He

sounded pleased but got straight to the point. 'What happened to the informant?'

'I just got in to Colombo, sir. We had to travel overland,' I said carefully. 'I brought the ... informant with me.'

'Give me your number,' he said abruptly. 'I'll call you back.'

I stood by the phone and picked it up when it rang again a few moments later.

'What does she have for us?' he asked immediately.

Kiriella smelled a coup!

'She claims she knows a precise location where her leader will be on a particular day and time,' I said slowly, picking my words. 'She says the building can be identified from the air.'

'Leader?' he demanded incredulously. 'Do you mean Prabakaran?'

'Yes.'

'When will this be?'

'On the sixth,' I said.

'Is this solid information?' I could sense the suppressed excitement in his voice.

'I think so, sir,' I said carefully. 'She claims she can give the exact co-ordinates. But she will only talk to DMI and wants to make a deal first.'

'What deal?' he demanded impatiently. 'What does she want?'

'A passport and a ticket to Canada,' I said carefully. 'Safe custody till she leaves.'

'Bullshit. Bring her in now,' he grated. 'I'll get the information out of her.'

You bastard, I have seen you interrogate suspects, with a

truncheon. They don't always survive, not intact anyway. You will get away with it too, because no one will know she was taken in. No one but me, and I'm part of the system.

My forehead felt damp. I knew I had to get this right.

'Sir, this will be a big operation involving the air force,' I said quietly. I tried to keep my tone very neutral.

'You know these fanatics. Under duress she might change just one co-ordinate. We will never be sure till it is too late,' I went on. 'They will blame you if the mission goes badly wrong.'

I paused to let this sink in. I then said:

'Why not just let DMI handle it? We'll get the credit anyway.'

He was silent for a while, turning it over in his mind. I held the phone tightly to my ear, my palm slippery with perspiration. The correct procedure, and common sense, dictated that the Director of Military Intelligence should handle the operation. It was just that Kiriella was such a glory seeker.

'Yes,' he said finally. 'Yes, perhaps that's best.'

I had been holding my breath. I let it out slowly and took another deep breath.

'I'll speak to the Colonel and try to reach the DMI,' Kiriella said. 'If he's in town, and if he agrees to see us, I'll arrange a meeting tomorrow morning.'

'Yes, sir.'

'But if DMI isn't available, we might as well handle it ourselves,' he went on. 'Then you'll have to bring her over tonight.'

I tried to think but my mind froze up again.

'Sir, we've had a really long day,' I said desperately. 'Can we leave it till tomorrow?'

'Oh, there's no need for you to come,' he said expansively. 'I'll send a vehicle for her. By morning she'll be begging to tell me things from her previous incarnation.'

You fucking sadist! You really want to get your hands on her, don't you?

'Yes, sir.'

'I'll call you back in half an hour,' he said cheerily and rang off.

I felt physically ill.

I put the phone down gently and turned towards the garden. I fought down the familiar fury welling up inside me. Anger wouldn't help us now. I tried to still my mind long enough to list my options.

I could send her away and say she'd escaped. But she didn't know Colombo at all. They'd hunt her down in a few hours. Maybe I could go with her. We'd certainly have a better chance and I knew how the security system worked. But we had nowhere to go. I'd have a good run but in the end we'd be caught. I would be sent to jail and she'd be on the rack.

The best I could do for her was to kill her quickly. Did I have the balls to do that? Maybe Kamala was right, I lacked the ruthlessness to be successful at this kind of work. There was a bitter taste of bile in my mouth. I leaned against the door leading out to the garden and stared at the darkness of the swamp. I could see Kamala and Pali chatting away, blissfully unaware of what was happening.

As I walked into the garden I heard Kamala laughing. Pali knows how to chat up and amuse women and he had turned on his charm for her. The bastard can discuss the most intimate subjects with a woman, even a perfect stranger, and she would accept it as amusing conversation. I'd expect to be slapped if I said the same thing.

Kamala was already at ease with him.

They turned to include me in their conversation and I made a special effort to appear casual, laughing on cue. But with a single glance, Kamala knew that something was dreadfully wrong, and that it affected her. I saw her jaw muscles tighten for just an instant and then the smile was back. She didn't say a word, trusting me to see her through it, whatever it was.

She trusted me.

At that moment my mind cleared and I knew what I had to do.

I was not going to hand her over to be brutalized, that was certain. If we had a meeting with the DMI, then fine, Kamala will have her chance of securing a deal. Otherwise I'd get as much money as I could from Pali and take off with her tonight. I had no plan and nowhere to go but all I needed was time to think it out.

I'd find a way. I always did.

I hadn't tasted alcohol for a long time. Pali had a bottle of Black Label on the table, a sure measure of the impression Kamala had made on him. He knew that my favourite tipple was Rockland Arrack and always had a bottle handy in case I visited. But today was special.

Pali packed a glass with ice and poured a generous measure of scotch on top. I yearned for that first anaesthetizing sip but I cupped the glass in my hands and waited. I leaned back in my chair and listened to them chattering away. No booze till I knew what the night had in store for us.

The phone rang in the drawing room. I took it slowly, standing up and walking deliberately towards the dining room.

Kiriella!

'Captain?'

'Yes, sir.'

'What's your address?'

Fuck. He's going to try it!

I gave him Pali's address. I had to.

'We're meeting DMI at 09.30 tomorrow, at headquarters. I'll send a vehicle for you at 07.30. Take her there directly.'

'Yes sir,' I said. 'And, sir, I need my kit.'

He promised to attend to it and rang off.

I wanted that drink now.

I felt the knots in the back of my neck easing slowly as I sank into the leather armchair. Kamala knew intuitively that the situation had changed because I could almost see the tension go out of her.

Banda came out with a platter of fried shrimp. Pali boy was laying it on.

'You have a beautiful house, Upali,' Kamala was saying. 'It's a shame to live here alone. You must get your family back soon.'

The bastard had already told her he was separated from his wife. He must have added that he was available too.

'Oh, I don't know,' he said, grinning lazily. 'Maybe it's time to start a new one.'

'Don't be foolish,' Kamala had a way of calling men morons without seeming to be offensive. 'You have everything a man can ever want but you are throwing it away, looking for something better.'

'If I had you, I'd not think of looking for something better,' Pali offered grandly.

Kamala tried to be severe but had to laugh in the end.

'You need to spend some time in Jaffna, or the Wanni, and see the conditions under which people live,' Kamala said, serious now. 'You must move with people who have lost their homes, lost their families. People who've lost their jobs and can't find work. Then you will learn to count your blessings. You take all these things so much for granted here.'

'Tell you what.' There is no suppressing Pali when he chatting up a girl. 'Take me to Jaffna and show me around. You know, I'll gladly suffer every hardship if you let me share your mat!'

'I might take you up on that,' Kamala said laughingly. 'Some day.'

We had dinner later, a simple meal of string hoppers and spicy curries. The steaming strands of rice flour arrived on the table in piles of ten. Most people find two piles quite enough for a meal. Kamala watched with resigned tolerance as pile after pile disappeared from my plate.

Pali made a great show of fussing over Kamala, offering coffee and dessert, but she said she was tired and excused herself. She went to her room soon afterwards and closed the door. Pali took me upstairs chatting easily as he settled down to watch TV in the living room separating the bedrooms. He knew very well that Kamala would not like me walking openly into her bedroom when he was around, so he was having his bit of fun with me.

I kept it up, pretending nothing was amiss. I collected

the newspapers and retired to my room mumbling something about being tired as well. My room opened on a small balcony overlooking the rear of the house. A crescent moon had risen now and reflected faintly off the reeds and patches of open water. Pali is fortunate indeed to own a house in a spot like this.

Brushing my teeth with mint toothpaste was an almost forgotten pleasure. I showered again and settled down to read the papers. The news about the war situation was censored. Yet, from what was not being said, I realized that the situation in Jaffna was critical. The camp at Elephant Pass was completely surrounded and cut off. If the Tigers were able to deploy their 152 mm cannon, our guns they'd captured in earlier battles, to cover our airstrip at Palaly, then the peninsula was lost.

I fell asleep thinking, for the first time, about the men in my regiment now trapped in Elephant Pass. I had to get back to them.

I woke up when she sat on the edge of my bed. She wore her special smile and a blue cotton nightdress that was too big for her. I just looked at her as she sat in a pool of light, trying to engrave the memory in my mind. We knew, without having to discuss it, how uncertain the future was. How dependent we were on people and events outside our control.

We dispelled our demons for a brief moment and fell into an exhausted sleep.

Something must have disturbed me because I woke up again later. Kamala was not there. I wondered if she had gone back to her room but surely she would have told me. I got up to check the bathroom and then noticed that the door to the balcony was open. When I looked through the door there was no one out there.

I was about to shut the door when something caught my attention. I saw her then, sitting on the ground at the corner formed by the balcony railing and the bedroom wall. She was curled into a ball, her head resting on her knees.

She didn't look up till I knelt beside her and touched her shoulder. She raised her face then and I saw the glisten of tears running down her face. I had never seen her cry before, not even when the poachers had attacked and assaulted her in the forest. It moved me in a way I cannot describe. I felt as though someone had thrust a hot needle deep into my chest.

'What's the matter, Kamala?' I drew her to me, holding her close. 'What happened?'

'We are in a minefield,' she said softly, as if to herself. 'I have to find a way out.'

'Don't worry about tomorrow,' I said confidently. 'I'll take care of you. I promise.'

'You don't understand. It is for you I must find a way out.' There was despair in her voice. 'There is no escape for me.'

'Nonsense,' I said. 'It will work out all right. You'll see.'

She would not speak after that.

I carried her back to the bed and held her close, feeling her body shudder from time to time. We drifted off to sleep like that.

28

4th April 2000

I could hear the koels.

When the koels began to call with that crazy intensity that precedes their breeding season, it also means the New Year celebrations are due soon. The Sinhala New Year is officially celebrated on the thirteenth and fourteenth of April but it is always, for us in the south, a whole week of revelry in the village. I felt a pleasant sense of anticipation.

Koels have a convenient practice of laying their eggs in the nests of crows. Crows, the smartest of birds, can never tell the difference between theirs and the koel chicks and raise the interlopers as their own.

Pali has been suspected of doing much the same thing with other people's wives.

I woke with a start and realized where I was. Kamala had gone, as she always did before the dawn broke. I lay there wondering what the day would bring. I shaved, showered quickly and went downstairs.

Pali was seated at the head of the table with the newspapers scattered around. Kamala was already there, seated on his right, a cup of coffee in her hand. She had selected a simple knee-length dress, using a broad belt to gather it around her waist. She looked at me gravely as I walked in and looked down again. Her expression was wan and strained.

'Morning, Wasantha,' Pali greeted me heartily, pushing the coffee towards me as I sat down. 'Did you sleep well?'

Pali tried to recreate the easy camaraderie of the previous evening but we were too tensed up and preoccupied to respond. Kamala toyed with her food, speaking only when spoken to. I served myself a full plate of hoppers and curry but derived little enjoyment from it.

The curries seemed strangely tasteless.

Someone rang the bell. Moments later Banda came to tell us that a soldier was at the door, asking for me. Kamala looked at me with resignation.

We were committed now.

I found a uniformed soldier standing outside with an automatic weapon slung across his shoulders and a canvas travelling bag in his hand. He saluted smartly and addressed me in Sinhala.

'Sir, I have your kit,' he said, handing the bag over. 'The vehicle is parked outside.'

'Give me some time to change,' I told him. 'Wait outside.'

When I changed and came downstairs again I found Kamala waiting in the lobby. She had a small sling bag on her shoulder that must have held a change of clothing and her toilet things.

'Are you ready?' My voice was slightly hoarse. 'We might as well get it over with.'

She just nodded.

Pali came down then. Even he was subdued, seemingly affected by the tension in the air. Kamala thanked him gravely for his help and hospitality. He took out a card and gave it to her.

'You can call me on these numbers at any time,' he said and I knew he meant it.

She took the card, then reached out and pressed her cheek against his. I saw that he was visibly moved. I just punched him gently on his shoulder as he saw us to the Land Rover parked outside.

There were two uniformed men in the vehicle. The soldier who had brought my kit was chatting with a tall, fairer man who turned out to be the driver. Both men saluted smartly and we climbed into the vehicle. I sat in front beside the driver. Kamala and the armed guard got in the back. Kamala sat just behind me with the guard opposite her on the other transverse seat.

The morning traffic was heavy with vehicles carrying people to work and school. My driver bullied the commuters shamelessly with his heavy vehicle, cutting in and out and using his horn incessantly. I turned to say something to the guard and found him staring at Kamala.

I wanted to lean over and tear his arms and legs off. Then I felt the futility of it wash over me. I had already surrendered control and her fate was now out of my hands. If I let my feelings show in any way, it would make her situation even more precarious.

The road became more and more congested till we came to a dead halt near Rajagiriya. A traffic cop was waving his arms up and down frantically, horns were being blasted without any let up and my driver was swearing under his breath. None of that was of any help, as there seemed to be a serious block further up the road.

'Methanin harawala Kotte pāreng yamu,' I told the driver.

Turn here. Let's try the Kotte road.

He was one of those professional drivers always in

a frantic rush to reach his destination, whatever that destination was. Once there, he'd have nothing to do but idle all day, chatting with other drivers who'd done exactly the same thing.

The man swung the Defender over the centre island and across the stream of traffic coming in the opposite direction. The cop at the junction wanted to come over and make an issue of it but, seeing that it was an army vehicle, changed his mind and ignored us.

A couple of twists of the steering wheel and we were on the Kotte road where the traffic was more manageable.

'Captain, we just went past a church. Can we go back there?' Kamala asked. 'I won't take more than a minute.'

I'd seen a small Christian church on the side of the road.

She'd told me she had abandoned her religion. Was she having second thoughts now?

The driver wasn't happy when I told him to turn back. He swung the vehicle in a sharp U against the oncoming traffic making an elderly man in a silver Nissan stand on his brakes to avoid a collision.

The doors of the church were standing open but there were no vehicles parked outside. The driver parked in the shade of a tamarind tree and Kamala climbed down. The guard moved to follow her but I motioned to him to wait. We watched her enter through the main door and disappear into the dim recesses of the building.

'Demala gäniyek neyda, sir?' the guard asked.

She's a Tamil woman, isn't she?

'Ow.'

Yes.

'Trasthawadiyekkda?'
Is she a terrorist?
'Nä. Withthikaruwek.'
No. She's a witness.

I had been watching some babblers hopping about the hedge in front of the vehicle. They are called the seven sisters because they always move about in small flocks, chirping noisily as they hunt for insect prey.

She was taking her time. I got down and walked towards the church.

It was dark inside but for a lamp, glowing red, by the side of the altar. Rows of pews stretched out on either side of the aisle before me. There was no one there.

Shit, shit, shit. She has lost her nerve and bolted, leaving me holding the can. Why hadn't she warned me?

Not wanting to march down the central aisle, I walked quickly down the open corridor on the side of the building, a simple rectangle without the usual wings. One glance was enough for me to see that the church was empty.

I was about to turn back when I saw her. She was stretched full length on the ground in the space between the first pew and the altar rails. I thought for a moment she'd had some kind of seizure. She had her face to the ground and, as I watched silently, I saw her body shudder from time to time. She got to her knees then and I saw her hands join in prayer, her eyes fixed on a large crucifix behind the altar.

I left her to it and went back.

She came out a few minutes later and climbed in. She seemed calm but I noticed that her eyes were puffed. She glanced at me and looked away quickly. We turned into the traffic once again, working our way down Horton Place and Green Path and then to Army Headquarters at Galle Face.

We were expected.

Just the same, Kamala was taken away by a woman soldier and subjected to a body search. Although she must have been prepared for it, it is never pleasant. Her eyes were glittering when she was escorted back a few minutes later. We climbed into the vehicle and were driven into the complex. The driver knew where he had to take us.

Army HQ is housed in a sprawling mix of modern, glass fronted, buildings erected haphazardly between gracious colonial style structures. The Directorate of Military Intelligence is in an airy building in the latter style with wide verandahs and high ceilings.

A grey-haired sergeant came out to meet me as I walked up the steps. Kamala followed me meekly, her pathetic little kit bag clutched in her hand.

'Sir, the Brigadier will see you in a few minutes. Major Kiriella from your unit is with him now.'

He glanced appraisingly at Kamala as he spoke. He then pointed to some worn wooden chairs that lined the varanda.

'Would you like to sit over there?'

The sergeant went back to his office overlooking the front steps. We were alone for the first time since we left Pali's house.

I turned to speak to Kamala, to prepare her for the ordeal ahead. I was shocked by the change in her. Her eyes were wide with anxiety and there was a faint sheen of perspiration on her forehead.

'Wasu, I have to tell you something.' Her voice was low and urgent.

'What is it?' I asked anxiously. 'You'd better tell it fast.'

'My information,' she whispered. 'It's a trap.'

'What the hell do you mean?' I demanded.

I felt as if the ground beneath me was slipping away, like quicksand.

'Won't your leader be there?'

'No,' she said unsteadily. 'No, he won't be there.'

She was looking into my eyes, pleading wordlessly.

I didn't notice that the sergeant had come out of his office and was standing behind me.

'Sir,' he said quietly, 'the Brigadier will see you now.'

'Just give me a minute,' I said urgently. 'I want to clarify something with this witness.'

Captains don't keep Brigadiers waiting.

He stared at me in surprise, hesitated for a moment, and went back to his office.

'Who will be there at noon on the sixth?' I demanded.

My voice was hoarse with tension.

'Ajay Devanand! He'll be there with a team of Indian journalists,' she said.

Dr. Devanand is a highly respected social worker from Chennai, India. He is involved in many programs to help the refugees who fled to South India to escape our civil war. He had often criticized the LTTE for human rights abuses.

'What's he doing in the Wanni?'

'They persuaded him to inspect their territory, to satisfy himself that they ran a humane administration, so that refugees could return.'

'And the real motive?'

'They want him dead, and they want your government to do the killing for them. There will be cameras filming your bombing attack. The footage will be used to turn Indian public opinion against your government.'

Bastards.

'You stupid fool, you will still be in custody,' I was yelling in a whisper. 'Have you any idea of what they will do to you when they realize that you have tricked them?'

She didn't answer.

'They will keep you screaming at the edge of death for days, weeks even,' I said desperately, trying to make her understand the mortal danger in which she had placed herself.

'Whatever they did to me, in the end I would die. Then it would be over,' she said calmly. 'I knew all that when I accepted the mission.'

I looked at her speechlessly.

'I had nothing to live for, then,' she went on. 'Only the mission mattered. I am expendable.'

Inside my head I was screaming, 'You are not expendable to me.'

'Even if you tell them the truth now, it will make no difference,' I said desperately, trying calm myself. 'They will still interrogate you as a hostile. You will suffer … permanent damage.'

'I suppose so,' she was resigned, fatalistic. "It doesn't matter.'

'So why are you telling me this now?'

The sergeant was back. His tone was urgent.

'Sir, the Brigadier wants to know what the hold up is. You'd better go in now.'

We turned to follow the sergeant.

'If the operation goes through, your involvement in bringing me here will ruin your career,' she whispered, 'and you will know that I betrayed you. I could not bear that.'

I had so many more questions.

I needed time!

Five minutes alone to come up with some plan, but there was no time left. The sergeant opened a door and ushered us into a spacious room. There was a large desk at the far end and behind it sat the Director of Military Intelligence, Brigadier Nalin Kularatne. Major Kiriella was seated in front of him and turned to look at us as we walked in.

I saluted them and stood to attention.

They were both staring at Kamala. That gave me a moment to study the Director, whom I had not seen before. He was a mild looking man with a thin face and jet-black hair, parted on a side and neatly brushed back. There was nothing menacing about him on the surface, nothing to support his reputation for utter ruthlessness. But there was a stillness about him that was ominous. His hands, now resting on the table, did not move at all. His eyes, brooding and reptilian, finally turned to me.

'Captain.' He had a soft, cultured voice. 'I'm told you have undertaken an arduous journey to bring this informant to us. Well done! We need more officers like you.'

'Thank you, sir!' I said formally. 'It is kind of you to say so.'

He nodded and went on:

'So this informant has some vital information to give us?'

'Yes, sir.'

'What is the nature of the information?'

'The precise location of a building where Prabakaran will be, on a specific day and time.'

'I see.'

There was no discernible change in his expression or tone.

'And what does she want in return for this information?'

'A new identity, passport, visa and passage to Canada,' I said. 'And protective custody till she leaves.'

He stared at me with his dead, unblinking eyes.

'Did she reveal the location to you?'

'No sir.' I was on safe ground here. 'She said she would only divulge that information to the Director of Military Intelligence.'

'Major Kiriella tells me we have very little time, so you must know when this is due to take place.'

'Yes, sir.'

I made a valiant effort to keep my voice steady.

'The sixth of April, sir, at 11.00 hours.'

We'd been together for nine days so I knew she was very quick and very professional. I'd only managed to throw her a straw, one hour in the time frame. She had to grasp it and make the best use of it.

And hope to be lucky!

The Brigadier stared broodingly at me for what felt like another eternity. I felt my face grow damp despite the air conditioning in the room.

Finally he nodded.

'We'll evaluate the information after we get a detailed statement from the informant. If we decide to mount an operation, and it is successful, we will certainly consider her requests.' He glanced at Kiriella and turned back to me. 'Once again, Captain. Well done! You may go now.'

The Brigadier had said 'statement' and not 'interrogation'. Did it mean he had accepted the story, at least for the moment? Was one hour enough to save her?

I didn't dare look at Kamala when I walked out. I wondered if I would see her again. The Major came with me and clapped me on the shoulder as we went down the steps.

'Well done, Wasantha.' He was in good spirits. 'I'll see you get credit for this operation.'

You pile of dog shit! You're alive at this moment only because you didn't have a chance to lay a hand on her.

This time Kiriella sat in the front of the Land Rover, and I climbed in the back.

'I was to fly to Jaffna today.' He turned and smiled at me. 'I now have permission to wait till this operation is over.'

'I would like to have a few days off, sir.' I was in no mood to fly back to Jaffna with the bastard. 'Will that be in order?'

'Let's get back to Brigade and brief the Colonel. I'll talk to him about your leave after that.'

The formal debriefing was handled by Major Munasinghe, a bureaucratic idiot from brigade HQ and it went on for more hours than I care to remember. When it was finally over I collected my clothes from storage, changed and went down to the gym. I tried to erase my anxieties by working out till my body was numbed in exhaustion.

I showered, changed and went down to the mess. I regretted it immediately.

Kiriella was there, as were a number of other officers. They treated me like a hero, shaking my hand and offering to buy me drinks. I had a couple but couldn't stand the conversation for long. I excused myself after awhile and went down to sickbay. The orderly obliged me with a couple of Valiums.

The workout and the Valium must have helped because I passed out as soon as my head hit the pillow.

29

5th April 2000

I had three days leave.

I couldn't even think of going home to my village. I called up a friend who worked for a branch office of an insurance company in Galle. He agreed to inform my mother that I was all right.

I collected my back pay and then hung around the operations room for a while, gleaning bits of information about the battle, all of it bad. I realized I was hungry and went to the mess. I ordered breakfast but when I sat down to eat, I found my appetite had waned, leaving me depressed and weary.

Another officer was going down to Army HQ and offered to take me into town. I accepted gladly and stayed in the vehicle till he reached the main entrance to the complex. I got off at the gate and crossed the road.

Army headquarters is located in a long strip of land bordered on one side by the Beira Lake and on the other by Galle Face centre road. The main entrance to the heavily fortified area is on Akbar road near Ceylon Cold Stores. Some shelters had been erected by the side of the lake to house the family members coming to HQ to ask for news of their soldier sons or husbands. With the battles raging in Jaffna, there were hundreds of people there already, milling about, faces drawn with worry.

I studied them from across the street. They were poor villagers from the south, most of them. Many were elderly women. My mother could have blended easily into that throng. Young wives too, clutching small children. It was always great to have your son or husband join the army. The paychecks, combined with the risk allowances for serving in a combat zone, finally lifted these families out of poverty and want. But it was when the sealed coffins started to come to the villages that the war became real.

The atmosphere of anxiety was palpable and it matched my own state of mind.

I walked away aimlessly and soon found myself on Galle Face Green. This is a triangular strip of land about a mile in length facing the open sea. The Galle Face Hotel stands at the base of the triangle and the old house of parliament at its apex. The green is packed with people in the evenings, families with small children mostly, coming to enjoy the fresh air. It was deserted now, in the blazing mid afternoon heat.

Except for the umbrella lovers!

I passed them as I walked slowly along the promenade. Young couples seated on the cement benches, huddled up against each other, and protected from the sun and the eyes of the public, by a single unfurled umbrella balanced on their shoulders. They only came here, and suffered in the heat, because they were poor and had no other place to go. But the cops would come from time to time and pick the whole lot up. I couldn't think of any rational explanation for that except sheer bloody mindedness and the sick pleasure the cops might derive from embarrassing the young women.

But they made me think of her. I could see the high, razor wire topped, boundary wall of HQ stretching along one perimeter of the esplanade. She was there, somewhere beyond that wall and out of my reach. Surely they wouldn't harm her, at least till the operation was over?

I tried to tear my mind away by looking the other way, out towards the sea. There was a stone plaque by the side of the walkway I hadn't noticed before. Some words were carved on it.

Galle Face Walk
Commenced by Sir Henry Ward
1856
and recommended to his successors
in the interests of
the ladies and children
of Colombo.

Would anyone look after the interests of my lady?

I turned and walked back. The Galle Face Hotel stands across the southern end of the Green and is one of the most famous landmarks in Colombo. I walked in because I was perspiring profusely and had developed a raging thirst. And because I had nothing else to do!

I stopped in the lobby for a moment to read a brass plaque announcing that the hotel had been in existence since 1864. I walked through to the open-air restaurant overlooking the sea and ordered fish and chips to go with a beer. The beer went down well so I took my time over it and then ordered another. But I couldn't face eating and pushed my plate away after a couple of forkfuls. I paid up and got out of there.

A three-wheel taxi deposited me at the Havelock Town post office. I mailed Mohamed Sadiq's ID back to him. At the last moment I had an attack of conscience and stuffed two thousand-rupee notes into the envelope. I also sent a money order to my mother.

I needed to get drunk.

I called Pali from a call box and he promptly invited me over. I took another three-wheeler to Pali's house and got there before him.

Old Banda let me in. I showered and found a sarong to change into.

I wandered into the bedroom Kamala had used. It had been neatly made up. I knew it wasn't Banda's handiwork so Kamala must have taken time to put everything in order before she left last morning. I checked the bathroom. The brown skirt and white blouse, now ragged and torn, had been washed and hung to dry over the bathtub.

Kamala had worn these clothes when she walked up to the barrier at Pallai. When had that been? A lifetime ago! I took the clothes down, sat on the edge of the bathtub, and held them to my face. They smelt of washing powder, all traces of the Tamil girl were gone. I felt my body start to shake.

I had one searing moment of clarity.

How many thousands of my countrymen had their children, parents and lovers taken in for questioning in the same way? How many real people, each loved and cherished by someone, had been taken away to be broken and brutalized? And all in the name of security! How many victims had found it useless to scream out the truth because no one believed them till they had been taken to the unbearable limit of pain?

And I had condoned, even supported, the practice.

Now it was my turn to feel the anguish and mind-destroying anxiety. I could not bear it.

Don't harm her, you bastards. If you do, I will find a way to kill all of you.

Useless, foolish thoughts! How would that help her?

I went downstairs and wandered out to the gazebo. I stared out at the swamp stretching into the distance. There was plenty of activity in the tall grass. A purple heron stood frozen like a sculpture of a javelin thrower. A couple of waterhens scampered about in the foreground. I heard a stork-billed kingfisher calling mournfully as it flew past. A couple of brahminy kites were circling the water, soaring on the last of the day's thermal currents. Kamala would have loved nothing better than to sit here and observe all this. With me!

Oh fuck it!

Pali tooted at the gate and Banda hurried to let him in. He saw me and waved, then went straight into the house. He joined me later and we watched the sun setting over the wasteland. Pali sensed my mood and didn't talk too much, just sat there in companionable silence.

He waited till dark before fetching the booze.

'What's the situation in Jaffna?' he asked quietly.

'It's very bad, Pali,' I said. 'I don't know how long we can hold out at Elephant Pass.'

'Will you be sent back there?'

'Yes, I have to rejoin my unit,' I said.

'What was Kamala's role in all this?'

I reflected on how much I could safely tell him. I

needed his help.

'She is an LTTE activist who's turned against them,' I said, selecting my words carefully. 'She is negotiating with the army to exchange some vital information for protection and a passage to Canada.'

'Have they agreed to the deal?'

'Tentatively,' I said. 'It depends on the outcome of an operation they have planned for tomorrow.'

'Will this … operation succeed?' Pali asked.

'I don't know,' I answered miserably. 'Probably not! So many things can go wrong.'

'What will her situation be, if it fails?'

'Very precarious.'

'I see,' he said seriously. 'Can we do anything to help her?'

I had been hoping he'd make the offer.

'Are you willing to take a big risk?' I asked, testing him.

'Is it important to you?' he responded.

We were sitting in the dark today, so I couldn't see his expression.

'Yes,' I said quietly. 'Yes. More than anything.'

'All right then.'

'By tomorrow afternoon I will know the outcome of the operation,' I said carefully. 'If it has gone badly wrong, they will detain her for interrogation. I will inform you then.'

'And?'

'No one has any receipt acknowledging her detention. She can just … disappear,' I said hoarsely. 'I want you to give details of her arrest to Amnesty International. I will tell you how to contact the local chapter.'

'The army will just deny they have her,' he observed.

'Then Amnesty will be helpless.'

'That's why I will leave a signed statement for them. The army won't be able to deny having her then.'

'Wasantha!' He was taken aback. 'That will wreck your career.'

'Just ten days ago, my career was my life,' I said sadly. 'Today it hardly seems to matter.'

We were quiet for a while.

I asked: 'Will you do it then?'

'Yes,' he answered readily.

'If the operation is inconclusive it's possible they will release her after a few days,' I went on. 'She has no one here and I will be in Jaffna.'

'So?'

'There's a good chance she'll come to you,' I said. 'You gave her your card.'

'What do you want me to do?'

'Help her to get a passport and apply for a visa,' I told him, straining to see his reaction in the dark. 'She'll need a safe place to stay.'

Was I expecting too much in the name of friendship? Pali had his own troubles.

'I'll see to it,' he said without hesitation. 'Don't worry about it.'

'It will cost a lot of money,' I said. 'I'll pay it back to you.'

'I know that, Wasantha,' he said quietly. 'I told you not to worry about it.'

'And Pali,' I said. 'She's off limits.'

He laughed.

'Yes machang,' he said. 'You have my word.'

I knew he was good for it.

We concentrated on the main item on the agenda after that. I must have eaten later but I don't remember too much about it, only getting up in the middle of the night to drink a gallon of water from the washbasin tap.

30

6th April 2000

The koels were at it again, louder than ever. The wretched birds seemed to have taken up residence in the mango tree outside my bedroom window. The curious ascending call, so loud and unmusical, and repeated endlessly, was calculated to drive a man with a bad hangover absolutely crazy.

I staggered to the shower and stood under the icy spray till I felt better. Not good, just a bit better. I found some A4 sheets in Pali's desk downstairs and sat down to write my statement.

By the time I heard Pali's cheerful whistle on the stairs I had it all down in black and white. Kamala's voluntary surrender to me in Pallai, our journey to Colombo and my handing her into the custody of DMI in the presence of Major Kiriella. I signed and dated the document.

The newspapers were heavily censored and gave no news of the ground situation in Jaffna. I settled for two cups of strong black coffee while Pali had his breakfast. He locked my statement away in his safe and promised to act on it the moment I gave the word.

I hugged him, something I had never done before, and walked quickly out of the house. I caught a three-wheeler outside his gate and had the man take me to Nugegoda. A bus from the terminus took me up to my regimental headquarters.

I went directly to the situation room.

A young lieutenant was the duty officer. I didn't know

him but had seen him around the base.

'I'm Mayadunne, sir,' he said, saluting smartly when I walked in. 'I'm glad you got back safely.'

'Thank you,' I said perfunctorily. 'I'm glad to be back. What's the situation?'

'The Tigers have cut the MSR from Pallai to Muhamalai. Troops from 53 division regained a section of the road and lost it again.'

So we no longer had a Main Supply Route to Elephant Pass.

'What about the alternate route,' I asked.

This had to be the track by the lagoon I'd used on that fateful night.

'Sir, the road through Kilali and Chava is open but the Tigers have infiltrated the area. So it comes under heavy mortar and RPG fire from time to time. There has been heavy fighting to keep the route open.'

'What is the situation at Elephant Pass?'

'We have lost the wells at Iyakachchi so there is a severe shortage of fresh water. With the supply route under attack all the time, it will be very difficult for them to hold on.'

'What about our men?' I asked anxiously. 'Is Captain Sirisena in charge?'

'Yes, sir,' Mayadunne answered.

'Casualties?'

'We've lost two men, sir,' he said. 'So far.'

I wanted to get back to my troops. I couldn't sit out the war in Colombo, when my men were fighting for their lives out there.

'Are you monitoring their radio?'

'Yes, sir but it's mostly propaganda,' Mayadunne said. 'The Tigers call this Operation Oyatha Alaikal Four.'

Oyatha Alaikal means Ceaseless Waves. That just

about described their battle strategy.

I wanted news of the air operation, and the best chance of getting that was to stay on the base. I wanted, even more desperately, to know how they were treating Kamala but there was no way of finding out. It would be out of character for me to make direct enquiries. They wouldn't tell me the truth anyway.

11.00 hours. No one at the base took the least bit of notice of that critical moment. I spent the early afternoon sitting in the mess, staring at a TV screen with the sound turned off.

I was summoned to the CO's office at 14.00.

The CO, Brigadier Sena Kuruppu, was a senior officer now nearing retirement. He was a sincere, if fairly unimaginative, leader who really cared about the welfare of his men. He was desperately concerned about the safety of our boys trapped in Elephant Pass. I was not surprised to see Major Kiriella there, seated across the table and smiling broadly.

'Well, Captain, you must have been waiting to hear the news.' The Brigadier was a slow speaker. 'The air force was on target, for once. We missed Prabakaran but we did get Srikantha and several other cadres. It was reported on their radio. I think we can count the operation as a fair success.'

I felt my chest exploding.

'Colonel' Srikantha was the LTTE military commander in the Wanni. Killing him was an important victory indeed, especially at a time when the LTTE was making such heavy inroads into Government controlled territory further north, in Jaffna.

And there was no mention of Indian dignitaries!

It had been a blind stroke of luck, but was it enough to save her?

We discussed the situation in Jaffna at some length. The CO wanted us to get back to our posts as soon as possible. Major Kiriella was to fly to Jaffna the next day. He would have to take his chances on the alternate route in order to rejoin our troops. I would, too, when my leave was over in two days time.

The ground water at Elephant Pass was far too brackish and drinking water was originally obtained from a couple of desalination plants. One of them had already packed up when I was posted to the camp and the other stopped working soon afterwards. They said something about the membranes being fouled due to poor pretreatment of the lagoon water. Since the spare membranes had not reached us on time, the engineers at Elephant Pass had simply pumped water from the fresh water wells situated at the village of Iyakachchi..

The very first operation the Tigers had undertaken was to capture the village and cut the pipes. Whatever the strategists did now, the camp was doomed. Sooner rather than later, they would have to abandon it and fight their way to the main fortification in Jaffna. If Jaffna could survive that long!

The Brigadier discussed plans and options for a tactical withdrawal of our men, if the high command decided to abandon Elephant Pass.

'It would be very helpful if we could have some contact with the villagers along the route.' The Brigadier knew that the order to abandon the camp would have a devastating political impact and would therefore be given only at the very last moment, when survival was impossible. By that time the enemy would have the only available escape route well covered. Attrition would be severe.

'No villager will speak to us now.' Kiriella was stating the obvious.

The Tigers would summarily execute any villager suspected of collaborating with government troops.

'What about Wasantha's woman?' the Brigadier asked suddenly. 'Maybe she will know something that will help us.'

Kiriella said: 'We can ask MI to question her about it.'

'I don't think MI will really be interested in the kind of information we need,' the Brigadier mused.

He stared out of the window for a moment.

My temple was throbbing.

Say it, you old bugger.

He turned and looked at me.

'Why don't you go over and have a word with her?' he suggested at last. 'I'm sure she will speak more freely with you.'

'Sir, what do we need to find out?' I asked carefully.

I didn't like his crack about 'Wasantha's woman', though he was probably using it only for want of a better expression

'The Tigers would have known that the coast road will be our only way out. She would have been in their loop when they planned this attack, so she might know something of their plans to cover it,' the Brigadier said. 'You know, Captain, any scrap of information might save a life.'

'I'll talk to her, sir, if you think it will help,' I said

neutrally, hoping my excitement would not show.

'Thank you, Captain,' he said. 'I know I can rely on you.'

I'd crawl on broken glass for a chance to talk to her.

'I'll have a word with DMI,' he continued. 'Stay in touch and I'll let you know the details.'

31

7th April 2000

I was standing on Hill Street at Dehiwela junction. I wore civilian clothes and held a blue file cover in my hands.

A battered white Toyota pulled up close to me. Two men were seated inside. The man in the passenger seat rolled down his shutter and looked at me carefully. A tar black face, wide forehead and a receding hairline.

'Captain Ratnayake?'

I nodded and he gestured to the back of the car.

They drove me to a housing complex off Hill Street called Lotus Grove. A developer had surrounded the entire housing estate with a high wall and entry was through a guardroom manned by a private security firm. The houses inside were laid out in neat rectangles facing a grid of connecting roads. It was a good place for a 'safe house'.

The driver and the other man stayed in the car. When I rang the bell, a grim woman dressed in a printed housecoat opened the door. I had a quick impression of graying hair, parted in the middle, and wound into a coil at the back of her head. Shrewd, unsmiling eyes examined me from behind rimless glasses.

She jerked her head, inviting me to step inside and shut the door behind me. She asked for the blue file and checked the letter my CO had provided. She gave it back to me without a word. She then unlatched another door and held it open.

It led to a sparsely furnished living room with French windows leading to a sunlit garden outside. I heard the door close softly behind me.

Kamala was seated on a sofa.

She stood up when I came in and looked at me gravely. A ghost of a smile flashed across her face and was gone. I found myself scanning her for signs of injury - face, fingers and toes. She saw my eyes move over her and smiled again. I felt lightheaded with relief.

She was all right!

She said softly: 'They told me you were coming, Captain.'

Was this room wired?

'Yes. My commander wants some information.' I kept my voice friendly but neutral. 'I've been sent to see if you could help us.'

She nodded, looking intently at me, waiting for my cue. I had to get out of that room!

'It's a bit stuffy in here,' I said. 'Shall we go out to the garden?'

She nodded again and led the way, stepping through the French windows. A high wall surrounded the small, well-tended lawn with its border of mixed foliage. In the centre was a mango tree throwing a circle of speckled shade on the grass. Some wrought iron furniture had been placed there, three chairs and a circular table.

We sat down there and I took out my notebook and pencil, pretending to glance at it.

'Are you alright, Kamala?' My voice sounded hoarse, even to my own ears. 'Did they hurt you in any way?'

'No. I'm all right, Wasu. Truly,' she said quietly. 'They questioned me for hours and hours. It was exhausting but they didn't resort to anything … physical.'

The ghostly smile came and went.

'You worried about me, didn't you?' she asked.

'Yes,' I said simply. 'I wouldn't want to live through the last two days again.'

'I am so sorry, Wasu,' she said. 'I have caused you so much pain and it was all my fault.'

'That's all in the past. I'm just happy you are all right.'

'We were desperately lucky, weren't we?' she observed. 'At least I was, that you picked that particular time.'

'Did they tell you any details?'

'Colonel Srikantha and at least five other cadres had been killed in the attack. He must have gone to check on the preparations. There has been no mention of the Indian visitors.'

'What is the reaction of DMI?' I asked. 'Are they satisfied with the results?'

'I was questioned by a Captain Ravith,' she said. 'He seemed very pleased.'

'What about your people?' I asked anxiously. 'Will they think that you betrayed them?'

'I have no way of knowing for sure. But, you know, there's a good chance they will put it down to a foul up by your forces,' she said thoughtfully. 'They don't have a high opinion of your Intelligence set up or your air force. They might think someone mixed up the times and got lucky.'

Arrogant bastards.

'So what happens next?'

'They've promised to have my papers ready in a week or two. I'm to stay here till then. I told you my friend lives in Vancouver Island. I want to go there.'

'You have Pali's card, don't you?' I asked. 'When they release you, I want you to contact him. Will you do that?'

'All right.'

'I've arranged for him to give you money and anything else you may need.'

'Where will you be?' She seemed surprised I wouldn't be here.

'My leave is over,' I said. 'I'm going back to Jaffna tomorrow.'

'Wasu, they can't send you back to Elephant Pass.' She was really agitated. 'That camp will fall at any moment. Can't you get a posting somewhere else?'

'My troops are there. You know I must be with them,' I said confidently. 'Come on! Don't worry about me, Kamala. I can't be killed.'

She stared at me in exasperation.

'Wasu, listen to me very carefully. Our people know the army will have to abandon Elephant Pass and retreat along the lagoon road. The fighters and guns are already in place, ready to ambush the troops coming out. It's a narrow road and there's no cover. It will be … hellish!'

'So?'

'I volunteered for this mission because I had nothing to live for,' she said gravely. 'I have a reason now. Please, Wasu, please take care! Don't try to be a hero. Just come out of there alive.'

'Does that mean that we have a … future?'

My chest hurt.

She looked down for a long moment. When she looked up at me again her eyes were anguished.

'No,' she said wretchedly. 'I am sorry, but no.'

'Why?' I asked hoarsely. 'Surely we can find a way'.

'Wasu, my people will always have their doubts about this operation. If they ever have the slightest suspicion that there was anything between us, they would know that it was not an accident. They would know that I have betrayed them.'

Her voice was full of despair.

'They will never forgive a betrayal. You know that.'

'We can protect you,' I said desperately. 'We can help you disappear.'

'There is no place on earth safe from them, so they will find me in the end,' she spoke softly, as if to herself. 'But that is not what I am afraid of.'

She looked up at me then.

'They will want a full accounting for Srikantha,' she said quietly. 'If they suspect that we have some relationship, they will kill you first, for your part in it and as an extra punishment for me. They will only kill me afterwards.'

'I can look after myself,' I said, 'You must know that by now.'

She shook her head sadly.

'Wasu, you don't really know my people, how determined they are. They will send their fighters, one after the other. They never give up. They need to succeed only once.'

'I will take that risk,' I said doggedly.

'You must listen to me. I would give up everything for a chance to go with you,' she said solemnly. 'I'll risk anything, except your life.'

'What are you trying to say?'

'I might find existence without you just bearable, provided I knew that you were safe. I could not live if I was the direct cause of your death.'

'So?'

'You must go now. We dare not meet again.'

I wanted to grab her and shake some sense into her. I wanted to rage against the forces that threatened us. I stood up and turned away from the upstairs window.

I forced myself to speak calmly.

'No. I can't accept that. There has to be another option. I .. will .. not .. give .. you .. up!'

'You are life to me. Do you think I would send you away if there was any other option?'

She was biting her lip.

'You must go. If I break down now they will suspect something.'

I wanted to stay and reason with her. I wanted so much to touch her, to comfort her. But anything I did now would put her in more danger. I knew I could help her only by leaving.

I forced myself to speak calmly.

'Once you get to Canada, will you write to me care of Pali? Promise me that, at least?'

She hesitated and finally nodded.

'Yes,' she said. 'I promise.'

My chest was knotted in pain as I walked away from her. Having stepped through the French windows, I looked back. She was still seated there, watching me. I let myself out of the house and walked towards the car. There was no sign of the old woman.

Kamala had advised Pali to count his blessings. I now counted mine.

We had negotiated the minefield, overcome countless threats and hurdles, and emerged miraculously unharmed. But we had come out on opposite sides of the minefield. Neither of us could find a way back.

Still, she was safe.

I had to be satisfied with that.

21st April 2000

News item.

Lt. General Srilal Weerasuriya, Commander of the Army, ordered Major General Lionel Balagalle, the Chief of Staff, to issue the withdrawal order for the troops at Elephant Pass. Maj. Gen. Balagalle dispatched the orders by hand but the courier returned, having failed to get through because heavy fighting had broken out along the alternate MSR. The order was then sent by radiotelephone and by fax to the GOC, Elephant Pass.

Brigadier Percy Fernando, Deputy GOC Elephant Pass, made preparations for the withdrawal and destruction of equipment and munitions at the fortification.

23rd April 2000

News item.

Troops began moving out of Elephant Pass just before noon on the 22nd of April. On leaving the fortification, the soldiers had to pass through a very narrow front. The alternate MSR came under heavy RPG and mortar fire and troops suffered heavy casualties. Brigadier Percy Fernando himself was hit by sniper fire and succumbed to his injuries.

Exhausted by weeks of continuous combat and the lack of water, many soldiers died of dehydration during the long retreat to Jaffna. Of the ten thousand men who withdrew from Elephant Pass, many hundreds lost their lives, many hundreds more were declared Missing in Action.

29th April 2000

Mrs. S. J. Asilin Ratnayake,
156/40, Temple Road,
Kirana,
Akmeemana

Dear Madam,

I write, with deep regret, to inform you that your son, Captain Wasantha Ratnayake, has been declared missing in action during the evacuation of the camp at Elephant Pass.

Captain Ratnayake was a brave and heroic officer. Eyewitnesses have reported that he was attempting to rescue one of his men, who had been injured by sniper fire, when the whole area was devastated by a heavy explosion.

We are making every effort to obtain more information and will not fail to keep you informed.

Faithfully

Sena Kuruppu (Brigadier)
Commanding Officer

Nihal de Silva

Email: wtrmrt@sltnet.lk

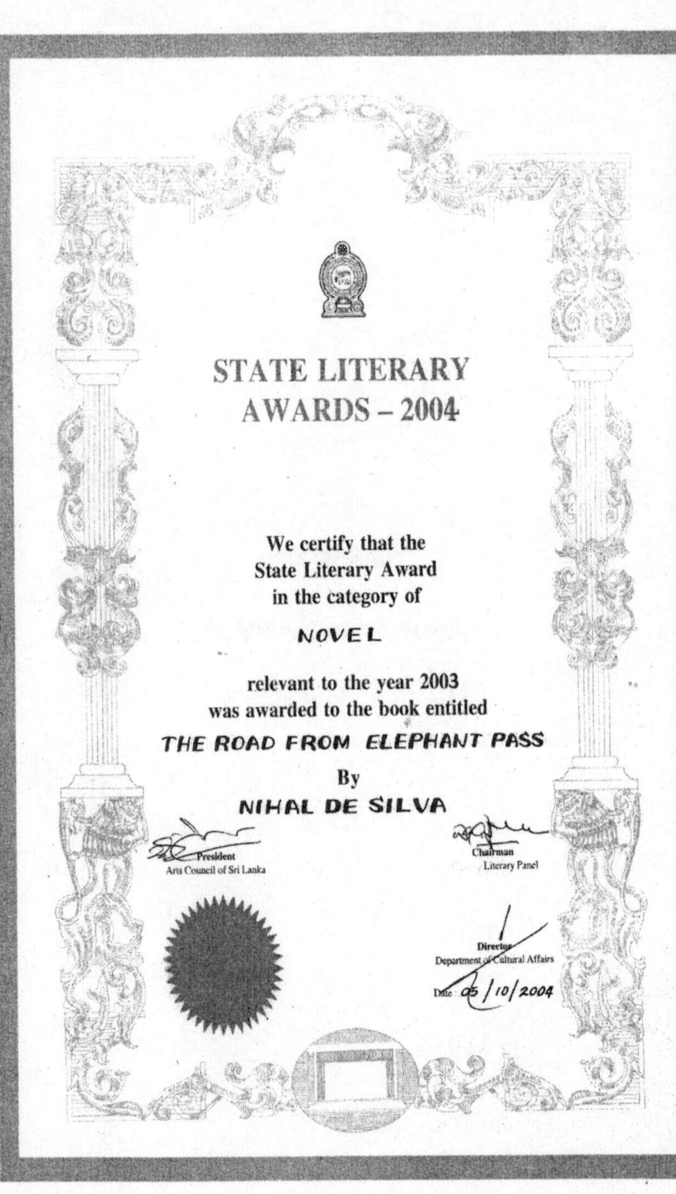

STATE LITERARY
AWARDS – 2004

We certify that the
State Literary Award
in the category of

NOVEL

relevant to the year 2003
was awarded to the book entitled

THE ROAD FROM ELEPHANT PASS

By

NIHAL DE SILVA

President
Arts Council of Sri Lanka

Chairman
Literary Panel

Director
Department of Cultural Affairs

Date : 05/10/2004

"Road from Elephant Pass"

BY

Nihal De Silva

**WAS THE WINNER OF THE GRATIAEN PRIZE
FOR THE BEST SRI LANKAN WORK
IN ENGLISH IN 2003**

CHAIRMAN OF THE TRUSTEES

CHAIRMAN OF THE JUDGES

The Far Spent Day

When Ravi returned after graduating overseas he wanted to help his father run their small family business. His well-meaning effort to stop a brawl escalates into a firestorm of violence as one party turns out to be the son of a Government Minister.

When Ravi is assaulted and hospitalized, his parents demand justice, but even this is considered an intolerable affront by the assailant's family. A series of ruthless attacks result in the death of Ravi's parents, ruin of the family business and loss of his home.

Driven to the edge of insanity by grief, Ravi fights back with the help of a young reporter, Tanya. But each strike only results in more violent and ferocious responses. When Tanya is also lost, Ravi prepares to carry out a final, devastating act of revenge.

But, looking within, he finds that the spiral of violence has also corroded his own soul....

The Giniràlla Conspiracy

COLOMBO IS UNDER A TERRIFYING THREAT

Sujatha Mallika, a girl from a remote village in the south, has been deeply traumatised by events in her own past. When she enters Jaypura University she faces and survives a sadistic rag carried out by a student union affiliated to a radical political party.

Even as she suffers the rigours of the rag, she is deeply impressed by the rhetoric of a messianic leader of that party who promises to sweep away the corrupt establishment and find a place in the sun for the rural poor. When the rag is over she joins the party and works hard to bring them to power.

Although deeply committed to their just cause, Sujatha is repelled by the violence the party uses to suppress its opponents and punish 'traitors'. She also becomes aware of a mysterious plan called the 'Ginirälla project' aimed at seizing power in the country. Dismayed and fearful, she leaves the party when she graduates from Jaypura.

As a journalist, Sujatha battles the demons of her own past even as she works to unravel the Ginirälla Conspiracy. What she finally uncovers is a plot so terrifying that it is almost beyond belief.

But the discovery comes too late for her, and for the city Colombo ...